Mrs Kimble

Jennifer Haigh grew up in a small town in Pennsylvania. She is a graduate of Dickinson College and the Iowa Writers' Workshop. She lives in Boston, Massachusetts. *Mrs Kimble* is her first novel.

Mrs Kimble

JENNIFER HAIGH

HarperCollins*Publishers*

HarperCollins*Publishers*
77–85 Fulham Palace Road,
Hammersmith, London W6 8JB

www.harpercollins.co.uk

This paperback edition 2004
3

First published in the USA by
William Morrow 2003

Grateful acknowledgement is made for permission to reprint the following:
Excerpt from "Turn! Turn! Turn! (To Everything There is a Season)" words
from the book of Ecclesiastes, adaption and music by Pete Seeger © 1962
(renewed) Melody Trails, Inc. All rights reserved. Used by permission.
Melody Trails, Inc. 11 West 19th Street, New York, NY 10011

A catalogue record for this book is available from the British Library

ISBN 0 00 715086 5

Set in Bembo

Printed and bound in Great Britain by Clays Ltd, St Ives plc

The author wishes to thank Claire Wachtel, Michael Morrison, Juliette Shapland, and Dorian Karchmar at Lowenstein Associates, for their extraordinary support of this book;

James Michener and the Copernicus Society of America, for their generous financial assistance; and

Dan Pope, for everything else.

The man died alone, in a baby blue Eldorado on Route A1A, waiting for the drawbridge to be lowered. As his heart seized, his foot lifted off the brake; the car crept forward and nudged the bumper of a lawn service truck. The driver of the truck radioed his office and waited for the ambulance to arrive. By the time it came, the man was already dead.

He had lived alone in a furnished apartment on Largo Boulevard with a sunny terrace and a view of the ocean; in the five months he'd lived there, no one in the building had noticed any visitors. In his apartment police found no books, no photos or personal correspondence, just recent newspapers and copies of the *Broward County Real Estate Guide,* a free publication distributed in boxes on the beach. In the bathroom were several bottles of pills, all unlabeled; according to the coroner, they were medications to lower blood pressure and cholesterol, slow a racing heart. The man had owned a dozen fine suits and three pairs of expensive running shoes. A neighbor said he'd risen at dawn each day to run on the beach. On the table next to his bed was a gold wedding band.

He'd been seen eating breakfast each morning at a coffee shop down the street—the same thing every day, black coffee and toast. He sat alone at the counter reading newspapers: a local daily, the *Miami Herald,* and the *Washington Post.*

How he spent the rest of the day, nobody knew. He was seen twice at a neighborhood drugstore, buying vitamins. He paid his rent with a personal check; five months ago he'd opened an account at First Florida bank. An associate at a local Cadillac dealership remembered selling him the car. He would remember it forever. The man had handed him sixty thousand dollars in cash.

He'd died on a Friday night, the beginning of the Memorial Day weekend. The Department of Motor Vehicles would be closed until Tuesday; pulling the man's driving record might have taken days, but the sheriff knew someone at the DMV. The man's Florida license was brand new; no address had been recorded from the Virginia one he'd surrendered. The Virginia DMV had an address on file but no phone number.

The body waited in the county morgue. Plaque in its arteries, an enlarged heart starved of blood. If no relatives were located, it would be buried in the municipal cemetery at the man's own expense. His checking account at First Florida contained half a million dollars.

The police kept trying.

VIRGINIA

1969

*C*harlie's mother sat cross-legged on the living room floor, her nightgown pulled over her knees, a spill of photographs scattered across the faded carpet. Years later he would remember the sound of the scissors' blades gnawing into the glossy paper, his little sister Jody wailing in the background, the determined look on their mother's face.

She had been drinking; her teeth were stained blue from the wine. She worked methodically, the tip of her tongue peeping out the corner of her mouth. The defaced photos she stacked in a neat pile: Christmases, family picnics, Fourths of July, each with a jagged oval where his father's face had been. One by one she slid the photos back into their frames. She climbed unsteadily to her feet and placed the frames back on the mantelpiece, the sideboard table, the naked hooks dotting the cracked plaster wall.

"Better," she said under her breath. She took Jody by the hand and led her into the kitchen. Charlie dropped to his knees and picked through the pile of trash on the floor. He made a pile of his father's heads, some smiling, some wearing a cap or sunglasses. He filled his pockets with the tiny heads and scrabbled out the back door.

His father was there and then he wasn't. A long time ago he'd taken them to church. Charlie could remember being lifted onto the hard pew, the large freckled hand covering his entire back. He remembered playing with the gold watchband peeking out from under his father's sleeve, and the red imprint it left on the skin underneath.

His father had a special way of eating. He rolled back the cuffs of his shirt, then buttered two slices of bread and placed them on either side of the plate. Finally he mixed all his food into a big pile—peas, roast, mashed potatoes—and ate loudly, the whole meal in a few minutes. Charlie had tried mixing his own food together, but found himself unable to eat it; the foods disgusted him once they touched, and his mother got mad at the mess on his plate.

His father made pancakes, and sucked peppermints, and whistled when he drove them in the car. On the floor of his closet, he kept a coffee can full of change. Each night lying in bed, Charlie would wait for the sound of his father emptying his pockets into the can, nickels and dimes landing with recognizable sounds, some tinny, some dry and dusty. It was always the last thing that happened. Once he heard the coins fall, Charlie would go to sleep.

$\mathcal{B}$ irdie was unwell. It was mid-morning when she opened her eyes, the room filled with sunlight. She rolled over and felt a sharp pain over her right eye. The other side of the bed was still made, the pillow tucked neatly under the chenille spread. She had remained a considerate sleeper, as if her sleeping self hadn't yet figured out that the whole bed was hers alone.

She lay there a moment, blinking. She had been dreaming of her childhood. In the dream she was small, younger than Charlie; she and Curtis Mabry, the housekeeper's son, had hidden in the laundry hampers. "You nearly give me a heart attack," said the housekeeper when she discovered them. "You're lucky I don't tell your mother."

Through the thin walls she heard movement, the bright tinkling music of morning cartoons. She lifted herself out of bed, her nylon nightgown clinging to her back. In the living room the children looked up from the television.

"Mummy," Jody squealed, springing off the couch and running to hug her leg. She wore shortie pajamas, printed with blue daisies.

Birdie wondered for a moment who'd dressed the child for bed. She couldn't remember doing it herself.

"Can I go outside?" said Charlie. He lay sprawled on the rug, too close to the television.

"May I go outside *please,*" she corrected him. "Yes, you may."

He scrambled to his feet, already in socks and sneakers. The screen door spanked shut behind him. Birdie unwrapped Jody's small arms from her leg. "Let me get you some breakfast," she said. The children seemed to lie in wait for her, to ambush her the moment she crawled out of bed, full of energy and raging needs. At such times it could be altogether too much—her stomach squeezed, the sign of a rough morning ahead—for one person.

She took Jody into the kitchen. It was a point of pride for Birdie: her kitchen was always immaculate. The room simply wasn't used. She hadn't cooked in weeks, hadn't shopped except for brief trips to Beckwith's corner store, to buy wine and overpriced loaves of bread.

She found the box in the cupboard and poured the cereal into Jody's plastic bowl, decorated with pictures of a cartoon cat. She opened the refrigerator and a sour smell floated into the kitchen. The milk had spoiled.

"Oops," she said, smiling brightly. She ought to pour it down the drain, but the very thought of sour milk turned her stomach; she left the carton where it was. She eyed the wine bottle corked with a paper napkin. Beside it an unopened bottle, the one she hadn't got to last night. She closed the door.

"Looks like it's toast for us," she said. She put two slices of bread in the toaster. She hadn't finished the bottle, so why did she feel so wretched? On Sunday night she'd had two full bottles, and not so much as a headache when she woke the next morning.

The toast popped, the sound a jolt to her heart. Perhaps she hadn't overindulged, just consumed unwisely. She'd already learned that red wine hit her hardest, that a small meal—toast or crackers— cushioned the stomach and allowed her to drink more. Beyond that, the workings of alcohol were still a mystery. It seemed to hit her harder at certain times in her monthly cycle; why, she couldn't imagine. She wondered if this were true for other women. She had no one to ask. Her mother was dead, and anyway had never touched anything stronger than lemonade. Her father's new wife probably did drink, but Birdie couldn't imagine talking to Helen about this or anything else.

"Butter?" Jody asked.

"Sorry, button." Birdie spread the bread with grape jelly and thought of the wine.

She would have been married eight years that Tuesday.

THEIR HOUSE sat back to back with the Raskins' house; a tall hedge marked the border between the two yards. Charlie stepped through a bare spot in the hedge and cut through the Raskins' backyard; then he crossed the street to the Hogans'. Mr. Hogan had already left for work. A single light burned in the kitchen window. Out back the Hogans' dog, Queenie, snored in her pen. Next door the Fleurys' German shepherd barked wildly—he barked at any- thing that moved—but Queenie didn't even stir. She was an old, fat dog, collie and something else. A heavy chain hung from her collar. Charlie wondered why the Hogans bothered. He couldn't imagine Queenie going anywhere.

He tiptoed toward the pen, where Queenie's bowl was filled with kibble. The nuggets were still crunchy. Later in the day they would be soft from sitting out in the heat. He filled his pockets with the kibble. He felt bad stealing from the Hogans, but Queenie was fat and lazy. Anyone could see she had too much food already.

From the Hogans' he went through the Arnetts' yard and into the woods. The path ran along a shallow stream. Earlier that spring a gang of older boys had built a dam there. He'd been watching the dam for weeks to see if more mud and sticks and rocks were being added. One of the gang, a mean, freckled boy named Jeffrey, had moved away; Charlie had seen the truck drive up to Jeffrey's house at the bottom of the hill. Since then the boys had neglected the dam. Charlie hoped that if he watched and waited long enough, they would forget the dam completely and it would be his.

He knew about moving. When he was little they'd moved to Richmond from Missouri. He remembered the kitchen full of boxes, his mother wrapping dishes in layers of newspaper. His father had driven the truck. Charlie had sat next to him on a box of books.

There had been no truck when his father went away, no boxes of dishes and newspaper that Charlie saw. He wasn't there when his father left. He was riding the bus to Pappy's house with Mama and Jody. When they came back his father was gone. Charlie was six then, had since turned seven. His father hadn't come back for his birthday. He hadn't come back at all.

He followed the creek upstream, to where six big rocks lay end to end, making a bridge across the stream. If he was careful he could cross without getting his sneakers wet. He'd always wondered if somebody had made the bridge, carried the heavy rocks to the middle of the stream, or if they'd simply been there forever.

On the other side he ran downstream to where the ground got swampy under his feet. He crossed the swamp to the empty house—

old, falling down, its windows covered with boards. Under the front porch lived a mother dog and her four puppies. He'd found the puppies when they were just born, silky, mouselike things with pinkish eyes and small, slick heads, snuggled in close to their mother's belly. He visited them every day.

He ran around to the front of the house. "Here, boys," he called softly. The black puppy, the friendliest one and Charlie's favorite, came first.

He reached into his pocket for a piece of kibble. The puppy came to him and mouthed it, its moist tongue sliding over his palm.

THE THING to do was make a list. In the past Birdie would write down everything: milk, hamburger meat, potatoes. Her husband would drive her to the A&P and walk down the aisles with her and they would talk about the prices of things; he'd lived on a farm as a boy and knew what was in season. Afterward he'd carry the bags into the house and place cans and boxes on the shelves; she'd separate the Green Stamps the cashier had given her and paste them into books. She had saved Green Stamps for years, redeemed them for a carpet sweeper, an egg timer she kept by the stove.

She'd kept busy then. She'd cooked his breakfast. *Eggs,* she wrote carefully. *Bacon.* She'd read to the children and made their lunches. *Cheese slices. Tomato soup.* While the baby slept she would dust or sweep or wash clothes. *Oxydol. Clorox bleach.* Every few days she'd wash two dozen diapers; the new disposables were too expensive, her husband said. After the laundry she'd start dinner. It seemed impossible, now, that she'd ever done so many things in a day.

Birdie looked at her list, written in wavy letters on the back of an envelope. The ink had begun to smear onto her sweaty hands. The complexity of the plan overwhelmed her: the driving across town, the finding of things in the bright aisles, the carrying of heavy bags from carport to kitchen. She sat for a moment with her head in her hands, her eyes leaking tears.

Jody appeared in the doorway. "Whata matter, Mummy?"

Birdie rubbed her eyes. "Nothing, button."

"What did you got on your face?"

Birdie peered at her reflection in the toaster. Her eyes seemed too far apart, her face round and flat as a dinner plate. There were splotches of bright blue around the eyes and mouth. She rubbed her face with sweaty fingers. Her hands were spotted blue, as with some rare disease.

"It must be this ink pen." She got to her feet and tossed the pen in the trash. She noticed then that Jody wore nothing but a diaper, and was suddenly ashamed. What kind of mother was she, letting her child run around the house half naked? What if someone should come to the door? What if—she tried to stop the thought, but couldn't—he should come back?

"Let's get some clothes on you." She drained her glass and passed through the living room. Charlie had come back and lay sprawled before the television. The children's room was a true disaster: toys scattered across the floor, tiny socks and underpants, small muddy footprints on the worn yellow carpet. She found Jody a clean sundress and ran a comb through her soft curly hair. She would take her children to the store, where she would locate the items on her list. People did this every day.

Birdie went to the dresser in her bedroom and took the envelope from the bottom drawer. Inside were four twenty-dollar bills, the last of the money her husband had left. She folded one of the bills and tucked it into her pocket.

"Charlie," she called. "Turn off the television. We're going to the store."

THE CAR was sweltering inside. Jody wailed when Birdie placed her on the black vinyl seat.

"Hot!" she cried.

"I know, button," said Birdie. Sweat bubbled up from her scalp and trickled down her forehead; she swiped it away with the back of her wrist. She felt a raging thirst. She couldn't remember the last time she'd driven the car. Weeks? Months? The hood stretched eternally in front of her. She felt like the captain of a large ship. Ahoy, she thought, turning the key in the ignition.

Nothing happened.

"It's just been setting awhile," she said to Charlie's serious eyes in the rearview mirror, his father's eyes watching her. She pumped the gas pedal a few times and turned the key again. The engine sputtered, but wouldn't turn over.

"Goodness," said Birdie.

"Why won't it go?" said Charlie.

"Child, I don't know." It was not a complicated operation, starting a car. She couldn't imagine what she'd done wrong. Again she turned the key and pumped the gas. From somewhere in the back of her head, she heard her husband's voice: *Don't flood the engine.* But it was too late; the car refused to start.

They climbed out of the car. Birdie noticed two bags of garbage waiting at the curb. For the second week in a row, the trash collector had forgotten her house.

"We'll walk to Beckwith's," she said. "Let me go get my handcart."

She left the children sitting on the stoop. Inside, she took the half bottle of wine from the refrigerator and drained it in several gulps. She located the handcart in the kitchen closet and wheeled it onto the porch.

BECKWITH'S WAS EMPTY that afternoon. The front door was propped open. A ceiling fan stirred up a limp breeze, the sweet dirty smell of baked goods and cigar smoke.

"Miz Kimble." Beckwith nodded from behind the counter. He was a stooped, indoorsy man, his skin and hair and eyes the same shade of gray, as if he'd been dipped in ash.

"Good morning," said Birdie. She'd already rehearsed it in her mind, how she'd go straight to the back of the store where the bottles of wine were arranged on a dusty shelf. She pretended to deliberate for a moment, then placed four bottles in the basket of the handcart.

"Having a party, ma'am?" said Beckwith.

Birdie kept her back to him.

"Why, yes," she said vaguely. She hated this man: his dirty little store, his tiny eyes that followed a person around the room. He was a gossip and so was his wife, a fat, slow-witted woman who sat in the front pew at church, arms resting on the shelf of her belly, the better to show her damp armpits to the entire congregation. Birdie pushed her cart down the aisle, trying to remember what else to buy. She picked up teabags, a tube of hand cream, a small jar of green olives. What else? she thought. She remembered the list and scrabbled through her pocketbook. When she found it, it was all but useless, the ink smeared; she could make out only a few words.

Chicken thighs, she read. *Hamburger meat.*

Well, that was a lost cause. Beckwith's hamburger was fifty cents a pound, shot through with fat and brown around the edges. You'd be hard-pressed to find sorrier hamburger in all of Richmond.

"Have you got any chicken thighs?" she asked.

"Just the whole." Beckwith pointed to the freezer case, where two small pale fryers sat wrapped in frosty plastic.

Birdie examined the chickens, her breath clouding the glass door. She felt light-headed, slightly unwell. She had always disliked cooking whole chickens, which looked entirely too much like what they were. A wave of nausea rushed though her. She leaned her forehead against the cool glass.

"You all right, ma'am?" said Beckwith.

"I'm fine," she murmured. "The heat."

"It's a hot one," said Beckwith. She wished he would disappear into the back room and do whatever shopkeepers did back there. Instead he watched as though she were some kind of criminal, as if there were anything in the sad little store worth stealing. She reached into the freezer and placed a fryer in her handcart. She was dimly aware of the children quarreling somewhere behind her.

"No!" said a small voice. Birdie turned in time to see Charlie wrench a jar of pickles from Jody's hands. Jody squealed with outrage. The jar broke loudly on the cement floor.

"Children," she whispered. No one seemed to hear her. She crossed the store in three large steps and grabbed Jody by the hand.

Somewhere in the process she lost her footing and slid facedown on the floor, bringing her daughter with her. Jody let out a wail.

"Mummy!" she cried. "You hurted me!"

THE JAR seemed to float in the air forever. Now, Charlie thought, and it obeyed, landing with a satisfying crash. The pickles looked soft and alive on the cement floor. For a moment he expected them to skitter away, like wild things that had been kept as pets.

He let out a cry as his mother lurched across the room and grabbed Jody by the hand. He was glad it wasn't him. She scared him when she grabbed, her fingernails leaving crescent-shaped marks on his skin. Once, when he was little, he ran into the street in front of a pickup truck. His mother spotted the truck and grabbed hold of his shirt just in time. *Look both ways,* she'd scolded him afterward. It seemed to Charlie that she was always clawing at him with that same urgency.

He backed away as she tripped on the rubber floor mat and fell, her dress flipping up to show the veiny backs of her thighs. For a moment he thought of bending over to smooth down her skirt. Instead he stood there wiping his hands on his pants.

She seemed dazed by the fall. She lay there without moving until the old man came and helped her up.

"You all right, Miz Kimble?" he asked.

She got to her feet. Tears ran down her cheeks. There was a blue ink spot near her mouth.

"I'm sorry," she said faintly. "I'll pay, of course." She rummaged in her pocketbook and handed the old man her change purse. "Take whatever you need."

The old man counted out bills and change and handed back the purse. "Can you make it home all right? You want me to drive you?"

Charlie imagined the old man's car. He would let Charlie sit up front and pick a station on the radio. Yes, he thought, watching his mother. Just say yes. But she was halfway to the door, dragging Jody by the hand.

"We'll manage," she said. She did not look back. Her handcart sat at the front of the store like an abandoned animal.

"Mama," Charlie called. He grabbed the handle of the cart. "You forgot."

His mother stumbled back into the store and took the cart from him. "We'll manage," she said again.

The street was busy at that hour. A line of cars idled at the red light. His mother walked unevenly, leaning on the cart. Jody toddled behind her, tugging at the hem of her dress. They crossed the street with painful slowness. Charlie held his breath as a car squealed to a stop just short of them, a big yellow car like his father's. The horn blared. Across the street an old woman came out of her house and stared.

"Land sakes," said his mother, blinking as if someone had woken her from a nap. "I'm so warm." Then she did a remarkable thing. She sat down right in the middle of the sidewalk. "Just for a minute," she said.

Charlie wanted to cry. His mother had broken the car. They'd gone to the store without buying one single thing to eat. Now she sat in the middle of the sidewalk, as if she planned to stay there awhile.

"Mama," he said. "I want to go home."

THE NEXT THING she remembered they were walking along the road. Charlie led the way, her little man; the baby trailed behind, holding the hem of Birdie's dress. The sun hung low in the sky, a perfect circle of orange pink. The daylight surprised her. It should have been much, much later. She was very tired.

She leaned heavily on her handcart, filled with packages she couldn't identify. She didn't remember leaving the store. She did recall rummaging through her purse and handing Beckwith her wallet, not caring how much money he took.

"Children, let's stop and rest awhile." She reached down to steady herself and sat heavily on the curb.

"We're almost home," said Charlie.

"I know, button. Your mama is just so tired." She closed her eyes and clamped her lips together. Stop, she thought, but it was no use: her stomach wanted to jump out of her mouth and into the street. She felt a small sticky hand on the back of her neck.

"Poor Mummy," said Jody, patting her hair. The sour smell of pickles filled the steamy air. Another wave rolled over Birdie, a potent mixture of nausea and shame. She leaned over and vomited quietly into the street.

The next morning his mother was awake when he came into the kitchen. She stood at the sink staring out the window.

"Good morning, button," she said.

Charlie could smell the stove working. His stomach cramped inside him.

"I'm making tea," she said. "Would you like some?"

Tea, he thought. He studied his mother's face, still smudged with blue. He had never drunk tea in his life. He thought she should have noticed.

"No, thank you," he said.

"I'm feeling better this morning." Her fingers raked at her hair, flat on one side of her head, soft and puffy on the other.

"That's good." Charlie looked around the kitchen for other signs of breakfast making. There was only a china cup with a string hanging over the side.

"Can I go outside?" he asked.

He cut through the hedge to the Raskins' yard, still wet with

morning dew. There was no light in the Hogans' kitchen. Charlie
went around back, but something was wrong.

Queenie was not in her pen.

He should have run away then. But Queenie's bowl was full of
fresh kibble. He thought of the black puppy, its moist tongue tick-
ling his hand. He was stuffing a handful of kibble in his pocket
when he heard the jangle of a chain.

"What are you doing?" said a woman's voice.

Charlie looked up. It was Mrs. Hogan, her head wrapped in an
orange scarf. She held a coffee cup in one hand, Queenie's chain in
the other.

"That's dog food," she said.

Charlie said nothing.

"Are you hungry?" she asked.

His face burned. Tears pressed behind his eyes. He dropped the
kibble back into Queenie's bowl. Then he ran.

He ran until his side hurt, through the Arnetts' yard, into the
woods, along the path. He crossed the stream, his feet missing half
the rocks. He ran downstream to the marshy ground, his sneakers
oozing cold water. The old house rose up in the distance, hiding
badly behind the trees.

Charlie stopped, breathing loud. Blood in his mouth: he had
bitten his tongue. "Here, boys," he called softly. The black puppy
came from under the porch and ran to him, ears flapping.

"I'm sorry," he said. His nose ran. He hadn't cried in a long
time, not since he was little.

The puppy licked his empty hands.

THE KITCHEN was dim in the morning, shaded by a small magnolia tree out back, the only thing anyone had bothered to plant on the barren little lot. Birdie poured her tea and went out to the yard for the newspaper. She hadn't read it in weeks. Each day she stacked it in the aluminum can they kept under the carport.

She winced as she sat at the table. A bruise bloomed on her right kneecap where she'd landed on the cement floor. She'd been embarrassed before. If she let herself, she could still burn over the awkwardness of adolescence, her first menstruation, the mortifications of childbirth. She could conjure up the bright hospital room, the breathstopping pain, strangers looking between her legs with clinical disinterest, the fat nurse who'd shaved her and given her an enema. In twenty-six years she'd accumulated a whole basketful of shame, a repository of palpitating memories she could dip into at any moment, each with the power to turn her hot and cold and sick with self-loathing.

Her eyes drifted over the front page. Her husband used to read the paper from front to back: national, local, obituaries, sports. He seemed to find pleasure in all the things happening in the world that had nothing to do with them, events so remote they seemed imaginary: wars in China, spaceships flying to the moon. Birdie pretended to be interested. In truth she found them—and at such times, him—dull and perplexing. She remembered the four bottles of wine in her handcart, still where she'd left it on the back porch. No, she thought. Not today.

She brought the basket down from on top of the refrigerator. She'd been tossing the mail there all summer. In it were at least a dozen bills: phone, gas, electric; one from the pediatrician who'd looked at Charlie's ears last winter. Birdie ripped open the envelopes with a rising sense of panic. She had a hundred dollars in the bank, another sixty in the house. He'd promised to send more, but hadn't yet. She sat staring at the pile of bills. Then she heard a knock at the door.

Him, she thought. But he had a set of keys; why would he knock?

She slipped into the living room and looked around. The floor covered with toys, a sofa cushion losing its stuffing. Sober for the first time in days, she noticed the defaced photographs hanging on the wall. Good Lord, she thought. Lord almighty.

She tiptoed into the children's room. Jody was asleep in her crib, her breathing soft and regular. Birdie peered through the Donald Duck curtains she'd ordered, long ago, from the Sears catalog. A strange woman stood at the door. She knocked again.

Jody sat up in her crib, her eyes wide and startled. "Whodat?"

"Ssshhh!" Birdie whispered, holding her finger to her lips.

Jody giggled with delight. "Ssshhh!" she repeated.

Birdie closed her eyes. Damnation, she thought. The woman had surely heard.

"Hello?" the woman called. "Anybody home?"

Birdie tucked the baby under her blanket. "You go back to sleep," she whispered. She shut the bedroom door behind her, smoothed her hair, and opened the front door.

The woman looked older than Birdie, with a double chin and a broad bosom. "Mrs. Kimble," she said. "I'm from the county department of family services."

Birdie's heart slowed, fluttered, sped up again. "The county," she said faintly.

"May I come in?" The woman wore a pants suit and a bright scarf at her neck. Through her white blouse Birdie could see the thick straps of her brassiere. She felt her own disadvantage: breasts hanging soft under her stained housedress, her breath stale, her armpits slightly oniony. She stepped aside and let the woman in.

THE COUNTY WOMAN took milk in her tea, a bad sign of things to come.

"I'm afraid I'm fresh out," said Birdie.

The woman peered over Birdie's shoulder into the empty refrigerator.

"It's my market day," said Birdie. "I'm out of everything." The four bottles of wine were on the back porch, safe in her handcart. The one thing she'd done right, thank you Lord. She closed the refrigerator door and carried the tea to the table.

"I'm sorry to come by unannounced," said the woman. "I tried to call, but the phone company said you were disconnected." She eyed the stack of bills on the table.

Birdie flushed. It was the redhead's curse, the transparent skin that hid nothing, not pleasure, inebriation, or shame. "That's nonsense," she said. "I called my sister this morning and it worked fine." In fact she had no sister, hadn't picked up the phone in weeks, couldn't remember the last time it had rung.

The woman frowned. "That's odd." She had a large nose, a faint mustache as fine as dust.

Birdie smiled. "People make mistakes."

"I suppose so, yes." The county woman stirred delicately at her tea. "Mrs. Kimble, I have to be honest with you. We've gotten calls from some of your neighbors. Folks are concerned about your children."

Birdie put down her cup. A splash of tea landed in her lap.

"That's ridiculous," she said. "The children are fine."

The woman smiled. "I'm sure they are. They almost always are. But two different people have called, so of course we have to check."

"Of course." Birdie wondered who would dare. Miss Semple, the nosy old maid across the street. Or Beckwith's fat wife—he might have told her what had happened at the store.

The county woman leaned forward in her chair. "Your husband works at one of the colleges, is that right?"

"Yes," said Birdie. "He's the assistant chaplain at Pennington."

"May I speak to him?"

"He isn't at home."

"He isn't?" The woman raised her eyebrows. "I figured he would be. The summer and all."

Birdie went to the sink. She wet a tea towel and rubbed the spot on her dress. She breathed deeply at the open window. The woman's perfume was making her queasy, sweet and fruity like summer garbage.

"He isn't at home," said Birdie. "He's in Missouri visiting his parents. His father is very ill." She flapped the hem of her dress to dry it. "He won't be back for another week."

"That's too bad," said the woman. "Too bad you couldn't have gone with him."

Birdie listened to the dripping faucet, the clock ticking loudly on the wall. The county woman pushed her cup and saucer away. "If you don't mind," she said, "I'd like to see the children."

Birdie imagined twisting the woman's bulbous nose until it came off in her hand. "Charlie is outside playing."

The woman looked at the clock. "It's lunchtime."

"We already ate. Josephine is taking her nap."

"I'll be very quiet." The woman stood and smoothed her jacket where it creased across her lap. Her belly was large and low. A mother's apron, Birdie thought, a phrase she remembered from long ago. She rose from her chair. Her bruised knee pulsed like a second heart. She led the way through the living room, stepping carefully around the train set, the wooden blocks. Jody was asleep in her crib. Her long eyelashes lay like butterflies on her cheeks; her small hand jammed in her mouth.

"There's my angel," Birdie murmured.

"How old is she?"

"Three and change. Four in November."

The woman's eyes darted around the room, resting on the diaper pail beside the crib. "She always wear a diaper? Or just when she sleeps?"

Birdie flushed. She'd started toilet training long ago, before her husband left. Now it seemed easier just to keep the baby in diapers.

"Oh no," she said. "Just when she sleeps."

She led the woman to the front door. Her face felt hot. There would be no more tea, no more discussion of lunches and diapers. The county woman trailed behind her. Birdie imagined her gawking at the photos on the wall. Well, let her, she thought. Let her look.

"I'm sorry you missed Charlie," said Birdie.

"I can wait."

"He usually plays in the woods all day. You know boys." She opened the front door.

"All right then." The woman hesitated in the doorway. "You might want to call the phone company. Get that business straightened out."

"I will," said Birdie.

Firmly she closed the door.

CHARLIE TOOK the long way home, avoiding the Hogans' yard. He crossed the street and followed the sidewalk up the hill to his house. The lady was standing on his front step when he came up the street. She shaded her eyes and smiled down at him.

"Are you Charlie?" she asked.

He said nothing. His feet felt raw. A blister had opened on his big toe.

"It's all right. I was just visiting with your mother." She sat down on the step and smoothed her white pants over her knees. "Are you coming home for lunch?"

His stomach hurt at the word. "Yes'm."

"What do you usually have for lunch?"

He couldn't think. All day long he dreamed of food, but now he couldn't think of a single thing. He looked at the lady's shoes.

"Pancakes," he said at last. "My daddy is making us pancakes."

The lady smiled. She wasn't pretty like his mother but he liked how she was: large and soft, like a comfortable chair.

"You wait right here." She crossed the street to a big green car and came back with a paper sack. "Here," she said.

Charlie looked inside. There was a meat sandwich, a slice of cake wrapped in plastic. He saw that the lady was giving him her lunch.

"You be a good boy," she said. "You mind your mother."

*D*rinking, Birdie remembered. Late summer at Hambley Bible College, her third-floor dormitory room stifling hot, rules for when you could eat or sleep or shower, the length of your skirt, what you could listen to on the radio. The dormitory a world of women: their voices, their laughter, damp stockings and underthings drying in the communal bathroom. After eight P.M., quiet hours: no speaking above a whisper, only studying. Exception on Wednesday, choir practice, the only time a Hambley girl was allowed to raise her voice.

Reverend Kimble directed the choir with watery strokes, eyes closed, a heaviness in his fingertips, as if they'd been dipped in something sweet and elastic. He was young, just past thirty; except for the elderly dean, he was the only man the girls had seen in months. After practice they crowded around him, giggling, asking questions. He had a remarkable voice, deep and resonant; he gave his full attention to each girl as she spoke, as if she were the only one in the room. He did not appear to play favorites, though there were rumors. A girl had been seen coming out of his office, a snooty blond from Charleston, tall and exquisite. For all her beauty she had a voice like a toad; she did not sing in the choir. Why, then, would she visit the reverend in his office? Publicly and privately, the girls could only imagine.

At practice they followed his hands with their eyes. The hands told them when to breathe, to release, to fall silent. Birdie had studied art history; watching him, she thought of the Pietà: Mary weeping over her son's crucified body, his naked arms smooth as milk, his chest delicately ribbed like the underside of a flower. She imagined Reverend Kimble's shoulders bare beneath his shirt, his body the long white body of Christ.

One evening he approached her after practice. "Vivian," he said. "Are you having problems with the descant?"

No one had ever called her anything but Birdie, a childhood nickname that had stuck because of her lovely voice. Vivian fit her badly, as stiff and chafing as a new pair of shoes. His eyes were a startling blue; they watched her closely, as though he could see through her skin. Blood rushed to her face.

"No," she said. "I can sing it."

"I know you can." He laid his hand over hers. "That's why I gave it to you."

In the spring he touched her again. Rehearsal with the windows open, filling the chapel with the muddy smell of life. Birdie's sinuses were swollen with allergies, her voice thick and nasal. She inhaled and felt a horrible squeeze in her chest. As a child she'd nearly drowned in the pond behind her house. She'd never forgotten the sensation, her lungs clutching for air and pulling in water instead. She grabbed a music stand for support and sent the pages flying, a sheaf of paper drifting to the floor.

The reverend sat her on the piano bench. Even in her terror she was aware of his arm across her shoulders. He dismissed the class with a wave of his hand and spoke to her in a soft voice. "Asthma," he said. "My brother had it as a child." He rubbed her shoulder through her blouse.

"You have a brother?" she said. She didn't care if he had ten of them. She would have said anything to make it last, the unexpected gift of his hand on her shoulder.

"Used to," he said. "He died as a child."

"I'm sorry," said Birdie. And quickly, before she could be afraid, she laid her hand on his thigh. "My mother died last year." Tears slipped down her cheeks. She wanted to lift her skirt and show him her knees, decorated with childhood scars; to tell him about the woman her father had just married, now using her mother's things. She wanted to take off her clothes and show him everything.

He kissed her on the mouth.

They were married on a Saturday morning in June, the day before her nineteenth birthday. She was three months' pregnant, not yet showing. They drove to a country church in North Carolina, where the pastor preached in shirtsleeves and owned a strawberry farm across the way. After the ceremony he sold Ken an old pickup truck for two hundred dollars. A week later they drove it to Pullman, Missouri, to live with Ken's parents. He'd been fired from Hambley; they had nowhere else to go.

*C*harlie hated baths, but for a long time his mother had let him alone. Then one morning he heard the water running, landing loudly in the tub.

"Charlie Kimble," his mother called. "You get in here this instant." His sister splashed in the water, dressed in soap suds. "Go on now," said his mother. "We haven't got all day."

Charlie shucked his shirt and pants and stepped into the tub. He knew there was no fighting it. Yet it was strange: he had never in his memory taken a bath in the morning. It didn't make sense. The whole point, he thought, was to go to bed clean.

His mother kneeled down beside the tub and rubbed the soap with a washcloth. Her hair was rolled in plastic curlers; pins criss-crossed at her hairline.

"Lord," she said. "You're filthy. You look like a little Indian." She took his arm and rubbed it with the cloth. "This is just a lick and a promise. We have to get you to the Semples'."

No, he thought. It was a clear, sunny morning; he'd started adding rocks to the dam in the creek. He knew a hundred better things to do than sitting on the sunporch with Miss Semple and her ancient mother.

"I don't want to," he said.

"I'm afraid you don't have any say in the matter. Rinse."

Charlie obeyed, sliding under the water up to his chin. "Why can't we have Dinah?" he asked. Any time his mother and father had gone out at night, Dinah Whitacre had come to sit for them. She was fourteen and danced to songs on the radio. She cooked frozen pizzas and let Charlie stay up as late as he wanted.

"Dinah's busy." His mother lifted Jody out of the water and wrapped her in a towel. "You sit in there and soak awhile. It'll save me some scrubbing."

TOGETHER THEY CROSSED the street. Charlie wore long pants that made his legs itch. His mother held Jody on one hip; a diaper bag hung from the opposite shoulder. She wore lipstick and a hat, a sign they were going somewhere unpleasant. Her heels clicked across the pavement and up the stairs to the Semples' front porch.

"You behave yourself," she whispered to Charlie, knocking at the screen door. "Be a little gentleman."

The door opened. A dusty smell floated onto the porch. "Good morning, all," said Miss Semple, holding the screen door open with a long arm. She was tall and thin, the sort of woman who'd been old for a long time. She wore a plain gray dress that nearly touched her ankles, black shoes as big as a man's. Eyeglasses dangled on a chain around her neck.

"I should be back by three o'clock," said his mother. "Four at the latest." She took the diaper bag from her shoulder and handed it to Miss Semple.

"Take your time," said Miss Semple. "We're always happy to have Charlie and Jody."

Charlie tried to catch his mother's eye. He hoped she would not take her time. But you never knew with her.

"We just finished eating," said Miss Semple. "Can I get them some lunch?"

Lunch, Charlie thought.

"Goodness, no," said his mother. "I don't want you going to any trouble."

Miss Semple smiled. Deep cracks appeared around her eyes, as if her skin wasn't used to such treatment. "Later on we'll have some tea."

Charlie's mother bent and kissed him. On his cheek he felt the waxy imprint of her mouth. "I'll be back soon," she said.

Miss Semple took Jody by the hand. "Come say hello to Mother. She's looking forward to seeing you."

They went into the house. Charlie glanced back at his mother standing at the corner, fumbling in her purse. A car whizzed past. *Look both ways,* he thought as she scurried across the street.

He followed Miss Semple past the dark parlor, toward the light of the kitchen. In all the times he'd been to the house, they'd never sat in the parlor, though once he'd sneaked inside the small, cluttered room and examined the photos hanging on the wall, women in bonnets, old men with long Semple faces. The windows were hidden by deep blue curtains. Everything else—the sofa, the fringed lampshades—was covered in plastic.

The kitchen smelled of toasted bread. Charlie glanced toward the stove: an empty pot, nothing more.

"Mother's out enjoying the sun," said Miss Semple.

They went out the back door to the screened porch. Sun streamed through the striped awnings, a hot green light. Mrs. Semple lay on the wicker sofa, her head propped with pillows, her bottom half covered with a crocheted afghan. She was old and enormously fat; through the afghan Charlie could see the outline of her thighs, round as hams. In front of her a tray table held a half-empty bowl of soup. Beside her a radio played organ music.

"Mother," said Miss Semple, touching her hand. "Look who's here. It's Charlie and Jody."

The old lady blinked. She was nearly blind. Miss Semple nodded at Charlie, his signal to speak. She had taught Sunday school.

"Hello, Mrs. Semple," said Charlie.

The old lady reached out to touch his face. She smiled, showing shiny pink gums.

"She's glad to see you." Miss Semple sat on the old glider, covered with flowered cushions. "Come sit next to me," she said to Charlie.

Jody dozed in Miss Semple's lap. The organ music ended and another program began, a man who believed the world had turned its back on Jesus.

"This is the Reverend Poundstone," said Miss Semple. "He's Mother's favorite."

Charlie watched the old woman and wondered how you could tell: Mrs. Semple appeared to be asleep. Finally Miss Semple got up from the glider. "I'm going to make us some tea," she said, lifting Jody in her arms. "Charlie, you keep Mother company."

Time passed. The Reverend Poundstone grew angry: grace would not wait forever. Between the two panels of the awning Charlie could see a narrow strip of sky.

Miss Semple reappeared carrying a tray. "Would you like some tea?" she asked. She set the tray on the table and settled back on the glider. The tray held a china teapot, three cups, and a plate of cookies.

Charlie considered. If he refused the tea, he might not get a chance at the cookies.

"Okay," he said.

Miss Semple poured the tea and added milk and sugar.

"Thank you," said Charlie. The tea burned his tongue and tasted like soap. Inside the scratchy pants his legs were slick with sweat.

Miss Semple offered him the plate. "Would you like a cookie?"

"Yes'm." He took one and put the whole thing in his mouth. It was small and hard, covered with powdered sugar. Once the sugar melted away it tasted intensely of lemon.

Miss Semple lifted Jody onto her lap. She grimaced. "Oh dear," she said. She looked down at her dress, now smudged with wet. "Somebody needs a change." She set Jody on her feet and took her by the hand, into the kitchen. "We'll be right back."

Charlie glanced at the old woman. Her eyes were closed, her lips wet with saliva.

"Wait no longer," urged the Reverend Poundstone. "The moment of salvation is at hand."

Charlie reached for the plate. He set it on his knees and ate the cookies two at a time. He ate until his teeth hurt and his lap was dappled with sugar.

TO BIRDIE, Harry Doyle looked large and wealthy. His hands were soft and clean. His fat pink face was impeccably shaved, the smooth skin of his neck pinched by a white shirt collar. He reminded her of her father.

"How do you do," said Birdie.

She let him shake her hand. She was more nervous than she would have imagined. The mere fact of dressing herself, riding the bus downtown. She hadn't worn stockings in months. In her wallet she carried three dollars.

"Have you done secretarial work before?" he asked. He was director of classified advertising at the paper.

"Yes." She looked down at her hands, folded in her lap. "My husband had a parish in Missouri for two years. I was the church secretary." It was largely true. She'd typed up the church bulletin each week, kept track of who sold raffle tickets in the spring.

"Minister," said Doyle. "He have a church now?"

"He's an assistant chaplain at the college." She allowed herself a smile. She'd had a little wine before she came, to help her relax. It was her first glass in two days.

Doyle looked down at a piece of paper on his desk. "You ever studied typing in school?"

"High school," said Birdie. That was an actual lie. She'd disdained the commercial classes, chosen art and music over book-keeping, French over shorthand. She'd learned typing on her own, on an old manual her father kept in the basement.

"This here's your typing test," said Doyle. "You type eighteen words a minute."

Birdie smiled again.

"I'm afraid I can't hire you," said Doyle. "Fifty words a minute would be the minimum."

Birdie leaned forward in her chair. The vinyl seat made a rude sound beneath her. "I'm out of practice," she said. "I could go home and practice and come back in a month or two."

"That's fine," said Doyle. "You do that, Miz Kimble."

. . .

AT THE CORNER she caught the bus, deserted at that hour, just her and an old colored woman who blew her nose in a checked handkerchief. Oh well, Birdie thought. Better not to dwell on it. Better to enjoy the remarkable feeling of riding alone on a city bus in the middle of the afternoon. She couldn't remember the last time she was truly alone, no baby tugging at her, no little boy asking where the bathroom was. A week had passed since the county woman's visit, yet Birdie still looked over her shoulder each time she left the house, wondering if the neighbors were watching. She'd taken a chance leaving the children with the Semples—who knew what Charlie might say to them?—but it was already done. She might as well take her time.

The bus stopped at an intersection; Birdie stepped down and crossed to the five-and-dime. Window signs advertised the specials: charcoal briquettes, roasted cashews, Breck shampoo. Through the glass she saw the long counter of the luncheonette. For the first time in weeks, she felt hungry. She went inside and sat at the counter, ordered coffee and pie.

"You want ice cream with that?" said the waitress, a thin, stooped woman with dyed hair and deep lines around her mouth. Ice cream cost a quarter more. Birdie reached into her purse and felt the three bills in her wallet.

"Yes, please," she said.

At the other end of the counter, two men in shirtsleeves were finishing their lunch.

"Whatcha doing for the Fourth?" asked the older one, a fat, bald man in a striped tie.

"Going to the shore," said the other. He was young and nice-looking. "I got a trunk full of firecrackers for the boys."

The men pushed away their plates. In a moment they would go back to one of the buildings on Canal Street, to do whatever men did in offices. Birdie had only the faintest notion of what her father called "bidness." Her grandfather had owned a vineyard that produced a sweet, cloudy white wine he called Tidewater Tea. Her father ran the vineyard as a hobby but made his living as a lawyer for the local school district, walking a mile each day to his office in town. Birdie's mother had never had a job, nor had any white woman she'd ever known.

Birdie looked out the window. Across the street a girl went into the hardware store. She wore shorts that barely covered her bottom, a man's shirt knotted at her waist.

"Will you look at that?" said the young man, the one with the firecrackers.

The waitress shrugged. "I think a woman ought to dress like a woman, myself."

"Those don't look like any man's legs to me," said the young man.

"They sure don't," said the old man. "But still."

Men's talk, Birdie thought: not intended for her ears. Still, it made her wonder. What would they say about her when she got up to leave? She looked down at her baggy skirt and shapeless blouse. Nothing, she realized; they would say nothing at all.

She hadn't bought the clothes herself. They had been chosen for her by Ken's mother, who hadn't considered Birdie's summer dresses fit for church or anywhere else. They'd spent a Saturday at Ferman's department store in Pullman, which sold tractor parts and animal feed as well as clothing. Ken's mother, enormously fat, wore dresses as big as tablecloths; she seemed to feel Birdie should wear the same size. She picked out skirts that hung nearly to Birdie's ankles, a billowing shirtwaist dress striped green like a porch awning.

Once, their first summer in Missouri, Ken had come home to find Birdie weeding the garden in a pair of Bermuda shorts. "What do you think you're doing?" he'd hissed. It was a small town; there were things the minister's wife simply couldn't do. She was not to wear shorts or leave the curtains open during the day or play the radio while she did housework. She could be friendly with the parish women, but not too friendly: she couldn't invite a particular one over for coffee, for example, or the others would feel snubbed. Above all she couldn't drink alcohol, not even the homemade wine her father sent at Christmas.

They lived in the parsonage with Ken's parents; his father had been Pullman's pastor until his stroke. He took over his father's duties; Birdie taught Sunday school and made covered dishes and sang in the choir. Twice a week she listened to Ken preach. My husband, she thought, wishing her old schoolmates were there to see her, the girls Reverend Kimble had not chosen. At school she had enjoyed their jealousy; she felt as though she'd been singled out for a prize. Now no one envied her. She spent her days caring for Ken's paralyzed father, bathing and feeding and reading to him. She and her husband slept in his boyhood room, the wallpaper printed with pictures of cowboys. They ate at the family table like two grown siblings.

The waitress sat at the counter and lit a cigarette. "Lord," she said to no one in particular. "It's good to sit."

Birdie smiled. She'd never learned how to strike up conversations with strangers. Her father did it naturally, casually; he made friends with every waitress, cashier, and salesman in the county. Her mother had been more reserved. Without anyone telling her so, Birdie understood that certain things, while fine for men, were unbecoming to women.

"Lord," the waitress said again. She was a different type of woman, the kind who talked to strangers all day long. It occurred to Birdie that the world was full of these women: girls who stood behind candy counters, shoveling cashews into tiny bags with an aluminum scoop; salesladies in lingerie departments, who wrapped up your new underclothes in layers of tissue. She had never paid much attention to such women; but suddenly, inexplicably, she envied them.

She glanced at the luncheonette window, at the HELP WANTED sign affixed with yellowed tape, the letters barely discernible, faded by the sun. She tried to imagine herself smiling at customers, taking down their orders with a pad and pencil. It seemed almost possible.

The men got to their feet. The older one took out his wallet and left a bill on the counter. "Take it easy, Fay," he called over his shoulder.

The waitress stubbed out her cigarette. "See you Monday," she called back. She stacked their dirty dishes on a tray, then reached for the bill the man had left and tucked it into her apron. No, Birdie thought. She could learn to take orders and serve food, but she hadn't been raised to take strange men's money. Her mother, if she weren't dead already, would have died from shame.

Birdie finished her pie and left a dollar on the counter. Outside the sky was bottle-blue, clear as glass; the sidewalks were busy with shoppers. She caught the bus, crowded now, at the corner. She found a seat next to a stout woman in a flowered hat.

Birdie settled into her seat. The bus was stifling; next to her the woman radiated heat. Across the aisle sat a young couple: the girl buxom and olive-skinned, like an Italian; the fellow blond and husky, a college boy. He leaned over and whispered something in the girl's ear, making her laugh. His hand rested on her suntanned thigh.

Birdie looked away, at the pedestrians waiting for the light to change, the mannequins gesturing in shop windows. She could almost feel the boy's hand warming her thigh, his mouth at her ear, his warm breath activating the nerves beneath her skin. Her husband had never touched her in public. He came to her silently at night, careful not to wake his parents on the other side of the wall. She remembered his cold hands under her nightgown, his breath hurried and shallow. Eyes shut tight, he seemed to disappear inside himself like a turtle retracting its limbs. The first few times, at Hambley, he'd withdrawn from her, making a mess on the floor; once they were married he simply left the mess inside her. Afterward he collapsed on the bed, exhausted, his skin perfectly cool and dry. She was mystified by his persistent interest in the act, which amounted to five minutes of intense concentration and a brief spasm that didn't appear pleasurable. She decided it was hopelessly beyond her, like geometry or algebra, yet another part of life she had failed to grasp.

Birdie glanced back at the couple. They were kissing now, the boy's hand tangled in the girl's dark hair. Birdie had never seen, up close, what kissing looked like. She watched, fascinated by the boy's clutching hands, the soft chewing movements of his jaw.

Next to Birdie the stout woman was looking too. "Heavens to Betsy," she murmured.

The bus trundled to a stop; a few passengers filed past. The boy and girl hurried to the front of the bus, flushed and giggling, the girl tugging at her short skirt.

"Good riddance," said the woman in the hat. She shifted indignantly in her seat. "There used to be such a thing as privacy, at least in our day."

Birdie looked closely at the woman. Her face was heavily powdered; she looked fifty, maybe older. She thinks we're the same age, Birdie thought. Birdie was twenty-six years old.

The bus stopped at the bottom of the street; the doors opened, admitting a blast of fresh air. Birdie got to her feet and stepped down to the curb, crossed the street, and climbed the hill. The sun heated the dark crown of her hat. She thought of the bottle of wine chilling in the refrigerator, so cold it would make her teeth hurt.

She glanced at her watch. She'd told Miss Semple she'd pick the children up at four. She had another ten minutes.

DRINKING, SHE THOUGHT of Evelyn Luck.

She hadn't thought of Evelyn in years. It was a special gift of hers: the ability to rewrite past disasters, to unhappen them in her mind. The worst debacles, her memory simply refused to record, so that there were periods of her life she barely recalled at all: her mother's illness, the long months after her death. Birdie's memories of Missouri stopped after the first year, when the gossip about Ken and Evelyn Luck started.

Birdie had never met Evelyn, but she'd seen her around: a small, narrow-shouldered woman with smooth dark hair and a sad, beautiful face. Evelyn and her husband were schoolteachers in the town; the year after Charlie was born they came to Ken for marriage counseling. It was a part of the pastor's job that Birdie couldn't fathom: strangers telling him their most intimate problems, asking his advice. She often wondered what Ken said to them, how their own short union could have given him any insight into other people's marriages. Most of the time she didn't feel married at all. They were apart all day; at night they slept in twin beds, Birdie in the bed that had belonged to Ken's dead brother.

Ken saw the Lucks twice a week at his office behind the church, a tidy room full of his father's old books. After a time he started seeing them separately. Once the Lucks had divorced, Evelyn continued to come for counseling, spending hours at a time in the pastor's office.

At first Birdie ignored the whispers at choir practice, the conversations that stopped when she came into the room. Then, little by little, she retreated. She quit the choir, the Sunday school, the church suppers and rummage sales. Pregnant again, she had a perfect excuse. She was in her fifth month when Ken was called before the parish council and asked to resign.

He never told her what was said at the meeting, and she never asked. He made vague references to wagging tongues, vicious gossip. She nodded sympathetically. That spring he wrote to an old seminary friend who'd become the dean of Pennington College. His parents would get along fine, he explained. By summer they were on the road to Richmond.

Life was different at the college, at least for Ken. He taught two classes a week, theology and Scripture; the rest of the time he spent in his campus office, counseling feuding roommates, arranging tutors for those failing math. He no longer comforted the sick and dying; instead he served on the Student Life Committee, planning prayer breakfasts and homecoming dances. He grew his hair, bought colored shirts to replace his old white ones. He became friendly with Walter Whitacre, the college president; they sang together in the faculty choir, and Whitacre's daughter Dinah sometimes baby-sat for Jody and Charlie.

Birdie spent the days alone. To her surprise she missed Ken's father, the helpless old reverend who'd watched her adoringly while she fed him. She found city life unsettling; walking alone downtown, the sheer volume of strangers intimidated her, the endless parade of faces she'd never seen before and would never see again. She rarely left the house; she had no one to talk to except the students who phoned each day to ask Ken's advice. Birdie began to recognize certain voices: the stammer, the Texas drawl. A particular girl called often, first several times a week, then every day. "This is Moira Snell," she announced each time, as if Birdie should recognize her name. Her husky voice became as familiar as that of the weather girl, a plump little blonde who stood in front of a Virginia map on television.

Then one morning the husky-voiced girl came to the house. She looked nothing like the weather girl: she was tall and thin, her eyes rimmed with dark liner, her hair the color of molasses, hanging straight and shiny down her back. She wore blue jeans and a blouse that left her shoulders bare. She wasn't wearing a bra.

"My husband has already left for work," Birdie told her; but the girl hadn't come to see Ken. She looked Birdie right in the eye. Her confidence was unnerving.

She'd come to tell Birdie that she and Ken were lovers.

. . .

COOKING SMELLS floated through the open window; next door Mrs. Gleason was preparing dinner. Birdie glanced at the clock. The children, she thought. I have to get the children. She stepped clumsily into her shoes.

The sun hung low in the sky, the feverish end of a hot afternoon. Birdie emerged squinting from the house, her legs soft and unreliable. In front of the house, the trash had piled up. Six, seven bags were heaped at the curb, ripening in the heat. Birdie looked up and down the street. At each neighbor's house sat a single neat bag.

She crossed the street to the Semples' and knocked at the door. Miss Semple answered, holding Jody by the hand.

"We were expecting you an hour ago," said Miss Semple.

Birdie smiled. Her teeth felt thick, her breath fruity. She'd forgotten to rinse with Listerine.

"I'm a little late," she confessed. "Did they behave themselves?"

"We-ull," said Miss Semple, her voice trailing off. She stepped back and let Birdie inside.

"What's the matter?"

"Charlie is under the weather," said Miss Semple. Behind her Birdie could see through to the sunporch, where a scrub brush sat in a pool of water. "We put him in the parlor."

"Goodness." Birdie followed Miss Semple down the dim hallway.

"It was very sudden. I don't know what came over him."

The parlor was dark and crowded with furniture: an ornate love seat, a highboy, an old Victrola draped with doilies. In one corner sat a cabinet full of china thimbles. Charlie lay on the brocade sofa holding a metal bucket.

"Sweetheart," said Birdie. "What happened?" She sat next to him and lay her hand on his forehead. "You're white as a sheet."

Charlie looked up at her with watery eyes. "Sick," he said. His breath was hot and sour. Birdie flushed. She turned to Miss Semple.

"I hope he didn't."

"I'm afraid so," said Miss Semple. The hem of her dress was wet, her face as white as Charlie's. Nothing in her ordered life had prepared her for the mess of a little boy's vomit.

"I'm so sorry. I had no idea he was ill."

Miss Semple's mouth tightened. "I need to check on Mother. She's a little upset."

She went out to the sunporch, her man's shoes silent on the carpet.

THEY CROSSED the street, Charlie holding Birdie's hand, Jody grasping the hem of her skirt. Once inside, Birdie sat Jody on the sofa.

"Come on," she told Charlie. "Let's get you out of those clothes and into bed."

"But I'm not sick anymore," he protested.

She looked closely at him. His color was back, his eyes bright; he seemed perfectly fine. Yet a boy didn't throw up for no reason.

"Charlie Kimble, what has come over you? Was it something you ate?" She bent down and untied his shoes. "You get right to bed. Later on we'll give you another bath."

She tucked Charlie in and went into the kitchen. The heat was oppressive; the empty wine bottle stood alone on the table. An engine rumbled in the distance, growing closer: the garbage truck.

Finally, Birdie thought. She peered out the window just in time to see it cruise past her house and stop in front of the Gleasons'. "For heaven's sake," she said aloud. She ran out to the front porch and hurried down the street. A colored man reached for the Gleasons' trash and tossed it into the back of the truck.

"Excuse me," she called. "I think you forgot my house."

The man turned to her, shading his eyes from the sun.

"I live at 507." She pointed to the house. "No one has picked up my garbage in weeks."

He squinted at her. "You paid the bill?"

Birdie thought of the basket on top of the refrigerator. "Of course."

The truck began to move. The man shrugged apologetically and broke into a slow trot behind it. Birdie followed him, her heels sharp on the pavement.

"I can pay you now," she called, though she couldn't. "If I pay you now, can you go back for it?"

"Sorry, ma'am. You'll have to wait until next week." He hopped onto the back of the truck. His uniform was the same dark green as the trash bags. The truck accelerated and turned at the bottom of the street.

Birdie glanced back at the house, the mammoth pile of trash advertising to the neighbors that she hadn't paid her bill. A curtain moved in the Semples' window. Birdie walked quickly back to the house, sure that Miss Semple had seen her running behind the garbage truck. Now what? she thought. Now what will I do?

C harlie made a slow tour of the neighborhood, cutting through backyards, looking for signs of dogs. The Gleasons had two terriers, the Raskins a toy poodle that stood in the window and yapped whenever Charlie crossed their yard, its jaws snapping soundlessly behind the glass. These dogs were no good to him; they were fed indoors. Other dogs—the Fleurys' German shepherd, the hounds Mr. Pitt kept for hunting—lived outside, chained to doghouses; but they were big and mean.

He scouted every backyard on his own street, and on the street below. He avoided the Hogans' yard, afraid Mrs. Hogan would see him through the kitchen window. Finally he approached the Fleurys' house.

The yard was strangely silent, the German shepherd nowhere to be seen. Charlie crossed the bare patch of dirt to the doghouse, near it a shiny metal bowl. His heart raced. The bowl was full of kibble.

Charlie was bending to fill his pockets when he heard a low

growl, a deep bark. The German shepherd was inside the dog-house, its large head and shoulders filling the small doorway.

He ran.

THERE WAS NOTHING in the refrigerator except a jar of olives; in the freezer, a chicken wrapped in plastic, hard and heavy as a bowling ball. Charlie was near tears. He hadn't fed the puppies in two days.

His mother came into the kitchen. "What on earth is that smell?"

Charlie looked down at his shoes. He had stepped in something as he ran from the Fleurys' dog.

His mother looked too. "Go outside and take off those shoes."

Charlie went out the back door and sat on the steps. He was sitting there when Mrs. Gleason came out of her house holding a pie tin.

"Hi, Charlie," she called across the fence. "Have you seen the cat?" A striped tomcat had been hanging around the neighbor-hood; every once in a while someone would give it milk.

"No'm," said Charlie.

Mrs. Gleason set the pie tin on her patio and went back inside.

Charlie waited. When he could wait no longer, he shimmied through the slats in the fence, into the Gleasons' backyard. Care-fully he picked up the pie tin. It was full of milk. He crossed into the Raskins' backyard and headed for the woods.

*T*he job was eleven to seven, Tuesday to Saturday. You bused your own tables and got minimum wage, plus tips. Not that tips were very frequent or very good, the waitress warned Birdie. Students were the worst: they complained that the soup was too salty or the malted didn't have enough chocolate syrup, then paid with exact change.

The waitress, Fay Burkitt, had worked at the luncheonette for six years. She seemed amused when Birdie came in and asked about the job. The Help Wanted sign had been hanging in the window for months; she'd forgotten it was there. "Sure," said Fay Burkitt. "Why not?" She took Birdie to the rear of the store to see the manager, Mr. Loomis.

He was a portly, round-faced man. A few lank strands of black hair lay across his glistening scalp. His lips moved as he scanned her application. "You forgot to put your phone number," he observed.

Birdie smiled. She'd left it off on purpose; she couldn't risk having her new employer find the phone disconnected.

"I feel so silly," she said. "I just recently moved and I can't remember the number. Not off the top of my head."

Loomis smiled back. There was a large gap between his front teeth. "We got to have your phone number."

"Let me see. I think this is right." She recited the number slowly, reversing the last two digits.

Loomis wrote the number down. "See," he said. "Nothing to it. All you needed was a little encouragement."

Birdie smiled again.

"Tell Fay to get you your uniform." He filed the application in a cabinet beside his desk. "We'll see you on Tuesday, Vivian."

Birdie flinched. She hadn't expected him to use her first name.

"See you then," she said.

Fay took Birdie into the back room and handed her a brown uniform on a hanger. A name, "Rose," was embroidered over the chest pocket. Rose was the last waitress, Fay explained; she and Birdie were about the same size. "She had a nice figure, like you," said Fay. "Not so big in the bust, but you're lucky."

Birdie flushed. Through the plastic bag she could see stains on the collar and the bodice.

"Try white vinegar," Fay advised. "That's what I do. Some of them won't come out no matter what, but you won't know until you try."

Birdie took the uniform and crossed the street to the bank. In her pocketbook was the forty dollars Mr. Loomis had advanced against her salary.

THE ALARM rang every morning at nine. Each time Birdie awoke in a panic. She got up and toasted three slices of bread, one for each of them; it was the only thing she could choke down so early in the morning. She dressed the children and took them across the street to the Semples'. Then she took the bus to work.

The first morning she arrived five minutes early, carrying her uniform on a hanger. That morning in her bedroom she'd looked at herself in the uniform and burst into tears. A waitress: the whole world would know she was a waitress. She found herself unable to walk out the door until she'd changed back into her own clothes.

The store was already open; at the register a young mother bought disposable diapers. Birdie slipped into the ladies' room and unbuttoned her blouse. The uniform was tight across her chest; it stopped two inches above her knees. She checked her reflection in the mirror, the name embroidered over the chest pocket. Rose, she thought. I'm not me. I'm Rose. She buttoned her own skirt and blouse over the hanger, then walked to the front of the store, to the luncheonette.

Fay Burkitt was already there, smoking a cigarette at the counter.

"Right on time," she observed. She eyed the hanger in Birdie's hand. "Oh, honey. Why don't you just wear it to work?"

Birdie flushed. "I don't know. I wasn't thinking."

Fay shrugged. "Suit yourself."

She showed Birdie the coffeemaker, the box of paper place mats, how to clip the sheets from her order pad to the metal carousel and spin them around to the Negro cook. She pointed out the location of the ice bin, the bus pans, the rags and ammonia for wiping down tables. Birdie wasn't to run the register, not just yet; someday, when they weren't busy, Fay would show her how.

An old man came in and sat at a table in the rear. "Go ahead," said Fay. "There's your first customer."

Birdie approached the table, order pad in hand, pencil shaking in her sweaty fingers.

"What can I get you?" she asked.

"Hello to you too," said the man.

"I'm sorry," said Birdie. "Good morning."

"Morning? It's almost afternoon." He glanced at the menu. "Hamburg and a Coca-Cola."

She wrote it down carefully on her pad and smiled. "Thank you," she said. It was just as she'd thought; there was nothing to it. She turned away.

"Miss," the man called after her. "Don't I get a glass of water?"

"Of course," said Birdie. "I'll be right back."

She hurried to the counter. In the minute her back was turned, three customers had come in. A woman in red sat near the window drinking coffee; at the counter, two men in plaid shirts chatted with Fay. Birdie reached into the ice bin and dropped a fistful of ice into an amber glass, then filled it with water from the pitcher. Nothing to it. She took the glass to the man's table and set it in front of him.

He crossed his arms over his chest. "I'm not drinking that."

Birdie blinked.

"Not after you had your hands all over it," he said. "You put your hand right in that bucket of ice. That ain't right."

"No I didn't," said Birdie.

"I saw you. Don't lie about it."

"I didn't," she repeated. She was near tears.

He stood up. He was a filthy old man; his cardigan sweater reeked of cigars. "That does it," he said. His yellowed dentures gave off a fungal smell. "Bad enough what you did, but then to go and lie about it."

"I'm sorry," she whispered.

"Count your blessings I don't call the board of health," he said, shuffling toward the door. "Young lady, count your blessings."

Birdie glanced at the counter. The men had stopped talking. The lady looked down at her coffee cup, then pushed it away. Fay looked at Birdie and nodded toward the back room.

"I'm sorry," Birdie said as the door closed behind them. "I wasn't thinking."

"You got to use the ice scoop," Fay said. "Didn't I show you the scoop?"

Birdie nodded. Her chest felt tight. Breathe, she thought. She exhaled slowly, fighting the squeeze.

"Look at you," said Fay. "You're turning purple." She touched Birdie's arm. "It's not that bad. Just don't do it again."

"Okay," said Birdie. Fay's hand felt small and bony on her arm, the delicate claw of a bird.

For two hours they worked nonstop. Birdie wrote orders on her pad and spun them around to the cook. She served tuna melts and egg sandwiches, rice pudding and slices of pie. Over and over she refilled coffee cups; the customers were crazy for coffee. Finally the tables emptied. She cleared the dirty dishes into the bus pan and wiped down the tables with ammonia.

"Lord," said Fay, sitting down at the counter. "I got to have a smoke. Come and have a seat."

"Is it always this busy?" said Birdie. Her back ached; there was a heaviness in her legs she hadn't felt since she was pregnant.

"It's the lunch rush." Fay slid open a pink plastic case and pulled out a cigarette. "You want one?"

"No, thank you."

Fay tapped the cigarette on the countertop and reached in her pocket for a matchbook. "Good for you. My husband was always after me to quit."

"You're married?" said Birdie.

"Divorced." Fay struck a match. "The day I got my papers was the happiest day of my life."

Birdie felt her pulse in her temples. "How long have you been divorced?"

"Four years. Almost five."

They stared out the window, watching the cars brake at the stoplight. Birdie had never met a divorced woman before, never seen up close someone who'd lived through it. What happened? she wanted to ask. Where did he go? Why did he leave?

A big blond man came through the door and sat at the other end of the counter.

"Look what the cat dragged in," Fay called, laughing. She stubbed out her cigarette and got to her feet. "Why don't you fill up those sugar bowls," she told Birdie. "It's next to the coffee filters, under the counter."

Birdie stood and smoothed the uniform over her behind. As she circulated through the tables, she noticed the blond man watching her, his pale blue eyes following her around the room. She was aware of her legs in the nylon stockings, the brown uniform tight across her chest. Her hands shook a little as she placed the sugar bowls on the counter and reached underneath for the sack of sugar, conscious all the time of the ring on her left hand, which her husband had placed there eight years before.

The counter was Fay's station; she joked with the man as she brought him a plate of french fries. "Looks like you had a rough night," she said, setting down the plate.

"You could say that." The man stuffed a french fry in his mouth and wiped his hand on his thigh.

Birdie went into the kitchen for the bus pan and cleared the coffee cups from her tables. She strained to hear their voices over the clattering dishes. The man spoke in a low rumble; Fay laughed sharply, like a crow's call.

Birdie carried the bus pan to the kitchen. The man was no longer watching her; he stared blankly out the window. She studied his faded denim shirt, his square, handsome face. His eyes tracked a yellow convertible turning the corner. She saw that his gaze was unconscious, instinctive. He reminded her of a hunting dog.

"Who was that?" she asked Fay later when they sat down for their coffee break.

"Buck Perry," said Fay. "He comes in for lunch sometimes." She inhaled deeply; smoke shot out her nostrils. In between drags she nibbled at french fries wrapped in a paper napkin, left over from the customers. Birdie wondered if they'd come from Buck Perry's plate.

"He's a charmer," said Fay. "All the girls love Buck."

Is he married? Birdie wanted to ask. The words sat inside her mouth. She gulped and swallowed.

harlie stepped carefully from rock to rock, holding the pie tin with both hands. He was getting better. Last time he'd spilled most of the milk. This time he spilled less than half.

He approached the old house and set down the milk. "Here, boys," he called to the puppies. Then he heard the noise. Near the house a truck was idling. A fat man leaned against it, smoking a cigarette. Charlie watched him cup his hand to his mouth and hold the cigarette there. In the distance he heard men's voices, the sound of splintering wood.

Charlie ran around to the front of the house. A different man carried an armload of boards to another, larger truck.

"Hey," said the man. "This ain't no place for you."

Charlie squinted past him, at the porch.

"This is a demolition," said the man. "You could get hurt."

Charlie found his voice. "There's puppies under the porch. They live there."

The man shrugged. "They going to have to find another place to live."

irdie had no wine for three days, but she remembered it was there. On the fourth day she came home from the luncheonette and opened a bottle. "Just a glass," she said as she poured, as if anyone was there to hear.

The next day she awoke with a headache, the alarm clock as piercing as a drill. In the kitchen the empty bottle sat on the counter. She found the last two slices of bread and dropped them in the toaster, one each for Charlie and Jody; her queasy stomach wouldn't mind going without. In the living room the children were already awake, watching a woman do exercises on television.

"Mummy!" Jody squealed.

Birdie winced. "Quiet, button. Mama has a headache."

She carried Jody to the bedroom and dressed her in a playsuit, squeezed her feet into sandals. Birdie sniffed.

"Lord," she said. "What's that smell?"

She ran to the kitchen, Jody toddling behind her. Inside the toaster the bread was perfectly black. "Damnation," she whispered.

The children had followed her into the kitchen and were sitting at the table, waiting.

"Butter?" said Jody.

"No, button," said Birdie. "No toast today. We can't eat it." She grasped the black toast with a tea towel and brought it to the table. "See? It's burnt."

"Burnt," Jody repeated.

Footsteps on the back porch, a brusque knock at the door.

"Whodat?" said Jody.

"Hush," said Birdie. She wasn't afraid, exactly; the county woman wouldn't use the back door. She peered out through the curtains. A colored man in workman's greens stood with his back to the window. Relief warmed her; if she were in trouble, they wouldn't send a colored man. She opened the door.

"Morning, ma'am. I'm from the gas company." He glanced at a clipboard in his hand. "I read your meter just now—you've barely used any gas all summer. I thought maybe something was wrong with the stove."

"I don't think so," said Birdie.

"If you like, I can have a look. It'll only take a minute."

Birdie stepped back and let the man into the kitchen. He bent down and opened the drawer beneath the oven. Birdie tossed the charred bread in the trash. With a white man in her kitchen, she'd never have done this. With a colored man she was not ashamed.

Jody climbed down from her chair and clung to Birdie's leg, staring silently. Birdie didn't understand at first. She thought nothing of having a colored man in her kitchen. She'd been raised by Ella Mabry, her family's Negro housekeeper; Ella's son Curtis had been like a brother to her. But Jody had lived her whole life inside the small house; she had never seen a colored person. She stared at the man in wonderment. Then, finally, she spoke.

"Burnt," she said.

Birdie flushed. The man glanced at the child and smiled. He pointed at his chest pocket, at the letters stitched in white thread.

"That's right," he said pleasantly. "That's my name. Bert." He smiled at Birdie. "She's a little one to be reading already." But Birdie's face gave them away, the redhead's flush radiating out from her hairline. Jody was a slow talker. So far she knew only a dozen words, which she repeated incessantly.

"Burnt," she said again, distinctly. She reached out to touch the man's dark forearm.

The man's smile faded. He straightened and turned on the gas, took a lighter from his pocket and held it to a burner. A blue flame appeared.

"The pilot light is on," he said. "Everything looks fine."

"Thank you," said Birdie, her cheeks burning.

She closed the door behind him.

BIRDIE LEFT the children at the Semples' and took the bus to work, a bottle of aspirin in her purse. At the luncheonette she drank ice water; the smell of coffee nauseated her. She leaned gingerly against the counter, letting the fan blow cool air on her face. Fay watched her closely but said nothing.

At the end of the lunch rush, Buck Perry appeared. He sat in his usual spot at the end of the counter. Birdie ducked into the back room and checked her hair in the mirror. Fay poked her head in the door.

"I'm out of smokes," she said. "Come keep an eye on things while I run across the street."

"Coming," said Birdie. She slipped off her wedding ring and tucked it into her pocket.

Perry sat hunched over his plate. "Can I get a refill?" he asked.

She approached him with the pot. He'd finished his meatball sandwich, a messy construction of bread and tomato sauce. The plate was as clean as if he'd licked it. He sat back on his stool and watched her fill his cup.

"How you doing?" he asked.

"Fine, thank you," said Birdie. His shirtsleeves were rolled to his elbows; his blond forearms were thick and suntanned. A flush built in her chest and washed over her throat, her face, up to the roots of her hair. Perry's eyes followed the same path.

"What's your name?" he asked. "You ain't Rose. I know that."

Her heart quickened. "Birdie."

"You're new."

"I started last week." Out of the corner of her eye, she saw two women come into the luncheonette and sit at one of the tables, their chairs scraping the linoleum. The sound seemed very far away.

Perry chuckled. "I bet Fay's happy. Since Rose left they been working her to death."

"Did you know her?" said Birdie. "Rose."

He grinned. "Why? What have you heard?"

"Nothing," said Birdie. "I just wondered where she went, is all."

Perry shrugged. "Got married, I guess. All the pretty ones do." His eyes went to her left hand. "You're not married?"

"No," she said, her heart pounding. She could not hold his gaze. Her eyes dropped to his hands, his thick fingers gripping the coffee cup. His fingernails were perfectly black. She turned away quickly.

"Excuse me," she said. "I have customers."

She left him sitting at the counter.

he car started with a great rumble. It smelled the same inside, old leather and peppermint and his father's hair cream. The smell engulfed Charlie like a warm bath. He'd forgotten the distinctive odor, the hollow tinkling of the turn signal.

"Can I turn on the radio?" he asked.

"Hold your horses," said his mother. "Wait until we get on the highway." She had a spot of red on each of her cheeks, like a giant rag doll. She frightened him, the floppy bonelessness of her, as if at any moment she might slump over the wheel or flop over sideways, her head lolling out the open window. But the car, his father's car, rolled smoothly down the hill. In the backseat Jody clapped her hands and squealed.

"What's that light?" Charlie asked. He pointed at the dashboard.

His mother looked down. "How should I know? Isn't it always on?"

"No'm," said Charlie. The light looked important, a glowing square of red.

"Never mind about that," said his mother. "First things first."

Ahead of them a traffic light turned yellow; she stepped hard on the brake. Charlie lurched forward, then fell back into the leather seat. He knew you only had to stop on red, but he didn't say so. He could see that she was nervous.

"We need bread and milk," he said instead.

"Whatever you want," said his mother.

Charlie made a list in his head: cereal, hot dogs, bologna for sandwiches. He didn't trust her to remember.

The A&P was cool and bright inside. The glass doors opened as if by some magic force. Charlie ignored the gumball machines, the wire cage of bright rubber balls. He led the way down the first aisle, grabbed a bunch of bananas and placed them in the shopping cart. His mother didn't seem to notice. She stood at the front of the store looking all around, blinking.

Charlie kept on. The sacks of potatoes were too heavy for him. He looked back. His mother stood near the cash registers, flipping through a magazine.

"Mama!" he cried.

She looked up, startled.

"Are you coming?" He'd tried for weeks to get her inside a store; now that they were here, she seemed to have forgotten how to buy things. He felt the first tears behind his eyes.

"Hold your horses," she said. But she put the magazine down and pushed the cart up the aisle.

Charlie raced down the next aisle. He wished he could carry more. He picked up a loaf of bread and a box of cookies. Then he saw the man.

He was at the back of the store, reaching into a refrigerator case of raw meat. His back was turned, but Charlie recognized the white shirt, the long hands, the wristwatch with the stretchy gold band. The man put down the meat and walked away quickly, his dark trousers moving with long steps.

Charlie followed him. The next aisle was crowded with mothers and children and babies in strollers. The man was already at the other end of it. He turned the corner and disappeared.

Charlie ran. He pushed through the shopping carts, the pocketbooks dangling from ladies' arms. What if the man had already left? What if he was in the parking lot, ready to leave without him, not knowing his boy was in the very same store?

Charlie scrambled around the corner, crying now. At the end of the aisle was his father, carrying a carton of eggs.

"Wait!" Charlie called. He could remember his father breaking eggs into a bowl for pancakes. He ran.

The man turned around.

"Daddy!" Charlie cried.

The man looked down at him, startled. "What's the matter, son? Are you lost?"

"Daddy," he said again, but something was wrong. The man was too old, his face too fat. He had brown eyes instead of blue.

"Son," said the man. His voice was grave. "Have you lost your father?"

*J*n the morning Birdie drove downtown. She tried not to look at the dashboard, the engine light an alarming red. Cars passed her on both sides; horns blared as she stopped at a traffic light. When the light changed she made a left turn from the righthand lane; the driver behind her yelled something out his window.

She found the garage at a busy intersection, not far from the luncheonette. "They won't charge you an arm and a leg," Fay had told her. "They're the only honest mechanics in Richmond."

Birdie parked in front and went into the office, a dirty little room redolent of cigarette smoke. On the wall hung a calendar, dating to the past December: a woman lay on her side at the foot of a Christmas tree, propped on her elbow, her other arm crossed beneath her large breasts. She was naked except for a Santa hat. From a radio somewhere, a sad male voice sang "Every Fool Has a Rainbow." Behind the counter a swinging door led to the garage.

"Hello," Birdie called out.

She waited. A cigarette burned in the overflowing ashtray. The phone rang, then stopped. A man in coveralls appeared through the swinging door. His bald head was smooth and glossy, like the plastic body of a doll.

"Keep your shirt on," he grumbled. He saw Birdie and reddened. "Excuse me, ma'am."

Birdie cleared her throat. "I'm having trouble with my car. The engine light is on."

The man glanced out the window. "That Pontiac there?"

"Yes." She was still shaky from the drive; her blouse stuck to her back like a bandage.

"Have a seat," said the man, "and I'll take a look."

The room was sweltering, the morning sun streaming through greasy panes of glass. She'd never been inside a garage before; her husband had handled the repairs. She had a sudden urge to walk down the street to the bus stop, leaving the car for the man to do with as he pleased.

She hated the car. Driving had been an ordeal from the start. She'd gotten her license four years before, after failing the test twice; Ken had insisted she keep trying, though she didn't see the point. He was an excellent driver; she was a happy passenger. She'd never imagined anything would change.

Birdie glanced out the window and saw Buck Perry coming up the sidewalk, keys dangling from his finger. He seemed to be looking right at her. She waved, but he couldn't see her behind the glare from the window. Hidden, she watched him come toward the garage. He was shorter than her husband, heavy through the arms and shoulders. His powerful thighs seemed ready to burst out of his blue jeans.

Perry disappeared around the side of the building. He must work here, she thought; the luncheonette was a few blocks away, an easy walk on his lunch hour. She thought of his thick arms in the denim shirt. Her husband had been slender and delicate; twice he'd wrenched his back and spent a week in bed, expecting his meals on a tray. Buck Perry looked strong as a horse. He looked like he could carry her on his shoulders.

The door to the garage swung open and the bald man emerged, wiping his hands on his coveralls.

"Looks like the transmission is about to go," he said.

Birdie blinked. She didn't know what a transmission was and didn't care; all that mattered was how much it would cost.

"Is it expensive?" she asked.

"You're looking at about three hundred dollars."

A lick of sweat trailed down her back. Three hundred dollars was what she earned in a month. Yet the car was the only thing of value she owned, the only thing her husband had left her.

"Parts and labor," said the man. "Give or take."

Birdie closed her eyes. "A transmission," she said. "Is it absolutely necessary? Can I run the car without one?"

The man howled. "Did you hear that?" he called into the back. "She asked can she run it without a transmission!" He turned back to Birdie and grinned; his teeth were bad. "Well, ma'am, let's just say I wouldn't advise it."

His rudeness stunned her. He stood with his hands on his hips, waiting. "Well, what do you want to do? Do you want me to replace it or not?"

"I can't afford three hundred dollars." Her eyes went to the calendar above the desk. The woman's nipples were the size of silver dollars, rouged to match her mouth. The door swung open and Buck Perry stood in the doorway.

"Are you the transmission?" he asked.

Birdie nodded yes.

"I think I can help you," he said.

here was only dirt where the house had been, a silent patch of bare ground. All afternoon a truck had hauled away bricks and boards and sharp slices of window glass. Charlie hid in the woods, knowing that the men, if they saw him, would chase him away. Crouching, he watched them load the truck. When it was full it would drive away and the men would stand in the shade, smoking cigarettes and talking in low voices, until the truck returned.

Finally the truck came back for the last time; the men piled into the rear and drove away, raising dust. Charlie got to his feet and walked through the woods, in a wide circle with the demolished house at its center. "Here, boys," he called softly. But the puppies didn't come.

He approached the crumbling foundation, half filled with splintered boards and chunks of plaster. He located the spot where the porch had been, the dark earth littered with nails and flaked paint and bits of glass. He reached into his pocket. That morning he'd gone back to the Hogans'; his pockets were full of kibble he'd taken from Queenie's dish.

"I'll leave it right here," he said loudly, piling the kibble into a neat mound. Though by then he knew the puppies were gone.

Somebody's watching you," said Fay.

Birdie looked up from the tray of water glasses she was filling. At the end of the counter, Buck Perry waved and smiled.

"Go take care of him," said Fay. "He needs a warm-up."

Birdie took the pot from the burner and refilled Perry's coffee cup. His blond hair, she noticed, was thick and wavy. (Her husband's had begun to thin.) It curled softly at the nape of his neck.

"How's the transmission doing?" he asked.

"Just fine," said Birdie. Perry had a friend who rebuilt transmissions on the side; he'd gotten Birdie one for almost nothing. He'd explained patiently what a transmission did, but Birdie didn't care. The car ran beautifully; the troublesome engine light had been extinguished.

"He's a card, that Jenks. The one that fixed your tranny. He plays drums in a dance band." Perry bit into his hamburger, half the sandwich in one bite; ketchup oozed out the other side. He seemed not to notice. He ate fast and intently, like a hungry dog.

"They're playing at the Vets this Saturday night," he said. "You want to come and hear them?"

Birdie's heart quickened. A date, she thought. He's asking me out on a date.

"That sounds lovely," she said.

Perry laughed. "Lovely it ain't," he said, "but it's a pretty good time."

*I*t was nearly dark when Charlie got home, heavy clouds low in the sky. A wind had started. Thunder rumbled in the distance. He'd been playing in the woods; the house felt small to him, hot and airless. His sister sat in front of the television, stacking wooden blocks.

"Where's Mama?" he asked.

"Where Mama?" she repeated.

He knocked at the bathroom door.

"Come in," his mother called. She stood in front of the mirror in a pale yellow dress. Her face looked strange to him: mouth painted red, eyebrows plucked thin. An empty glass sat on the edge of the bathtub.

"Do I look pretty?" she asked.

"Yes'm," said Charlie.

She sprayed a cloud of perfume into the air and walked into it; Charlie tasted it, flowery, in his mouth.

"A little scent goes a long way," she said.

The doorbell rang. "That's Dinah," she said. "Button, go and let her in."

Charlie ran to the door. He'd forgotten she was coming. They hadn't had a baby-sitter in a long time.

"Remember what I told you," his mother called after him.

"Yes'm," said Charlie. If possible he was not to say anything about his father. If Dinah asked—and only if she asked—he could say his father was visiting in Missouri and would be back soon.

Charlie opened the door. Dinah came in holding a grocery bag. Pizzas, he thought. Last time she'd made them frozen pizzas.

"Hi, buddy," she said, messing his hair. "Long time no see." She looked around the room. "What happened to the pictures?"

"I don't know," said Charlie. His mother had taken them down from the wall; the plaster was dotted with bare hooks.

His mother came out of the bedroom holding a string of pearls. "Can you help me with this?" she asked Dinah.

She turned her back and lifted her hair; Dinah clasped the pearls behind her neck.

"You look nice, Mrs. Kimble," said Dinah. "Is it a special occasion?"

"I think I hear my ride," said his mother. She bent to Charlie and Jody and gave them each a kiss. "You be good now. You listen to Dinah."

She rushed out the front door, leaving a trail of perfume. Dinah went to the living room window and peered out from behind the curtain.

"What are you looking at?" Charlie asked.

"Nothing," said Dinah.

THE WIND had stopped; the evening was still and muggy, the sky clouded over with gray. Birdie stood on the front step waiting for

Buck Perry. It was the Saturday before Labor Day, the last wearing of the white shoes. She smelled meat cooking, a charcoal fire. The neighbors were having a barbecue.

Through the open windows she heard the children laughing; they wouldn't miss her at all with Dinah Whitacre there. Poor Dinah, she thought; poor homely child. She felt bad for the girl, so timid and awkward; Dinah who would have been pretty if it weren't for her birthmark. It was so ugly Birdie could barely look at her, a jagged purple stain that covered half her face.

Birdie had called her at the last minute; she'd had the phone reconnected after her first paycheck. She dreaded the obligatory chitchat with the girl's mother. Married to the president of the college, Grace Whitacre knew all the faculty comings and goings; she would know Birdie's husband had quit his job and might even know why. Luckily, Dinah herself had answered the phone. She was a mannerly girl, raised properly, not like some others Birdie could name. (That girl on the downtown bus, draped all over the college boy; Moira Snell, braless in her peasant blouse.) Dinah's shyness seemed appropriate to her age; in her presence Birdie felt like an adult, a sensation she rarely felt.

She breathed deeply; the yellow dress felt tight across her chest. She'd picked it off a sale rack three years ago when she was pregnant with Jody; that morning she'd cut off the price tag still dangling from the armpit. The dress was a size too small; her breasts had never shrunk back down to their old size. Still, it was the only thing she owned that didn't hang to her ankles.

Her hand fluttered to her throat, to the pearl necklace her mother had left her. It was a short strand, meant to fit close around the throat; her father had given it to her mother as an engagement present. Birdie had worn it only a handful of times: her own wedding day, a couple of dinners at the Whitacres'. Her married life had provided few occasions special enough. Then, this afternoon, something had come over her. Why not? she'd thought as she took the necklace from its leatherette case. Birdie Kimble, what are you waiting for?

A dusty green sedan appeared around the corner; engine rumbling, it pulled up to the curb. Birdie's legs shook as she made her way down the porch steps. At the curb she waited, but Perry didn't get out of the car. Finally she opened the door herself.

He lounged in the driver's seat, so far back from the wheel that he was nearly lying down. He wore black pants and a pink shirt, open at the throat; his hair, slicked back from his forehead, showed comb marks.

"Well, look at you," he said.

The car was low to the ground; Birdie held down her dress as she slid into the seat beside him.

"I should have brought my umbrella," she said. Her heart worked furiously. "It looks like rain."

"Nah," said Perry. "You won't need it."

He shifted gears and backed smoothly into the street. The engine seemed uncommonly loud; Birdie slid down in her seat as they passed the Semples' house.

"Did you have any trouble finding me?" Birdie asked. It was the only thing she could think of to say.

"Hell no," said Perry. "I've lived in this town my whole life."

In a moment the neighborhood was behind them. Perry hummed softly with the radio: muted horns, a deep Negro voice. His hands pattered on the steering wheel. Freshly shaved, his skin looked moist and childlike. He smelled strongly of cologne. They drove away from the city, to where the traffic thinned out and bars and storefronts were separated by occasional houses, patches of grass. Perry drove fast and expertly, his left elbow hanging out the window. Twice he reached forward to change the radio station, gripping the steering wheel between his knees. He seemed to have forgotten her.

The Vets was set back from the road on a wide lot worn bare in places. Perry parked and came around to open Birdie's door. She heard music in the distance, the silvery hiss of a cymbal. Perry placed his hand at the small of her back. She picked her way across the reddish dirt, worried about her white shoes. The sky had darkened; the air was very still.

"Storm coming," said Perry.

The Vets was loud and dark inside, packed with people and their smells: perfumes, liquor, cigarettes, sweat. Men stood smoking and talking at the entrance. Perry pushed through them, his wide shoulders cutting a path; he took Birdie's hand and pulled her along behind him. They crossed the dance floor to a table at the back, where a couple sat with their backs to the wall. On the table were cigarettes, glasses of beer, an empty pitcher.

"This is Lou and Marie," said Perry. He had to shout over the music. "Everyone, this is Birdie."

"Birdie," said Marie. "That's cute." She was a sharp-faced blonde.

"It's a nickname," said Birdie. She eyed Marie's snug sweater, the silver heart dangling from a chain into the dark hollow between her breasts. In her dress and pearls, she felt like a chaperone at a dance.

"I'm just Marie," said the blonde. "I don't have a nickname."

"That's what you think," said Lou, winking. He was older and balding.

"Hey!" Marie squealed, giving him a shove. Her small eyes were rimmed with black liner. For a moment Birdie thought of Moira Snell, the hateful girl who'd seduced her husband. She pushed the thought away.

"They're cooking tonight," Lou shouted to Perry. "They're really cooking."

Birdie craned her neck toward the stage. The combo had four pieces—piano, guitar, drums, and bass. The singer was a colored man in a dark suit.

"Which one is your friend?" Birdie asked.

"Drums," said Perry. He pulled up an empty chair from a neighboring table. "Have a seat. I'll be right back."

She sat, the vinyl seat sticky beneath her thighs. Lou and Marie said nothing; they sat watching the band over her shoulder. Finally she turned her chair a little to face the dance floor.

Perry returned with a pitcher of beer and two glasses.

"None for me, thanks," said Birdie.

"You sure?" said Perry. "Why not?"

"I don't care for beer."

"Suit yourself." He tilted a glass and filled it. Across the table Lou and Marie leaned close together. Birdie sat with her chin in her hand, watching the dancers. When the music slowed the floor filled with swaying couples; afterward the band would pick up the tempo and only a few would remain. The steps were new, nothing Birdie recognized. She had not seen anybody dance in years.

"How long have you two been going together?" Marie asked.

"What time is it?" said Perry, and laughed.

The room was hot, everything—the floor, the chairs, the table-top—coated with a sticky film, as if thousands of beers had been spilled there. Birdie blotted her forehead with a napkin. Her nylon slip felt slick against her back; soon she would sweat through the yellow dress. She eyed the pitcher of beer.

"Look at her," said Marie, blowing smoke out of the side of her mouth. "She's dying of thirst. Go get her something to drink, for Christ's sake. Be a gentleman for once in your life."

"All right, all right," said Perry. He got up and went to the bar.

Marie leaned forward in her chair. "I've known him a long time. Since we was kids." She stabbed out her cigarette in the ashtray. "You're in for a good time. Wait and see."

Perry returned with a glass. "I got you a rum and Coke."

"Thank you," said Birdie. The drink was cold and sweet; she took half the glassful in one gulp.

"Whoa," said Perry. "You *are* thirsty."

The band lurched into a slow song Birdie recognized. She watched the dancers shuffle to the music, clinging to each other like shipwreck survivors. When the music picked up, Perry glanced at her. "You wanna dance?"

"Buck's a great dancer," said Marie.

Birdie looked out at the dance floor, the dancers twisting at the hips. She'd learned the box step as a girl; she could waltz and fox trot; but this was a different kind of dancing entirely.

"I don't know how," she said.

"Don't know how?" said Perry.

"It's been a long time." Dancing was forbidden at Hambley; and after she was married, she hadn't danced at all. She smiled apologetically. "No, thank you."

Perry shrugged. "How about you?" he asked Marie. "Lou won't mind."

She glanced at the bar, where Lou stood smoking. "Mind, hell. He won't even notice." She got to her feet. She wore a sleeveless sweater and a short skirt; her bare legs were long and slender. She kicked off her shoes and followed Perry to the dance floor. The music quickened. "'We're going to wait till the midnight hour,'" the Negro crooned into the microphone. "'When there's nobody else around.'" Perry took Marie's hand and swung her toward him, then away; for a big man he was surprisingly graceful. Marie's body moved like water, a smooth rippling of hip and shoulder. Only her hair remained still, a firm tower of blond, sculpted as a wedding cake.

Birdie drained her glass. Perry's legs were quick and rhythmic; the loose black trousers sat low on his hips. He twirled Marie, then pulled her close, their bodies merging at the pelvis. A Hambley girl had once whispered to Birdie that dancing was nothing but dry intercourse. At the time, the remark had baffled her. Now, watching Perry and Marie, she understood perfectly.

When the music ended, Perry and Marie came back to the table, laughing and breathless.

"Whew," said Marie. "You got me good that time."

Perry sat next to Birdie. He was very close; she smelled soap, alcohol, sweat. "Looks like you're dry," he said. "Let me get you another one."

"Yes, please," said Birdie. Across the table Marie fanned herself with a napkin. She tugged at the V of her sweater; sweat glistened on her suntanned chest.

"You're a good dancer," said Birdie.

"You're sweet." Marie refilled her glass from the pitcher; foam slipped over the rim. "Oops," she said. She lowered her mouth to the glass and slurped away the excess.

Birdie smiled. If Jody or Charlie had done such a thing in public, she would have been mortified; but watching Marie it seemed perfectly reasonable—more logical, certainly, than wiping the glass with a napkin, which would make a sticky mess.

Birdie giggled. Marie looked at her, quizzically at first; then she too began to laugh.

Perry returned with two glasses and sat down next to Birdie. "What's so funny?"

Marie laughed louder, a shrieking sound.

"Nothing," said Birdie.

"I brought you a spare," said Perry. "Save me a trip."

"Thank you," said Birdie. She gulped the drink.

"We're going to take a short break," the Negro said into the microphone. His voice was very deep. "Back in ten."

"Excuse me," said Birdie, getting to her feet. She wove her way through the crowd. Her legs felt loose and warm; the drink was stronger than she'd imagined. In the ladies' room she waited for a stall, her bladder heavy as a melon. Women stood three deep at the mirror, brushing, powdering, fixing lipstick. A short brunette teased her fallen beehive with a rattail comb.

Some time later she was walking across the room; time had begun to quicken and slow, back to its old tricks. Thunder rumbled in the distance. "It's raining," the Negro crooned into the microphone. "Another rainy night in Georgia."

Birdie approached the small stage; she stood at the edge of the dance floor, swaying slightly to the music. The singer was young, handsome in his dark suit; his hair was neatly parted, slicked with something to make it shine. He's about Curtis's age, she thought. She hadn't seen Curtis Mabry in nine years, had never seen him as a grown man. He might, she thought, look exactly like this.

She turned and made her way through the tables, her hand trailing over the backs of empty chairs. The crowd had thinned; couples headed toward the door, hoping to beat the storm. Across the room Marie's blond hair was bright as a lighthouse; the rest of the room bobbed like a boat on a choppy sea. I'm drinking too much, Birdie thought.

Perry looked up from the table. "Where have you been? We thought you fell in."

Outside, a clap of thunder sounded. The Negro sang: "Seems like it's raining all over the world." Then the room went dark. The air filled with gasps, laughter, a smattering of applause.

"Ooh!" Marie squealed from across the table.

"Power's out," said Perry. Then, without warning, Birdie felt his hand on her thigh, his mouth at her ear, breathing warmly. In the next moment the lights came back; the room filled with groans. Instantly Perry's hand was gone, so abruptly she could have imagined it.

Lou got to his feet and reached for Marie's hand.

"Where do you think you're going?" said Marie. "Things are just getting interesting." She lit the wrong end of a cigarette and tossed it, disgusted, into the ashtray.

Perry stood. "Us too. Time we hit the road."

Birdie rose. She felt unsteady on her feet. "It was nice meeting you," she said to Marie. She still felt the imprint of Perry's hand on her thigh.

"You two be good," said Marie. "Don't do anything I wouldn't do."

They made their way to the door. To Birdie the crowd seemed liquid, parting gently to let them pass. Outside it was raining hard, the drops shattering where they hit the pavement.

"Oh no," said Birdie.

"It's just water," said Perry.

He took her hand and they ran across the parking lot, puddles bursting beneath their feet. I'm drunk, Birdie thought. Her foot landed hard in something cold.

"Wait," she cried. "My shoe." She ran back and retrieved the white pump, lying on its side in a puddle. She slipped it back on and followed Perry to the car.

"Jesus," he breathed, slamming the door behind him.

Inside the car was quiet, the clatter of raindrops muted. Birdie raked at her wet hair. She was soaked through, her dress plastered to her skin, the outline of her slip clearly visible through the wet fabric. She crossed her arms over her chest.

"Don't," said Perry. Then he reached across the seat and pulled her close. For a second she panicked; he was squeezing her too tight, her lungs wanted to expand but couldn't. He kissed her hard on the mouth. His sour breath was oddly fragrant, like swallowing perfume. His cheeks were rough with invisible beard, a blond man's trick.

"You're shivering," he said.

"Cold," she said. Her legs felt heavy and lifeless, like something she'd have to carry. Perry eased her back across the seat and slid on top of her.

"Better?" he said.

She couldn't answer him; they were joined at the mouth, an airtight seal. If she wanted to she could blow him up like a balloon; he would float above her, filled with her breath. She closed her eyes. Music in the distance; her body warmed where their chests met, a moist pocket of heat.

His hand slid between them and fumbled at the buttons of her dress. "I've been waiting for this all night." He pushed her slip aside and lifted out a white breast.

"Pretty," he said, and lowered his head to her chest. His mouth was warm; it seemed to pull a string inside her. In a moment she would unravel completely.

He reached under her dress, rough palms snagging her stockings.

This can't be, Birdie thought.

"Relax," said Perry.

The vague thrill of his mouth at her ear. She closed her eyes and thought of him and Marie dancing, hands touching, the proximity of their hips, the colored singer crooning into the microphone. His mouth was suddenly delicious. With her eyes closed the car seemed to spin; she imagined it boring into the earth like a corkscrew, scattering red dirt, screwing them down into the ground.

S he woke to the sound of bells, the bells of the Catholic church on the other side of the river. The sun lit the sky as if nothing unusual had happened. Birdie shifted, a small movement of head and neck. Her mouth was dry; pain covered her right eye and pulsed at the roots of her hair. She had been dreaming of Curtis Mabry.

She sat up carefully and saw her yellow dress crumpled into a ball at the foot of the bed. Naked, she felt under her pillow for her nightgown and pulled it over her head. Her arms were crossed with sheet marks, her chest red and blotchy, scraped raw by Perry's beard. She could still feel every place he'd touched her; her skin seemed unnaturally soft, like unbaked dough.

No, she thought. Usually this was enough, this single word. But this time memory came in a wave. Perry's mouth against her ear: "I'll bet you're a natural redhead," he'd said, fumbling at her garter belt. "There's only one way to tell." His weight on her, pressing her down, slowly rocking. "Don't worry," he said. "I'll be careful." At the end he withdrew from her, turned away in the dark. A single breath escaped his throat. A sound like raindrops on the vinyl floor mat, heavy as pearls.

Birdie's hand went to her throat. She sprang out of bed and picked up the dress from the floor. A button was missing from the bodice; stains decorated the skirt. The fabric gave off a smell, cigarette smoke and something else, dirty and sour. Her eyes dusted the room: nightstand, floor, top of the bureau. She reached for her pocketbook dangling from the doorknob; inside was lipstick, a wallet, nothing else. In the bureau drawer the leatherette case was empty.

She went into the living room holding her head. The house was quiet as a crime scene. The children were still asleep; Dinah must have let them stay up late. Birdie glanced around the room. The girl had straightened up: the crocheted afghan was folded over the back of the sofa, the dolls and blocks and miniature cars packed neatly into the toy chest. Birdie recognized her white pumps at the doorway, the toes pointed toward the door as if they were on their way out.

She crept into the kitchen. She'd come home hungry; she remembered, vaguely, making herself a sandwich. Now crumbs littered the table, a loaf of bread getting stale; she hadn't bothered to close the bag. An open jar of mayonnaise sat on the counter, a fly perching on the rim. Nausea twisted her stomach.

She had lost her mother's pearls.

here have you been?" said Miss Semple. "We've been waiting for you all morning."

She stood in the doorway looking over Charlie's shoulder, into the house. *Don't let her in,* his mother had told him.

"Mama's sick," Charlie said. "She's not going to work today."

"Where is she?" Miss Semple asked. He could see she wanted to come in; how he was supposed to stop her, he had no idea.

"Sleeping," said Charlie. She'd been sleeping for two days.

"I see," said Miss Semple. "Is she well enough to make you something to eat?"

"Yes'm," said Charlie. For two days they had eaten apples, bread and jelly.

Miss Semple frowned. "All right then. You keep an eye on your sister. Make sure she stays quiet so your mother can rest."

"Yes'm."

"And get to bed early tonight. The school bus comes at seven-thirty. You don't want to be late your first day of school."

"Yes'm," said Charlie.

He closed the door. The living room was dark; his mother had drawn the blinds and wanted them kept that way. He thought of turning on the television but decided no. It was the last day of summer, his last day to add rocks to the dam. Yet he wasn't sad; he didn't mind going back to school. The puppies were gone; they no longer needed him. And the school cafeteria made delicious lunches, barbecue sandwiches and sloppy joes.

"Charlie," his mother called.

He ran to the door of her bedroom. "I didn't let her in," he said.

"Good boy." His mother sat up in bed. Her face looked large and puffy. Beside the bed was an empty bottle.

"You mind your sister," she said. "I'm going downtown."

SHE GOT OFF at her usual stop but took the long way around the block. She'd called and told Fay she was sick; it wouldn't do to go traipsing past the luncheonette window in the middle of the afternoon. The day was cool and sunny, the air flavored with fall. A whole season had passed, as if she'd been in bed for months instead of a couple of days.

She crossed the street to the garage and went into the office. The air was thick with cigarette smoke, the same acrid smell she'd washed out of her yellow dress. Her head began to pulse; she felt loose and jangly from the wine.

A man appeared through the swinging door. "Ma'am?" he said. "Can I help you?" A smudge of black grazed his cheek. It was a moment before she recognized him. He was the one who'd wanted three hundred dollars to fix her car.

"Yes," she said firmly. "I would like to speak to Buck Perry."

"Right now?" He eyed her strangely. She hadn't taken the time to change, just pulled a sweater over her housedress. Still, he had no business staring. She, at least, was clean.

"Please," she said.

He turned toward the swinging door. "Hey, Buck," he yelled. "There's a lady here to see you."

Perry came through the door in dirty coveralls. His eyebrows lifted when he saw her. "Well, hello," he said. "This is a nice surprise." He wiped his hands across his chest; they were black with grease.

Birdie's head throbbed. She thought: I let him touch me with those hands.

"I stopped by the luncheonette to see you," he said. "Fay said you were home sick."

Birdie blinked. He was a thief; she'd expected him to be nervous.

"I believe you have something of mine," she said.

"I do?"

"Yes." Birdie watched him closely.

"What's that?"

"The last time I saw you"—her voice faltered, then recovered—"I was wearing a valuable piece of jewelry."

"You were?"

"A pearl necklace." She felt tears behind her eyes but willed them back. Her voice came out in a whisper. "It belonged to my mother."

Perry frowned. "Did you lose it?"

Birdie nodded.

Perry ran a hand through his hair. "Did you call over at the Vets? Maybe somebody found it."

"I didn't lose it at the Vets." It was true; she was nearly sure. "It must have been later. In your car." Her face heated. She could not look at him.

"I didn't find any pearls," he said.

Something broke inside her.

"Are you sure?"

"Of course I'm sure." Perry frowned at her. "What are you getting at? Are you saying I took them?"

Birdie turned to go.

"Wait!" said Perry, but she didn't listen. She ran out the door, into the street, and kept running. Tears trailed down her cheeks: for her mother's pearls, for everything she had lost.

*D*rinking, she remembered Curtis Mabry.

When they were both eight, Curtis had come down with chicken pox; his mother kept him home from school—the colored school—for a week. They'd hidden together under Birdie's porch; she made him rub his arms and legs against hers so she'd get chicken pox too. Somehow they'd both escaped with a single scar, a faint circle at the corner of one eye—Curtis's left, Birdie's right. Something they'd have for the rest of their lives, marking them forever alike.

Once, the summer they turned seventeen, they went swimming at night. Birdie could still conjure up the feeling of it, a heaviness in her arms and legs, a slow dilation of her senses not unlike being drunk. There was a warmth about him, a heat underneath his skin that bled into her if they were close enough. They had always played together, run wild in the woods while Curtis's mother cleaned or cooked. The play had simply changed.

That night the pond shone flat as a mirror under the moon. They had the thought at the same time; their minds had always worked alike. "Let's go," said Curtis. It was always Curtis who pressed, who took liberties, Birdie who said no and no and no until he covered her mouth with his and did as they both wanted.

"I can't," she said.

He didn't try to coax her. He kicked off his shoes and fumbled with his trousers. Birdie heard a buzzing in her ears. In the moonlight his skin looked as white as hers. She covered her eyes and was immediately sorry, but it was too late. He was in the water too fast.

And then she did something she could not have predicted. She unbuttoned her blouse. The water was warmer than the air, the same temperature as her blood. The loamy mudsmell seeped into her hair.

When they touched it was like touching her own body. From childhood they had been the same height; their arms and legs and hands were still perfectly congruent. Only the centers of them were different, aching, fascinated, every part of them heated to the same temperature by the sunwarmed pond.

C harlie got off the school bus and climbed the hill to his house. With him was Greg McGough, a new boy who'd moved from Kentucky. The first day of school Greg had shoved Charlie into a wall and made his nose bleed; the second day Charlie was waiting for him in the lunchroom. Their teacher stopped the fight and kept them both after school; that afternoon Greg's mother picked them up and drove them home. After that Charlie and Greg were best friends.

Greg's dad was a truck driver. He drove all over the country, to Texas and back, once to California. Each time he brought back a souvenir for Greg: a water gun, an Indian arrowhead, a dead mouse pickled in a jar. Charlie pictured Greg's dad like Artemus Gordon, his favorite character from his favorite TV show, *The Wild Wild West*.

"He's coming home tonight," Greg told Charlie as they walked. It was a Friday. "Tomorrow me and him are going to Luray Caverns."

Charlie had never been to Luray Caverns, but he'd heard about it at school. He was impressed.

"I bet your dad's been there," said Greg. "I bet the bus goes all the time." Charlie had told Greg his dad was a bus driver, that he drove a Greyhound all over the country and only came home at Christmas.

"Sometimes," said Charlie. They arrived at his front step.

"You can come with us if you want," said Greg.

"Really?" said Charlie.

"I'll call you on the phone." They had exchanged phone numbers; the whole second-grade class had been required to memorize their own numbers and addresses.

"See you tomorrow," said Greg.

"Yeah," said Charlie. "See you." He reached under the doormat and unlocked the front door, then replaced the key under the mat. It was a new rule: Charlie was to go in and out through the front door only; he was to lock it behind him. "You never know," his mother had told him. "Someone could come and take your sister while she's sleeping." Charlie couldn't imagine anyone wanting his sister, but he usually remembered to lock the door.

Inside, he put down his book bag and took off his shoes, then went to the door of his mother's room and peered through the crack. She was still in her nightgown, a pillow over her face. His sister lay curled next to her, but she was not asleep. Her eyes brightened when she saw Charlie.

He held a finger to his lips. "Come on," he whispered.

Carefully Jody crawled out of the bed. She could be quiet when she wanted to, quieter than Charlie. She knew better than to wake their mother, who would be in a bad mood.

They went into the kitchen. Charlie found bread and grape jelly in the refrigerator and made a sandwich of the last two slices of bread. He cut the sandwich crosswise and gave half to Jody.

"Don't make a mess," he said, though it was already too late: after one bite her mouth was slick with purple.

In the living room the telephone rang. Charlie stood and listened. Luray Caverns, he thought. From the bedroom his mother groaned.

"Don't answer that," she called to Charlie. "It isn't anybody."

"Yes'm," said Charlie. He knew she was right; Greg couldn't be home yet. He finished his sandwich and went to the bedroom door. She was sitting up in bed, a dazed expression on her face.

"We're out of bread and milk," he said.

She rubbed her eyes. "Where's my pocketbook?"

Charlie took the pocketbook from the doorknob and approached the bed. His mother took out her wallet and handed him a five-dollar bill. She had begun sending him to the store.

"Bring me back a bottle of wine," she said.

THE SCREEN DOOR slammed. Birdie closed her eyes and waited for sleep to come. The phone rang again; a chill climbed her back. For two days she'd called in sick at the luncheonette. The second day it was Mr. Loomis, not Fay, who'd answered. "What exactly is wrong, Vivian?" he'd asked irritably.

"The flu," said Birdie. "A bad case of flu."

"You been to the doctor's?"

"I'm going today. I have an appointment."

"How about you bring us a note from that doctor."

After that she didn't call the luncheonette at all. Let Loomis think what he wanted. She had a young child in public school; every other day, it seemed, he came home with a sniffle. It was exhausting, raising children with no help from anyone; naturally her resistance was down. She was so angry with Loomis that she forgot she didn't have the flu at all, that she'd made the whole thing up.

Finally the ringing stopped. Birdie sat up and fumbled beneath the bed for her slippers, then gave up and walked barefoot across the carpet, noticing a splotch of purple where she'd spilled some wine that morning. She found a sweater on the floor and buttoned it over her nightgown. Then she heard a deeper ringing, the two tenor notes of the doorbell.

She froze. It was probably nothing. The day before she'd hidden in the bedroom closet; when she emerged, she saw two little girls descend her front steps and ring the Gleasons' bell next door. She recognized their green hats and knee socks: Girl Scouts selling cookies.

She tiptoed into the children's room and peered out from behind the curtain. The county woman stood on the doorstep talking to a man in a suit. Birdie sank to the floor, hand over her mouth. She could barely hear their voices over the pounding of her heart.

"It's three o'clock," said the woman. "Where could she be?"

"The boy was in school today," said the man. "I called and checked. Maybe she went to meet him at the school bus."

The floorboards creaked.

"Something is very wrong," said the woman. "I've been trying to call her all week. I'm scared to death for those children."

Birdie looked at the clock. The children would be back any minute. She pictured them climbing the hill, Charlie with a bottle of wine in his hand. Please, she thought. No.

The seconds ticked off. Charlie's alarm clock was shaped like a football. Each morning a voice inside it shouted "Hike!" getting him up for school.

Finally the man spoke. "We can't wait around all day. We'll have to come back."

There was a creaking of floorboards, a shuffling of shoes. The county woman's high heels descended the porch stairs. A car started at the curb, then pulled away.

A moment later Birdie heard footsteps on the back porch. The screen door opened.

"Mummy!" Jody cried.

Birdie rushed into the kitchen, her legs shaky with relief. She scooped Jody into her arms.

"You aren't mad, are you?" said Charlie.

Birdie leaned against the refrigerator, grateful for its support. "Why, button?" she said. "Why would I be mad?"

"You said to come in the front." His brow wrinkled, a mannerism of his father's.

"It's all right," said Birdie. "Just this once." She reached into the paper sack Charlie had set on the counter.

"I didn't get milk," he said. "I ran out of money."

"That's fine," said Birdie. She took the wine bottle out of the sack. "Mama's going to take a bath."

A CORK POPPED; water rushed into the tub. Through the thin floors Charlie heard the water pump in the basement, ticking like a bomb. He sat in the living room looking at the phone. Brian Norton, who'd gone that summer, said Luray Caverns were as old as the dinosaurs. The caverns tunneled deep into a mountain; you could get lost in them and never find your way out. Inside the caverns were fossils, pools of water, ancient bones. Brian Norton hadn't seen any bats hanging upside down, but Charlie thought there must be, if you knew where to look.

The water stopped. Charlie went to the bathroom door. It was open a crack. His sister sat on the floor with crayons and a coloring book; his mother lay in the water with her eyes closed, the bottle of wine balanced on the edge of the tub. He went back to the living room. When the phone rang he held his breath, waiting for his mother's voice; but it did not come.

Heart racing, he picked up the phone. "Hello?" he said. He had not answered the phone in a long time; it made him nervous. Please, he thought. Luray Caverns.

"Hello?" said a lady's voice. "Charlie, is that you? This is Grandma Helen."

"Oh," said Charlie. "Hi, Grandma."

"Hi, honey." Her voice shook. "Let me talk to your mother."

"She's sleeping."

"You go and wake her up then. It's very important."

"Yes'm." He went to the bathroom and knocked at the door. In the tub his mother stirred. He opened the door a little. "Mama?"

She groaned and rolled over on her side; she was like a big slow fish kept in a tank.

"Mama," he said, louder this time.

She sat up in the tub. "Charlie Kimble," she said, crossing her arms over her chest. "What's the matter with you? Close your eyes this minute."

Charlie did. "Grandma Helen is on the phone."

"Damnation. What did I tell you about the phone?" She stood, her back to Charlie, and wrapped herself in a towel. For a moment she lost her footing, then caught herself against the wall. She stepped out of the tub and went into the living room, leaving a trail of wet footprints.

"Hello, Helen," she said into the phone.

Charlie followed. His sister stuck her head out the bathroom door. "Whata matter?" she said.

Their mother let out a cry then; in the next moment she dropped the towel. It was a thing Charlie would remember forever: his mother standing naked in the middle of the living room, dripping wet from the bath as if her whole body were weeping.

HER FATHER was named John Wilkes Bell, for the man who shot Lincoln. He was a big red-haired man who'd been to war and married late. He met Birdie's mother at a wedding in Charleston. He was at that time forty-six years old.

He wanted a son but settled for a daughter. He taught Birdie to ride and shoot; he took her fishing and hunting, sometimes inviting Curtis Mabry, the housekeeper's son, to come along. Then she turned fourteen and began to change; her father became polite and careful, as though she might break. There was no more fishing after that, no more hunting; her father's rifle was locked away in the hall cabinet, silent behind the glass.

In the winter Birdie's mother got sick; for a year father and daughter tiptoed around the dark house, waiting for her to recover. During that time Birdie's father seemed to forget her entirely, as if what he'd always suspected, the basic fragility of women, had been confirmed. After her mother's death the house stayed dark. Every morning her father walked to his law office in town; every evening he came back drunk, was fed by Ella Mabry and put to bed in his clothes. By the time Birdie went off to Hambley, she no longer knew her father. She hadn't known him in a long time.

He drove her to Hambley himself, a hot August day in the middle of a drought, dust in her hair and in her mouth, through the open windows a smell of hay. She would study sacred music; she would learn to play the organ. There had been no discussion of whether or why. Her father had arranged everything himself.

While she was away at school, he married a widow he'd met on a trip to Richmond. Birdie found out that winter when she came home for Christmas vacation. When they pulled up to the house, Helen was standing on the front porch, hugging herself in a homely gray coat. She was tall and plain, with a long equine face and dull brown hair cut short like a man's. At dinner she sat in Birdie's mother's chair. Once Birdie had walked past her father's bedroom and seen Helen at the dressing table using her mother's hairbrush.

After Christmas Birdie went back to Hambley. By summertime she was married and pregnant, living in Missouri with someone else's parents.

THEY RODE to the bus station in the rain; the taxi cost three dollars. Birdie tipped the driver, then paid for their tickets with her last twenty. She'd already spent her one paycheck from the luncheonette: phone, electricity, the rebuilt transmission for the car. As they waited for the bus, she gave Charlie a quarter.

"Go get yourself a soda pop," she said.

It was done: her last dollar broken into coins. She felt the urge to celebrate. All summer long she'd waited for this, the end of the end, when whatever it was she'd been dreading for months would finally happen. Here I am, she thought. Come and get me.

Then she remembered that her father was dead.

THEY SAT at the front of the bus, Charlie and Jody and their mother; over the driver's shoulder they could see the road stretching in front of them. The driver wasn't tall but he had dark hair, thin on top. He looked a little like Charlie's father.

His mother leaned against the window, holding Jody in her lap; her hair was still damp from the bath, leaving a wet mark on the glass. Underneath the seat was a small suitcase packed with their clothes. Through the window Charlie watched the streets go past: stores and offices, then houses, then woods and open fields. The sky was beginning to darken. He'd drunk a whole bottle of grape Nehi at the bus station; his stomach hurt from the bubbles.

The bus ride took three hours. "Montford, Virginia," the driver announced. Grandma Helen was waiting for them inside the station. She wore an old coat over her dress; her long face looked pale and tight. "Where's Ken?" she asked. "Isn't he coming?"

"He's in Missouri," said Charlie's mother. "Visiting his father."

They drove to the house in Pappy's station wagon, loud inside from the rain. They drove through the small town and out the other side of it, a long country road that wound through a forest.

"We never even got him to the hospital," said Grandma Helen. She explained how Pappy had been upstairs shaving, how she'd never even heard him fall. It was the water that finally got her attention, seeping through the kitchen ceiling. Pappy had left the water running; the sink overflowed, the drain clogged with soap.

"I kept trying to call you, but no one answered," she said. "I was about to send a telegram. There must be something wrong with your phone."

They turned off the road onto a dirt path paved with chunks of red rock. The path looked beaten smooth by the rain; on either side of it, the ditches overflowed with pinkish mud.

For supper they had ham sandwiches and coleslaw. His mother wore a dress and stockings. Halfway through the meal she turned to Grandma Helen.

"Where's Ella?" she said. It was the first she'd spoken since the bus station.

"I'm afraid we won't have her until Monday," said Grandma Helen. "It's unfortunate timing. Her boy—what's his name?"

"Curtis," said Charlie's mother.

"Curtis is getting married tomorrow." Grandma Helen reached for Charlie's plate and heaped it with more coleslaw. "A girl from Alabama. He met her down there when he was in the service. Apparently her people are all staying at Ella's, though I can't see how that's possible in such a small house. Ella said she'd be cooking all weekend. "

Charlie's mother said nothing. She did not eat, just moved the food around her plate with a fork. A while later she pushed away her plate and went out the back door.

THE RAIN had stopped; a pale moon glowed through the wet clouds. Birdie left her shoes at the back door and stepped into a pair of her father's boots. The boots were cold inside, worn smooth all around; he'd had them specially made to fit his large feet. Daddy, she thought. For the first time in hours, something nipped at the edge of her. She exhaled; the feeling passed.

She followed the dirt road to the pond, nearly black in the low light. In the distance an owl hooted; the frogs and crickets were strangely silent. She peered through the woods. Through the trees she could make out the lights of Ella Mabry's house, a tiny bungalow on the other side of the forest. She heard strains of music in the distance, a barking dog, full-throated Negro laughter.

She squatted at the edge of the pond; the hem of her dress grazed the muddy ground. Her father had taught her to swim in the pond, his big hands under her belly as she kicked and smacked at the water. "Don't let go," she told him a hundred times. "I won't," he said a hundred times back. Then once she looked back and saw him ten feet behind her and realized she was swimming. Her mother was terrified of water; she sat in a lawn chair and covered her eyes as Birdie and her father splashed and ducked. "I can't look," she'd say, peering between her fingers. Finally she stopped coming; she lived indoors the bright afternoons, the folded lawn chair gathering dust on the back porch.

Birdie circled the pond, protected on three sides by dense forest. In summertime it felt perfectly secluded; only when the leaves fell did you notice how close the house was. Anyone swimming in the pond would be clearly visible from the dirt road, but that had never mattered; the road was seldom traveled during the day and never at night. Birdie looked back toward the house and imagined a figure coming down the dirt road, a big man with a heavy step.

Her father had been drunk the night he found her and Curtis in the pond. He'd left his car downtown at the Legion and walked back to the house. Except he hadn't stopped there; for reasons she never understood, he'd walked past the house and continued down the dirt road, his footsteps quiet on the gravel. He must have seen them first and gone back to the house for his hunting rifle.

She and Curtis sprang apart when the first shot rang out, the water suddenly cold against her chest, her thighs, all the parts of her that had been touching him. Even before she knew what was happening, she was sick with the loss of him.

"Daddy!" she cried.

He fired another shot into the air, wild-haired, his face white in the moonlight, tears streaming down his cheeks.

"Get out of here, you nigger bastard," he barked. Then he lost his footing on the muddy bank.

"Run!" Birdie cried. "Run!"

Curtis tore through the water: a slick flash of skin, a gasp of breath. Her father stumbled, then righted himself. He fired a third shot. Curtis disappeared into the woods, leaving his clothes behind.

The rest her memory skipped: weeks, a month. The next thing she remembered the summer was over, and her father was driving her to Hambley.

*T*he doorbell woke her, the first of the covered dishes. All morning long, women would come with baked hams, chicken and dumplings, casseroles of every description. When Birdie's mother died the church women had filled the chest freezer with food; she and her father had eaten sympathy casseroles for a month.

Hushed female voices filled the downstairs hallway and floated up the steps: Sally Beauchamp, Birdie guessed, or Marion Simpers or Betsy Peale. She had gone to school with their daughters; as a girl she'd been to birthday parties at their houses. The women had lived in Montford their whole lives and knew more about Birdie's family than she did: which great-grandfathers had drunk or gambled, made money or lost it, hit their wives or fallen asleep in church. There was nothing malicious in their talk. Montford's only movie house had closed when Birdie was small; for entertainment there were four churches and the public library. Under such conditions gossip was inevitable.

There was a knock at the bedroom door. "Birdie," Helen called. "Mrs. Peale would like to say hello."

"I'm not dressed," said Birdie. "Please thank her for me. Tell her I'll see her in church."

Her dark dress hung in the closet, losing its wrinkles. They want to get a look at me, she thought. They want to see what an abandoned woman looks like. Since moving to Richmond she'd visited Montford three times, just her and the children; Ken could never be persuaded to come. She knew perfectly well how it looked to the Betsy Peales of the world—her turning up with two babies and no husband. At the time it had enraged her. *I'm married!* she'd wanted to shout when she passed them in the street. *I have a husband!* Now she knew the gossips had been right all along.

She slipped on a housecoat and went downstairs. The children sat at the table dressed and ready, eating scrambled eggs.

"Where's your grandma Helen?" Birdie asked.

"Upstairs," said Charlie. He wore long pants and a white shirt; next to his plate lay a child-size blue necktie.

"Where did that come from?" Birdie asked.

"Grandma." Charlie covered his toast with a thick smear of butter. "Do I have to wear it?"

Birdie heard rapid footsteps overhead, Helen bustling about the bedroom. She looked up. The kitchen ceiling was cracked in one corner, the plaster beginning to crumble: the spot where the bathroom sink had overflowed.

"Bring it with you," she told Charlie. "You can take it off after church."

She sat at the table between the children, watching them eat. Footsteps climbed the back porch, a knock at the kitchen door. Through the lace curtains she saw familiar brown eyes, a dark, heart-shaped face.

"Ella!" she cried.

She opened the door. Ella Mabry wore the same black dress she'd worn to Birdie's mother's funeral. She'd put it on especially for the visit. She'd have to change again when she got home, Birdie thought, something festive to watch Curtis get married in.

"Little Birdie." Ella opened her arms and hugged Birdie to her chest. "I had to come and see you. I been feeling bad all morning." Her hair smelled of cooking and lilac perfume; her shoulders felt very small. Birdie's throat tightened. Age had worn away at her like a bar of soap. One day she would simply disappear.

Ella looked around the kitchen, at the covered dishes sitting on the counter. "You going to have your hands full with the luncheon."

"We've got lots of food," said Birdie. "I'm sure it will be fine."

"They can come eat they own casseroles, isn't that right?" Ella chuckled. "Better put them in the icebox. You don't want to leave them setting out."

Birdie busied herself with the casseroles. Her back to Ella, she asked, "How's Curtis?"

A brief silence: forks on china, Jody slurping her milk.

"He doing just fine," said Ella. "I guess you know he getting married today."

Birdie's chest ached; a lump rose in her throat. "Helen told me. A girl from Alabama, is that right?"

"Maple," said Ella. "Her name going to be Maple Mabry. Isn't that something?"

Birdie turned to Ella. "Do you like her?"

"She's a good girl. Not like that other one." Ella glanced at the children and lowered her voice. "You know he got a little boy already, from that girl he was fooling around with. He seven years old already."

Birdie's heart raced. "I didn't know."

Ella beamed at Jody and Charlie. "Look at these children. How they growing." She gave Charlie's shoulder a squeeze. "This one look a little skinny to me." She took the frypan from the stove and scraped the rest of the eggs onto his plate.

"I wished I could stay and help," she said. "I wished I would have known."

"Don't you worry," said Birdie. Her voice shook. "You go on now. Go and have a good time at that wedding."

She clasped Ella again, a quick contact of chest and shoulders.

"Your father was a good man," said Ella, "even with his faults."

And she turned and was gone.

THEY FILED out from under the tent, past the big box where Pappy lay. Charlie followed his grandma Helen; he made a game of keeping up with her long legs, taking two steps for each of hers. His sister watched him over his grandma's shoulder, thumb in her mouth like a baby.

The box was closed but Charlie had seen inside earlier, at the funeral parlor. He hadn't wanted to, but his mother made him. Come say good-bye to your pappy, she'd said. The man in the box was wearing a suit. Charlie had never seen Pappy wear anything but an old brown sweater; in summer, a blue checked shirt.

At the edge of the cemetery, cars were lining up.

"Birdie," said Grandma Helen. "You go and ride up front." She pointed to the big gray station wagon they'd transported the box in. The chrome hubcaps and bumpers gleamed like silver; the back windows of the car were hung with curtains. "They'll take you back to the house."

"No," said his mother. "You go ahead. I'll take Daddy's car and meet you back there."

"Are you sure?" said Grandma Helen.

"Of course. You take the baby. Charlie can ride with me."

She took him by the hand to Pappy's big sedan. The car started with a powerful sound. His mother turned sharply, struggling with the steering wheel. The car rolled down the road, leaving the others behind.

"Where are we going?" said Charlie.

"To town. I need to stop at the store."

It was a small town: churches, a gas station, a flashing red light at the main intersection to slow the traffic. A little grocery store sat at the corner, no bigger than a garage. His mother parked at the curb and stepped into the street, leaving the engine running. In a moment she came out of the store with a paper sack.

"Hold this a minute, button," she said. "Just till we get out of town."

Charlie looked inside the bag, though he already knew what it was. The two bottles of wine sat heavy in his lap. His mother drove past the post office, the fire station, the newspaper stand. They passed under the flashing light and followed the road that led to Pappy's.

Outside the town they pulled over to the side of the road.

"Let me have that sack," said his mother.

The bottle had no cork; she screwed it open with her bare hand. She took a long drink from the bottle and sat a moment with her eyes closed. Then she took off her hat and tossed it into the back-seat.

"Roll down your window," she said. "Get some air in here."

Charlie did. They got back on the road.

"Where are we going?" he said.

"Back to the house." She took another drink from the bottle. "There's a whole houseful of people waiting for us."

"What people?" he asked.

His mother laughed. "Just people."

She stepped on the gas, filling the car with wind. Her hair blew crazily around her head; it seemed like something separate from her, a cloud of reddish smoke. On either side trees rushed past; farmers' fields, houses and barns. The car raced past the dirt road to Pappy's house; Charlie recognized the mailbox marked J. W. BELL disappearing behind them.

"You missed the turn," he said.

"We're taking the scenic route." She drank, then set the bottle in her lap and gripped it between her thighs. Her hands were white on the steering wheel. The road curved sharply, then climbed a steep hill. The engine roared.

"Hang on to your hat," she said, though Charlie wasn't wearing one and hers lay on the floor behind the seat. At the top of the hill, the road dropped sharply into a hollow. His stomach lurched as they sailed down the hill. His mother laughed; wine splashed from the bottle into her lap.

They followed the road up another hill. At the top the car slowed.

"Why are we stopping?" he asked.

"I want to enjoy the view." She cut the engine and stepped out, taking the bottle with her. Charlie followed and sat next to her on the hood. They stared down into the valley, at a small house surrounded by parked cars. Chairs had been set up in the front lawn.

"What are they doing?" he asked.

"They're getting married." Down in the valley people settled into the chairs. His mother pointed to the house. "See them? That's the bride and groom."

Charlie squinted. A dark couple stood on the porch, the woman in a white dress and hat. For a long time his mother didn't speak, just sipped quietly from the bottle.

"Button," she said finally, "get me that other bottle."

Charlie got the sack from the car and handed it to her. She lay her empty bottle on the ground; the opening was caked with her lipstick. Then she opened the new bottle and took a drink. Down below the people began to clap. A wind blew through the valley and up the hill, carrying voices, music, laughter.

"That's it," said his mother. "It's done."

She slid off the hood, stumbling a little.

"It's these shoes." She bent over and took them off, leaning on the car for support. Then she tossed her shoes in the backseat and sat heavily behind the wheel. The engine started with a roar. She pulled onto the road, scattering gravel; they headed back the way they had come. His mother drove faster now; the engine roared as they climbed the first hill.

"Mama," said Charlie. "Who were those people?"

His mother accelerated; the car charged down the other side of the hill, gaining speed.

"We were best friends," she said. "Me and him played together when we were little."

Ahead of them a pickup truck appeared around the curve.

"Move over," Charlie yelled. "There's someone coming."

"Good Lord," said his mother. She turned the wheel sharply to the right, just before they hit the curve. The truck swerved out of their way, missing them by inches; the car spun off the road, a horrible squeal. Then everything was quiet.

His mother lay flopped over the steering wheel, the bottle of wine at her feet. Somehow her hat had landed in her lap.

"Mama?" said Charlie.

She lifted her head. Her face had a look he'd seen before, as if she'd just woken from a nap. She opened the car door and staggered out. They had landed in a farmer's field.

"Let's go," she said.

"What about the car?"

"I don't want it."

Charlie got out of the car. His mother walked strangely, a cut bleeding at her forehead. They walked through the field, their feet sinking in the moist earth. She was barefoot but seemed not to notice. He reached for her hand. They walked up the hill and crossed the road, to the dirt path that led to Pappy's house.

The house was surrounded by cars. His mother stopped and patted at her hair. Grandma Helen appeared on the porch.

"Birdie!" she cried. "What in God's name happened?" She ran down the porch steps and across the lawn. Charlie had never imagined she could move so fast.

"I wrecked Daddy's car," his mother said.

"My God." Grandma Helen bent and took Charlie's face in her hands, pulled back each of his eyelids and looked at his eyes.

"Did you hit your head?" she asked.

"No'm," said Charlie.

Grandma Helen stood and embraced his mother. "Oh, Birdie."

His mother began to cry. A small crowd had assembled on the porch.

"Ken is gone," she said into Grandma Helen's shoulder. "He left in May. And I can't go back to Richmond because they're going to take away my children."

Joan

FLORIDA

1969

S he met him at a swimming-pool party in late October, in Florida a time of clear days and cool evenings, when women draped cotton sweaters over their shoulders and men remembered snow tires and dead batteries, the bitter winters of Newark or Philly or Hartford, Connecticut, the places they'd left behind. Joan Cohen, recently of New York, had never minded the snow; she still believed she would return.

The party was given by Dick and Nancy Snell, a couple Joan had known a short time. Besides Joan, they'd invited Hal and Dot Beckley, pleasant, suntanned people who shared their interest in gardening and the weather. The Snells and the Beckleys were young by local standards; they were all under fifty.

Joan sat in a chaise longue overlooking the pool; she was the only one not wearing a swimsuit. The air smelled of chlorine and citronella. Nancy Snell and Dot Beckley splashed in the water, their bodies slick in colorful nylon. Hal Beckley sat on the flagstone rim, smoking.

Dick Snell approached Joan's chair, bringing two drinks. "Here you go," he said, sitting at the foot of the chair. "Any offers on that house of yours?"

"One," said Joan. "We're still negotiating. I'm hoping to close by the holidays."

Dick chuckled. "Wait till you see the winter down here. You'll change your tune. You'll never want to leave."

Joan smiled. She'd been in Florida five months, at first settling her father's estate, lately just reading novels and walking on the beach. She'd known all along she couldn't stay. There were no bookstores; the local paper she found inadequate. She was thirty-nine years old, her neighbors of retirement age. If she hadn't met Nancy Snell at a hair salon, she'd have no friends at all.

"Have you heard from Moira?" Joan asked. Moira was the Snells' older daughter, who'd dropped out of college to drive cross-country with a friend.

"A couple of postcards." Dick looked down into his drink. "She's out in California somewhere. Nancy's worried sick about her."

"She's probably having the time of her life," said Joan, then noticed Dick's face. That's exactly what he's afraid of, she thought.

"You know what I think?" said Hal Beckley, butting his cigarette on the cement. "I think the girls should go topless."

Giggles from the pool, squeals of protest.

"Why not?" said Dick. "We're all friends here."

Nancy Snell was the first to let go; her bikini top landed with a wet slap on the cement. She was a small blonde, cute and toothy. Her breasts were the size of cupcakes.

Dick whistled approvingly. "That's my girl!" he called. The Snells had been high school sweethearts; their youngest child had just gone off to college.

He turned to Joan. "What about you?"

"No thanks."

"Come on." He placed his hand on her bare foot.

"No, really. I'll pass." Joan hugged her sweater around her and sipped her drink, a sweet concoction of mangoes and rum.

Dick stood and peeled off his shirt. He was still in navy shape at forty-six; except for the line of gray hair dividing his chest, he could have passed for thirty.

"Finish that drink," he said. "You might change your mind." He jumped into the pool with a tremendous splash.

"Watch it!" Dot Beckley yelled. She raised her arms to shield her bouffant hairdo, her flat brown nipples peeking above the surface.

"This isn't fair," said Nancy. "Giving them a show for nothing." She tore through the water, breasts bobbing, and made a grab for Dick's swim trunks. Dot clapped and squealed. They'd all been drinking for hours.

Dick disappeared underwater, surfaced, then tossed his wet trunks across the pool. "All you had to do was ask."

Hal Beckley lunged for Nancy Snell, dunking her slick blond head. In a moment she reappeared, shrieking with mock outrage. He lunged again; she shoved him aside, cocking her head.

"What's that noise?" she said. "It sounds like a car."

"Nice try," said Hal. "You won't get away from me that easy." Again his arm crossed her bare chest; again her head disappeared beneath the water, giggling and sputtering.

"Mom?" a voice came from inside the house. "Dad?"

For a moment everyone froze. Dot let out a little cry. Dick Snell tore across the pool for his trunks. The women fumbled with bikini tops.

At the rear of the house, the French doors opened. A girl

appeared in the doorway, lugging a knapsack. Behind her stood a tall man in ragged blue jeans.

"Mom?" she called.

Nancy Snell had ducked beneath the water. She reappeared, tugging at her bra straps.

"Moira," said Dick. He had tucked himself into his swim trunks.

"Surprise!" said Moira.

"It certainly is." Nancy climbed out of the pool wearing a tight smile.

"Come meet your future son-in-law." Moira clutched the man's arm, beaming. "Mom, Dad, this is Ken Kimble."

THE SNELLS and the Beckleys showered and changed; they sat around the pool in Bermuda shorts, drinking colas. Dick Snell fired up the barbecue grill. The mood on the patio was polite and restrained.

Joan stood behind Dick at the grill. "Where's the happy couple?" she asked.

Dick grunted. "Inside getting cleaned up. Could take a while, from the looks of them." He turned the steaks with a long fork; juices dropped, hissing, onto the coals.

"What's he like?" Joan asked. "Moira's fiancé."

"No idea. I never laid eyes on the guy until today." He stared morosely at the meat.

Joan glanced across the patio. Moira appeared through the French doors in a patchwork sundress.

"Joan!" she cried, running across the patio.

"Hi, honey," said Joan, embracing her. They'd met the previous spring, when Moira was home on college break. Nancy Snell had asked Joan to take the girl to lunch, to advise her on a career in journalism. They'd eaten at a seaside restaurant and spent the afternoon chatting and laughing. Joan had found Moira lively and articulate, brighter and better informed than either of her parents. She was unhappy at her small Virginia college; she found her classmates narrow-minded and politically apathetic. She planned to suffer through another two years and join the Peace Corps after graduation—though her father, she told Joan, would have a fit. That summer Joan was stunned to hear that Moira had dropped out of school.

"I want to hear all about your travels," said Joan.

"It was fantastic," said Moira. "We drove all the way up the coast, from Los Angeles to Vancouver. We picked grapes in Monterey, with these beautiful Mexican families who are here illegally because the government won't give them papers. Ken actually speaks Spanish. You're going to love him. Ken!" She was sunburned, a little breathless; her wet hair smelled of strawberries.

The boyfriend came through the French doors with Nancy Snell, who paused to point out shrubs and trees and exotic ferns. He was tall and slender; his lank dark hair hung to his shoulders. He wore faded jeans and a colorful cotton blouse.

Moira rolled her eyes. "Mother," she called. "He doesn't need the whole garden tour."

Nancy and the boyfriend approached the grill. Moira hooked a finger through one of his belt loops.

"Baby, this is Joan. I told you about her. The writer for *Newsweek*."

The boyfriend offered his hand, his grip cool and firm. He'd looked younger from a distance. Up close, Joan could see that his hairline was receding; deep grooves curved from his nostrils to the corners of his mouth. His eyes were a startling blue.

"Glad to meet you," he said. "I'm Ken Kimble."

Moira fingered the fabric at his wrist. "Isn't his shirt fabulous? All the Mexican ladies fell in love with him. One of them embroidered it herself."

"Coming through," Dick Snell barked. He stepped between Moira and Kimble, carrying a plate of steaks. Behind him trailed the rich smell of beef.

"Oh, Daddy," said Moira. "We don't eat meat. We're vegetarians."

Dick Snell didn't answer. He carried the platter to the table.

"It's okay," Kimble said softly. "We'll adapt."

They sat at wrought-iron tables overlooking the pool: Joan and the Beckleys at one table; the Snells, Moira, and Kimble at the other. The Beckleys had a Lhasa apso; they bemoaned the dearth of competent dog groomers in Palm Beach County. At the other table Dick Snell hunched over his plate, sawing at his steak; Moira picked at her potato salad. Her mother explained the gardening challenges presented by August rainstorms, sandy Florida soil. Kimble nodded attentively.

"What kind of grass is that?" he asked, pointing. "All your neighbors have it too. It seems to be everywhere down here."

"Bermuda grass," said Nancy. "It's perfect for this climate. It has deeper roots, so it holds the water better."

Kimble gave a low whistle. "Amazing," he said. "You're a walking encyclopedia."

Nancy beamed. "It's so nice to have a man around who's interested in gardening. Dick couldn't care less."

"It's fascinating stuff," said Kimble. "You could go into business giving gardening advice. Really. You'd make a fortune around here."

True enough, Joan thought. She paid plenty to have her garden maintained; she wouldn't know where to begin taking care of it herself.

"I have a question," she said. She pointed to the tall flowering shrub that bordered the patio. "What's that plant over there? With the red flowers?"

Nancy laughed. "Why, they're oleanders. You've got them yourself, in your backyard."

"I thought so." Joan helped herself to more fruit salad. "There's something wrong with mine. The leaves are all curled up, and there's some kind of black stuff on them."

"Aphids," said Nancy. "Sounds to me like aphids."

"Oh, no," said Dot. "Not *aphids!*"

A cool breeze blew across the swimming pool. The citronella candles flickered.

"You've got to take action," said Dot. "This is serious, Joan. They're insidious little creatures. If you give them an inch, you'll never get rid of them."

Kimble and Moira stood and excused themselves. Hand in hand they disappeared into the house.

*J*oan awoke with a racing heart. It was late morning, the bedroom filled with sunshine. She'd been up half the night worrying; she always slept poorly the night before a doctor's appointment. In the distance she heard the mechanical grind of a lawn mower; in her dream it had been the hum of aphids, a thousand tiny mandibles sucking at her oleanders. She put on a robe and went barefoot down the spiral staircase, across the cold marble foyer, through the cavernous kitchen and out the back door.

She passed the swimming pool and hot tub, the patio damp beneath her feet; beyond, a flagstone path bisected the grassy lawn. The path was lined with fig and mango trees, plus a host of flowering shrubs Joan couldn't identify. Her father had taken no interest in the yard; a lawn service had looked after the trees and flowers. Since his death she continued to pay the monthly bill. Every Friday a uniformed gardener came to mow and water.

The oleanders grew thickly around the perimeter of the yard; they'd been blooming since summer, a fragrant explosion of red blossoms. Joan stared at the top branches, their narrow leaves shiny in the morning sun. The hedge was ten feet tall; its dense leaves screened the yard completely from the neighbors' view. She examined a leaf. It was gnarled and discolored, coated with a sooty substance. On the lower branches the growth seemed to be thinning; soon the neighbors would be able to see her through the shrubs, at least from the knees down.

She went back inside and dialed the gardening service. A shrill woman answered the phone.

"I need some advice," said Joan. "Something is killing my oleanders."

The woman asked Joan's name and address. "We'll send someone over to spray this afternoon."

"Thank you," said Joan. Then she went upstairs to dress for the doctor's.

SHE PARKED in the lot behind the hospital and went in through the back entrance. Her appointment was in the rear wing—the Ava Cohen Cancer Center, built with her father's money after her mother's death. The wing held a hundred beds, a laboratory, and four operating rooms. Recently they'd added radiology facilities; a week ago Joan had stood there bare-chested for the X ray of her breast.

She passed the chapel, the nurses' station, the portrait of her mother hanging in the hallway. She was twenty feet from the radiology area when she recognized Dot Beckley coming toward her in the corridor.

"Joan?" said Dot. The question in her voice: *What are you doing at the cancer center?* Then her brow cleared. "I didn't realize your family was still involved with the hospital."

"Oh, yes," said Joan.

"I had an appointment, myself." Dot pointed to a small Band-Aid at her hairline, several shades lighter than the brown skin underneath. "I had a little spot removed."

"Goodness," said Joan. "Nothing serious, I hope."

Dot waved airily. "Oh, no. I get them all the time. The sun, they say." She fumbled in her purse for cigarettes and shook one out of the pack. Her hands were brown and creased, studded with gold rings.

"I'm glad I ran into you," she said. "I've been meaning to call. Hal's brother George is visiting for the week. We want you to join us one night for dinner." Dot lowered her voice. "He's recently divorced. We've told him all about you."

"How nice." Joan glanced at her watch. "Dot, I've got to run, but why don't you give me a ring at home? That way I can check my calendar."

"Sure. I'll call you this afternoon."

"Wonderful," said Joan. By then she'd have thought up an excuse.

THE NURSE poked her head into the examining room. "Miss Cohen," she said. "Dr. Sugarman will be right with you."

"Thanks," said Joan. She sat on the examining table in a flimsy hospital gown, her clothes neatly folded on a chair. She glanced at her watch; she'd waited half an hour already. Come on, Zuckerman, she thought. This made her smile. Her father had deplored

Jews who Americanized their names; for a second she'd sounded just like him.

The door opened.

"Hi, Joan," said Sugarman, manila folder under his arm, the tails of his white coat flapping behind him. He was young and handsome, always a little disheveled: tie loosely knotted, cuffs rolled back to show his tanned forearms. Had she met him on the street she would have found him attractive; but as a doctor he was all wrong. She preferred the dour demeanor of her surgeon at Sloan-Kettering, whose sonorous voice seemed to acknowledge the gravity of what had happened to her.

He pulled a stool up to the examining table. "I had a look at your chest film. Everything looks great, Joan."

Thanks, Larry, she thought. She and Sugarman were the same age; it irked her that she was "Joan" and he was "Doctor." She'd despised doctors her whole life, in direct proportion to her parents' admiration of them. Her father had wished his son to become one and his daughter to marry one. Her mother had revered her surgeons until the end, even when it was clear they'd failed to save her life.

Joan untied her hospital gown and turned her head. Though she avoiding looking at it herself, she didn't mind showing Sugarman her scar, a puckered trail that led from her breastbone to her right armpit. It was the other part she dreaded: him looking at her remaining breast, round and as innocent as a baby. Him seeing her the way she used to be.

"The tissue looks very healthy," he said, feeling along the incision with his fingertips. "You've healed nicely." He let the gown close over the scar. "Now let's have a look at the other one."

Joan's face warmed. He was like an arrogant fraternity brother, the Harvard boys who'd descended on Radcliffe for dances and mixers. She remembered a particular one who hadn't even kissed her, just asked her to take off her blouse, too sure of his own attractiveness to bother seducing her.

He pushed aside the gown; her eyes darted around the room. There were two photos on Sugarman's desk. In one, towheaded boys posed in front of a sailboat; in the other, the doctor embraced a buxom blonde in a strapless evening dress. Jewish boys and their blondes: her brother was obsessed with them, a different one each time Joan saw him. She closed her eyes and imagined Sugarman in bed with his wife, palming those enormous breasts. She wondered if his hands moved in the same circular path, unconsciously feeling for lumps.

"Are those your kids?" she asked.

"Yep," he said. "The little Sugarmen." The motion of his hand changed; he felt her breast in straight lines radiating outward from the nipple. You won't find a thing, she thought. She'd examined her breast herself that morning. Every morning. She felt for lumps six or seven times a day.

She looked down at his curly dark head. She'd gone gray in her mid-twenties; she wondered if Sugarman dyed his hair too. Finally he closed the gown and tied it at her throat, like a mother bundling her child against the cold.

"Okeydokey," he said. "Let's have a look at that arm. Lift them both as high as you can."

Joan imagined lecturing Sugarman like an angry schoolmarm: Grown men do not say "okeydokey." She stretched her left arm overhead, her right arm to eye level.

He whistled through his teeth, a startling sound. "Pretty good," he said. "How does it feel?"

"Pins and needles."

He scribbled something on her chart.

"You've made remarkable progress. There's almost no swelling, and your range of motion is excellent." He closed the folder. "Any questions I can answer?"

Joan eyed her clothes piled on the chair, her silicone breast hidden among them.

"Can I go now?" she asked.

SHE WAS thirty-nine years old, the age in a woman's life when questions begin to answer themselves. By chance or choice she hadn't married; she wasn't sure which. If pressed she'd answer vaguely: *I was doing other things.* She was often pressed, at cocktail parties, in job interviews, by the aging uncles who'd sat shiva for her father the previous winter. In those days the question struck nobody as rude: *Why aren't you married?*

Other things. She'd graduated second in her class (Radcliffe, 1952; the first-ranked girl was also Jewish, as Joan's father liked to point out.) Jobs at newspapers—copy girl, assistant to the women's-page editor of a suburban daily on Long Island. (It hadn't yet occurred to anyone that women might read the entire paper.) Then she went to work at the *Times*. She was the only female reporter in her bureau, which suited her. She enjoyed men; men trusted her. Joan laughed easily; she was hardworking and direct; she was not a prude. She had a good figure and a handsome face—her father's dark eyes, his strong nose. A certain type of man found her attractive: dynamic, aggressive men, as devoted to their careers as she was to hers. By happy coincidence, this was the sort of man she liked.

From age twenty to thirty-eight she had twelve lovers, more than she would ever admit. A few had lasted a year or two; they remained her dearest friends. They called her each year on her birthday, men who'd married someone else.

Only one had met her parents. A year out of Radcliffe, Joan met a young law student named Howard Resnick. He was the first Jewish boy she'd ever dated; she brought him home one night to dinner. Her father wore a vest to the table; her mother, already ill, roused herself from bed, put on lipstick, and looked, for one evening at least, herself. After dessert they listened to records in the parlor, all six Brandenburg Concertos. Her father and Howard Resnick sat across from each other in overstuffed chairs, their long legs crossed at the ankle; the resemblance was almost familial. A month later Howard proposed marriage. Joan saw clearly the life ahead of her—babies and keeping house, a life like her mother's—and said no. Her father was heartbroken. She wasn't used to disappointing him; the sole aim of her childhood had been to make him proud. In school she'd excelled in all subjects; she had played the violin. She was more son than daughter, the dutiful son her brother, Ben, refused to be. (Four years younger, he wouldn't go to Hebrew school. He befriended the neighborhood boys, Irish and Italian, and repeated the eighth grade.) Her father's disappointment was too much to bear. She never brought home a man again.

Of all her lovers, only two had mattered. The first: Morris Brown, a married editor at the *Times;* they still spoke on the phone each month, wrote notes at the holidays. The second: Claude Tirat, a philosophy student she'd met in Paris when she was covering the student protests. Not for any particular qualities he possessed, but because it was he who, in bed, had found the lump in her breast.

She had the surgery on a snowy day in December. The roads were glazed, the cabs barely running; she took the bus across town to Sloan-Kettering. She told no one. Her mother was dead; she had no close girlfriends. All the important people in her life— co-workers and boyfriends, her brother and father—were men. If the cancer had been located elsewhere—her liver or intestine, blood or bone—she might have told. But she remembered her father's discomfort during her mother's illness: two mastectomies, long years of doctors and hospitals, and still he couldn't bring himself to say the word *breast*.

In a week she was back at work, shaky but relieved. Her life proceeded much as it had, strung along by interviews and deadlines and weekly phone calls to her father, who'd retired to Florida. But she was exhausted. She began missing deadlines, handing in copy that didn't come close to her former standards. Many nights she couldn't sleep; when she did she dreamed of her mother, gray and motionless on the bed where she'd died.

Months passed before her editor noticed. When he did, he assumed she was hooked on drugs, which was fine with Joan: the magazine world ran on gossip, and she'd rather be known as a pill junkie than a cancer victim. That spring she took a leave of absence from the magazine. Then her father died of a sudden heart attack, and Joan was on a plane to Florida.

AT HOME she undressed and slipped into her bathing suit. She'd found it in New York, at a tiny shop on Third Avenue that catered to exotic women: the maimed, the very fat, the pathologically modest. The friendly Hungarian owner could order you a turtleneck bikini, a suit with a built-in girdle, or, if you preferred, a bathing dress from the 1920s with a skirt that hung to your ankles. Joan's suit, a plain black one-piece, was cut high under the arms; on the right side of the chest, a hidden inner pocket held an inflatable breast. (The silicone one she usually wore was too dense; it refused to bob to the surface the way a real breast would.) Every afternoon she inflated the fake breast with a plastic straw, each time marveling at the absurdity of wearing a balloon against her chest.

Outside she slipped off her caftan, grateful for the sun on her back, the looming protection of the oleanders. Easing into the water, she exhaled slowly. It was her favorite moment of the day.

She swam every afternoon, sixty laps of sidestroke: thirty fast laps on her strong left side, thirty slow ones on the weaker right. The previous winter, after the surgery, her right arm had been weak and mostly numb, swollen to twice its normal size. The physical therapist in New York had given her exercises to do. Twice a day she walked her right hand down a wall from eye level to waist height, an excruciating process. She wore long sleeves to her father's funeral, a voluminous black overblouse to accommodate her swollen arm. Now, eight months later, the swelling was nearly gone.

She breathed deeply. She'd quit smoking just before the surgery; she could cross the pool underwater on a single breath. As she swam her mind wandered, freed by the languid rhythm of the stroke. She thought of summer camp in the Catskills, tearing across the lake amid the splashing of a dozen other girls, the sound fading as she left them all behind. Solitary swimming had bored her; she needed someone to race. When the other girls refused, she raced the boys. She liked those races even better.

She shifted to her right side, exhaling slowly, sinking into the pain. At the *Times* she had raced with boys every day; she had fought for everything she got: every raise, every byline, every column inch of precious space. At *Newsweek* the egos were even bigger, the competition more fierce; but there too she had won.

Some of the boys had minded; there was no doubt about that. She'd been passed over countless times, seen lesser reporters sent to Israel, to Greece, places her editor deemed too dangerous for a woman. But she kept pushing; she did not let up. Finally, in the spring, they sent her to Paris to cover the student uprisings. She let the boys chase down cabinet ministers (a losing battle; French politicians had no time for the foreign press). In her jeans and dark sweaters she passed for a student; each day she rode the Métro to the Nanterre campus or walked the narrow streets around the Sorbonne. One day she heard Danny Cohn-Bendit speak in the Place St.-Germain-des-Prés; afterward she pushed through the crowd and walked several blocks at his side. In her Radcliffe French she told him she was a Cohen too; amused, he gave her five minutes. She wrote the piece that afternoon; it appeared three days later, a half-page breakout embedded in the cover story. She'd managed to articulate the students' concerns, to convey the frenetic mood in the streets; she'd captured Cohn-Bendit's distinctive voice, his sharp wit. When she held the issue in her hand, her own initials stamped on the slick pages, she thought, I have done something. She'd celebrated with Claude Tirat that night, a miraculous evening that began and ended in bed.

That night, his hands exploring her body, Claude found the lump.

"*Qu'est-ce que c'est?*" he'd whispered. "*Ça te fait mal?*"

No, she told him: it didn't hurt. Later, alone, she examined it: a hard, rubbery nodule just below the nipple. In June the red and black flags came down from the Arc de Triomphe; Joan went back to New York and made an appointment with her internist.

"Excuse me," said a nearby voice.

Joan looked up, startled. A man stood on the patio in a bright green uniform.

"Hi," he said. "I'm with the lawn service."

She felt a sudden chill. She hadn't heard the truck in the driveway, or the man's footsteps on the cement. He could have been watching her for half an hour.

"I'll be right out." She stood at the shallow end and removed her swim goggles, then glanced down at her chest. Once, months ago, she'd gotten out of the pool, toweled off, and gone into the kitchen to make herself a sandwich, all without realizing that her right breast was still floating in the water, clear and shiny as a jellyfish.

She made her way to the edge of the pool, squinting through the afternoon sun. She was halfway up the ladder before she recognized the man's long face, his slender build. It was Moira Snell's fiancé, Ken Kimble.

"Ken," she said. "How nice to see you."

She stepped onto the cement, streaming water. The black swimsuit clung to her like a second skin. A breeze blew across the patio.

"Joan," he said. "I didn't make the connection. They only gave me a last name and an address." His gaze skimmed her body, stopped for a second on the erect nipple of her left breast.

"Let me put on some clothes." She crossed the patio and slipped into her caftan, wondering if his eyes followed her legs. She still had good legs.

"Sorry to startle you," said Kimble. "I tried the bell, but no one answered."

"No problem." She turned to face him, safe inside the billowing fabric. "I didn't realize you worked for the lawn service."

"It's my first day." His eyes swept over the tiled pool, the hot tub, the bronze sculptures of exotic birds along the perimeter of the patio. "This is a beautiful place."

"It was my father's." She rubbed her hair with a towel. "It's a little extravagant for my taste, but he was in real estate. He had an eye for fancy houses." In the bright sunlight Kimble looked older than he had at the Snells'; he must be her age, at least. What on earth, she wondered, was he doing with Moira?

"A movie star should live here," he said. "Greta Garbo. Someone like that."

Joan blinked. Her father had bought the place from the estate of just such a person, a silent film actress who'd come east when her looks and career faded. The woman had been a recluse; she'd surrounded herself with beautiful houseboys and never ventured beyond the patio. It was, Joan thought, a sad story.

"Let me show you the oleanders." She led him down the flagstone path to the blooming hedge. Her right arm tingled from shoulder to fingertip. "They're not doing very well. It looks like something is eating them."

Kimble approached the hedge and examined a blemished leaf. He caressed it gently, then rubbed his fingers together. He turned the leaf over and peered at the underside.

"Aphids," he said softly.

"I thought so." Joan peered over his shoulder. "What's that black stuff?"

"Mold. The aphids leave honeydew on the leaves, and pretty

soon it gets moldy." He knelt and examined the soil at the base of the shrub. She noticed his hair was sparse on top.

"Can you get rid of them?" she asked. "The lady at the service said you could spray them."

Kimble frowned. "We *could*—there's a spray for everything these days. But that stuff is pure poison." He glanced toward the house. "Do you cook much?"

"A little." In New York she'd subsisted on coffee and cigarettes, diner food and deli sandwiches. Only recently had she tried her hand at the stove. She'd fired her father's cook and borrowed a stack of cookbooks from the public library. So far the results had been disappointing.

Kimble smiled. "If you want, I can make you a bug spray that won't contaminate the groundwater. You probably have all the ingredients in your kitchen."

What a strange thing to do, she thought. What an odd person. Yet for the first time in months she was intrigued. "Sure," she said. "Why not?"

She led him across the lawn, through the sliding glass doors and into the kitchen. His bright blue eyes seemed to take in everything: the marble countertops and tiled floors, the double oven and eight-burner stove.

"You could open a restaurant here," he said.

Joan laughed. "You haven't tasted my cooking."

Kimble reached for a copper pot from the overhead rack, filled it at the sink, and placed it on the stove. His sneakers were silent on the tile. He moved with quiet assurance, as if he'd spent his whole life in her kitchen.

"Do you have an onion?" he asked. "And some garlic?"

"I think so." She opened the refrigerator and rooted through the crisper drawers. She handed him an onion and a head of garlic, left over from her one sad attempt at a tomato sauce.

"What can I do?" she asked.

"Just stand there and look pretty."

Joan laughed, pleased in spite of herself. If a man had said such a thing to her a year ago, she would have rolled her eyes. Now, somehow, it struck her as charming.

"I'm surprised to see you," she said. "I didn't realize you and Moira were planning to stay in town."

"It's a nice place. Beautiful climate." He looked closely at her. "Why? You don't like it?"

"It's lovely," she said hastily. "But it's an older crowd down here. There isn't much to do at night if you're single." Her face warmed. Why did I say that? she wondered. Why did I tell him I was single?

"Anyway," she said, "I'm glad you're getting settled. You found a job pretty quickly."

Kimble chuckled. "Nancy gets the credit for that. She helped me cram for the interview. They were astounded by my knowledge of gardening. They hired me on the spot."

He whistled softly as he puttered around her kitchen, a tune she faintly recognized. It had been all over the radio a few years back; Joan couldn't identify the singer, but she remembered the words: *Unto everything there is a season*. Something like that.

"What's that song?" she asked.

"The Byrds," he said, and began to sing. "To everything, turn, turn, turn, there is a season, turn, turn, turn, and a time for every purpose under Heaven." He sang unself-consciously; his deep voice serious, almost reverent. The sound seemed to her larger than his body, vibrant and full of emotion.

"You have a terrific voice," she said.

He shrugged. "Thanks. I'm not much for popular music, but that one stuck with me. I guess I like the sentiment." His eyes met hers. "Everything happens for a reason."

"You believe that?" said Joan.

"You don't?"

"I used to," she said slowly. Her prosthesis felt heavy against her chest. "Now, honestly, I think it's a load of crap."

Kimble laughed. "You're an honest woman." He peeled a clove of garlic and dropped it into the pot. "What changed your mind?"

"Nothing specific." Her face felt warm; all along her right arm the pins and needles returned. "Just that, well, it's easy to believe in destiny when you're young and everything you want lands in your lap. It's when life starts taking things away from you that you start to question—" She hesitated.

"The fairness of things?"

"Yes." She crossed her arms over her chest. "But not just that. You start to question the logic. And once you do you realize that anything could happen to anyone. There's no order at all."

Kimble considered this. "It's not immediately obvious, I'll give you that. But if you're patient it eventually becomes clear. It's all in the way you look at things. Life never takes away something without giving something back." He grinned. "You strike me as an impatient woman."

She laughed. "I can't deny that."

He dropped another garlic clove into the pot.

"Smells good," she said.

"I think so too. I guess that says something about us." He took a knife from the butcher's block and cut the onion into quarters. "There's an old Chinese proverb I heard once. 'He who is afraid of garlic is afraid of pleasure.'"

She laughed again, her face warming. "Who doesn't like garlic?"

"Moira can't stand it. Even the smell of it makes her sick."

Joan's smile faded. She'd forgotten, for a moment, that the charming man who'd commandeered her kitchen was engaged to a teenager.

"How is Moira?" she asked.

"Not so good. Her folks are giving her a hard time. I think they'd rather not have me staying in their house."

"Really?" said Joan. "You and Nancy seemed to hit it off."

"Oh, Nancy's a sweetheart. It's Dick who can't stand me."

Joan thought of Moira's father slicing into his steak. She'd had the impression he wanted to do the same to Kimble.

"It must be a shock for them," she said. "The engagement. But I'm sure they'll get used to the idea."

"I suppose so." Kimble rinsed his hands under the faucet. "Where's your spice rack?"

She opened a cupboard. "I don't have much. What do you need?"

"Cayenne pepper."

She handed him a shaker of red pepper flakes. "Will this work?"

"Close enough." He took the shaker and sprinkled it over the pot of water.

"Now what?"

"Let it simmer for an hour." He wiped his hands on his pants. "I'm supposed to mow the lawn while I'm here."

"Oh," said Joan. She'd forgotten, briefly, what had brought him to her house. I could talk to him all day, she thought. It occurred to her that she hadn't enjoyed a conversation so much in months.

"It won't take me long," said Kimble. Lightly he touched her shoulders, moving her out of his path. His touch startled her.

Except for her surgeon and Dr. Sugarman, no man had touched her in a year.

"I'll start the lawn," he said. "By the time I finish, our bug spray will be done."

JOAN SLIPPED out of her swimsuit and into the marble tub. She hadn't used it in months, preferring quick showers in the tiny bathroom down the hall. The house was full of strange creakings; the last time she'd taken a bath, each small noise had seemed amplified as she lay in the tub. But that afternoon was different: she was not alone. The mower buzzed in the distance, Ken Kimble tending to her lawn. A breeze floated through the open window, carrying the clean smell of cut grass.

She sank into the steamy water; heat seeped into her arms and shoulders. She closed her eyes and thought of his voice filling her kitchen. He is just outside, she thought. A moment later she was asleep.

When she opened her eyes, the water had cooled; the house was silent. She sat upright in the tub. A draft brushed her bare skin.

The bathroom door was wide open.

Panic shot through her like an electrical impulse; she lurched out of the tub, splashing water onto the floor. She saw at once the grotesque picture she'd made: lolling naked in the water, her devastated chest exposed.

She reached for a towel and peered out the window. The mower stood silent in the driveway.

She dressed quickly and hurried downstairs. In the kitchen the pot was gone from the stove; clearly he'd come back into the house.

He had a light step; he could have crept up the spiral staircase without waking her.

He came upstairs, she thought. He stood there looking at me.

She went out through the glass doors. Kimble stood at the edge of the lawn, squirting the oleanders with a spray bottle, still whistling the same tune. She approached the hedge. Kimble turned and smiled.

"There you are," he said. "It stinks, but it'll keep the aphids away. At least until it rains."

Joan's heart raced. Inside the house, a door slammed.

"The wind's kicking up." Kimble glanced at the house. "Looks like you left some windows open."

Relief washed over her. The wind, she thought: it must have been the wind.

"I was taking a bath," she said.

"Must have been some bath," he said, eyeing her. "You're glowing."

An odd sensation filled her, familiar but nearly forgotten, an intoxicating mix of anxiety and pleasure. This is ridiculous, she thought. What's wrong with me?

"I guess I fell asleep," she said.

"I hope I didn't wake you, banging around in the kitchen like that." He gave the oleanders a final squirt, then handed her the bottle. "Keep this in the refrigerator—it should last for a month or so. Make sure the gardener sprays them again next week."

"Won't you be back next Friday?" said Joan.

"I don't know." His eyes were very blue; they held hers just a second too long. "They don't make the schedule until the night before. They just send whoever's available, unless the customer requests somebody specific."

"I see," said Joan.

He fumbled in his pocket, keys jingling. "I finished the lawn and the watering, so you should be all set." He gave her a little salute. "Keep an eye on those oleanders."

He disappeared around the hedge, the way he had come.

*H*ealthy," said George Beckley. "Everyone down here looks so darned healthy."

Joan glanced around the room at the fit, middle-aged couples gliding across the dance floor. They were eating dinner in the Flamingo Ballroom of the Orange Grove Hotel, a double date: Hal and Dot Beckley at one end of the table; Joan and Hal's brother George, a car salesman from Pittsburgh, at the other. Twice Joan had begged off, claiming a migraine; the third time she gave in. She was a single woman with no job and no family; there were a limited number of excuses she could reasonably invent.

"It's the sun," said George. "Nothing like a little sunshine for the complexion." He was broad and fair-haired, square-jawed like a cartoon hero.

"No need to tell this one," said Hal, nodding toward his wife. "She's out there three, four hours a day." He winked at Joan. "You ought to come over sometime and join her. We've got a wall around the garden now. Complete privacy."

Dot laughed, a dry, crackly sound. "No tan lines." Her hair was freshly set, the bangs swirled artfully over the bandage at her hairline. She butted her cigarette with a spotted brown hand.

The music ended; the dancers on the floor offered polite applause. The orchestra swept into a familiar tune, the opening bars of "String of Pearls."

"That's our song." Hal stood and reached for Dot's hand. "My dear?"

Dot smiled. "We believe in romance."

George shook his head, watching Dot's flat behind as she and Hal made their way to the dance floor.

"They're something else," he said. "Married thirty years, and they can't keep their hands off each other. You don't run into that every day, let me tell you." He drained his glass. "You ever been married?"

"No," said Joan.

He reached for the wine bottle. "I was. Twenty-one years in June."

"That's a long time."

"Is it?" He refilled his glass. "We were high school sweethearts. I always knew I'd marry her."

Don't ask, Joan thought, but she couldn't help herself. He so clearly wanted to tell her.

"What happened?" she said.

George raised his hands. "What happened? What happened was we had three children, a beautiful house, a perfect life. What happened was I gave her everything a woman wants."

"Forgive me," said Joan. "It's none of my business."

George sighed. "Truth is, I don't know what happened. A friend of hers got divorced, a girl from the neighborhood. I could say that was why, but I'd just be guessing." He corked the bottle with a napkin. "How about you? How come you never got married?"

Joan blinked. She could think of no concise way to explain it: the years of dating, the (long, now) series of boyfriends. She'd watched all her Radcliffe friends succumb, leave promising jobs in banking or publishing for marriage and houses in Connecticut. By the time she was thirty-five, Joan was the only one still out in the world.

"It's complicated," she said. "I was always so busy." Toward the end she'd traveled constantly. Often her editor phoned late on a Sunday night; the next day she'd be on a plane to Europe.

Across the table George Beckley looked perplexed.

"I guess it was never important to me," she said finally.

Dot and Hal returned to the table.

"Look at you two," said Dot. "Deep in conversation. What are you talking about? If you don't mind my butting in."

"Joan here says she's too busy to get married," said George. "What do you think about that?"

Dot squeezed Joan's shoulder. "Joan's a career girl."

George leaned back in his chair, peering at her like a scientist examining an exotic specimen. "No kidding. A career girl."

"I think it's perfectly wonderful," said Dot. "In fact, if I had it to do over again, I might be a career girl myself."

Hal chuckled. He grasped his lips between his thumb and forefinger. "Watch me button my lip. I'm not saying anything."

Dot leaned close to Joan. "Don't pay any attention to him, honey. He's living in the Dark Ages." She lit a cigarette. "Have you talked to Nancy lately?"

"Not since the pool party," said Joan. "She must be busy, with Moira in town."

"Oh, honey. You haven't heard." Dot lowered her gravelly voice. "You didn't hear it from me, but apparently Moira and her boyfriend—what's his name?"

"Ken," said Joan.

"Moira and Ken got themselves an apartment together on Ocean Avenue." Dot's eyes widened. "The wedding isn't for months. Can you imagine?"

"Really?" said Joan. She hadn't seen Ken Kimble since the day in her kitchen; the next Friday a different gardener had come to spray the oleanders. She'd considered calling to request him specifically, but changed her mind. If she asked for him by name, he was sure to hear about it.

"Nancy's heartbroken. And of course Dick is fit to be tied." Dot frowned. "I don't know how this could have happened. He seemed like such a nice fellow."

Across the table Hal grunted. "A hippie, if you ask me."

Dot giggled. "I thought he was handsome."

"He needs a damned haircut," Hal grumbled.

"Oh, don't be an old fogey. That's the look nowadays." Dot turned to Joan. "Of course, I'm old-fashioned too. It's wonderful to be young and in love, but for heaven's sake, can't they be discreet about it?"

Joan smiled absently. She remembered Ken Kimble standing on her patio, how he'd sized up her father's house in a single glance: *A movie star should live here.* His deep voice filling her kitchen, resonant and warm; his blue eyes bright with curiosity, missing nothing.

"He seems a little old for Moira," said Joan. "Did Nancy ever tell you how they met?"

"She doesn't know. Moira won't tell her anything." Dot sighed. "First she quits college, and now this."

Across the table George stared into his glass. "My wife wanted to go to college," he said suddenly. "Can you believe it? We've got two kids at Penn State, it's costing me a fortune, and all of a sudden she wants to go to college."

Joan's eyes drifted across the dance floor. The orchestra was packing up. Through the arched doorway a line formed at the coat-check window, husbands collecting their wives' furs. November had come; at night the temperature dropped to fifty-five degrees.

"What did she want to study?" she asked.

George frowned.

"In college," said Joan. "What did your wife want to study?"

"Beats me," he said.

THEY DROVE through town, George hunched over the steering wheel of Hal's Eldorado. Hal and Dot had stayed behind at the Orange Grove; he'd booked the honeymoon suite and slipped the key into Dot's baked Alaska—further evidence, Joan supposed, of their shared belief in romance.

You two be good, Hal had joked as he handed his brother the car keys. *Or at least be careful.*

"It's this one," Joan said, pointing. "First house on the right."

George pulled into the circular driveway. Promptly she reached for the door handle. "It was nice meeting you," she said.

"Wait a second." George cut the motor. "I'll walk you to the door." He followed her silently up the curving walk, his hand at the small of her back.

At the door Joan offered her hand. "It was a lovely evening."

George grasped her hand with both of his. "Hey," he said. "I'm sorry for going on about my ex-wife like that. You don't need to hear that." His face was very close, broad and earnest under the porch light.

"I haven't been on a date in twenty-one years," he said. "I don't know how to act anymore."

"Don't be silly," said Joan. His large hands were very warm, trapping hers inside them. "You're terrific company."

He stepped closer. "You're a good sport. I never met a girl like you."

He's going to kiss me, she thought. She took a step backward, into the stucco wall. Her legs felt dead; blood pounded in her temples.

He bent and covered her mouth with his. The wall at her back radiated heat, still full of the afternoon sun. His chest pressed against hers, the silicone breast heavy between them. She turned her head away.

"What's the matter?" he said.

"I'm sorry," she whispered. And then, recovering herself: "It's late. I should go."

He stepped back from her, so abruptly she nearly fell over. "Okay, then," he said, red-faced. "Good night."

He turned his broad back to her and headed toward the car.

IN THE KITCHEN she mixed herself a drink, sipped it as she undressed. She lay in bed waiting for sleep, feeling her breast for lumps. The skin was smooth under her fingertips. She was perfectly healthy.

She closed her eyes and saw George Beckley's face. He didn't interest her; he was the sort of man she wouldn't have looked at twice, before. At least she didn't think so. Her old self was fading. She could barely remember the way she used to be.

She had loved men. At twenty she'd lost her virginity to an English professor. He was much older, thin and gray-haired; he had adored her body, treated her like a goddess. After that, boyfriends: writers, journalists, the young lawyer Howard Resnick, whom her father had wanted her to marry. She'd worked with Morris Brown for six years before they went to bed. The delightful shock of seeing him naked, the secret parts of a man she'd known a long time. In the summer they would sleep on the roof of her fifth-floor walkup, waiting for a breeze. One freezing night in November they made love on an old army blanket. They lay there afterward watching the first snow of the season, the tiny flakes melting instantly on their warm faces, leaving behind wetness, a lingering thrill. They did not fall in love; what grew up between them was an intense loyalty. He was the dearest friend she'd ever had.

They had all loved her. Yet a year ago she'd lain alone in a hospital room waiting to die, the men who loved her conspicuously absent. She had pushed them all away. Young, foolishly sure of her power, she'd always imagined there would be others.

Now what happens? she thought. Who's going to want me now?

EARLY IN THE MORNING a noise woke her. The room was still dark; the alarm clock read 5:15. On the bedside table sat an empty glass. It smelled of tonic water, astringent as men's cologne.

Joan sat up in bed and listened. She'd been sleeping deeply; the nightcap—her first in a year—had helped. In the distance she heard water running. The pool, she thought groggily. Something's wrong with the pool. She slipped on a robe and padded downstairs to the kitchen, unlocked the sliding doors. Across the patio a shadow moved.

"Who's there?" she called out, her heart hammering.

A man stepped out from behind the hedge, holding a garden hose.

"It's me, Joan. Ken Kimble."

He'd come to check the bougainvillea, he explained: it was caterpillar season, and he'd noticed a few holes in the leaves the time he'd visited.

"It's five o'clock in the morning," said Joan.

"I know." He coiled the hose loosely and hung it on the wall of the toolshed. "I'm sorry I woke you. I must have scared you half to death, prowling around your yard in the dark. Please forgive me."

Joan frowned. She was very confused; her brain didn't function before nine.

"Ken," she said. "Come have some coffee."

THEY SAT at the kitchen table, cups of coffee between them, Kimble's back to the glass doors. Behind him the sky had begun to lighten. A pale glow spread at the horizon. He sugared his coffee and spoke in a flat voice. He and Moira had been fighting; for two nights in a row she'd put the chain on the door, locking him out. He slept in the apartment in the afternoons when she was at work. She was as a lifeguard at the country-club pool.

"So where do you spend the night?" said Joan.

Kimble smiled sheepishly. "In the truck."

"You can't be serious."

"It's not that bad." He sipped his coffee. "Anyway, that's why I came so early. The sooner I get everything done, the sooner I can go back to the apartment and sleep."

Joan put down her cup. "It's none of my business," she said, "but what's the problem? Why is Moira so angry?"

Kimble hesitated. "Things are bad with her parents," he said finally. "Her father especially. So I suggested we postpone the wedding awhile and let them get used to the idea. Not forever. Six months. A year at the most."

"And?"

"She went crazy. She wants to get married right away." He ran a hand through his lank hair. "I don't understand it. She's nineteen years old. She's got all the time in the world."

Nineteen, Joan thought: half my age. She'd been a virgin at nineteen, editor of the Radcliffe poetry review. She'd imagined herself an adult.

"Have you ever been married?" Kimble asked.

For God's sake, she thought. Again with this question.

"No," she said, more sharply than she'd intended. "And I never felt like I was missing anything. There's more to life than getting married."

Kimble clapped appreciatively, as though she'd performed a magic trick. "Brava," he said. "That's exactly what I'm talking about. I keep telling Moira she should go back to school, figure out what she wants to do with her life. Women have so many opportunities today. She could be anything she wants. Look at you."

Joan flushed. She'd spent years explaining herself to the George Beckleys of the world, men mystified by the choices she'd made. To Ken Kimble she'd explained nothing; yet he seemed to understand.

"I wish Moira could talk to you," he continued. "She's getting some bad advice from her mother. Nancy's a sweet lady, but she's led a sheltered life. Every day the two of them go shopping for a wedding gown. It's all they talk about."

Joan thought of the Moira she'd met that spring, restless and independent, ready to join the Peace Corps. Joan had envied her then, the discoveries awaiting her, her youth and energy and radiant health. The world had changed in marvelous ways. For her, anything would be possible.

"This doesn't sound like Moira," she said.

"I know. I barely recognize her anymore." Kimble set down his cup and pushed back his chair. "Anyway, I've taken up enough of your morning."

"Nonsense," said Joan. She had no plans—for the day, the week, the rest of her life. "I'm not very busy these days."

He rose from his chair and grimaced. "Whoa." He gripped the edge of the table and placed a hand at his lower back.

"What's the matter?"

"Back spasm." He was suddenly pale. "I get them every once in a while."

"Sit down," said Joan, touching his shoulder.

"Actually, sitting is worse." Beads of sweat appeared on his forehead. "That's probably why I got it, from sleeping sitting up."

"Why don't you lie down on the couch?" said Joan.

"Maybe just for a minute."

She laid a hand on his shoulder and steered him toward the living room. He eased himself onto the couch and stretched out his legs. His face relaxed.

"Better," he said.

"Just lie still." Joan sat on the edge of the sofa. "Can I get you an aspirin? Would that do any good?"

"No." Kimble closed his eyes. "Sometimes heat helps."

"I think there's a heating pad upstairs." She rose from the sofa. "I'll be right back."

She hurried upstairs, to the dark bedroom where her father had slept; he'd used a heating pad for his arthritis. The bed was neatly made, the curtains pulled as if someone was sleeping. She peered into the walk-in closet, still hung with his suits; the thought of giving them to charity made her chest ache. There was no heating pad on the closet shelves. She couldn't bring herself to look through the dresser.

She tried the next room, and the next. There were six spare bedrooms in all—six empty closets, six beds with clean linens, as if guests were expected. Joan had never slept in any of them. In five months she hadn't had a single guest.

She found a hot water bottle in one of the bureaus and filled it at the bathroom sink. Outside, the early light was clear and gentle, the garden loud with birds. She hadn't risen before ten o'clock in months, yet she felt rested and full of energy. There were eggs and bacon in the fridge; she could make them breakfast.

"Ken," she called from the stairs, "can I make you something to eat?"

She went into the living room and stood at the foot of the couch. Kimble lay perfectly still, arms crossed over his chest. She'd slept next to plenty of men, watched them gape and drool and snore; but in sleep Kimble looked handsome and composed. His mouth was closed, his breath silent. Long eyelashes lay on his cheeks. She had never seen such eyelashes on a man.

Suddenly his eyes snapped open; he inhaled sharply, as if she'd startled him.

"I'm sorry," said Joan. "Did I scare you?"

He sat up carefully. "I must have fallen asleep."

"I couldn't find the heating pad. I brought you a hot water bottle instead."

"Perfect," said Kimble. "Can you put it under my back?"

Joan knelt beside the couch, her heart beating loudly. His shirt had escaped from the waistband of his trousers, revealing a slice of white skin. Carefully she slid the bottle underneath him, her wrist grazing his flesh. His skin was surprisingly cool.

"Thanks," he said. "That feels great."

She sat back on her heels. "Ken," she said. "I hope you don't mind my asking, but how much longer are you going to sleep in that truck?"

"I don't know. Depends on Moira, I guess." He shifted, wincing. "Sooner or later she'll come around."

Joan took a deep breath. "I had a thought," she said. "You're welcome to stay here until you and Moira work things out. I have plenty of room."

Their eyes met.

"That's very kind," he said. "But I wouldn't want to put you out."

"I have six spare bedrooms." The insistent tone of her voice surprised her. "You couldn't put me out if you brought all your relatives."

Kimble smiled. "In that case," he said, "I'd love to."

*K*en Kimble rose at dawn. From down the hall Joan heard the trilling alarm clock, the gentle creak of bedsprings, the soft patter of water on tile. She lay drifting in and out of sleep and imagined him standing under the shower, the white skin of his back turning pink under the spray. His tread was silent on the stairs; after the shower stopped she heard nothing until the truck started in the driveway. Her days unfolded as they had before—walk on the beach, afternoon swim—but now there was an endpoint. At five o'clock Ken Kimble would come home.

She had dinner waiting when he walked in the door, each day a new recipe from *The Joy of Cooking*. She'd never cooked for a man before and found that she liked it. She avoided the complicated dishes—the soufflés and cream sauces, anything that involved stuffing—and produced passable roasts, hamburgers, breasts of chicken. The first night she'd remembered too late that he was a vegetarian; she apologized for the lamb chops and offered to make him something else.

"Are you kidding?" said Kimble, his mouth full. He cut into the meat as if he ate it all the time. "This is terrific."

He ate quickly, barely chewing; he held his fork with an overhand grip. Five minutes later he pushed away his plate. "I'm stuffed," he announced. He'd left a lamb chop and most of his potatoes.

"What's the matter?"

"Nothing. Everything was wonderful." He rubbed his flat belly. "I'm watching my weight."

Joan glanced down at her plate; she was still eating her salad. "I'm a little slow," she said.

"Take your time."

He seemed happy to entertain her while she ate; he described in detail the elaborate houses he'd visited that day, the difficult clients he'd encountered. He was an excellent mimic, able to reproduce the New Jersey accents of his matronly clients, the rolled consonants of his Cuban coworkers. After dinner they divided up the newspaper and read together in companionable silence. "Listen to this," he'd say periodically. Then he'd clear his throat and read to her—sometimes just a headline, an inane comment by a public official; other times an entire editorial. He was knowledgeable about world affairs; his political views mirrored Joan's. Her whole adult life she'd read the paper alone, over morning coffee. Now she reserved this pleasure until evening, when she could share it with him.

"Did anybody call?" he asked one night as they lingered at the table. "I told the lawn service they could reach me at this number."

"No," she answered.

He never mentioned Moira Snell, and Joan never asked.

. . .

THE NEXT AFTERNOON while she was cooking, the telephone rang. She answered it clumsily, pinching the receiver between her ear and shoulder.

"Hello?" she said.

The line was silent.

"Hello?" she repeated.

At the other end a radio was playing; she heard laughing, splashing, the soprano cries of children.

"Moira?" she said. "Is that you?"

A soft click as the caller hung up the phone.

ONE NIGHT Joan tried something different for dinner, fillets of sole with orange sauce. A complicated recipe, but her confidence had grown.

At five-fifteen she glanced out the window, waiting for the truck in the driveway. Traffic was gentle as a rule, but even in Palm Beach County, bottlenecks could happen.

By six o'clock the sauce had cooked down to nothing; the fish looked fragile and desiccated in the pan. The unread newspaper lay on the table. Joan dialed the lawn service; no answer. A strange anxiety gnawed at her stomach. He'd been in town only a few weeks; he never spoke of any friends. There was only one place he could be. The days were getting shorter. Moira would be home from work by now, the pool closed for the day.

She waited until dark. The night was cool and damp; she dressed in slacks and a dark sweater—her reporter's uniform, now worn to spy on a man she barely knew. In her father's car she drove the three miles to Ocean Avenue, a broad, busy street lined with inexpensive restaurants and tourist motels. Among them were several large stucco buildings, dotted with flimsy terraces. Ken and Moira's apartment could be in any one of them; she had no idea of the address. She turned into the first complex on her right and circled the small lot, looking for his green lawn service truck.

She drove slowly in and out of parking lots, headlights off to avoid attracting attention. Then she remembered what she was driving: her father's baby blue Cadillac, polished to a sheen; as conspicuous as an airplane among the vans and Volkswagens and beat-up sedans.

She reached the last white stucco building on the strip. A sign out front said COCO PALM COURT. In the distance she saw the lights of a gas station; beyond it Ocean Avenue stretched dark and empty for miles, nothing but swampland on either side. She turned into the parking lot and cut the motor. For the first time in months, she wished for a cigarette. She was aware that something had taken hold of her.

She glanced at her watch. The lot was full of cars; the residents of Coco Palm were home for the night. A door opened and a pregnant woman emerged, carrying laundry; a long-haired couple threw a Frisbee across the parking lot. In the courtyard children teased a small dog. Cooking smells floated through the open windows; a baby's cry, the driving beat of rock music. A pennant in a window read FLORIDA ATLANTIC UNIVERSITY.

Joan rolled down her window to let in the noise. She was a city girl, raised in apartments; she missed the companionship of the neighbor's television set, the comforting footfalls of the couple upstairs. She dreaded going back to her silent house, the ruined dinner on the stove. A week before, she'd been fine; she'd accepted her solitude, made peace with it. Kimble's arrival had changed everything. She couldn't bear to be without him.

She started the engine and drove to the gas station. The Cadillac guzzled fuel; she'd burned a quarter tank casing Ocean Avenue. When no attendant appeared, she stepped out of the car and peered into the front window. A sign dangled behind the glass; the station was closed.

Joan went back to her car. In the distance she noticed a cinder-block building farther down the road. The parking lot was dark, but a few of the windows blazed with light. She got into her car and drove toward it, her hands weak on the steering wheel.

In front of the building sat the green lawn service truck.

THE NEXT MORNING she awoke to a silent house. The clock ticked loudly; the leaves of the date palm scratched the window-pane like a pet demanding attention. Her throat burned; her mouth tasted dirty. An ashtray overflowed on the bedside table.

Joan sat up in bed, still wearing her dark sweater; her silicone breast was slightly askew. The evening came back to her in an instant. She'd parked outside the cinder-block building on Ocean Avenue and sat there for a long time. Dim light flickered in an upstairs window—a candle, she supposed. Finally she stepped out of the car. The outside door was locked; she stood there a moment, staring through the glass into the lobby, at the bank of mailboxes just inside the door. She couldn't make out the names on the boxes, except for one marked with a strip of masking tape. On it someone had written in large block letters: "Snell/Kimble." Afterward she'd driven across town in search of cigarettes. She'd sat in bed and smoked them one after the other, a whole pack in a matter of hours. When the cigarettes were gone she went to sleep, leaving the front door unlocked.

She rolled over, hoping for sleep; then, in the distance, she heard a motor. She sprang out of bed and went to the window just as the lawn service truck turned into the driveway.

She reached beneath her sweater to adjust her breast, then slipped on a pair of slacks. Her face in the mirror shocked her, the fine smoker's lines around her mouth. She wasn't a kid anymore; her skin could no longer hide a poor night's sleep. Her hairdresser had talked her into a darker color; in the morning light her black hair looked false, lifeless, like the synthetic curls of a doll. The pixie cut was also a mistake—it had never suited her strong face. She swiped at her hair and hurried downstairs.

Kimble met her on the front step, dressed in jeans and his Mexican blouse. He had showered; his hair curled wetly over his collar.

"Hi," he said.

"Hi." She bent and picked the newspaper from the stoop, feeling light-headed. Nerves tingled in her hands, the aftereffects of nicotine.

"I'm about to make coffee," she said. Her voice was pleasant but cool. "Would you like some?"

"Sure," said Kimble, following her inside.

In the kitchen she filled the coffeepot with water. The whole house smelled of fish; she'd left the pan of sole on the counter all night. Kimble's eyes went to the sink, filled with crusted cookware.

"No work today?" said Joan. "You're not wearing your uniform."

"It's my day off." His eyes met hers. "Joan, I need to talk to you about last night."

She turned her back to him and filled the sink with hot water. "What about it?"

"I should have called. You went to all this trouble making dinner, and I didn't even show up."

"Don't be silly," she said. "I was going to cook anyway. Believe it or not, I eat even when you're not here." She pulled on her rubber gloves and squirted soap into the sink. "How's Moira?"

"She's all right."

She rinsed a glass and placed it in the drainer. "I take it you've worked out your differences."

"Not exactly." He reached around her and shut off the faucet. "Look at me."

Her heart quickened. She turned to face him.

"I feel like a heel for what I did last night," he said. "You've been nothing but generous and this is how I repay you."

"It's no big deal," said Joan. An unfamiliar tightness in her throat. Don't cry, she thought. Whatever you do, don't cry.

"There's something you should know," he said. "Moira and I are finished. The wedding is off."

Joan's heart paused, then reset itself.

"What happened?"

"Things haven't been good for a while." He was very close, his mouth crusty white at the corners; he had just brushed his teeth. "I've never told you this, but I'm a little older than Moira."

No kidding, Joan thought. "Really?" she said.

"Yes," said Kimble. "She seemed so mature I didn't think it would be a problem. I guess I was wrong."

"I'm sorry," said Joan.

His eyes met hers. "Everything happens for a reason."

She turned to fill the sink. "What will you do now?"

"I only came to Florida because of Moira," he said, "but I like it here. I'm going to stay."

Joan waited.

"I'll need to find an apartment," he continued. "I've taken

advantage of your hospitality long enough. You said I could stay here until Moira and I worked things out, and I guess we have."

Joan wet a sponge and scrubbed at the spattered stove top. "What will you do? Keep working for the lawn service?"

"I don't think so." She could tell by his tone that he found the idea ridiculous. Clearly he was an educated man. It occurred to her that he'd lived a whole life she knew nothing about.

"Actually," he said, "I've always been interested in real estate."

"Really?" she said. "My father was in real estate. Did I ever tell you that?"

"No."

She thought a moment. "My uncle has an agency in Coral Gables. Maybe he could help you out."

"That would be great. Joan, I don't know how to thank you." He eyed the newspaper on the counter. "Would you mind if I borrowed your paper? I need to start looking for an apartment."

"Sure," she said.

He took the paper and sat at the kitchen table. She noticed he held the pages at arm's length. *He needs reading glasses*, she thought.

"Ken," she said.

He looked up from the paper.

"You don't have to leave. I don't want you to." She swallowed loudly. "I like having you around."

He rose and crossed the kitchen, bent and kissed her cheek.

*O*n Christmas Eve they ate dinner on the patio. Joan made baked beans and potato salad; Kimble grilled hamburgers for their guests. Joan's brother, Ben, was visiting from New York; he and his new girlfriend, Lynda, had flown in the night before. A statuesque Lutheran girl from Minnesota, she was a stewardess for TWA; she'd just finished telling them how she'd finagled Ben a seat in first class. It was a kick, she explained, when a passenger was *allowed* to grab her ass.

"How long have you been a stewardess?" Joan asked.

"Three years. It beats waiting tables, I can tell you that." Lynda tucked her blond hair behind her ear. Ben kissed her loudly on the cheek, a tremendous sucking sound that made her squeal with laughter. He'd grown stouter and hairier, his plump pink face half hidden by a dark beard. He raised his can of beer toward Joan.

"Merry Christmas," he said.

"L'chaim," said Joan. They hadn't shared a Jewish holiday since their mother died; but their whole lives Christmas had brought them together. As children they'd tried unsuccessfully to ignore it;

as adults they'd planned parties around it, at Joan's apartment in Manhattan or Ben's in Brooklyn. The year before Joan had spent Christmas in a private room at Sloan-Kettering. Lying in her hospital bed, drifting in and out of sleep, she'd fought the urge to phone her brother: *I'm in the hospital, Ben. I have cancer.* Shame stopped her. She couldn't tell a soul.

Lynda rose and stripped off her T-shirt. Her round breasts spilled over her bikini top.

"I'm going in for a swim," she announced. "Anybody coming?"

"Still digesting." Ben caressed his belly like a pet. "What about you, Ken? Go have a swim."

"Sure," said Kimble. "Why not?" He stood and pulled off his shirt. His chest was slightly concave; his sternum protruded like something painful.

"Man, don't you eat?" said Ben.

"You bet. Your sister's a terrific cook." Briefly he touched Joan's shoulder. "I'll be back in a minute."

Ben studied Joan from across the table. From his pocket he produced a small tin. "You're looking good," he said. "This place seems to agree with you."

"It does." Joan watched Lynda bounce a few times on the diving board, breasts quivering, then dive expertly into the water, a perfect jackknife. Kimble descended the ladder at the other end of the pool. In the dark she couldn't see whether he watched Lynda's magnificent chest.

"She's pretty," said Joan.

"Isn't she, though?" Ben opened the tin and began to roll a joint. "So when are you coming back to New York?"

That week her editor had called, asking the same question; her leave of absence had run out and her only options were to quit or return. *I'm sorry,* she'd told him, watching Ken through the window, planting chives at the base of the oleanders—a permanent solution to the aphid problem. *I can't go back there. My life is here now.*

"I'm not," she told Ben.

He looked up from his rolling paper. "You're joking."

"What's so incredible?" She watched Kimble cross the pool, swimming toward Lynda. "I don't need the money, and I don't miss the aggravation."

Ben frowned. "What are you going to do with the rest of your life? Sit around the pool with some aging hippie?"

Joan watched the pool. Kimble had disappeared underwater. He surfaced for a breath, then vanished again.

"That's not fair," she said quietly, afraid he might overhear. She hadn't discussed her decision with him; things were too good between them to risk such a serious conversation.

"I mean it." Ben lit the joint and took a drag. "Tell me. Where did you find this guy?"

Please, Joan thought. Don't ruin it. She hadn't seen her brother in ten months, not since their father's funeral.

"Ken and I are just friends." She inhaled deeply. She hadn't smoked marijuana in a year; she'd forgotten it could smell so sweet.

"Oh, right. Friends." Another drag; he held the smoke in a long time. "Nothing like a wealthy friend with a great big house. A friend who doesn't charge rent." He reached across the table for her hand. "Don't get offended. I'm trying to look out for you. You're a wealthy woman now. You have to be careful."

Joan withdrew her hand. "Ken's not interested in my money. He has a job."

"Mowing lawns?" Ben offered the joint; Joan shook her head no. She knew Ken's opinions on pot smokers.

"That's just temporary," she said. "He's looking for something else."

"Like what? A paper route?"

Joan stared at him. "This isn't like you. Since when are you so concerned with money?"

"I'm not. I'm concerned about you. You've always known how to look out for yourself. What's happened to you?"

The question hung in the air. Joan hugged her caftan around her, conscious of the silicone breast against her chest.

"You don't know him," she said finally. "You don't know the first thing about him."

"True enough," said Ben. His eyes went to Kimble and Lynda, crouched at the shallow end of the pool, their slick heads bobbing at the surface. Kimble spoke softly; Lynda nodded and smiled. She seemed mesmerized by his voice.

"Do you?" he asked.

$\mathcal{T}$hey drove to Coral Gables in her father's car, Kimble behind the wheel. It was a brilliant Saturday morning, crisp and sunny; they were expected at her aunt and uncle's for lunch. Joan closed her eyes. Through the windows the winter sun warmed her skin; her limbs felt heavy and languorous. She hadn't been a passenger in a long time. She'd forgotten how pleasant it could be.

She glanced across the seat at Kimble. He'd driven the car once before, when she had a big grocery order and needed help carrying the bags. He was a tall man, like her father; the first time he slid the seat back from the dashboard to accommodate his long legs, she'd felt a pang of recognition.

"You look tired," he said as he turned onto the highway.

"A little." She fatigued easily since the surgery; she could no longer function on a few hours' sleep. The night before she'd lain awake, remembering Ken at the dinner table: shoveling mashed potatoes into his mouth, the cuff of his Mexican blouse tipped with gravy. His beard had grown in completely; his hair was long enough for a ponytail. She thought of the way her brother had described him—an aging hippie—and knew her uncle Floyd would see him the same way. Floyd was a hardhead. If Ken planned to show up in Coral Gables with a ponytail, they might as well save themselves the trip.

When she woke that morning, Kimble's truck was gone; an hour later he'd appeared with a fresh haircut.

"What do you think?" he'd asked, turning to show the neat nape of his neck. "Would you buy a house from me?"

"Wow," said Joan. His hair was thinner than she'd realized; a bare spot had opened at the crown. She'd never been attracted to bald men, but on him it was somehow different; she appreciated his high forehead, his long, intelligent face. "You look terrific."

He looked down at his faded jeans, worn and stringy at the cuffs. "Will I be all right like this? I don't have a suit."

She eyed his long legs: a thirty-six inseam, maybe thirty-eight.

"Come with me," she said.

They went upstairs to the master bedroom, cool and dim behind the thick curtains. She opened the closet. Her father had taken good care of his clothes; there were suits she recognized from twenty years before. She thought, Everything happens for a reason.

"These were my father's," she whispered.

She reached for a linen jacket on a hanger, next to it the matching pants. Her father had worn them to her college graduation.

"Try this," she said. "It's an old one. He was thinner then."

Kimble took the suit and disappeared into the bathroom. He came out a moment later, buttoning the jacket over his T-shirt.

"Does it fit?" he asked.

Joan covered her mouth, afraid she would laugh or cry. Her father's clothes didn't merely fit. They suited him perfectly.

. . .

THEY ARRIVED in Coral Gables ten minutes early. Unlike Joan's father, Floyd Cohen had no taste for glamour. He and his wife had lived in the same modest rancher for twenty years, though he could have bought the biggest house in the neighborhood, with cash.

"Uncle Floyd," Joan said at the door. "This is my friend Ken Kimble." Her palms were moist; she felt like a teenager bringing home a date.

"Welcome," said Floyd, extending his hand. *Kimble?* she imagined him thinking. *What kind of name is Kimble?*

"Your aunt Cookie is in the kitchen," he said. "Come and say hello."

They went inside and sat in the parlor. The house hadn't changed in twenty years. Joan recognized the ornate lamps and threadbare rugs, the dark, heavy furniture Floyd and Cookie had brought down from their house in Newark. On the coffee table was a crystal candy dish filled with butterscotch disks; Cookie ate them compulsively. The house had an odd medicinal smell that had nothing to do with age. Floyd and Cookie had smelled that way for as long as Joan could remember.

"Cookie," Floyd called. "Joanie and her friend are here."

Cookie emerged from the kitchen. "Joanie!" she cried. She was stout and firmly corseted; her broad bosom jutted forward like the prow of a ship.

Joan embraced her. "Hello, Aunt Cookie."

Kimble got to his feet. "Pleased to meet you."

"Sit, sit," said Cookie. Her knees made a cracking sound as she lowered herself to the sofa.

"How've you been, Auntie?" said Joan.

"Better than them up there. I heard on the radio this morning: fourteen degrees in Newark." She scrabbled in the candy dish for a butterscotch. "How's your brother, dear heart?"

"He's fine," said Joan. "He was just down for a visit."

"Still with the girlfriend?"

"A new one." Joan's eyes went to Kimble. After their swim, he and Lynda had chatted for over an hour, her breasts bobbing between them in the hot tub. *Do you think she's pretty?* Joan had asked after the guests went to bed.

Not especially, he'd answered. *She's not my type.*

Floyd sat back in his chair and eyed Kimble. "Joanie says you're interested in real estate. Ever sold anything before?"

"In a manner of speaking." Kimble's voice seemed deeper than usual; he sat erect in his chair. "I used to be a teacher."

"A teacher," Cookie said, beaming.

Joan smiled. She'd only just learned this herself. "At school," he'd said when she asked how he and Moira had met; only when she pressed did he admit that Moira had been his student. Since then Joan had tried to imagine him at the head of a classroom. Was it the old, long-haired Ken who had taught school? Or the new Ken, crisp and distinguished in her father's suit?

"Young people today are different than they were in our day," said Kimble. "Teaching them requires a lot of persuasion."

Floyd grunted. "They're spoiled rotten. They know nothing about life."

"That's right. They don't know what they want, but they want it right now. It makes them difficult customers."

Floyd nodded. Finally he stood.

"Let's not bore the ladies with talk of business. How about we get some fresh air?" He led Ken through the kitchen and out the back door.

Cookie turned to Joan. "And you," she said. "How are you getting along? All alone in that big house."

"I'm just fine," said Joan. Through the window she watched the men walk around the garden. Ken stood taller than usual; his bearing was almost military. "I go swimming every day. The weather has been lovely."

Outside Floyd stopped at a rosebush. Ken squatted and felt the soil beneath it. Joan relaxed a little. He was at his best talking about plants.

"Your beau is very handsome," said Cookie.

Joan colored. "He's not my beau. Really, Auntie, we're just friends."

"What are friends?" said Cookie, waving her chubby hand. "Why be friends with a man?"

"I've been single for a long time."

"Too long." Cookie reached for another butterscotch. "Your father worried about you. It broke his heart that you never married."

"I know," said Joan.

"You and your brother." Cookie shifted on the couch. "We talked to Ruthie today. She and Phil are expecting again."

"That's wonderful," Joan said, steeling herself. There was no avoiding the subject of her cousin Ruth, married to a doctor in Scarsdale, New York; no avoiding the unspoken comparisons.

"She's your age, you know," said Cookie. "She'll be forty in August."

Joan glanced out the window. Ken stood at the rosebush, gesturing as he spoke; she'd never seen him talk with his hands before.

Floyd nodded slowly. He clapped Ken's thin shoulder as they walked back toward the house.

"I know it's a touchy subject," said Cookie, "but for you it's not too late. Trust me, dear. There's still time."

THE SKY reddened behind them as they drove back toward the coast. Kimble would take the real estate exam in the spring; then he would go to work for Floyd.

"I feel like celebrating," he said. "What do you say I buy you an ice cream?"

"Great," said Joan. Ridiculously, she felt nervous. They'd lived under the same roof for weeks, but except for a trip to the grocery store they'd never been out together in public.

He parked in front of an ice-cream parlor a few blocks from the beach. The girl behind the counter filled their cones with strawberry ice cream.

"Uncle Floyd loved you," said Joan. "He doesn't usually take to new people." Especially gentiles, she nearly added, but didn't. "I've never seen anything like it."

"I like him," said Kimble. "He's a crafty old guy."

They sat at a table near the window. "He and my father were partners for years," said Joan. "They used to have a furniture store in Brooklyn. Then my father came down here and got into real estate. A few years later Floyd joined him."

"Interesting." Kimble crunched his cone loudly; Joan had never seen anyone devour an ice cream so fast. "Why Florida? If you don't mind my asking."

"The climate. My mother was ill—" She nearly said *with breast cancer,* but stopped herself. "And I guess they were sick of the winters in New York."

Kimble smiled. "Is that what happened to you? Got sick of the snow?"

"Not exactly." Joan hesitated. "I can't explain it. I came down for my father's funeral and I can't seem to leave."

Kimble finished his cone and wiped his hands on a paper napkin. Just then Dot Beckley and Nancy Snell came into the store. They were loaded down with shopping bags, laughing throaty laughs.

Joan felt hot and clammy, slightly ill. They hadn't seen her yet; she could easily slip out the side door. No, she thought. We haven't done anything wrong. She forced herself to speak.

"Hi, girls!" she called out. "How have you been?"

Dot smiled nervously. Nancy looked stricken.

"Fine, thank you," Nancy said icily. She turned to Dot. "Will you look at him, all cleaned up? I barely recognized him."

An awkward silence followed. The girl behind the counter watched with interest. Finally Kimble spoke.

"How's Moira?" he asked.

"How dare you." Nancy approached their table. "You broke her heart. How she's doing is none of your business."

Ken crumpled his napkin into a ball; his half of the table was littered with crumbs. "Well, give her my best," he said, perfectly calm.

"You've got some nerve." Nancy turned to Joan. "And you. Moira thought the world of you. She wanted to be just like you."

Joan's throat closed. "She's a wonderful girl."

"What's wrong with you, Joan?" said Nancy. "Are you so desperate for a man that"—she eyed Kimble—"*anyone* will do?"

"You don't understand." Joan's cheeks burned. "I wish you'd let me explain."

"I suppose I should thank you. My daughter was going to marry this schemer, for God's sake. At least she got to see his true colors before it was too late."

Kimble rose and grasped Joan's elbow. "Let's go."

"Wait," said Nancy. Her eyes met Joan's. "Don't worry about Moira. She'll be just fine." She lowered her voice. "I don't know how you got mixed up with this gigolo, but if I were you, I'd worry about myself."

THEY RODE back to the house in silence. In the driveway Joan stepped out of the car.

"I'm exhausted," she said. "I'm going upstairs to lie down."

She went inside and climbed the stairs to her bedroom. As she reached the door, Kimble called her name. She turned; he was right behind her. He placed his hands on her shoulders. They felt cool through the fabric of her blouse.

"What's the matter?" he asked. "Is it what Nancy said?"

Joan's heart raced. "It's not just Nancy. The whole world thinks so. My brother. My aunt. Everyone."

"Everyone thinks what?"

Her face felt very warm. "They think we're lovers."

"Joan." His hands tightened on her shoulders. "Which part bothers you? That people think we're lovers? Or that we aren't?"

This isn't happening, she thought as he bent and kissed her. He pulled her close and slipped his hands under her blouse.

"Don't," she said faintly.

"Why not?" His hands were cool and dry on her bare back; he slid them around front and placed them over her bra. "Because of this?" Gently he held her breasts, the warm, living left one, the cold, unyielding right.

"Do you think I care?" he said. "Do you think it makes any difference?"

He kissed her chastely, his lips cool. Behind the silicone her chest burned, the place where her breast had been.

"How did you know?" she whispered. Her mind raced. He'd seen her in her bathing suit, the day he sprayed the oleanders. The day she fell asleep in the bathtub and woke up with the door wide open.

"Does it matter?" said Kimble.

She let her mouth open under his. Her hands climbed his back; through his shirt she felt his ribs. He was right: it didn't matter at all.

He led her down the hall to his bedroom. Quickly he shed his shirt and pants. He pushed her back on the bed and removed her skirt and stockings. For a year she'd wondered how it would be, undressing for a man again. She held her breath, waiting for him to unbutton her blouse.

He didn't. He made love to her bottom half; occasionally he caressed her breasts through her blouse. He treated them both equally, though one thrilled at his touch and the other felt nothing at all. His body was long and thin, his skin perfectly cool.

It was over quickly.

"I'll be right back," he said.

He disappeared into the bathroom, closing the door behind him; in a moment she heard the shower running. She lay alone in the bed, half dressed, her silicone breast still held in place by her bra, wetness pooling on the sheet beneath her. A fly buzzed near her ear; he'd left a window open. It's done, she thought. She had made love to a man; it was still possible. In her terror she'd been unable to move; but somehow—she felt the sheet—she had pleased him.

euben Goldfarb was her father's rabbi. Joan had met him only twice, at each of her parents' funerals. He was a genial man, bright-eyed and quick to laugh; but in Joan's mind his bearded face was the face of death.

"Joan," he said, pressing her hand. "Wonderful to see you. How long are you in town?"

"Actually, I live here now." Mentally she ticked off the holidays—Rosh Hashanah, Yom Kippur, eight months of Sabbaths. Eight months' worth of failures to appear at Beth Israel.

The rabbi's eyebrows shot up. "How wonderful." His eyes darted from her to Kimble.

"Rabbi," said Joan. "This is Ken Kimble. My fiancé." The word sounded strange on her tongue. He'd proposed suddenly; they'd been engaged for two days.

Goldfarb extended his hand. "Congratulations. I had no idea." He gestured to a low sofa across the room. "You want to talk about a marriage service, am I right? Please. Sit down."

They sat. Goldfarb nodded toward Kimble. "I take it from your name that you are not Jewish."

"Oh, no," said Joan. "Ken's mother was Jewish." As she said it she felt herself beaming; she couldn't help it. She'd discovered this bit of information by accident; her uncle Floyd had mentioned it one night when they'd gone to his house for dinner. *Why did you tell Floyd and not me?* she'd asked Ken afterward. *I didn't think it would matter,* he'd replied. A few weeks later he proposed.

"My parents weren't religious," said Kimble. "So I don't know the first thing about being Jewish."

"Even so." Goldfarb shifted in his chair. "Under Jewish law the child of a Jewish mother is himself Jewish, regardless of the father's ancestry or the religion practiced in the home."

Joan exhaled. It would be all right. Goldfarb would marry them; they could have the ceremony in her backyard. She hadn't been to temple in years; for three Yom Kippurs she had failed to fast; yet she wanted to stand under the chuppah beside her new husband, the familiar prayers raining down on them both. It was a thing she'd always known in her heart: if she were ever to marry, it would be to a Jewish man. If Ken were Christian, she might have said yes anyway. (Maybe. Probably. Of *course* she would have, but without the same conviction.)

"I take it you were raised a Christian?" said Goldfarb.

"No." Kimble glanced at Joan. "I wasn't raised anything. That makes it simpler, doesn't it?"

Goldfarb considered this. "Simpler because celebrating your marriage in a Jewish ceremony would not conflict with any religious beliefs of your own?"

Kimble nodded.

"Simpler, yes," said Goldfarb. "Certainly it makes things simpler."

1972

oan Kimble was bleeding.

She'd felt it coming all morning but told herself it was something else. Years ago she'd waited for her period with the same mixture of anxiety and hope, but for different reasons. At Radcliffe, only one infamous girl had a diaphragm; the rest relied naively on the calendar, resorting to hot baths and vinegar douches when they were late. Joan was never late; she'd always been lucky. Now she wondered whether it was luck at all, or simple biological failure; whether her body had ever mastered that most basic of female chores, the production of an egg.

She dressed and went downstairs to call Ken's office. "Is my husband there?" she asked the secretary.

"He's out showing a house right now. Shall I have him call you?"

"That's okay," said Joan. "It's nothing important."

She padded into the kitchen for more of Rosa's Cuban coffee, the marble floors cool under her feet. Ken had hired Rosa soon after the wedding to cook and maintain the house; it was simply too big, he insisted, for Joan to do everything herself. He was adamant about keeping the place, though Joan would have been just as happy a few miles inland, in a little bungalow with fruit trees out back. Without the expense of maintaining the house, Ken wouldn't have to work at all; they could live on the income from her father's investments. Joan imagined them spending every day together, swimming and reading and sleeping in the sun.

"It wouldn't be right," Ken said each time she proposed the idea. "I've got to earn my keep."

Her analyst had helped her understand that his male pride wouldn't allow it; that if he was sometimes preoccupied with business the way her father had been, it was only because he wanted to prove himself to her. Already he'd achieved enormous success—in four years he'd doubled the agency's profits—but even that wasn't enough for him. Since Floyd's death Ken had branched into commercial development; his newest project was a beachfront hotel. He talked constantly about casinos and shopping malls, a proposed golf resort in Boca Raton. Joan could barely keep up.

AT NOON he came home for lunch. They ate at the glass-topped table Joan had bought for the patio.

"I hope it isn't too rare," she said as Rosa brought out salads and steaks. "Tell Rosa if you want her to cook it some more." They ate meat all the time now; Ken's vegetarianism had gone the way of his long hair and Mexican blouse. Joan was privately horrified at the way he preferred his beef, cooked to a leathery gray—a taste he must have acquired growing up in the Midwest. She found herself thinking often of the Midwest, a place she had never been. She blamed the Midwest for Ken's atrocious table manners, his Spartan work ethic, his reluctance to talk about his feelings, all the parts of her husband she would never understand.

"Looks fine," Ken said. "A little heavy for lunch, though. I missed my run this morning." He'd recently taken up jogging; he was concerned about his weight. Joan couldn't understand it. For as long as she'd known him, he'd been as lean as a greyhound.

He dug into his Cobb salad. A piece of avocado shot across the table.

"How did your meeting go?" she asked. Lately he'd been showing an oceanfront villa in West Palm. At just under a million, it was a tough sell, but he enjoyed the challenge.

"Great," he said. "The husband is dragging his feet, but the wife is ready to sign." It was always the same story: Ken did his best selling to wives.

Joan cut into her steak. The meat was bright red inside, barely warm—just the way she liked it. She tried to listen as he described an apartment he'd listed, a tenth-floor oceanfront condo in Delray Beach. It reminded her of dinners with her father, who complained about taxes and zoning laws while her mother nodded patiently and Joan and Ben kicked each other under the table. Lately she'd been lonely for her brother, hundreds of miles away. They had barely spoken since her wedding.

Ken reached into his mouth, fished out a piece of gristle and lay it on his plate. "What's on your agenda for this afternoon?"

"Dr. Sugarman." Joan made a face. "My six-month checkup."

Ken said nothing. They never spoke of her breast cancer; after two years of marriage, he still hadn't seen the scar on her chest.

"I suppose I should tell you," said Joan. "I got my period this morning. Six days late. I was sure this was it." Her gynecologist had told her to expect it, given her age: her cycles would become gradually less regular until they stopped altogether. She'd never repeated this to Ken.

She was dying for a child. For two years it had crept up on her, like a thief trying all the doors and windows, looking for a way in. She found herself noticing children at the beach, the shopping plaza, the playground across from the hair salon. She'd become fascinated with Rosa's granddaughter, a chubby four-year-old named Marisol who watched her with enormous eyes and hid behind Rosa's skirt when Joan spoke to her. Sometimes, through the kitchen door, she heard Marisol laugh, a bright arc of sound that bubbled through the air like water from a fountain. Alone in the big house all day, she could think of nothing else. Recently she'd had a birthday card from her cousin Ruth in Scarsdale, pregnant with her third child. Ruth was forty-two, the same age as Joan. It was another reason to hope.

"Maybe next month," said Ken. He pushed his steak away and sat back in his chair.

"Maybe," said Joan. He always froze up when she talked about the intimate functions of her body. She supposed women didn't do this in the Midwest.

"Aren't you going to eat your steak?" she asked.

They both looked down at his plate, the barely touched meat lying in a pool of blood.

SUGARMAN'S HAIR had begun to gray. He sat on a low stool, examining Joan's left breast—more roughly than necessary, she thought. Or maybe she'd become hypersensitive. She wasn't used to being touched.

"Ouch," she said.

"Premenstrual tenderness?"

"No." She shifted on the examining table; the paper cover crinkled beneath her. "I got my period this morning. I'm not happy about it."

Sugarman looked at her quizzically. "I don't understand."

"I'm trying to get pregnant." *You idiot,* she nearly added.

His eyes widened. "Pregnant?"

"For God's sake," Joan snapped. "Don't look at me like that. I'm not that old." Her eyes went to Sugarman's desk. His boys in baseball uniforms, teenagers now. A new photo of the blond wife, this time holding a baby.

"I didn't mean that." Sugarman's eyes sought hers. "I wasn't even thinking about your age. But you've had breast cancer. No matter what your age, pregnancy would pose some risks."

"Risks of what?" Her pulse was loud in her ears.

"There haven't been any controlled studies," he said. "But when a woman is pregnant, her estrogen levels go through the roof. If there are any abnormal cells in your remaining breast, all that estrogen is going to make them grow."

"So?"

"So there's a chance your cancer could recur."

Joan stared him. There were fine lines at the corners of his eyes; finally he'd begun to age. But he is a young man, she thought. He will live a long life.

"No," said Joan. "That's crazy. I haven't had cancer in four years."

"Three years."

"Three and a *half.*" Pressure behind her eyes, a threat of tears. "Four in December."

"Four in December," Sugarman said gently. "Look, I'm not trying to scare you. I probably should have mentioned this earlier. But at your age—" He broke off. "It didn't occur to me that you were considering it."

Joan drove home into the blinding sun. Storm clouds behind her: it was the last week of the hurricane season. She hadn't thought of her cancer in a long time. At some point in the past few years—she couldn't say when—she'd stopped grabbing her left breast, obsessively feeling for lumps. She felt, if not quite whole, then healthy and content. She had a husband, a home, a life she'd never imagined.

She pulled into the driveway. The garage door was open, Ken's Eldorado parked inside—he must have come home early, to squeeze in a jog before the storm. He met her at the door, dressed in running shorts.

"How'd it go at the doctor's?" he asked.

"Make love to me," she said.

Thunder rumbled in the distance. He looked over her shoulder, at the threatening sky.

"I want to squeeze in a run before the storm hits," he said. "How about a rain check?"

*T*hey made love every Sunday. First they went out to dinner.

Mulligan's was the best steak house in Boca Raton; that Sunday the parking lot was packed with cars. As always Joan had reserved a table for five o'clock. She had no interest in the early bird special; her concern was more urgent. Ken needed two hours to digest after dinner, and by nine o'clock he'd be asleep for the night. If sex were to happen, it had to occur before eight.

They parked in front and went inside, expecting the usual crowd of elderly couples; instead the place was filled with men. They stood four deep in the entranceway, waiting for tables. Their dark wool suits and sober ties looked out of place in the winter sunshine, relics of a colder climate.

The hostess showed the Kimbles to their usual table, a wide booth in the corner of the dining room. Joan scanned the menu, though she knew it by heart. They came to Mulligan's every Sunday; the other local restaurants specialized in seafood, which Ken refused to eat. If it were up to him, they'd have every meal at home, Rosa's meat loaf seven days a week.

An unfamiliar waitress approached with glasses of ice water. She was young and heavily made up, sleek in a strapless dress. As Joan knew he would, Ken smiled warmly.

"Busy tonight," he said.

"You got that right." She set down the glasses. "There's a conference in town."

Ken ordered for both of them, T-bones and baked potatoes; his eyes darted briefly to the girl's cleavage. The waitress shimmied away, the dress tight across her behind.

"What an odd crowd," said Joan.

He shrugged. "Lot of bad suits."

She glanced around the room. The tables were filled with men in dark jackets: a few gray ones, lots of browns, one forest green. Her eyes stopped on a fat man in a bow tie.

"That man is looking at you," she said.

Ken looked up. His mouth tightened. "A client, maybe."

"Do you recognize him?"

"Why should I?" he snapped. "I can't keep them all straight." He stood up abruptly, nearly upsetting his water glass.

"I'll be right back," he said, heading toward the washroom.

Joan waited. The young waitress swept past, carrying a platter of steaks. Once the aroma would have made her hungry, but no longer; she was sick to death of steak. She glanced at her watch. Ken had been gone nearly ten minutes.

"Excuse me, ma'am," said a deep voice. It was the fat man, now approaching the table. "The gentleman who was sitting here. I could swear I know him from somewhere." He spoke slowly, a Southern drawl.

"He's my husband," said Joan.

"Then you would know." The man smiled. "Did he by chance study at Bethany Biblical Seminary? Class of forty-eight? He's a dead ringer for my old roommate."

"I'm afraid not," said Joan.

"Are you sure?"

"Very sure. My husband and I are Jewish."

The man colored. "Sorry, ma'am. I didn't mean to offend you."

"It's okay," said Joan. "You didn't."

"Beg pardon." The man's face was very red. He turned and lumbered back to his table.

A moment later Ken reappeared. He looked very pale.

"Are you all right?" said Joan.

"I think I'm coming down with something." He did not sit.

"Oh, sweetheart." He had a delicate stomach; everything made him queasy. "How about some ginger ale?"

"I think we'd better go home."

Joan slid out of the booth; Ken reached into his wallet and laid a five on the table. "For the girl," he said. Joan was about to point out that she'd only brought them water, but stopped herself. He was stingy with their usual waitress, who was stout and fiftyish. Only young, pretty waitresses got generous tips.

He hurried out the back door, Joan close behind him. He reached the car first, backed out of the parking space before she could close the passenger door.

"Sorry about this," he said. "I feel lousy."

"Poor baby," said Joan. She clutched her door handle as they peeled away from the curb. Only then did she notice the sign out front:

MULLIGAN'S WELCOMES THE SOUTHEAST BIBLE CONFERENCE.

. . .

KEN WENT immediately to bed. Later, when Joan slid in next to him, he lay flat on his back, snoring softly. She curled up beside him and pressed her chest against his shoulder. Since her marriage she'd wore the silicone breast constantly, even at night.

"Hi," she whispered.

His eyes snapped open. "Hi." It still amazed her, how alert he was the moment he opened his eyes. No grogginess. His body operated at only two settings, awake and asleep; there was nothing in between.

"I'm glad you're awake," said Joan.

"I wasn't."

"Sorry." She reached under his pajama jacket and ran her hand across his chest. Absently he patted her thigh.

"I have an early meeting tomorrow," he said. "I set the alarm for five."

"Five?" she repeated. He jogged most mornings before work; his discipline astounded her. She'd tried to adopt his schedule but found it impossible; she went to bed when he did, then lay awake for hours watching him sleep. "Why don't you stay up for a while?" he often asked. "You can always sleep in." But Joan would not. If she gave in to her nocturnal nature, they'd never make love again. She would never get pregnant.

He closed his eyes; she persisted, stroking his chest. "Come on. It'll only take a minute." She was joking, though of course it was true: in five minutes he'd be in the shower; in ten, asleep.

The irony was lost on him. "I'm wiped out," he said.

Joan sighed. She was days away from ovulating; next Sunday would be soon enough. She laid her head on his shoulder.

"The funniest thing happened in the restaurant," she said. "When you were in the rest room, that man came over and asked about you."

"What man?"

"The man who was staring at you."

"No kidding." He closed his eyes. "Who was he?"

"I didn't get his name." She chuckled. "He said you looked like someone he knew in—what did he call it? Bible school? Isn't that bizarre?"

"Very strange," he said. "I guess I have a double."

He turned to her and took her in his arms.

*P*regnancy affected her in strange ways. Her vision improved. Her hair straightened. She cried easily, something she had never done; nearly every night she dreamed of her mother. As if she were waking from a long sleep, she began to remember her old life, her years as a journalist. How she had lived.

She remembered late nights, bottles of wine, Leonard Cohen on the hi-fi. Traffic. Taxis. Men in suits, strange and thrilling men who watched her as she passed. She remembered crossing the park on cool mornings, her legs alive in dark stockings, walking with a purpose.

At the end of her first trimester, she went back to New York for a visit. "I'll be fine," she told her aunt Cookie, who'd taken to phoning her every day. She had no morning sickness; she felt healthier than she had in years. She asked Ken to come along—it seemed like the right thing to do—but he was meeting with developers about the new golf course; after months of negotiations they were close to a deal. "Maybe next time," she said, hiding her relief.

She booked a room at the Plaza—like a tourist, she thought; but she had nowhere else to stay. For the first time in her life, she had no relatives in New York. Her parents' Brooklyn apartment had been sold; her brother had moved to Washington, D.C., where he'd made a career of harassing the government, marching in protests and getting himself thrown in jail. Staying with friends was not an option; she hadn't told anyone she was coming. She would have felt foolish saying so, but she wanted to observe New York when New York wasn't looking.

It was easy to do. For a whole day she wandered the streets: her old neighborhood, the newsstand and deli, the bookstore where she'd met Howard Resnick, the young lawyer she might have married. "That's where Mother used to live," she told the child inside her. "That's where she used to work." Late in the afternoon she walked through midtown: past the *Times* building, the watering holes they'd frequented after hours. The taverns were filled with new faces—still journalists, presumably, but unfamiliar and impossibly young. Among them were women in short skirts, long hair hanging down their backs. Five years ago Joan had been a rarity; in certain establishments she'd turned heads simply by sitting at the bar. Now women were everywhere.

She went into a tavern and ordered tomato juice. It felt good to sit. She hadn't walked so much in years; in Florida she drove everywhere. Around her women knocked back martinis and short glasses of Scotch; they watched themselves in the mirror over the bar, smoking, preening, laughing. Joan took a cab back to her hotel; in the large tub she soaked her aching legs. The next day she called Morris Brown and invited him to lunch.

"JOAN," HE SAID.

He got to his feet and took her in his arms. Out of habit she stood on her toes; her husband was very tall. But Morris was short and thickly built; they had always stood eye to eye.

"It's good to see you," he said. His neck smelled of shaving soap and something else, something deeply familiar, like a place she'd visited as a child. Stop, she thought. Morris had never seen her cry.

"Thanks for coming," she said, breaking the embrace.

"Are you kidding me? I wouldn't miss seeing you for the world."

They sat. The restaurant was dark and smoky, a reporters' hangout; Joan had eaten a hundred lunches here, hamburgers and garlicky pastrami. On Fridays, drinks after work; packs and packs of cigarettes.

"I ordered you a martini," said Morris.

I'm not drinking, she could have said. *I'm pregnant.*

"Thanks," she said instead.

"God, Joanie." He reached across the table for her hand. "God, you look good."

A flush washed across her chest. Ken complimented her all the time (had at the beginning, anyway; lately not so much), but it never affected her like this. Her scalp tingled; she felt almost faint. She took a sip of her martini; a sip wouldn't hurt.

"I'm fat," she said, though she wasn't. She'd gained eight pounds so far, mainly in her face and chest. Her silicone breast no longer matched the other one; she'd taken to wearing a padded bra, the stuffing removed from one side. She had let her hair grow; Ken preferred it long.

"You're gorgeous," said Morris. He offered her a cigarette; she shook her head. "It's been a long time."

"It has." She'd invited him to the wedding knowing he wouldn't come, knowing the invitation was a breach that probably offended him, not because he was jealous but because she'd left what they both loved. "How are things?"

That was all it took. There'd been a break-in at Democratic National Committee headquarters in Washington; a bunch of crazy Cuban nationalists, it had first appeared. Then one of the burglars turned out to be the security coordinator for Nixon's reelection committee.

"This is just the beginning," said Morris. "There's more here than meets the eye." Joan nodded eagerly, devouring it.

"These are crazy days," he finished. "God, Joanie, you'd be in your element. A muckraker like you."

Sadness filled her like a sickness. She hadn't expected this, hadn't wanted it. She'd only wanted a last look back.

"Anyway." Morris raised his glass. "To Joan Cohen."

"Kimble," said Joan. She regretted it immediately.

"Sorry." Morris took a long drink. "How's the husband?"

"He's fine. He's—" He's what? she thought. Selling mansions? Building a golf course? Ken's business deals bored her beyond words. Morris, she knew, would feel the same way.

"He's fine," she repeated.

Morris sat back in his chair. "I can't believe you're married." An awkward silence. "That didn't come out right."

"That's okay." Joan looked down at her glass; she had finished her martini. "Neither can I."

"I'm jealous as hell." Morris drained his Scotch; the waiter came with another. "That sounds crazy, doesn't it? Me, the one who was married all those years. Here I am. Jealous as hell."

Joan looked around the restaurant, at the pale, keen faces—not a suntan among them, though some were rosy from the booze. The room was suddenly loud: jazz, urgent voices, laughter; the dull roar of traffic outside. Morris's eyes followed hers.

"Do you miss it?" he asked.

"No," said Joan. Tears burned behind her eyes. "I don't miss it at all."

Later Morris hailed her a cab. The taxi idled; on the rush-hour sidewalk they clasped each other, annoyed pedestrians stepping around them. She inhaled deeply, filling her lungs with the smell of him, some piece of him she could take back with her.

That night, in the airplane rest room, she began to bleed. When the plane touched down in Miami, she was no longer pregnant.

THERE IS a superstition among Jews about taking the future for granted. Buy blankets and booties for an unborn child, and you risk putting a *kineahora*—a jinx—on the pregnancy. Joan had laughed when her aunt Cookie warned her, but she'd obeyed nonetheless. She hadn't bought so much as a diaper.

She lost the baby anyway.

The child, had it lived, would have been a girl; the doctor said there was no way to tell, but in her heart Joan was sure. Privately she'd named the baby Ava, after her own mother. Joan imagined her tall, with Ken's blue eyes, an athletic girl who did not play the violin.

She imagined Harvard for her daughter, not Radcliffe. Ava would have studied physics, philosophy, discrete math; she would have understood the movement of the planets, the invisible workings of the universe, all the things her mother did not.

Ava would have lived a long life. She would have inherited nothing from her mother to prevent this. She would have traveled the world unafraid; perhaps she would have joined the Peace Corps, as Moira Snell had wanted to do. If she'd wanted to, she could have fallen in love. She would have surrendered nothing.

S ummer came.

Joan lay awake a long time, restless despite the sleeping pills, the Valium for her nerves, the Midol for her menstrual cramps. Since the miscarriage her periods had been agony. "It'll pass," her gynecologist had assured her. She was in the early stages of menopause; in another year her cycles would stop altogether.

Rain nicked the windowpanes; the shadow of the date palm darkened her husband's face. A face, by now, as familiar as her own. They'd celebrated their second anniversary that spring.

Ken stirred; the ceiling fan blew a lock of hair across his forehead. He was always so careful about his hair. She imagined he resembled his father: the blue eyes, the straight nose. His mother would have been small and dark, with a round behind and a broad shelf of bosom. Like Joan's own mother, the original Ava; like her aunt Cookie. It was the way all Jewish women seemed to end up, the way Joan herself was starting to look. She'd gained weight and didn't care, eight pounds from her brief pregnancy and ten more besides.

She'd never met any of his family. He'd invited no one to the wedding; his parents were dead, his few boyhood friends scattered all over the big squarish states of Kansas and Nebraska and Iowa. Except for Joan he was alone in the world. Or almost. He'd been married before—a youthful mistake, he said, hardly worth mentioning. She'd never asked about his first wedding, if the bride wore white, if she was, in fact, a virgin. He never spoke about past lovers, and Joan didn't press: she had too many of them herself to be comfortable swapping histories. Yet she'd never married any of hers.

Joan rolled over on her side, kneading the soft flesh between her hipbones. They never spoke of the child who'd died. The way her gynecologist explained it, miscarriage was common in the first trimester—nature's cruel quality control, a sign that something serious was wrong with the baby. Ava's death could not have been prevented; Joan's one martini with Morris Brown was not to blame. She chose to believe otherwise; she held herself responsible. The alternative was to believe evil happened for no reason, that fate was perverse and sadistic and humans powerless against it.

She watched her husband in the dark. They hadn't made love since she lost the baby; she'd stopped reaching for him and he seemed not to notice. He did not need her. She wondered, briefly, why he didn't; if his needs were being met elsewhere.

She felt a quickening in her chest, a flash of pain.

JOAN SAVED birthday cards, ticket stubs, snapshots taken in photo booths. She'd kept her grade school report cards, her grandfather's violin, her father's army discharge papers. Years ago, in New York, she'd rented a storage space for her old yearbooks and photo albums and pressed corsages, the zippered bags of twenty-year-old dresses, the crates of her mother's china. Recently these treasures had been shipped to the house in Florida. They filled the attic and the crawl space above the garage, cardboard boxes labeled "Mexico Trip" or "High School" or simply "Mother".

One morning after Ken left for work, Joan put on a robe and went into his dressing room, a small alcove off the bedroom. She opened the walk-in closet and flipped on the light. His suits hung in neat rows, matching vests and jackets and pants on cedar hangers. Joan fingered a sleeve. Except for a blue seersucker he'd bought on a whim, they were exquisite fabrics: linen and silk, tropical-weight wool in shades of cream or beige. In the seersucker he looked seamy and slightly quaint, like a crooked politician or a door-to-door salesman. "I'm not crazy about the seersucker," she'd finally told him. He had never worn the suit again. She was surprised that he'd kept it.

On the closet floor sat a neat row of suede bucks and light-colored wing tips, impeccably polished; beside them, an antique spittoon she'd given him for his birthday, to hold his pocket change. His shirts hung along the opposite wall. There was nothing in the closet Joan didn't recognize. It had all come from Harrison's Men's Store, where Ken had an account.

She opened a dresser drawer. Inside were running shorts, carefully folded; in the next drawer, colorful bikini briefs. The other drawers were filled with socks, handkerchiefs, swim trunks; all new, from Burdine's downtown. She couldn't have said what she was looking for: a note perhaps, a phone number written on a scrap of paper. But Ken was a prudent man. If he was having an affair, he'd be careful not to leave a trace.

In the bottom drawer she found the ratty jeans and tank tops he'd worn when they first met, folded with the same care as his new silk handkerchiefs. At the bottom of the pile was his Mexican blouse. Joan held it to her cheek, stroked the colorful embroidery. The fabric felt soft and somehow alive, like a person's skin.

That was all. The old clothes were all he'd retained of his previous life. In forty-four years he hadn't saved a single letter or photograph, not a shred of evidence that he'd ever gone to school or held a job or kissed a girl, much less married one.

Joan refolded the blouse and laid it carefully in the drawer. She was about to close it when she saw something in the back pocket of a pair of cutoffs. She slid her hand inside. It was a black-and-white photograph of two children sitting on a porch swing. The boy wore short pants and a striped T-shirt; on his lap sat a baby of indeterminate sex. The children were fair-skinned and serious; they squinted into the sun. On the back of the photo, in neat cursive: *Charlie and Josephine, September 1967.* The letters were round and careful, a woman's hand.

Joan stared at the photograph for a long time, too absorbed to hear the car in the driveway, the front door opening, Ken's tread on the stair. When she looked up he was standing in the doorway.

"Joan," he said softly. "What are you doing?" His voice was calm, his face blank. A muscle twitched below his left ear.

What could she say, sitting on the floor with his denim cutoffs in her lap, the dresser drawer hanging open? She stumbled to her feet, wishing she had dressed. He looked rich and powerful in his silk suit. In her old bathrobe she felt at a disadvantage.

She took a deep breath. "I was looking through your clothes."

He smiled. "Why would you do such a thing?"

The smile reassured her; he wasn't angry at all.

"Who are Charlie and Josephine?" she asked.

Ken's face did not change. Seagulls outside; in the distance she could hear the ocean.

"They're my children," he said.

*C*harlie would remember it for the rest of his life, the quiet hum of the baby blue Cadillac trundling down the dirt road. It was late summer and hadn't rained in a month; the car raised a cloud of dust as it traveled down the path. He stood in the yard watering pepper plants from a china basin. His grandma Helen had planted them in June, right before she died. His mother seemed to have forgotten them, but Charlie would not. He watered the plants every other day. All by himself he kept them alive.

A man wearing a pale suit stepped out of the car. He came toward Charlie in a bright cloud of dust, the particles lit up by the early sun.

"Good morning, son." He was two heads taller than Charlie, who that spring had been the tallest boy in the fourth grade. "Where can I find your mother?"

"She's inside," he said. It was her day off from work; she wouldn't rise before noon.

The man squinted in the sunlight. "Can you take me to her?"

Charlie headed down the dirt path to the house, the man following. Jody sat on the back porch playing with a toy truck.

"Hi," she called.

"Hello," said the man.

"This is a cement mixer." She reached out to show him the truck. "I had a dump truck but I lost it." Her face and hands were dirty. She would talk to anyone; she couldn't help herself.

The man said nothing. Charlie opened the screen door and the man followed him inside.

BIRDIE SAT at the table in her nightgown, drinking wine from a jelly glass.

"Hello, Vivian," he said.

She got to her feet, upsetting the glass. For years she'd imagined what she would say. (*You will burn in hell forever.* And *You are a poor excuse for a man.* And *We're fine without you, just fine.*) When she spoke, none of these things came out.

"Good Lord," she said. "What happened to your hair?"

They stood there a moment, staring at each other. Charlie watched them from the doorway, eyes wide.

"Mama?" he said.

"You run along," said Birdie. "Go keep an eye on your sister."

"Is everything all right?"

"Go ahead, son." His voice was deeper than Birdie remembered. He wore a beautiful seersucker suit.

The screen door slammed. For an instant she thought she was dreaming. But no: she would not have dreamed him bald.

"I've been driving all morning," he said. "I went to Richmond looking for you."

A slow drip, the wine she'd spilled dripping from table to floor.

"I asked around the neighborhood. Nobody knew where you'd gone. I took a chance and drove down here."

"Daddy died," she blurted out. "We live here now."

"I see." His eyes went around the kitchen, to the dishes piled in the sink.

"You're looking good," he said.

Her hand went to her hair; it hadn't been washed in a week. Like most things, this day had caught her off guard. She had not seen him in three years.

"Thank you," she said faintly.

"Let's clean this up," he said, swabbing the table with a tea towel. "Then we can sit down and catch up."

"WHO WAS THAT?" said Jody. She had abandoned her truck and stood at the door, peering through the screen.

"Nobody." Charlie refilled the basin at the outside tap and headed toward the garden.

She followed him. "What does he want?"

"I don't know." He splashed water over the tomato plants. A few of them drooped in the sun; he'd have to tie them up to spikes, the way Grandma Helen had done.

"I'm going in the house," Jody announced.

"Wait!" He grabbed her by the shirt. "Stay here."

"How come?"

"Because." He couldn't say it out loud; he wasn't sure. "Go get that old coffee can on the porch. I'll let you water the turnips."

"Really?" she said. It was Charlie's garden; he rarely let her near it.

They watered the turnips and cucumbers and pole beans and

collards, the mint and chives and parsley and dill. Six times Charlie refilled the china basin. When there was nothing left to water, he wiped his hands on his pants.

"All right," he said. "We can go in now."

Just then the screen door opened. The man came down the porch steps and gave them a brief wave.

"I'll be back in a little while," he called out.

He got into the baby blue Cadillac and drove away.

BIRDIE SAT in the bath, soaking. She heard the screen door slam, the children's footsteps rumbling up the stairs. A knock at the bathroom door.

"Mama's taking a bath," Birdie called out. "She'll be out in a minute." She rubbed her shoulders with a washcloth, her grimy ankles, her heavy white breasts.

"Who was that man?" Jody called through the door.

Birdie hesitated. She hadn't decided what to tell the children. She rubbed her wet hair with a bar of soap.

"That was your father," she said.

A long silence. Finally Charlie spoke.

"Where did he come from?"

"Florida," said Birdie. He had a parish down there, his own congregation; the parsonage was surrounded by orange trees. "Wait till you see it," he'd told her. "Summer all year long." Birdie couldn't imagine such a thing. She supposed she'd get used to it.

"Go and get yourselves dressed," she said. "Your father will be right back. He's taking us out for an ice cream."

"Then what?" said Charlie.

Birdie slipped her head underwater to rinse out the soap. She had asked about his girlfriend, the hateful Moira Snell; they had parted company ages ago. She sat up and squeezed the water from her hair.

"After that," she said, "we'll see."

THE MAN came back that afternoon in the same striped suit, carrying a bunch of carnations. Charlie's mother went to the door. She wore lipstick and a flowered dress. She put the carnations in a jar of water and rubbed at a spot on her collar.

Charlie and Jody watched from the parlor, in Sunday clothes. Charlie watched carefully. He had to make sure the man was his father.

He'd been six years old when his father left; yet he remembered almost nothing. His grandma Helen had told him this was natural; his father leaving was a shock to his system. Still he kept trying, squeezing hard the way he did at school when he couldn't see the chalkboard. (He had glasses but wouldn't wear them.) He could bring up only two faint memories. A time when they were picking elderberries for jelly and Charlie tripped and fell, spilling his bucket of berries. His father had knelt to pick them up; all Charlie remembered was the top of his head, the comb marks in the thin black hair, the white scalp beneath. This man was almost bald; the little hair he had was gray, not black.

Another time they'd walked in deep snow. It was high, above Charlie's knees, and cold where it slid into his rubber boots. His father had carried him on his shoulders, but here again Charlie couldn't recall a face. All he remembered was the whiteness, the thick soft blanket over the houses and trees, the whole world shrunken and quiet.

Now the man stood close to Charlie's mother. He grasped her elbow and murmured something in her ear. She ought to know if it was him; but Charlie had no faith in her. She barely managed to get herself to work in the morning. Each day it was Charlie who woke her and made sure she didn't go back to sleep, who walked her to her job at the dry cleaning store in town.

His mother took the man's arm. "All right," she chirped. "Who wants ice cream?"

They rode in the man's car to the Dairy Freeze out on the highway. The car was silent inside, the velvety backseat wide as a sofa. Jody bounced up and down and squealed with delight. She was six and didn't understand anything.

"Quit it," said Charlie. Then he remembered. The two adult heads rising above the front seat; the man's head nearly touching the roof of the car, his long neck craning forward from the headrest. It wasn't much, but Charlie didn't need much.

The man was his father.

They got twisted cones, brown and white, and sat at a picnic table in the parking lot. His father paid for everything. His mother ordered vanilla custard and forgot to eat it; Charlie watched it melt in the paper cup. Then they rode back to the house.

"You children stay outside for a while," his mother said. "Play outside until it gets dark." She led Charlie's father into the house. The screen door slammed behind them.

"What do you want to do?" said Jody.

"Nothing," said Charlie, but he got a rubber ball from under the porch and kicked it to her. Jody couldn't throw and couldn't catch; she'd duck if you tossed a ball in her direction. Back and forth they kicked the rubber ball. Charlie watched the house, checking the windows for signs—of what, he wasn't sure.

"This is boring," he said after a while. "I'm going to Terence's." He cut through the woods to his friend Terence Mabry's house. He wanted to show Terence the big blue Cadillac, parked behind the house as if it had always been there. He allowed Jody to follow. He could see she had nowhere else to go.

The Mabrys' truck was gone; a single light burned in the kitchen window. Charlie and Jody wandered into the backyard and sat on the swing set. The rusty chains scattered flecks of brown on their good clothes. At dusk the bug sounds started abruptly, as if someone had put the needle on a record. Charlie picked out cicadas, katydids, the low gargling of bullfrogs.

"Can we go home now?" Jody asked.

"Let's wait awhile," he said.

IN THE KITCHEN the light was fading; Birdie and Kimble sat with glasses of wine. She'd panicked when he found the bottle in the refrigerator, but he didn't seem upset. He cleared the clutter from the table and poured them each a glass. She had never seen him touch alcohol.

"To our family," he said, raising his glass. "They're terrific kids. You've done a magnificent job."

"Thank you," she said.

"I know it hasn't been easy." He set down his glass. "We had our problems, but I was wrong to leave like that. I've regretted it every day since. I wonder if you could find it in your heart to forgive me."

Birdie frowned. In her opinion they'd had no problems at all until Moira Snell appeared on their doorstep; but she wasn't about to split hairs. He had come back; he had admitted he was wrong; and she was tired. Tired of worrying about the roof (it leaked), of walking to town in the rain (she'd sold the Pontiac ages ago). Since Helen's death she'd had the cooking and shopping and laundry to do, on top of her loathsome job at the dry cleaner's. She'd had enough of this life. She was ready to be a wife again.

"I want to talk about the future," said Ken. "Our future as a family."

Birdie lifted her glass to her lips and found it empty; Ken refilled it without a word. His own glass was still full.

"I'd like to take the children on a vacation," he said. "Maybe take them down to Florida."

"Vacation?" Except for trips to Missouri to visit his parents, they'd never gone anywhere together. Long drives made Birdie carsick; he must have forgotten that. Still, if a vacation was what he wanted, she was willing to try.

"That sounds lovely," she said. "I'd like to get away."

"I didn't mean that." Ken fingered his glass but didn't drink. "I was thinking it would be just me and the children. The three of us. Give us a chance to get to know each other."

Birdie set down her glass. Outside a mockingbird trilled, a final aria before nightfall.

"What about me?" she said.

He reached across the table for her hand. "We have to be careful. All this is going to be an enormous shock to them. Little Josephine doesn't even remember me. I'd like to spend some time alone with them before—" He squeezed her hand.

"Before what?"

"Before we turn their lives upside down."

His hands were cold. Far away, in the town, a fire whistle shrieked; somebody's house or barn was burning.

He smiled. "Well? What do you say?"

Birdie felt flushed, clammy; a headache starting at her temples. "I'm sorry," she said. "I can't let you take them."

A muscle twitched in his jaw.

"Be reasonable. I'm their father. I'll take good care of them." There was a slight edge to his voice, a tone that meant he was losing patience.

"Of course you would," she said hastily. "I know that. It's just—" Her mind raced. "They start school in a couple of weeks."

"Don't worry. I'll get them back in time." He raised her hand to his lips. "See? Problem solved."

Birdie closed her eyes. The kitchen was stifling, the wine going to her head; she hadn't eaten except for a few bites of ice cream. If she refused he could disappear in an instant, drive away in his glorious car. Then what would she have?

"Well," she said. "If you think it's for the best."

Again he squeezed her hand. "You're a wonderful mother, Vivian. The children are lucky to have you."

Her cheeks felt very warm. "When can I come to Florida?"

"Let's not get ahead of ourselves. One thing at a time." He stood and pulled her to her feet.

"Now that everything is settled," he said, "come here."

He drew her close; she did not resist. The divorce had never seemed real to her; she'd burned the papers when they came and never told a soul. In her mind he was still her husband. She felt wobbly on her feet. She leaned heavily against him as they climbed the stairs.

Her bed was unmade and piled with clothing. She'd tried on a dozen dresses that afternoon before settling on the flowered one.

"I'm sorry about the mess," she said.

He placed the pile on a chair and pulled her down to the bed, slipped out of his trousers like a snake shedding its skin. He unbuttoned her dress and reached inside; for what seemed like hours he nuzzled at her breasts. Curtis, she thought. The name was magic to her; it always brought about the desired result when she was alone. But this time nothing happened. His movements stopped; he collapsed with a shudder. Finally he rolled off her and lay at her side.

"I need a shower," he said.

THE HOUSE was dark. For a moment Charlie panicked, but the car was still there, silver in the faint light.

"Come on," he whispered to Jody.

They went in the back door. The kitchen was dark, the parlor deserted. They climbed the stairs, feeling their way along the wall. Their mother's bedroom door was closed.

Jody reached for the knob. She had always slept with their mother.

"Don't," said Charlie. "You can sleep with me." Their mother never shut her door. He understood that it was closed for a reason.

They tiptoed into his room and slid under the covers. Jody's thumb crept into her mouth and in a moment she was snoring. Charlie would tease her about it in the morning. For now he let her sleep.

hey were to mind their manners in Florida—*please* and *thank you* and *I don't care for,* not *I don't like.* They were to mind their father no matter what, with no back talk.

Charlie's mother followed him through the house as he finished his cereal and brushed his teeth and packed his shorts and T-shirts in the old suitcase. They were to bathe when asked. They were to bow their heads for grace before supper as they'd done when Grandma Helen was alive. Being a preacher, their father might want them to pray all the time. They weren't to tell him they never did this at home. They were to enjoy themselves and think of their mother waiting for them when they came back.

"Why aren't you coming?" Charlie asked, though he was glad she wasn't. His mother made him nervous; there were too many things that could go wrong.

They wouldn't give her any days off from the dry cleaning store, she said. And for the moment at least, she needed to keep her job.

She kept on talking right up until the Cadillac appeared at the end of the dirt road. His father had gone to fill the tank with gas. He got out of the car but left the motor running.

"What are we supposed to call him?" said Charlie.

"Why, child," said his mother, "you call him Daddy."

THEY WATCHED their mother fade away until she was just a tiny waving thing in a yellow dress, her hair a bright splotch of red against the pale sky. She'd cried when they got in the car. Their father had kissed her long on the mouth. Neither Jody nor Charlie had seen her be kissed before. Jody stared. Charlie turned away, embarrassed.

In a moment they were on the road. Jody lay stretched out across the backseat. Charlie sat up front with his father. The scenery flew past them on both sides, at a speed that made Charlie dizzy. They whizzed past the Baptist church, the corner where he and Jody caught the school bus, the road their mother walked to work. They passed the radio tower, the Dairy Freeze, the Mail Pouch Tobacco sign on the Deakins' barn. Charlie watched the speedometer, the red needle hovering at seventy.

"How's school?" said his father.

Charlie hesitated. The question was confusing; school didn't start for two weeks. Jody poked her head between the two front seats.

"I'm going into second," she said, and for once Charlie was grateful for her patter. "I already know how to times and divide."

"Good for you," said their father.

Once started, Jody wouldn't shut up. She named every boy and girl from her first grade class. She counted to a hundred by fives, to thirty by threes. She sang a song called "The Polly-Wolly

Doodle." Charlie was no longer grateful; he imagined pulling her hair until she cried. He looked out the window at the strange fields, cotton on one side of the road, soybeans on the other. They'd been driving only ten minutes and already he recognized nothing at all.

His world was small; he knew it was. When he was little they'd lived in Richmond, and twice a year they'd ridden the Greyhound bus to the country to see Pappy and Grandma Helen. He remembered the grand adventure of those trips, the crowds at the station, the small rest room in the back of the bus, reeking of disinfectant; the stops at Howard Johnson's, where his mother would buy them caramels to eat on the ride. A map at the bus station showed every Greyhound depot in America, hundreds in all. Someday, when he was older, Charlie planned to ride a bus through every one of them.

He watched his father's hands loosening and tightening on the steering wheel. The hands were brown, as if he'd been in the sun all summer. A thin band of white circled one of his fingers.

"What happened to your ring?" said Charlie.

His father looked down at his hands. "I lost it."

"How did you lose it?" said Jody.

"In a rest room somewhere." The hands opened and closed, opened and closed. "I was washing my hands and it got slippery from the soap and went down the drain. It was an old ring. It belonged to your grandfather."

After that he was quiet. A while later Charlie asked if they could play the radio. His father turned it on and found a news station; Charlie didn't ask if he could change it. In a few minutes the news turned to static. His father didn't seem to notice.

In the afternoon they stopped at a diner. "Order anything you want," said their father.

Jody and Charlie got hamburgers and french fries and Cokes. Their father had a salad and a bowl of tomato soup. He opened a package of saltines and crumbled them in his fist, then dropped the crumbs into the soup.

Charlie bowed his head and looked down at his fries. The paper place mat was printed with the words "Bless this food." He waited.

"What's the matter, son?" his father said. "Something wrong with your sandwich?"

Charlie looked up. His father was already hunched over his bowl. A drop of red liquid ran down his chin, as if he were bleeding at the mouth.

"No," said Charlie. He bit into a french fry. Next to him Jody had already dismantled her hamburger: meat to one side of the plate, doused with ketchup; bun and lettuce to the other side.

His father slurped the last of his soup and moved on to the salad. He stabbed a tiny tomato with his fork; it jumped off the plate and rolled across the table. Charlie pretended not to notice.

THEY DROVE until it got dark, then parked in front of the Dixie Maid Travel Court. Jody was asleep in the backseat. Charlie followed his father inside the office. Behind the desk an old man smoked and watched a fight on television. He took a twenty-dollar bill from Charlie's father and handed back change and a key.

"Got any newspapers?" said Charlie's father.

"You can have this here," said the man. He handed over a folded paper, the cigarette still bobbing in his mouth.

"Go get your sister," said Charlie's father.

He ran outside and pounded on the rear window with his fist. "Come on," he said. "We're going in."

The room was hot and dark. Charlie flipped on the light, the same kind they had in their kitchen at home, a fluorescent tube bent into a circle. His father fiddled with an air conditioner bolted inside one of the windows. It came to life with a loud rattle. There were two beds covered with flowered spreads.

"Which one do you want?" said his father.

"I don't care," said Charlie.

Their father sat on the one near the door. He took off his shoes and lined them up under the bed. He sat back on the bed and unfolded his newspaper.

"Can we watch TV?" Charlie asked.

"Sure."

The set took a while to warm up. Charlie turned the dial, but there were only two channels. He found the fight the man in the office was watching, then sat on the bed next to Jody, who was curled up small and facing the wall, her thumb in her mouth. When the fight ended he slid under the covers, happy to be in bed without bathing or brushing his teeth. His father went into the bathroom. Charlie closed his eyes and listened to the running water, the flushing toilet. His father came back to the bed. He picked up the phone and dialed a long number. "Hi," he said.

Charlie opened his eyes. The room held a greenish light, from the glowing sign outside.

"South Carolina, somewhere. We stopped for the night. They're both sleeping now."

Trucks whizzed past on the highway, a mighty sound. The air conditioner rattled like a snake.

"I won't keep you. I just wanted to let you know we're on the road. We'll be there tomorrow around three." He turned away and lowered his voice; Charlie could barely make out the words.

"Me too," he said, and hung up the phone. Through slitted eyes Charlie watched him take off his pants and drape them carefully over a hanger. He wore purple undershorts. He got into bed and turned off the light.

Charlie opened his eyes. He wasn't tired at all. In the distance he heard highway noises, crickets. A newscast droned in the next room. He thought of his mother back in Virginia, alone in the big house. She'd been different with his father there: laughing too much, smiling for no reason. He thought of her at the Dairy Freeze, the melting custard, the plastic spoon tipped with orange from her lipstick.

He listened to the bubbly breathing on both sides of him. Jody and his father had the exact same snore. For a moment he was jealous. He knew he was nothing like his father.

He climbed out of bed in slow motion, careful not to make a sound. He tiptoed into the bathroom and closed the door before turning on the light. His father's things were spread out on the counter: toothbrush, Listerine, a bottle labeled "Multiple Vitamins" and another that said "Pierre Cardin." A gold watch ticked loudly, like a bomb about to explode. Near the sink lay a silver-handled razor. Charlie held it an inch from his cheek. He practiced tracing it over his face the way men did on television.

He crept back into the bedroom and climbed under the covers.

oan sat on the patio, smoking—something she never did when Ken was at home. He had the nose of a bloodhound; if she sneaked a cigarette with her morning coffee, he could smell it on her clothes ten hours later. But that night he was in South Carolina with his children; she was free to do as she pleased.

For nearly a week she'd waited to hear. The first day he'd phoned collect from a truck stop in Georgia. He had nothing to report, but just hearing his voice had comforted her. After that, three days of silent torment, in which she imagined him alone with his ex-wife. (Vivian, he'd finally admitted when Joan swallowed her pride and asked. She couldn't say why, but she had to know the woman's name.)

Joan butted her cigarette and lit another. The night was damp and moonless, loud with bugs; the smoke seemed to keep the mosquitoes away. He'd called that evening from a hotel, his voice so low she could barely hear him: Charlie and Josephine were asleep in the room. "Why not spring for their own rooms?" she nearly asked, but stopped herself. Maybe, for once, he wasn't being cheap.

The man hadn't seen his children in four years; maybe he just wanted to keep them close.

It was a lot to process. Her husband had deceived her, had kept his children—their names and ages, their very existence—a secret. "Why?" she'd demanded that day in his dressing room. "Why on earth didn't you tell me?"

At first his explanations made no sense. Vivian wouldn't let him see the children; he thought it best to withdraw from their lives. For weeks Joan cross-examined him; then, finally, he told her the truth. Vivian had left him for another man, and he'd lied to Joan to hide his humiliation. It didn't excuse his deception, of course; but she forgave him on the spot. She pitied him; more than that, she recognized a blessing when she saw one. They had lost their own child, their Ava; but they would still have a family together. She would be a mother after all.

At first he had balked when she suggested custody. "I can't," he said. "She's their mother."

"Some mother," said Joan. "What kind of mother keeps her children away from their father?"

"We can give them a wonderful life," she told him again and again. "It was meant to be."

She stood and stretched, longing for a swim; the pool glowed invitingly with underwater lights. After the miscarriage she'd lost interest in swimming. Now, five months later, she could no longer squeeze into her mastectomy suit. She glanced around. No one could see her. The oleanders had died soon after the wedding; now the pool was surrounded by a brick wall.

Why not? she thought. The neighbors' windows were dark. Ken was far away, her greatest fear—that he would see her mutilated chest—no impediment.

She slipped off her caftan, the wet air gentle against her skin. Naked, she dove into the water and broke into a fast crawl. It was a strange feeling, swimming without her prosthesis; she felt a drag on her left side, the weight of her healthy breast. She rolled onto her right side and tried the sidestroke. Breastless, her body cut cleanly through the water; she felt curiously light. This is what it would be like, she thought, to swim as a man.

She climbed out of the water, slightly winded; she'd been sneaking cigarettes for months. Her body felt warm and loose. She wrapped herself in a towel and went upstairs.

The room was nearly finished. The day Ken left, the paper hangers had come; the next day Burdine's delivered the bunk beds. She'd bought colorful curtains to match the new wallpaper, special child-size hangers for Charlie and Josephine's small clothes. (Josephine, she marveled. What kind of woman names a child Josephine?) The children were ten and six, still young enough to share a bedroom; they'd need their own rooms eventually, but she supposed that could wait. She knew from her attorney that custody hearings were complicated, that fathers rarely won; but Ken would be the exception. Getting the children to Florida was the first step.

A warm breeze blew through the window, a child's good-night kiss. Naked, Joan stretched out on the bottom bunk. For once she fell easily asleep.

ello," Ken called. His voice echoed through the big house. "We're here."

Joan got to her feet, her heart pounding. They were two hours early. She'd just sat down to lunch on the patio, Rosa's seafood salad and grilled pineapple.

"Coming!" she cried, her stomach seizing. For weeks she'd waited for the children to arrive. Now, somehow, she wasn't ready.

She rushed inside, through the kitchen and dining room and into the foyer. Ken stood in the doorway holding a scruffy cardboard suitcase. His pants were wrinkled, his shirt collar gray with sweat. He looked exhausted. The children were bigger than she'd expected, skinny and strikingly pale.

"Well, hello there," she said. "I'm Joan." She'd given a lot of thought to what they should call her; this seemed like the best solution for now. "Welcome to Florida."

She swooped across the room and gave them each a hug, nearly tripping over her caftan. Josephine offered her cheek politely, but Charlie was stiff in her arms. She ought to have known better, she realized that; no little boy wanted to be mauled by a grown woman.

She turned to kiss her husband and found him halfway up the stairs. Panic rose in her throat. No, she thought. Don't leave me alone with them.

"I'm going for a run," he said. "I'll be back in an hour." He had left the suitcase in the foyer.

She took a deep breath and turned to the children. Josephine's hair was carrot-red, her skin white as chalk. Charlie's hair was curly and red-gold. They must take after Vivian, she thought. Nobody would ever mistake them for my children.

"Well," she said brightly. "What a long journey you've had." Journey? she thought. What am I? A fairy godmother?

"I'm hungry," said Josephine.

"Didn't you have any lunch?" Joan smiled. Lunch was easy enough. "I was just sitting down to eat. Rosa always makes extra."

She led them through the house. "Rosa," she called into the kitchen. "Can you bring out some lunch for the children?"

They went outside to the patio.

"Look!" Josephine whispered.

The children stared at the swimming pool. It shimmered blue in the sun, the water striated with light.

"Can we go swimming?" said Charlie. It was the first he'd spoken.

"Sure," said Joan. "After lunch. You can swim every day, if you want."

Charlie knelt and felt the water, frowning thoughtfully; his concern appeared almost scientific.

"We can make it warmer," she said. "Or colder, if you like."

"How do you do that?" said Josephine.

"With a heater, stupid." Charlie splashed her legs; she squealed loudly, a sound that could shatter glass. "Or you add cold water to make it cold."

Rosa appeared and placed two more plates at the table.

"Come have some lunch," said Joan.

The children sat. They peered suspiciously at their plates.

"What is it?" Josephine asked.

"Seafood salad." Joan took a bite from her plate. "It's delicious."

Josephine wrinkled her nose. "It smells funny. Ow." Charlie had kicked her under the table.

"What about you, Charlie?" Joan asked. "Do you like seafood?"

"I don't care for it," he said.

Just like their father, Joan thought.

"That's okay," she said. "Rosa can make you something else."

JOAN SAT in a lawn chair at the edge of the pool, watching the children splash in the water. Sweat streamed down her back; the sun had risen high overhead. Charlie dove headfirst in cut-off blue jeans. Josephine followed in a pair of shorts, her bare chest as flat and featureless as her brother's. She held her nose and landed with a splash. They had each eaten a cheese sandwich; too late, Joan remembered some rule about swimming after eating. I have children now, she thought. I have to learn these things.

Charlie was a strong swimmer, his skinny little body long and luminous underwater. His sister turned somersaults like a baby seal. They didn't talk to Joan; they seemed completely occupied with the water and each other. She recalled how she and Ben had played as children, inventing games and stories, speaking in a language all their own.

She checked her watch. They'd been at it for only an hour; she'd never imagined time could pass so slowly. She watched them intently, fearing that at any moment Josephine would disappear underwater and not come back up. Her jaw hurt from smiling. She wondered where her husband was.

"Watch me!" Josephine cried.

Joan sat up in her chair; it was the first time either child had acknowledged her presence. She watched Josephine dive beneath the surface; a moment later her legs shot up into a perfect hand-stand. Joan applauded loudly.

"Big deal," said Charlie. He climbed out of the pool and jumped back in, hugging his knees to his chest for a tremendous splash.

"That was wonderful, Josephine!" Joan called.

Charlie snickered loudly. "Yeah, _Josephine_. Good job."

"Shut _up!_" she squealed.

"What's the matter?" said Joan.

The child squinted at her, shading her eyes. "Nobody calls me that. My name is Jody."

"I'm sorry," said Joan. "I didn't know."

Finally Ken appeared, showered and red-cheeked after his run.

"How are you holding up?" he called to Joan; but instead of sitting at the foot of her chaise longue as he usually did, he pulled a chair over from the table and sat at the edge of the pool.

"So far, so good," said Joan. Then she noticed his hands.

"Ken," she said. "Where's your wedding ring?"

He looked down at his hands.

"I was going to go for a swim in the ocean," he said. "It was too choppy, though."

Joan frowned. "You never take your ring off when you swim."

"Sure I do." His eyes followed Charlie as he bobbed beneath the water and surfaced with Jody on his shoulders.

"What are they wearing?" he asked.

"Shorts. They don't have swimsuits."

"Oh." Ken shifted in his chair; his discomfort was almost palpable. He's embarrassed, Joan thought—embarrassed to see his seven-year-old daughter swimming bare-chested with her own brother, her small pink nipples as innocent as violets. It was ridiculous.

"Silly old dad." She leaned over to kiss him; suddenly he got to his feet.

"Maybe you could take them shopping," he suggested. "Get her a bathing suit. Whatever else they need. "

His reluctance to kiss her in front of the children surprised her. Her own parents had been affectionate with each other; she'd assumed all parents were.

"Sure," she said. "But what will you do?"

"I've got to go to work."

*I*t was the light that woke him, the clear early light, at once paler and hotter than the sun in Virginia. His sister snored softly in the bottom bunk. In the distance he heard a quiet rushing, the squawk of unfamiliar birds. The air was filled with sound.

Charlie climbed down the ladder and dressed: T-shirt, shorts, the plastic sandals Joan had bought him. His sister stirred but didn't wake. He crossed the hall and went down the strange staircase. His father sat on the marble floor, legs stretched out in front of him.

"Good morning, son," he said.

"Morning." Charlie watched him bend forward and grasp his ankles with his hands. "What are you doing?"

"I'm about to go for a run." His father stood and stretched his arms overhead.

"Can I come?" said Charlie.

"If you want."

The morning air was damp, as if it had just rained. They crossed the road and climbed a wooden staircase. Tall grass grew all around, waving softly in the wind. At the top of the stairs they stopped.

"That's it," said his father. "The Atlantic Ocean."

He broke into a run, across the soft sand to where the ground was firmer, packed wet from the waves. Charlie followed, clumsy in his new sandals. His father moved at an easy pace, breathing evenly. He didn't seem to be working hard, but his legs were very long. Soon it was impossible to keep up.

Finally Charlie stopped. He took off his sandals; the water was stunningly cold. It wasn't blue as he'd expected, but gray and silver; it rolled violently toward him, then back out into forever.

Nothing was the way he'd imagined it, the way his mother had told him it would be. His father hadn't asked them to pray or do anything else; since arriving in Florida they'd barely seen him. After swimming, Joan had taken them shopping. All afternoon they had walked through a maze of interconnected, air-conditioned stores, more stores than Charlie had ever seen in his life. His father hadn't appeared at dinner—he was working late, according to Joan. Charlie wondered what type of work a preacher did on a Friday evening. It seemed impolite to ask.

He watched the man grow small in the distance, running along the darker sand where the ocean met the shore. Charlie had never seen an adult run before. He thought of himself and Terence, racing through the woods that connected their two houses. He'd give anything to show Terence the big Cadillac, the swimming pool. They'd left Virginia so quickly; there had been no time to say good-bye.

He turned and looked back at the massive house, pale pink in the morning light. The front door opened; Joan appeared on the step and picked the newspaper from the lawn. Besides the sandals, she'd bought him an ice cream at the shopping plaza, and a mask and snorkel for swimming underwater in the pool. He couldn't remember the last time an adult had bought him something for no reason. Unlike his mother, Joan stayed with them every minute; not once since arriving in Florida had they been sent outside to play. Charlie supposed she'd been hired to look after them—like Dinah, the baby-sitter they'd had in Richmond.

"Joan loves children," his father had said as he parked the Cadillac in the driveway, a path of crushed seashells leading to the house.

AFTER BREAKFAST they drove to Disney World, just her and the kids. (Ken had three properties to show; Saturday was his busiest day of the week.) It was nearly dusk when they got home from the park. Ken still hadn't returned.

"Can we go swimming again?" said Charlie.

"Not just now." Joan's legs ached; all afternoon she'd raced back and forth between the roller coasters and the teacups, the merry-go-rounds and the Ferris wheels. Charlie loved the bloodcurdling rides; Jody preferred the gentler ones. Joan would have preferred a stiff drink and a comfortable sofa. Her head ached from Jody's piercing squeal. She hadn't been so tired in years.

At seven they sat down to dinner. At Joan's request Rosa had made pizza. Already they'd eaten hamburgers twice. Joan wasn't sure what else a child would like.

"Where's my dad?" Charlie asked.

"He's at work," she said.

His brow wrinkled. "Maybe we should wait."

"He said he'd be late. He said to start without him." It wasn't true, but she didn't care. She'd held enough dinners for Ken to know it could be a long wait.

They ate in silence. Unlike his father, Charlie had excellent table manners—his mother's influence, Joan supposed. Vivian had had less success with Jody. The girl dismantled each slice of pizza with her fingers. She made separate piles for cheese and pepperoni, then licked the tomato sauce from the bare crust. Joan tried not to watch.

Finally Charlie spoke. "Do we have to go to church tomorrow?"

Joan looked at him quizzically.

"It's Sunday," he said. "My mama said we'd have to."

Rosa came to clear the plates. Joan hesitated. So Vivian was Christian: yet another thing Ken had failed to mention.

"Do you *want* to go to church?" she asked carefully.

Charlie looked down at his plate. "I'd rather not."

She smiled, relieved. "Then you don't have to."

"But what about my dad?" he asked. "Doesn't the minister *have* to go?"

"Minister," she repeated. A sick feeling spread through her stomach. "Who told you he was a minister?"

"My mama," said Charlie.

Jody beamed. "We never go to church."

"Shut *up*," said Charlie. His eyes met Joan's. "You mean he isn't one?"

Just then Joan heard the Cadillac in the driveway. "Here he comes," she said. "Why don't you ask him yourself?"

The front door opened.

"We're in the dining room!" Joan called out. She noticed a strange quaver in her voice. No way was he going to bolt upstairs and take a peaceful shower. Not after this.

Ken came into the dining room, crisp in a linen suit, his starched collar snug at his throat. A cleric's collar, Joan thought.

"I was going to change clothes," he said.

Her heart raced. "We just finished dinner. Sit down and have some dessert."

He sat. Rosa brought out dishes of strawberry shortcake. Joan watched him across the table. He glanced at his watch.

"How was your day?" he asked the children. "Did you have a good time?"

"It was okay," said Charlie.

Okay? she thought. They'd eaten hot dogs and Sno-Kones for lunch; Charlie had ridden the roller coaster eight times. Surely that was better than *okay*. It wasn't as if Vivian had ever taken them to an amusement park. Charlie had said so himself.

"That's good." Ken picked out the strawberries from his dessert, leaving the whipped cream behind; he was as bad as Jody. "What's on the agenda for tomorrow?"

Joan put down her fork. For the past two days he'd gone to the office, adhered to his jogging schedule. He'd gone about his business as if his children weren't even there.

"You're asking *me?*" She rose quickly, her napkin fluttering from her lap to the floor.

"I'm going upstairs," she said. "To take a bath."

SHE SAT in the tub for a long time, remembering. Their wedding, Ken handsome in his tallis and yarmulke, breaking the glass beneath his feet. After the ceremony her uncle Floyd had embraced him. "He's like a son to me," he'd said to no one in particular. "The son I never had."

Early in their marriage they'd attended services together; sometimes at Beth Israel, but usually with Floyd and Cookie in Coral

Gables. Twice they'd gone to her uncle's house for seder. Then Floyd had died, a sudden stroke. Joan and Ken hadn't been to temple since.

She closed her eyes, picturing her husband's face—his blue eyes, his straight nose. He'd been vague about his past: his years as a teacher, where he'd gone to school. The University of Missouri, he'd said the first time she asked; another time, she was fairly certain, he'd said Missouri State. She thought of the man at Mulligan's Steak House, the one who'd recognized him. His old roommate, she thought. From Bethany Biblical Seminary. A stranger had told her the truth; she had simply refused to hear it.

Her husband was not Jewish.

WHEN KEN came into the bedroom, she was sitting at the dressing table in her bathrobe, drying her hair with a towel. She wanted a drink but was afraid to pour one. The glass decanter was a wedding gift from her brother; it seemed unutterably fragile. Everything around her seemed ready to break.

"What was that all about?" said Ken.

"All what?"

He stepped out of his trousers and draped them over a hanger. "Leaving me with the children like that. What am I supposed to do with them?"

Her heart beat as fast as a sparrow's. "I've had them for two days straight. I thought you might enjoy a few minutes of their company. They are *your children*."

"Wait a minute." His eyes narrowed. "You were the one who was so hot to get them down here. I thought I'd never hear the end of it. Now you're complaining?"

Joan put down her comb. Her pulse was loud in her ears. Just say it, she thought. She took a deep breath. "Charlie asked if we'd be going to church tomorrow."

"What?" said Ken. "Why would he think such a thing?"

"Apparently Vivian told him we would be."

Ken stared at her. He seemed puzzled but calm.

You lied to me, she wanted to say. *You told me you were Jewish.*

"Vivian," she said instead. "Your ex-wife. The one you just spent three days with." She was exhausted, near tears.

Ken frowned. "Is that it? You're jealous of Vivian?" He sat at the foot of the bed. "Be reasonable. I haven't seen the woman in four years. I couldn't drive off with the children just like that." He snapped his fingers. "It took a little persuasion."

"I'll bet it did," said Joan. "I'll bet you were much more persuasive without your wedding ring."

"Joan." He reached for her; she brushed his hand away. She tightened her bathrobe around her and went downstairs.

CHARLIE LAY in the top bunk. Their father had sent them to bed early; it wasn't even dark yet. From across the hall he heard low voices, his father's and Joan's. Even with the door closed he could tell they were fighting.

"What are they saying?" Jody whispered.

"I don't know," he said.

A while later the voices stopped. His sister's breathing deepened; in the distance the ocean whispered. Charlie sat up in bed. Outside the moon was full, the sky fuzzy and starless. He stared out the window for a long time. The garden was filled with strange trees, shapes he couldn't identify. He thought of the three slices of strawberry shortcake downstairs in the refrigerator. "Rosa made extra," Joan had told him. "If you get hungry, help yourself."

He crept down the staircase and into the dining room, then peered through the archway, into the kitchen. Joan sat at the counter with her face in one hand, a burning cigarette in the other. Her shoulders shook; even from behind he could see she was crying.

He heard footsteps on the stairs, his father's voice. "Joan? Honey, where are you?"

Charlie felt suddenly sick. If he turned back now, he'd run right smack into his father. He looked around. The doorway was flanked by small trees in clay pots; he crouched behind one of them, making himself small. He held his breath as his father swept past.

"Are you smoking?" his father asked.

Joan turned to him. Her face was red from crying. "Obviously," she said. "Obviously I'm smoking."

His father took the cigarette from her hand and stamped it out in an ashtray.

"You've been under an enormous strain," he said, stroking her hair. "I should have seen that." He sat on a stool next to her. "You have nothing to worry about with me and Vivian. That was finished long ago. She means nothing to me now."

Charlie thought of his mother flushed and pretty in the flowered dress, hanging on his father's arm. His mother standing in the backyard, waving as they drove away.

Joan sniffed loudly, a moist, slurry sound. "Do you love me?"

"You're my wife. Of course I love you."

He leaned over and kissed her. A long kiss, like the one he'd given Charlie's mother two days before. Charlie thought of the man's hands, the band of white skin where a wedding ring would be.

"I've made a mess of things," said Joan, wiping her eyes. "I don't think the children like me."

"Sure they do. You've been great with them. It just takes a little time, is all." He stood and offered her his hand.

"Come on," he said. "Let's go to bed."

Charlie held his breath as they passed through the doorway. He listened to their footsteps climbing the staircase, a door closing upstairs. Finally he tiptoed up the steps to the room where his sister slept.

"Get up," he whispered, shaking her. "It's time to go home."

THEY WAITED until dark, then waited some more. Finally they crept down the stairs, Charlie carrying the old suitcase. The moon had risen; a cold light bathed the marble floor, pooling softly in the thick white carpets.

"Be careful," Charlie whispered. All he needed was for Jody to miss a step and fall headfirst down the iron stairs. He thought of a cartoon he'd once seen, a cat's head bumping along a staircase, each step sounding a different tone, like a large xylophone. His sister's head would make a hollow noise; she was that stupid.

They reached the bottom stair and tiptoed across the foyer. Charlie turned the dead bolt and the heavy door opened with a creak.

"Which way do we go?" Jody whispered.

"Don't worry. I know." Over and over they'd passed the bus station in the car, driving back and forth from the shopping center and again on the way to Disney World. Charlie hoped he could find it in the dark. He fingered the three twenty-dollar bills in his pocket. It was an enormous sum of money, more than he'd ever held in his hand at one time. He'd stolen it from a straw pocket-book Joan had left on the sofa. It bothered him a little—he wanted to steal from his father, not Joan—but they were in a hurry, and it was too good to pass up. Sixty dollars would be enough to buy their tickets home. At least he hoped so.

At the end of the drive they went right. Charlie glanced back at the big house, the dark window where his father and Joan were sleeping. The ocean thundered; the path of crushed seashells glowed under the swollen moon. He paused for a last look at the baby blue Cadillac. Then he turned his back on the house.

THEY WALKED a long time, down winding streets dotted with fancy houses, then along a stretch of highway. In the distance the ocean breathed, like a large animal sighing in its sleep.

"Are we almost there?" Jody asked.

"Almost." It might have been true; he didn't know one way or the other. Charlie shifted the suitcase from one hand to the other. His shoulders ached from carrying it, as though someone had tried to tug his arms from their sockets. He looked up at the sky. The moon had disappeared; a gauzy film covered everything, heavy and damp.

"It's raining," said Jody.

A drop landed on his face, warm as a tear.

"Is not," he said.

The air smelled of pavement; a moment later lightning streaked across the sky. Then the heavens opened.

"Now what?" Jody wailed.

"Keep going," said Charlie.

IT WAS after midnight when they found the bus station. "Go sit down," he told his sister. Then he approached the counter. Behind it a man lounged in his chair, reading a newspaper.

"I want to buy some tickets," said Charlie.

The man put down his paper and looked around. "Where are your parents?"

"My mama's not here," said Charlie. "She's sick."

"What about your dad?"

"He's dead."

The man frowned. "Where are you headed, son?"

"Montford, Virginia."

"Virginia. Why would a boy be going to Virginia in the middle of the night?"

Charlie squirmed. His wet T-shirt was plastered against his back. "To see my grandma."

"All by yourself?"

"Me and my sister."

The man glanced over Charlie's shoulder. "Does your grandma know you're coming?"

"No." Charlie handed the man his sixty dollars. "It's a surprise."

The man took his money. "Well, there's no bus until six in the morning."

"That's okay," said Charlie. "We'll wait."

JOAN SLEPT late that morning; when she awoke Ken had already left for his run. She stood at the window watching him, the August sun warm on her face. He ran along the water's edge, the low tide erasing his footprints, wiping away all trace of him. He lied, she thought. Someday, perhaps, she would forgive him. In the meantime she had the children.

She wrapped herself in a robe and headed downstairs. "Rosa," she called out, "could you make Charlie and Jody some waffles?" It had been her favorite breakfast as a child, hers and Ben's. She ought to have recalled that sooner. It's not so difficult, she thought. She'd been a kid once herself; all she had to do was remember.

Rosa appeared at the bottom of the stairs. "How many waffles?"

"I'm not sure. Charlie has a big appetite." Joan turned and headed back upstairs. "Let me see if they're hungry."

She tapped at the bedroom door. "Jody! Charlie, are you awake?"

THEY SAT at the front of the bus, the engine grinding beneath them. Charlie shivered in his damp T-shirt, wishing for a sweater. He'd abandoned the suitcase, left it in someone's front yard when it became too heavy to carry. He knew, but didn't care, that his mother would be angry. He thought of his room, his own bed. Once he was home she could yell at him all she wanted.

He glanced over at his sister, asleep in the seat beside him. She had no more sense than a baby; he had to watch her every minute. When he came back from the ticket counter, she was talking to a man who'd given her a quarter. She'd told him all about the big pink house, the swimming pool, the stuffed alligator Joan had given her as a present. "You dope," Charlie hissed when the man went away. Their mother had warned them about talking to strangers.

Charlie closed his eyes. He'd stayed awake all night in the hard plastic chair, listening to Jody snore, worrying about the twenty dollars he had left in his pocket; and now that they were safe inside the bus, he couldn't fall asleep. Through the window he watched the sky lighten, the morning clear and streaked with pink.

I'll sleep when we get home, he thought.

ineahora.

K The Burdine's truck came promptly at nine. Joan stood in the doorway of the bedroom, watching the men separate the bunk beds where Jody and Charlie had slept. She did not cry as the men struggled down the spiral staircase and loaded the beds into the truck. She signed the clipboard they offered and handed them each a twenty. The truck backed out of the driveway and disappeared down the road.

She sat in the empty room, smoking. The bright new wallpaper looked garish in the bare light. She'd already returned the curtains to the store.

A week had passed since the children ran away. She'd been in tears when Ken came back from his run. "Call the police," she said. "Tell them it's an emergency." He'd insisted on looking for them himself; an hour later he'd called her from the bus station. A clerk there had sold a little boy two tickets to Virginia.

"Can we go after them?" she said.

"No," said Ken. "I'll have to call their mother."

He made the call in private, from his office. Joan didn't object. She'd stopped caring whether Ken spoke with his ex-wife, what the two of them said to each other. None of it matters, she thought. Just let the children be safe. It occurred to her that she was praying. The next day Ken told her that Charlie and Jody had arrived in Virginia. Joan, once again, was alone with her husband.

Destiny, she'd learned, was written in the heavens; a person couldn't take what the universe didn't wish to give. Her own child had been taken away; in her pain she had tried to take someone else's. A perverse act, malignant in its selfishness. One that God would not permit.

She never told Ken what his son had said, never confronted him about being a minister. He had lied to her about the deepest thing; their marriage was founded on a lie. But she had lost everything else. He was all she had.

She found the lump in bed one night as he lay sleeping beside her. She wasn't surprised. She'd been waiting for it all along.

Dinah

WASHINGTON, D.C.

1979

They met by accident on a snowy day in January, a dark afternoon when the street lamps came on at three o'clock. To Dinah Whitacre, who did not believe in accidents, their meeting seemed fated. Their paths had already intersected once—years before, in Richmond, when she was just a girl. For it to happen a second time required an alignment of large forces, a rare convergence of time and weather and traffic. To call it a coincidence seemed ludicrous.

The bus was late that morning, and crowded. Dinah crammed into a seat in the back, her thick down jacket insulating her from the strange bodies on either side. Next to her a stout man folded the *Post,* elbowing her puffy side. Over his shoulder she scanned the headlines: "Record Snowfall Pummels East Coast."

The bus stopped at a red light; on both sides the avenue was glutted with cars. She glanced at her watch. In a few minutes the first lunch customers would arrive. In four years she'd never been late for work; her punctuality had won her the approval of the chef, who was not easily pleased.

The light changed; the bus lurched forward. Just then a second bus appeared at the cross street; a moment later it slid, spinning, into the intersection. Brakes squealed; Dinah was thrown forward against the seat ahead of her. At the front of the bus a baby wailed.

"Is everybody all right?" the driver shouted.

Debris littered the aisle: pocketbooks, bag lunches, an open briefcase spilling papers across the floor. A small crowd had formed on the sidewalk. In the distance a siren screamed. She slid out of her seat, legs trembling, and stepped across the clutter in the aisle. Around her passengers grumbled, swore, rubbed their necks. She reached the front of the bus.

"Let me out," she told the driver, a broad man in uniform.

He stared at her face. "You sure you're okay?"

It's a birthmark, she wanted to say. *I've had it my whole life. You don't get a birthmark in a bus accident.*

"I'm fine," she said.

He pulled a lever to open the doors. She hurried down the steps and into the street. Running was impossible in her chef's clogs; she walked as fast as she could, careful not to slip on the icy sidewalk. The low sky was moist and dark: more snow on the way.

The restaurant, Emile's, sat at the corner of two busy streets, its front windows glowing under a blue awning. Behind it the alley had just been plowed; a wall of dirty snow blocked the rear door of the restaurant. Stamping her feet, she went in through the front door, something she hadn't done in years.

The dining room was half full; customers occupied the prime tables at the windows. The hostess looked up from her podium. She was a slim, dark-haired girl with beautiful skin.

"Jesus," she said. "What happened to you?"

Dinah peeled off her jacket. "What do you mean?"

"Your mouth," said the hostess.

Dinah touched her lip, sticky with blood. "The bus crashed," she said, blotting her mouth with a glove.

At the window a customer looked up from his menu, a very thin man in a dark suit. He had a long face and brilliant blue eyes. Dinah met his gaze and he nodded, a slight inclination of his bald head. There was something familiar in his face.

"You'd better go back. Emile is worried about you." The hostess smiled, showing perfect teeth. "He figured if you were late something horrible must have happened."

Dinah went through the swinging doors, pulling off her down jacket. Underneath, her white coat was wrinkled, her neckerchief slightly askew. In the kitchen the four line cooks were already in place. The prep cook chopped an onion loudly, a precise, mechanical sound.

"Here she is," said the sous-chef. "We were starting to wonder."

"Sorry I'm late." Dinah looked Emile in the eye but didn't explain. Nothing made him angrier than an excuse.

"Go wash your face," he said. He took a plate from the line and stuck a fork into the gratin; he was meticulous about tasting the food.

In the staff washroom she rinsed her mouth, glad she hadn't bothered with makeup. She rarely made the effort to cover her birthmark; everyone at Emile's knew what she looked like. She thought of the customer in the dark suit, whose eyes had held hers a second too long across the room. Nothing new there: she'd always gotten noticed. In the street, in the grocery store, children gaped and pointed. "Don't stare," their parents whispered, not realizing they were staring too. But this man's look was different, as if he recognized her. It seemed unlikely. She spent fourteen hours a day in Emile's kitchen. After five years in Washington she knew almost no one.

She dried her face and went back to the dining room, where the hostess stood chatting with the bartender.

"There was a man sitting alone." She pointed to the table by the window. "In the first seating. Did he have a reservation?"

The hostess frowned, rippling her smooth forehead. "I can check."

Dinah followed her to the podium. The hostess reached for her reservation book, traced down the page with a perfect red fingernail. Her skin was as pale as milk. She must live on vanilla ice cream, Dinah thought; rounds of Camembert, crème anglaise.

"A little old for you, isn't he?" said the hostess.

Dinah colored. "It's not that. He looked familiar, that's all."

"Here it is," said the hostess. "He comes in now and then for lunch. His name is Ken Kimble."

SHE LEFT Emile's at one-thirty in the morning. It was snowing as she walked down the avenue toward the bus stop, large wet flakes that melted the instant they touched her skin. She boarded the bus at the corner and sank into a seat, thinking of Reverend Kimble.

She hadn't thought of him in years. As a teenager she'd baby-sat for him and his wife. She'd doted on their redheaded children—Charlie especially—but it was her crush on the reverend that kept her coming back. At the time, he was like no one she'd ever known: a grown man, but as different from her stern father and stodgy uncles as he could be. Her father wore half glasses and suspenders, black wing tips and starched white shirts; the world he lived in was black and white, a dour place devoid of surprises. Reverend Kimble seemed to live in glorious color. She remembered his bright ties, his crazy patterned shirts. He kept his hair longer than other men—in back it touched his shirt collar—and in the winter he wore turtlenecks and a suede jacket.

He was the only adult she knew who cared about music. Driving her home at the end of the evening, he'd hum softly with the radio. His favorites were the same as hers: the Byrds, the Beatles, Joni Mitchell. He never bothered her with meaningless questions about school or teachers, as adults usually did. When he spoke it was about real things: the war, the upcoming election, the injustice of the draft. He expected her to have opinions and listened carefully to what she said. Sitting in the car next to him she'd felt perfectly comfortable—her pretty side exposed, her birthmark hidden by the dark.

The mark began at her temple, a purple stain that washed over her right eye and cheekbone and ended at her jaw. Her whole life it had been the size of her hand; as her hand grew, so did the purple stain. As a girl she'd spent hours examining it in the mirror: the gradations of color, the odd topography. She'd had a jigsaw puzzle as a child, a map of the United States; her birthmark was the exact shape of Minnesota, its jagged eastern border cutting across her right cheek. Back then there was no concealing it; her mother wouldn't let her wear makeup. "It's not natural," she'd once told Dinah. "We all go through life with the face God gave us." It was the only time in Dinah's memory that an adult had mentioned the mark. Her parents treated it as a secret; teachers and neighbors avoided looking her in the face.

Only Reverend Kimble was willing to admit it was there. Once, driving her home from baby-sitting, he'd asked her about it. He had pulled into her parents' driveway; as she reached for her door handle, he stopped her. "Wait," he said, his hand on her shoulder. He had never touched her before.

"Where did it come from?" Lightly he touched her cheek. "Have you always had it?"

"Yes." She couldn't look at him; her skin burned beneath his fingers.

"Don't let it bother you so much," he said. "You can get it taken care of someday."

She had never heard of such a thing.

"There are doctors who specialize in cosmetic problems," he explained. "Plastic surgeons." He smiled; he seemed amused by her ignorance.

"My mother would never let me," she said.

"You'll be eighteen in a few years. Then you can do as you please."

Her voice quavered. "Is it expensive?"

He shrugged. "Whatever the cost, it would be worth it. You're a beautiful girl."

His words stayed with her for years. Each night as she lay waiting for sleep, she tried to re-create the evening in her mind—the tone of his voice, his hand on her shoulder. Soon the memory was worn as an old photograph, the edges fuzzy from frequent handling; she worried that she'd gotten the words wrong, forgotten some nuance of his face or voice. Finally she wondered if she'd made the whole thing up.

Dinah stared out the bus window: snow melting on the slick pavement, streetlights reflected in the wet. She'd been stunned to learn he'd left his wife and children; but in a way it made sense. She had never understood what he saw in his wife, who was very much like Dinah's mother, a woman who wore pin curls and said things like "Oh my stars." Once, when she was baby-sitting, Dinah had rifled through the drawers in the Kimbles' bedroom. Mrs. Kimble wore the same kind of underwear Dinah's mother did: hideous brassieres with pointed cups and thick straps, nylon panties as big as grocery sacks. With shaking hands Dinah had opened the smaller bureau, the one that held Reverend Kimble's clothes. His underwear was neatly folded, colorful briefs in thin cotton.

Her parents had never told her where Reverend Kimble went; she overheard them talking one night after she'd been excused from the table.

"It isn't your fault," her mother had said.

"Tell that to the Snells," said her father. "The girl is nineteen years old. They didn't send their daughter to a Christian college to have her run off with the chaplain."

"What kind of a girl is she? The Snell girl. What kind of a girl would do that?"

"A troublemaker. Worked up about the war. A hippie kind of girl."

After that it had all made sense. The reverend had left his wife and children, it was true, but there was a good reason: he had fallen in love. Not only that, he'd chosen someone not much older than Dinah; a girl who stood for all the same things she privately believed. You could almost say he'd picked someone just like her.

Dinah got off the bus and climbed the hill. She'd lived in Glover Park for three years. It had once been a genteel neighborhood, the brick row houses owned by middle-class families who'd lived there for generations. Now those families were gone, the houses divided into small apartments. The tenants were mostly young and poor, a transient mix of students and dropouts. Burglaries were common; at least once a week she was awakened by sirens.

She gathered the mail and climbed the stairs to her apartment. She'd bought the house for virtually nothing; she paid her mortgage by renting the first floor to two Georgetown medical residents, an Indian couple named Ann and Dillip Patel. At the top of the stairs she fumbled with a second set of locks. The house had been burglarized twice in two years; after each break-in she'd added an extra lock to the door. Inside, she undressed and stepped into the shower. Though she wore it in a tight chignon, her long hair absorbed the kitchen smells; unless she washed it first she'd be unable to sleep.

She wrapped her hair in a towel and sat at the kitchen table to sort through the mail. She found the invitation among a stack of bills and magazines. The Calvary High School five-year class reunion, to be held in the school cafeteria the first of June. The envelope had been mailed to her parents' address in Richmond; her mother must have forwarded it. Oh, Mother, she thought. Don't you ever learn?

She worked her way to the bottom of the stack, putting aside the electric bill. Finally she stood and lit the gas stove. For a moment she held the invitation to the burner. Then she dropped it, flaming, into the sink.

In the bedroom she slipped between the cold sheets. The wind howled outside, a lonely sound; she sensed movement in the rooms beneath her. Dinah rarely saw the Patels; she knew them only through their noises—dish washing, laughter, the low hum of the radio. She was grateful for their presence below her, a buffer between her and the street.

Her aching back released into the mattress. Beneath her the noises grew louder. She heard them several times a week: a soft whimpering, like an animal's cry; the rumble of a deeper voice. Dinah held her breath. She waited for the usual cadence, the rhythmic thud of the headboard against the wall. Dillip was slender and soft-spoken; she imagined he would be very gentle.

The sounds quickened. Dinah closed her eyes and thought of Dillip's skin, the hard muscles of his legs—in the summer he rode his bicycle in terry-cloth shorts. He was studying to be an obstetrician; he would know her body better than she did herself.

A small cry, a sudden silence. Dinah imagined the heat of his mouth, his hands on her face, loving and uncritical; hands that ushered newborn babies into life. She closed her eyes. Outside, snow floated down from heaven. Somewhere, not far away, Reverend Kimble was sleeping.

Calvary High, named for the mountain where Christ was crucified. Dinah was tortured there, mocked and mortified. Only years later did she realize that the school was aptly named.

During her final year at Calvary, the senior English class read *Beowulf;* afterward, a boy named Ted Nally nicknamed her Grendel. The name caught on. By springtime even freshmen, who'd never read about the hideous monster, were tormenting her with the name.

Grendel. Grendel.

It stalked her in the hallways, on the school bus; it passed through the cafeteria line like an evil rumor. At school assemblies she calculated the length of the stage. Forty feet, she guessed; she wondered how quickly she could walk across it to receive her diploma. At Calvary, graduating seniors endured a full week of festivities: a day-long religious retreat, an awards banquet, a traditional commencement ceremony, and a baccalaureate dance. A smorgasbord of public humiliations, it seemed to Dinah.

The night of the banquet she rode to the school with her parents. Her mother's heels clacked against the tile floor, echoing through the empty corridors. She had made them identical dresses, pale yellow with full skirts and voluminous sleeves. They looked, Dinah thought, like backup singers from *The Lawrence Welk Show.*

The cafeteria was decorated with crepe-paper streamers; a banner across the back wall congratulated the class of '73. The overhead lights had been extinguished, the cafeteria tables hidden under silky fabric. Handwritten place cards seated the families alphabetically, the Whitacres next to the Warrens and the Welds. Sue Warren and Carolyn Weld were best friends; for four years Dinah had sat behind them in class, listening to them laugh and whisper.

Dinah sat closemouthed as the salads were served. Candelabra flickered at the tables; in the dim light the cafeteria looked like a different place. Only the smell was the same, a sickening blend of floor cleaner and fried fish. Dinah's mother chatted with Mrs. Weld: *What lovely decorations,* and *Thank goodness it stopped raining,* and *Don't the girls look beautiful?* Listening, Dinah hated her ease and cheerfulness, her ability to invent conversation with strangers. At the same time she was proud, glad her classmates could see that her mother, at least, was normal.

Across the table Sue and Carolyn sat with their heads together, whispering. Dinah's mother smiled.

"What are you girls giggling about?"

"Look at Dinah," said Carolyn. "She's the same color as the tablecloth."

It was true: her foolish dress and her lank hair were the same pale shade of yellow. Only her birthmark stood out, purple-red. A color that belonged on the inside of a body, not fit for public viewing.

"Why, she is, isn't she?" said her mother, still smiling like an idiot. "What do you know about that?"

Dinah picked at the stringy roast beef, the overcooked green beans. Her father spoke in a low voice to Mr. Warren; a moment later they went outside to smoke.

At the podium the vice-principal announced the chemistry prize, the awards for history and Spanish and math; then the Most and Best awards. A week before, in homeroom, they had voted for the boy and girl with the nicest smiles and the most pleasing personalities; the smartest and best-looking; the likeliest to succeed. In Dinah's opinion, none of her classmates had pleasing personalities; she filled out her ballot in under a minute. (Her pick for cutest couple: Nixon and Brezhnev. Secretariat, most likely to succeed.)

The winners were announced; at each name Sue and Carolyn applauded and laughed. Carolyn wore a nervous smile; she was a shoo-in for Best Looking. Dinah's mother clapped too, though she didn't recognize the names. She applauded warmly as Ted Nally accepted his award for Class Clown. Don't clap for him, Dinah thought. He's ruined my life.

"And now the award for Most Athletic," said the vice-principal. "In keeping with the times, we're now presenting this award to both a boy and a girl." He smiled. "For those of you who don't know, the Calvary girls' tennis team has just wound up its inaugural season. And let me tell you, those ladies can play."

It was a bald-faced lie. Only six girls had signed up for the team; three had never held a racquet before. To Dinah's knowledge, the vice-principal had never attended a match.

"The award goes to Paul Ackerman—" said the vice-principal.

A large, neckless boy lumbered to the podium.

"—and Dinah Whitacre."

Dinah froze. A hundred heads swiveled in her direction. No, she thought. This isn't happening.

"Dinah!" her mother cried. "Isn't that wonderful!"

She glanced helplessly around the room. Ted Nally sat two tables away, his beady eyes watching her. Her face warmed, a wash of heat radiating outward from her left eye. She knew she blushed oddly, her birthmark darkening to a deep blue.

Her mother touched her shoulder. "Honey, go up there and get your award."

"I can't," she whispered.

"Of course you can." Then Dinah's mother did a horrible thing. She stood and offered Dinah her hand.

"Come on," she said. "I'll walk up there with you."

"Mom," Dinah hissed. The room seemed very loud; blood pulsed furiously in her face. *"Please. Sit. Down."*

She got to her feet, thinking *Soon, whatever is going to happen will already have happened.* Her legs shook as she made her way through the tables. When she reached the front of the room, the chant began. Softly at first, then with increasing urgency.

"Grendel. Grendel."

Out of the corner of her eye she saw her father standing in the doorway, pipe in hand, a confused look on his face.

At the podium, the vice-principal shook her hand and handed her a small trophy. She smiled mechanically.

"Grendel. Grendel."

"That's enough," the vice-principal said sharply into the microphone.

The chanting stopped, but the laughter only escalated. At the back of the room, Ted Nally clapped loudly, his fat face flushed and triumphant.

Dinah returned to her seat. Across the table Sue and Carolyn were red from laughing. Dinah did not look at her mother; she sat holding her trophy, waiting. Finally the graduates were dismissed to the auditorium to don their caps and gowns; the parents were to stay behind for coffee and dessert. Dinah followed her classmates into the hallway. Then she turned down a corridor and ran.

She ran past the library, the school nurse's office, the classrooms for algebra and English and Bible study and French. Never again, she thought. I will never see any of them, ever again.

At the end of the corridor was the entrance to the gymnasium; opposite it, a glass case full of trophies won by boys who played sports. Dinah's own small trophy felt heavy in her hand. She threw it at the display case with all her strength.

The glass shattered loudly, an exquisite sound, random and musical, like an orchestra tuning. She wondered if her classmates heard it in the auditorium, Sue and Carolyn and Ted Nally; she hoped, fervently, that they had. She picked up her trophy and went out the front door.

The act of vandalism made the local papers; the culprit was never found.

Dinah never saw Calvary High again. In August, her father drove her to Washington, D.C.; together they carried cratefuls of records into her dorm room at American University.

In September, Billie Jean King trounced Bobby Riggs in a tennis match people called the Battle of the Sexes.

In October, tired of being stared at as she applied makeup in the dormitory bathroom, Dinah Whitacre quit school and went to work at Emile's.

$\mathcal{T}$ he Friday lunch crowd was voracious. At one o'clock Dinah ran out of the special, tomatoes stuffed with seafood salad. She peered into the dining room. To do a head count, she told herself. To see if the crowd had thinned.

Reverend Kimble wasn't there.

In the cold kitchen she mixed cooked squid and capers and cherrystone clams, enough for a second batch of salad. From the walk-in she took a tray of hollowed-out tomatoes, expertly carved by the prep cook. The tomatoes were wet and ripe, easily torn if you crammed in too much seafood. It was the sort of task she usually loved—at culinary school she'd excelled in presentation—but that day it seemed futile. In five minutes the salads would be eaten and forgotten; the customers would move on to the main course. Why not just put the seafood on a plate?

The tomatoes stuffed, she went into the walk-in to check on her salmon. As garde-manger, she was responsible for all cold foods served at Emile's: raw oysters and salads and crudités; in the summer, chilled peach soup and macédoine of fruits. Twice a week she smoked a whole Alaska salmon or cured it with herbs for gravlax. For two days she'd soaked this one in a special marinade; now, finally, it was the proper color. She drained off the marinade and arranged the salmon in the smoker, then filled the bottom pan with a mixture of wood chips and lit the burner. At the other table the pastry chef filled profiteroles with cream.

She'd worked at the restaurant for four years, ever since she'd dropped out of college and her father had stopped paying her rent. The usual jobs open to young girls—waitress, supermarket cashier—were, for her, impossible: she was paralyzed by the thought of making small talk with customers, carrying trays of food across a roomful of strangers. Finally she'd answered an ad for kitchen help. Emile had hired her on the spot.

She'd been surprised to find the kitchen full of men. Emile staffed the dining room with stunning hostesses and waitresses, but felt the kitchen was no place for women. "Nobody can see you," she'd once heard him tell a pretty job applicant. "It is a waste of beauty."

She started as a prep cook—at Emile's, everybody did. Her first day Emile had diced a red pepper and placed a single, perfect cube on the table in front of her. "Like this," he said. "Each piece exactly like this." Soon she could pare an apple in ten seconds; the peel came off in a single perfect strip. Emile encouraged her to apply to culinary school, let her arrange her shifts around her class schedule. After she graduated he hired her full-time.

Now the cold kitchen was her domain; she preferred its relative calm to the chaos of the main one, crowded with line cooks, hot from the grill and Emile's fiery temper. She shared the space with the pastry chef, an impassive Swiss who rarely spoke. The cold kitchen smelled of cucumber and melted chocolate; she couldn't imagine a better smell.

· · ·

THE LUNCH RUSH ended; at four o'clock the staff broke for dinner. The main kitchen smelled deliciously of Emile's cassoulet, a hearty stew of white beans, sausages, duck legs, and pork.

"Another leg, please," said Dinah as the line cook filled her plate.

"*Encore?*" he said, incredulous.

Dinah reddened. "Yes, please." She rarely had to ask, but he was new to Emile's. The other line cooks knew her appetite.

She sat at the long table, her plate mounded with cassoulet. She'd always been a hearty eater: eggs and flapjacks for breakfast; seconds of everything, plus dessert. As a little girl she'd asked for two sandwiches at lunch, yet remained painfully thin; her mother finally took her to a doctor, fearing she had a tapeworm. "She's a growing girl," the doctor said. "It'll catch up with her." So far it hadn't; at twenty-three she was slim-hipped as a boy.

She dug into the cassoulet. The pork was tender, the house-made sausages seasoned with garlic and fennel. The line cooks piled in across from her, then the prep cooks and the executive chef. There were twelve men all together, not counting Emile and the pastry chef, who ate standing up. Deep voices filled the small kitchen, a ragged blend of English and French.

"My God," said one of the line cooks. The hostess had come into the kitchen in a short skirt. "*Les jambes qu'elle a!*"

Deep laughter, a whistle, grunts of approval. Dinah smiled, embarrassed.

"There you are," said the hostess, coming toward Dinah. "I saw your friend yesterday. He came in for lunch."

"*Ça alors,*" said a line cook. "Little Dinah has a friend."

Dinah blushed. "Ignore these cavemen," she told the hostess. She lowered her voice. "Are you sure it was him?"

"Positive." The hostess sat down, so close Dinah could taste her perfume. "He asked me out."

No, Dinah thought. But the hostess had a stunning figure, the coveted hairstyle of a famous TV actress. Of course Reverend Kimble would find her attractive.

"Dinner, dancing, the works," said the hostess. Then she noticed Dinah's expression. "Oh, don't worry! I told him no. But he's pretty smooth. I see why you like him."

"He's a wonderful man." Dinah glanced around the kitchen. The others had finished their cassoulet; a few stragglers remained, swabbing their plates with crusty bread.

"Where do you know him from, anyway?" the hostess asked.

"He used to work with my dad. At Pennington College, in Richmond. He was the college chaplain."

"Chaplain?" The hostess frowned. "Not this one. He's in real estate. He's got a big agency downtown."

"Are you sure?"

"Positive." The hostess stood to go. "I guess you've got the wrong guy."

"Oh well," Dinah said lightly. "Looks like you turned down a date for nothing."

"That's okay," said the hostess. "He's not my type."

LATE THAT NIGHT, climbing the hill to Glover Park, Dinah saw a police car parked in front of her house.

She sprinted up the front steps. The first-floor lights were on. The front window was broken, the porch covered with jagged glass.

"Hello?" she called out, her heart racing.

In the hallway the Patels' door was ajar. Ann Patel sat on the worn sofa, a colorful shawl around her shoulders. Her husband sat next to her, still in operating scrubs. They were talking to a policeman.

"Are you the owner?" the officer asked. His eyes lit briefly on Dinah's birthmark.

"Yes. I'm Dinah Whitacre." She looked around. Broken glass littered the floor; at the front window the curtains hung askew. In one corner was a mass of extension cords; the appliances they'd been attached to were gone. "What happened?"

Ann Patel's eyes met hers. "I am sitting in the kitchen reading the newspaper and I hear a noise. I come into the living room and I see two men in face mask." She pantomimed pulling on a ski mask.

"Oh God," said Dinah.

"One of them go in the bedroom and I hear him tearing everything apart," said Ann Patel. "The other one tell me to sit down; he unplug the TV and the record player. Then he want to go upstairs; I tell him I have no key. That's when he show me the knife."

"We've had a number of these smash-and-grab robberies in the neighborhood," said the officer. "It's mainly juveniles, drug addicts, that type of thing."

"I see." Dinah turned to Ann Patel. "They didn't hurt you, did they?"

"No, thank God," said Dillip, rubbing his wife's shoulder through the shawl.

"You got some good locks on that upstairs door," said the officer. "They tried to force it. Lucky for you that dead bolt held."

"That's good, I guess." Dinah avoided the Patels' eyes, ashamed that her own apartment hadn't been touched.

"What happens next?" she asked. "Can you catch them?"

"I'll file a report," said the officer, "but without a positive ID it's pretty unlikely."

Dinah nodded stupidly. They'll be back, she thought. It's just a matter of time.

"We've had two break-ins in the last year," she said. "Isn't there something else you can do?"

The officer shrugged. "Put some bars on that window. No way would I live in this place without bars."

"I cannot live behind bars," said Ann Patel.

Her husband adjusted the shawl around her shoulders. "You've been very kind to us," he said to Dinah. "But we can't continue to live in this neighborhood. It's simply too dangerous. My wife is expecting a baby."

Dinah thought of the noises late at night, the rhythmic thud of the headboard against the wall. "A baby," she said softly. "That's wonderful."

Dillip got to his feet. "We're going to stay with some friends until we can find another apartment. I know this is not your fault, but you understand our position."

"Yes," said Dinah. "Of course I understand."

THE MOON was full that night; Dinah lay in bed listening for noises. The locksmith had come and gone; he'd charged her a hundred dollars to install an iron grate over the front window. "A hundred dollars?" she'd repeated; but she'd written the check. After he left she covered the window with plastic to keep out the draft; she'd call someone in the morning to replace the glass.

The old windows whistled, leaking frigid air. The rooms beneath her were perfectly silent. She thought of Ann Patel, pregnant, making love to her husband the night before. The idea shocked her. She'd never imagined that a pregnant woman could have sex. It was, she suspected, just the beginning of what she didn't know.

She thought of the man who wasn't Reverend Kimble, his blue eyes fixing hers with an expression she couldn't decipher. She closed her eyes and listened. Outside the street was loud with traffic. Hundred of cars, thousands, any one of which might contain the two men who'd robbed the Patels. There were two dozen houses on her street, two dozen on the next. For reasons she couldn't imagine, they had chosen hers.

She lay awake for hours, alone in Glover Park.

*T*he next thing should not have happened.

It was a Tuesday morning, her first day off in weeks. Dinah should have been at home in bed, sleeping until noon. Instead she made a special trip downtown to pick up her paycheck, afraid of bouncing the check she'd written the locksmith. And that morning, crossing the alley next to Emile's, she was struck by a car.

The bumper hit her at knee level; her foot landed on a dark patch of ice. The car braked sharply; a horn sounded. She slid gracelessly to the pavement.

The car door opened. "Are you all right?" the driver called out.

She was more embarrassed than hurt; her heavy down jacket had cushioned her fall. A small crowd had gathered; the contents of her pocketbook—keys, loose change, hairbrush—lay scattered around her on the sidewalk.

"I'm fine," she said, sweeping the coins into her purse. "I slipped on the ice."

The man got out of his car and offered his hand.

"Thank you," she said as he helped her to her feet. Then she looked up into the brilliant blue eyes of Reverend Kimble.

"Dinah?" he said. "Good Lord, it really is you."

"Reverend Kimble?" Her cheeks burned; she wished she had put on makeup.

"Are you all right?"

"I think so." Her heart beat furiously. "I can't believe it's you."

"In the flesh." He smiled. "I saw you in the restaurant the other day. I knew it had to be you."

Her cheeks burned. Of course it was me, she thought. Who else has a map of Minnesota on her face? She pushed the thought away.

"I just had lunch there," he said. "I was asking about you."

"You were?"

A horn sounded, a delivery truck idling in the alleyway.

"I should move my car," he said.

"Of course." She took a step and stumbled; a sharp pain shot up her right shin. He grasped her elbow to steady her.

"It's my ankle," she said. "I must have twisted it."

"Lean on me," he said, sliding his arm around her waist. "I'll take you to the hospital."

THEY WAITED in the emergency room of Sacred Heart Hospital, an overheated corridor loud with bustle, the steamy hiss of radiators. Periodically the doors sprang open and a stretcher wheeled in, flushing the room with cold. They waited a long time, but Dinah didn't mind; she could have sat there for hours listening to him talk. He'd been in Washington two years, developing commercial properties: two office towers, a hotel. She pretended surprise, though she already knew this from the hostess. The rest of that conversation—his asking the hostess for a date—she preferred not to think about.

"Enough about me," he said finally. "What are you up to these days? Husband? Children?"

"God, no." Dinah felt herself blush.

"Of course," said Kimble. "Plenty of time for that later."

"I guess so." She smiled, red-faced. "What about you? You never remarried?" She had noticed his hands: no wedding band.

"My second wife died," he said. "I'm a widower now."

Dinah nodded mutely. Her mother would know how to respond; she was fluent in the language of condolences and congratulations, perfectly at ease at weddings and funerals. Dinah had always dismissed such talk as superficial. She wished, now, that she'd paid attention.

"How are the kids?" she asked. "Charlie and Jody. They must be teenagers now."

"I suppose so," said Kimble. "It's hard to believe."

"Do they still live in Richmond?"

"I don't think so." He shifted in his chair. "Last I heard, their mother had taken them to live in the country, but they may have moved since. We aren't what you'd call a close family."

"That's too bad," said Dinah. She supposed it was. One of the sous-chefs was divorced, but never spoke of it. Other than that she didn't know any divorced people.

A nurse appeared pushing a wheelchair. "Dinah Whitacre? The doctor will see you now."

"I'll come with you," said Kimble.

Dinah got quickly to her feet. A breathtaking pain shot up her leg. "Jesus," she hissed. Then blushed, remembering he'd been a minister.

The nurse took her arm and guided her to the wheelchair; pain radiated up her leg. They rolled down the hall and into an examining room, Kimble following close behind. A doctor in green operating scrubs extended his hand. He stared intently at her birthmark, as if that were the emergency.

"It's my ankle," she said flatly. "I fell on the ice and sprained my ankle."

"Gotcha," he said, still staring at her face. He pulled up a wheeled stool and rolled up her pant leg. "Does this hurt?" He pressed gently at her ankle. She cried out in pain.

"I guess that's a yes," he said.

She looked down at her foot. "What is it? A sprain?"

"I doubt it. We'll have to take some X rays, of course, but I'm pretty sure your ankle is broken."

Dinah closed her eyes. Sweat ran down her forehead; she felt suddenly ill. "Broken?"

"Yes. We'll have to set the bone and put you in a cast. And of course you'll have to stay off it for a while. Are you a student?"

"I work in a restaurant."

"Not for the next couple of months, you don't."

Dinah leaned forward in the wheelchair, head in her hands. She thought of the hill she climbed every night from the bus stop; the steep stairs leading to her apartment; fourteen hours a day on her feet in the kitchen. Her life left no room for illness or injury; she'd never even owned a car. She had always taken her independence for granted, never seeing how fragile it was.

"Don't worry. It looks like a nice clean break." The doctor

stared again at her face. "That's quite a hemangioma you've got. I've never seen one quite like it."

Heat spread over her face and chest. She was intensely aware of Reverend Kimble watching her.

"What did you call it?" she asked.

"Hemangioma. It means the blood vessels in the skin are very dense and twisted." The doctor leaned close to her, squinting. "I've seen these marks before, but none this severe. Has it ever been treated?"

"No," said Dinah.

"A colleague of mine at Georgetown is leading a study you might be interested in. He's gotten some terrific results using a device called an argon laser." The doctor stood. "I'll be right back. I'm going to see about getting you some X rays."

Dinah nodded, trying not to cry. She thought of lying alone in her empty house, footsteps on the stairs, strange men forcing the door. How she would protect herself when she couldn't even run.

Kimble sat on the doctor's stool. "Are you all right?"

"I can't take two months off from work," she said. "My boss will have a fit. He'll probably fire me."

"Because you're injured?" He frowned. "That doesn't seem fair. Can't someone else do your job for a while?"

"It's hard to explain," she said. "It's not like a regular job. And my apartment—" She stopped. Tears came and she let them, too tired to hold them back.

"Here," said Kimble, offering a handkerchief. The gesture struck her as quaint, something her father would have done. No one her age would carry a handkerchief.

"This is so embarrassing," she said, choking.

"Don't be silly." He took her hand in both of his. "I nearly ran you over. It's my fault you're in this mess. Naturally I'll take care of you."

"There's nothing you can do."

"Nonsense. You'll need money, a place to stay. It's the least I can do."

She stared at him. His hands were long and cool; she wished she could place them on her flushed cheeks, all the parts of her that burned with shame.

"Oh, no," she said. "I can't let you do that."

"Of course you can." He squeezed her hand. "You just concentrate on getting better. I'll take care of the rest."

Dinah handed back the handkerchief.

"Keep it," said Kimble.

She tucked the soggy thing into her pocket. A fresh wave of blushes covered her cheeks.

"I just had a thought," he said. "Since you're going to be home recuperating anyway, why not do something about this?" He touched his cheek. "Maybe have that procedure the doctor was talking about."

Her face burned. "It probably costs a fortune."

"Don't worry about that," said Kimble.

The doctor returned, followed by a nurse. "All set. Let's wheel you down to X ray."

Dinah's heart pounded. "That friend of yours," she said. "The one who's doing the study. Do you think he could help me?"

"Maybe so," said the doctor. "I can put you in touch with him, if you like."

Dinah's ankle throbbed; beneath her down jacket her turtleneck was soaked with sweat. Again Kimble squeezed her hand.

"Yes," she said. "I'd like that very much."

1994

*A*t the time it meant nothing to her: another black-tie dinner at a downtown hotel, another night of tedious speeches and polite chitchat. Dinah had no idea she'd return to that night in her memory, re-create it fifty, a hundred times, as if the recollection held some sign she ought to have seen, some prefiguration of what would later happen. That night she noticed only that the room was too warm, the food a bit heavy; that everyone around her was growing slowly drunk on an indifferent cabernet. In those respects it was an evening like count-less others. In fifteen years of marriage, she'd accompanied Ken to many such affairs; at least once a month she was on display, trotted out like a prize mare at a county fair.

They'd been photographed twice outside the hotel: Ken joking with the photographer, Dinah smiling between chattering teeth. The next morning she'd see herself in the paper—tall, pale-haired; her bare shoulders lean and sculpted. The caption would identify her only as his wife; this would irritate her, though what else was there to say? Wife, mother of his teenage son; envy of his aging business associates, who kissed her unnecessarily each time they met and occasionally cornered her for a drunken embrace. Dinah was thirty-nine but appeared younger; Ken was sixty-five and looked it: too thin, his skin leathery from jogging in the sun. He enjoyed the raised eyebrows when they appeared together in public, the sly smiles of well-dressed men. Dinah did not. She felt like the punch line to a dirty joke.

There were three hundred people in the grand ballroom that night: chairmen of boards, prominent black clergymen, wealthy Washington couples, white-skinned and white-haired. She'd counted them between the salad and the surf and turf. At five hundred dollars a head, it was a nice haul for the Single Candle Foundation, the charity that had named Ken its Man of the Year. With them at the head table sat the secretary of housing and urban development, congressmen from Maryland and Virginia, the mayors of Washington and Richmond and Baltimore. Sitting across from the mayors, Ken talked more than he ate. Dinah eyed his untouched lobster tail; if they were dining alone, she'd steal it from his plate. The lobster was tender and succulent, sweet as butter; but Ken turned up his nose at seafood. The only fish he'd eat was tuna from a can.

"My lovely wife grew up in Richmond," he told one of the mayors, giving Dinah a squeeze. "You can see why I feel indebted to the town." He reached into his jacket for a business card and scrawled something on the back of it. "Call me in the morning. I'm in the office by seven."

Dessert appeared, a slice of apple pie drizzled with caramel sauce. The filling was nicely tart, the golden crust exemplary. Lard, Dinah thought approvingly: the secret to a flaky crust. She glanced at Ken—he had high cholesterol and should be warned—but couldn't catch his eye. It wouldn't matter. He obsessed over his weight; he rarely touched dessert.

"How can you eat like that and look like that?" asked the secretary's wife, a sausage-shaped woman in a green satin casing.

"I can't help it," said Dinah. "I'm always hungry."

Coffee was served; the speeches began. First came the mayors, the congressmen; then the Reverend Elmore Blanks, pastor of the Southeast AME Zionist church.

"My opening act," Ken whispered, leaning close to Dinah.

Reverend Blanks was a squat man with a booming voice; with evangelical zeal he touted the accomplishments of the Homes Project, the nonprofit company Ken Kimble had founded. For nearly five years he'd bought foreclosed properties in burned-out neighborhoods, restored the houses, then resold them to poor families at reasonable prices. Reverend Blanks praised the determination of these families, their persistence in the face of adversity, their willingness to hope against hope. Then he introduced the Man of the Year.

The room crackled with applause as Ken took the stage. He adjusted the mike to his height and waited for the room to quiet.

"I am somewhat embarrassed to be standing before you tonight." His voice was quiet and serious, empty of theatrics. "I have not led an exceptional life."

Here we go, Dinah thought. Simple Midwestern values.

"I was raised in a hardworking family with simple Midwestern values," he continued. "My parents weren't sophisticated people, but they gave me the tools to accomplish whatever I set out to do in life.

"I chose to sell real estate—not a bad way of making a living, but not an especially noble way either."

He stopped and scanned the crowd, his eyes passing over the silver heads.

"I have never lain awake at nights listening to gunfire, fearful for the lives of my children."

His voice grew louder.

"I have never tried to raise a family in a violent neighborhood, where drugs are sold *on every corner.*"

He rapped the podium for emphasis. Under the table Dinah did likewise, her right fist silent against her left palm.

"So I'm not going to talk any more about myself. Instead I'm going to introduce you to some folks who have fought the hard fight and won."

He pointed to the back of the room, a sweeping gesture of his long arm. At a table in the corner was a black family: a young woman, two little boys, and an old lady.

"Meet Charmaine Watkins," he said.

The woman got to her feet with effort. She was dark-skinned, with cherry-red hair. She looked nine months pregnant.

"Miz Watkins and her family live in a newly refurbished row house in southeast Washington, in a neighborhood where no one has lived in their own private residence in thirty-three years. The Watkinses are in that house as a result of her own courage and character, not because of anything I've done. So if you want to honor somebody tonight, how about honoring them."

The applause was thunderous.

"Thank you," he said.

IT WAS TEN-THIRTY when the banquet wrapped up, a half hour later before Ken shook all the hands offered to him. He and

Dinah walked toward the parking garage down the block. He handed her the keys. His night vision was poor; he disliked driving after dark.

She backed his Lincoln Town Car out of the tight space. It was ridiculous for city driving, a sluggish boat that required a space and a half on most streets and couldn't be parked at all in Georgetown; but Ken liked big cars.

She turned onto New Hampshire Avenue and cut northeast through the city. Ken reclined his seat and in a moment began to snore. He was up at five every day, on the treadmill by five-fifteen. He slept the deep sleep of a farmhand, a man with a clear conscience. She glanced across the seat at him, his long forehead illuminated by the streetlights. Though his face was gaunt, running had kept him trim and vigorous; at sixty-five he moved with an athlete's grace. Only his teeth had failed him. Several times that summer she'd answered calls from his dentist's office, reminding him of upcoming appointments. Then one day he'd come home with shiny white dentures. He never said a word about them. She pretended not to notice.

She turned off the highway into Great Falls, Virginia. Their house loomed in the distance, a cavernous Tudor at the end of a cul-de-sac. A large house, with five bedrooms and six baths; too large for a family with just one child. When she turned into the wide driveway, Ken awakened with a gasp. He always woke that way, his eyes wide and startled, as if he'd been caught in a compromising act.

"We're home," she said.

They went inside. The house was dark but Dinah sensed that their son was awake. Brendan was a nocturnal creature; he went to bed at eleven as directed, but she knew it was only an act, that late at night he listened to music on his headphones or crept silently around the house.

There was a strip of light beneath his bedroom door. Dinah knocked softly and waited. She opened the door a crack. Brendan sat on the floor staring at the television, the volume turned low.

"Hi," she said.

"Hey," he answered, his lips barely moving. His flannel shirt hung open; underneath it a black T-shirt stretched tight across his belly. A late-night talk show flickered on the screen.

"Sorry we're late," said Dinah. "The speeches ran long."

Brendan ran a hand through his hair. He had a terrible haircut, long on top and shaved nearly bald on the sides, as if he'd had recent brain surgery. *You paid for that?* Ken had asked when she brought Brendan home from the salon.

It's just hair, she'd answered, though she hated the style too. *It'll grow back.*

Brendan changed the channel to a music video. A bare-chested rap singer shook his fingers at the camera. Behind him women cavorted in a swimming pool.

"I talked to your headmaster," she said. Brendan had failed Spanish and math for the semester; unless he made up the classes over the summer he'd have to repeat ninth grade. "You don't have to go to summer school. You can get a tutor instead."

"Forget it," he said. "I'd rather go to summer school."

"Okay. I'll call the realtor in the morning." They'd rented a beach house in the Outer Banks for all of July. "She can find us a place for August instead."

"Don't bother." Finally he looked at her. "I don't want to go anyway." He turned back to the screen, his gray eyes bleary and unblinking.

"Get some sleep," she said softly. "We'll talk about it in the morning."

She closed the door and rubbed her eyes, exhausted; talking with her son had that effect on her. He's a teenager, she told herself, remembering her own miserable adolescence; but the thought did not comfort her. He'd be a teenager for another five years. She wasn't sure she'd survive it.

She slipped off her shoes and tiptoed to the bathroom, where she dabbed her face with cold cream. The foundation and powder melted away; underneath it, the right side of her face was an angry pink, like a bad sunburn. It was all that remained of the purple stain. Ken had paid for the argon laser treatments before they were married; it was, she later realized, a part of their courtship. Only after the six treatments did they become lovers.

She wiped off the cream and examined her skin. Recently, for her thirty-ninth birthday, he'd offered to pay for more treatments. He'd read about a new technique in the *Post* and asked a doctor friend about it. Apparently a new gadget, the pulse-dye laser, could eliminate the discoloration of Dinah's skin.

"Look at this," he'd told her, showing her the article. He pointed to the Before photo. "Her birthmark was even worse than yours. And look at her now." He left the clipping on her dressing table; Dinah tucked it away in a drawer. Two months later she still hadn't seen a doctor.

She went into the bedroom and unzipped her silk dress, one Ken had recently bought her. He kept her sizes on a card in his Rolodex; before each big event he came home with a department store box. The dresses were always bare and slinky, styles she wouldn't choose for herself; but Dinah didn't object. She detested shopping. If she vetoed his choice, she'd have to buy something herself.

She draped the dress over a chair. Ken lay still in the king-size bed, hands crossed over his chest. Early in their marriage it had bothered her, how they never touched while they slept. Now she couldn't imagine it otherwise.

She slid under the covers. In a moment his cold hand found her thigh.

"You're awake," she said.

"Too keyed up to sleep. Miz Watkins and her struggling family." He chuckled. "Was it too much?"

"I guess it had the desired effect."

His hand slid under her T-shirt. She was expecting it; after parading her around in public he usually made a grab at her. Unless, of course, she had her period. Then he wouldn't touch her with gloves on.

He fingered a slow circle around her nipple. He never kissed her anymore, not since the teeth. She understood. Still, the hand was too abrupt for her. She resisted the urge to shrug it away.

SHE WAS thirty-nine years old, a woman living with her choices. She had married a successful man; she had borne him a child. These seemed to be the last things that would ever happen to her.

She led a comfortable life. Each morning she dropped Brendan off at his private school. Afterward she played tennis; she was a top-seeded Masters player at their club in Reston. She had a magnificent garden, help with the house if she wanted it (she didn't). Yet sometimes—while cooking dinner, or driving home from the club after a match—she imagined what could have been. How her life might have turned out if she and Ken had never met.

She had never returned to Emile's kitchen. Her ankle had healed slowly, badly; agonizing months of painkillers and physical therapy. Ken had done everything to help: sold her house in Glover Park at a slight profit, offered her the first floor of a town house he owned in Georgetown, rent-free for as long as she needed it. By the time her ankle healed, they were engaged.

They were married by a judge on the island of St. Thomas, a thousand miles away from anyone who knew them. Dinah's parents disapproved of the marriage; their absence was a relief. She wore flowers in her hair, a nervous but happy bride.

A single photo exists of their wedding, a snapshot taken by the judge's wife. In it they stand shoulder to shoulder in front of the courthouse, Ken in a pale suit, Dinah in a white sundress, her hair braided by a woman who sold trinkets on the beach. She'd just finished her laser treatments; in the photo her skin looks perfectly smooth. She didn't know it, but she was a beautiful woman.

*I*t was a gorgeous point.

Across the court Wayne Day sprang from foot to foot, like a heavyweight boxer in the ring. Dinah took her time placing the shot, deep to Wayne's left. He snagged it narrowly, nicked it with the edge of his racquet. She knew by the sound that it wouldn't clear the net.

"Goddamnit," he hissed. "Good shot, Dinah." They met at the net, a brief clasp of moist hands. His breath smelled of coffee. Sweat rolled down his neck.

"That was a hell of a point," said the club manager, watching from the sidelines. He was a tennis player himself; often he lingered to watch them play.

"Thanks." Dinah's arm still vibrated from the impact, the satisfying collision of ball and racquet. "Another set?"

"Jesus," said Wayne. "You're killing me. I can barely walk." He said this every time they played; it was never true. He was fast for a big man, graceful and strong.

"I should get going," he said. "I have clients this morning." He gave his head a shake, like a dog drying its coat. A drop of his sweat landed on her throat.

"Are we on for tomorrow?" she asked.

"Yep," he called over his shoulder, loud enough for the club manager to hear. "See you tomorrow."

In the weight room Dinah dropped to the mat and stretched: calves, thighs, hips, groin. She paid special attention to her right ankle; since her fall on the ice years before, it was prone to stiffness. She took her time, breathing deeply into each stretch. Then she pulled on a sweatshirt and drove to Wayne's house. His German shepherd no longer barked when she pulled into the driveway. The dog recognized the sound of her car.

Wayne was getting out of the shower when she arrived.

"I'm all sweaty," she said, kicking off her shoes.

"Come here," he said.

THEY'D BEEN lovers for a year. They'd met in the club mixed doubles league, a random pairing in the annual round-robin. "I know you," Wayne said when they were first introduced. It took her a moment to place him: when she and Ken first moved to Great Falls, he'd given Brendan tennis lessons.

"Of course," she said. "I remember you."

They played tennis once a week, then twice, then every day. Wayne was the better player—he'd been an intercollegiate champion at Georgetown—but Dinah was the real competitor. That summer they placed first in the league.

After every match they went out to breakfast. Starved, flushed from exertion, hair wet from the shower, Dinah felt curiously at ease. She never wore makeup to the club; Wayne had seen her naked face, the angry ghost of her birthmark, and didn't care. Together they devoured eggs, bacon, stacks of pancakes. He was the first man she'd ever met who ate more than she did. Though he maintained a legal practice, he never seemed to work; he'd spend the whole day with her if she let him. She was glad for the company; since moving to the suburbs she was too often alone.

One morning he failed to show up for a match. He phoned her at the club: dead battery, he explained. She went to his house with jumper cables. They got his truck running and went immediately to bed.

She was overwhelmed by the strangeness of his body, its heat and smells. To her astonishment he talked to her as they touched. *What do you like? What can I do?*

At the time she had no answer. Since then they'd made love a hundred times; she had learned every inch of him, and of herself.

AFTERWARD THEY LAY in bed, moisture cooling their skin. Summer was ending, the morning light tinged with sadness.

"I missed you," he said.

"I missed you too." She and Brendan had gone to the Outer Banks after all; she hadn't seen Wayne in a month.

His arms tightened around her. "How was Cape Hatteras? Did Ken ever show?"

"He couldn't make it. Busy, as usual." She rolled onto her side, away from him. She would talk to him about Ken, but not in bed. It made her think too much about what she was doing.

"Sorry." Wayne curled up behind her, wrapping her in heat. "Explain it to me again."

She did. The thought of living on alimony repulsed her; yet independence seemed impossible. She had a half semester of college and a diploma from culinary school; the only decent-paying job she could get meant working nights and weekends. Brendan had gotten into enough trouble already. Without parental supervision there was no telling what he could do.

"At least now he has a good mother," she said. "If we got divorced, he wouldn't even have that."

"That's awfully convenient," said Wayne.

She extricated herself from his arms. "It's not convenient at all. That's exactly my point."

Wayne sat up. "I don't get it. I don't see how you can compromise yourself that way."

Dinah stood, naked except for the neoprene brace on her ankle; she wore it for tennis and rarely bothered to remove it before they made love.

"Of course you don't," she said, pulling his T-shirt over her head. "You've never been married."

The Godfrey Day School wasn't the best private high school in Fairfax County, just the most expensive. Ken and Dinah had chosen it together, but only Dinah had been inside: for open houses, conferences with teachers, and, lately, meetings with the headmaster. "I don't have time today," Ken always said when she asked him to come along. Yet he made time for the things that interested him: work, social functions, predawn runs on the treadmill.

That October morning Dinah drove Brendan to school. She parked in a visitor's space behind the library, where he was serving in-school suspension. A teacher had caught him in the woods behind the school, smoking cigarettes with another boy in the middle of the afternoon.

They sat in silence, the motor idling. A silent rain nicked the windshield.

"It's stupid," said Brendan. "Sitting there all day, doing nothing. It's a waste of time."

"You cut class," said Dinah. "You must have known you'd get in trouble."

"It wasn't class. It was a pep rally." Brendan stared out the window. "I don't care about the football team. Why should I have to go to a pep rally?"

"It's not just that," said Dinah. "You were smoking. After everything we talked about." That summer she'd noticed cigarette burns on one of his T-shirts; she'd lectured him for an hour about the dangers of nicotine. He'd sworn he'd never smoke again.

Brendan opened the passenger door. "Can Sean drive me home?"

Sean Guthrie was his only friend, a junior who'd just gotten his driver's license. Dinah questioned Sean's skill as a driver, but the school was only ten miles from home; she let Brendan ride with him as long as it was daylight.

"Okay," she said.

He slammed the door and climbed the stairs to the library. Dinah watched him go, big and slow in his oversize jacket. In the past year his face had changed; his other features had failed to keep up with his new nose and chin. His haircut was just dreadful. Still, he was a handsome boy, if only he'd smile. If only he'd stand up straight.

Puberty had hit him suddenly and violently. First he'd grown long and gangly; then his body had expanded into his baggy clothes like rising dough. As a boy he had loved the beach; Dinah remembered him sturdy and compact, hurling himself into the waves and whooping with delight. Now he refused to swim at all. The last time she'd dragged him to the pool at the club, he wouldn't take off his shirt.

In the space of a few months, he'd grown slow and sullen. He wore the same clothes day after day: tattered flannel shirts, scrubby T-shirts that hadn't fit him in a year. Ken made pointed comments about his sudden weight gain: "Don't they have gym class at that school?" and "How can one kid put away so much pasta?" It confirmed something Dinah had known for years, a basic truth about her husband's character: he disliked unattractive people. He'd staffed his agency with handsome associates; his secretaries over the years had resembled fashion models. When their son was small and cute, he'd been a mildly attentive father. Now that Brendan was heavy and awkward, Ken wanted nothing to do with him.

Dinah backed out of the parking lot. The library windows glowed with fluorescent light. She imagined Brendan hunched over a book, pretending to read; leaning back in his chair, whistling. The day before he'd fallen asleep and the librarian had scolded him for snoring. He'd told Dinah this with visible pride, his new deep voice thick and phlegmy. It was the longest conversation they'd had in a week.

He'd become strange to her, a thing she'd never imagined could happen. All through his childhood they'd been uncommonly close. They'd lived in the District until he was ten; every Saturday she'd taken him to one of the museums on the Mall. He liked Natural History best, Air and Space a close second. He was fascinated by the names of things: dinosaurs, planets, the moving parts of planes and locomotives. Together they pored over encyclopedias, *National Geographic,* field guides to birds and trees and marine mammals. His curiosity was a shining thing, educating her in a way that her own schooling had not. She thought of him running through museum corridors, calling her to come and see the giant ant farm, the anacondas; the stuffed carrier pigeons, long extinct, dead and gone forever. Ken couldn't spare the time to go along; he'd never seen the fossils or the primates or the miniature *Spirit of St. Louis* hanging in the Smithsonian. Back then he'd handled a few residential properties, million-dollar places in Georgetown. Every weekend he was busy showing houses.

Dinah turned off the highway and into Great Falls. They'd left Washington at Ken's insistence; he had a fondness for grand houses, the larger and more ostentatious, the better. She'd resisted the idea of moving to the suburbs; she hated the lookalike houses, the neighborhood associations with their silly rules. It was the yard that sold her on the move: a wide expanse of grass, big enough for barbecues and baseball. Big enough for a growing family; they'd postponed a second child for too long.

The barbecues never happened. The commute lengthened Ken's workday by two hours; Dinah bought a microwave oven to reheat his dinners. Alone in the big house, she found herself waiting: for Brendan to come home from school each day, for a second child to fill her life with chaos and purpose and joy. Then, finally, it happened. "I'm pregnant," she told Ken, inarticulate with delight.

"No, you're not," he said calmly. Then he explained. He'd had a vasectomy years before, just after Brendan was born. He hadn't felt it necessary to tell her about it.

She never forgave him. He had lied to her; worse, he'd robbed her of everything in life she wanted. Her period came the following day, two weeks late. That summer she met Wayne Day on the tennis court.

Dinah pulled into the driveway. The phone was ringing as she opened the door. Later she'd remember that the ring seemed louder than usual, as though the call was unusually important. The voice at the other end was deliberately calm.

"Mrs. Kimble?" said the woman. "This is Great Falls Memorial Hospital. Your husband has had a heart attack."

*D*inah drove to the hospital in the rain, aware of every sound: the scrape of windshield wipers, rubber peeling off the wet pavement. She drove with spectacular correctness, signaling, shifting, lightly tapping the brake, as if by filling each second with small, impeccable action she could influence the outcome of the day.

The doors of the inpatient wing swung open with a flourish, as if they'd been waiting for her a long time. Inside, well-dressed women chatted in the sunny solarium. A large plate-glass window offered a view of the grounds: a man-made lake and spindly new maples; acres of fresh sod, smooth as carpet.

She gave her name at the desk; the nurse said something with a slow mouth, as if she were speaking to a deaf person. Dinah followed her down the corridor. She felt as though she were walking on water.

In the room an old man lay in the bed. His eyes were closed, his skin a delicate film over the blue veins of his forehead. He looked as if he'd been dead for a day. Dinah smiled helplessly at the nurse. Words eluded her, the polite words to explain that this was not her husband.

The man was breathing; the sheet rose and fell where it covered his chest. On the table next to the bed was a blue plastic container labeled with masking tape: KIMBLE. Dinah looked again at his face, the pale lips and sunken cheeks.

"We took his teeth out for him," said the nurse. "They always look so different without them."

"Yes," said Dinah.

"Your father has a strong heart. He stabilized pretty quickly."

"He's my husband."

The nurse colored. "Excuse me. I shouldn't have assumed."

"That's okay," said Dinah. "You didn't know."

"There's a pay phone down the hall, in case there's any other family you need to notify." The nurse glanced toward the bed. "He's going to be out for a while, but you can sit here as long as you want."

Dinah pulled a chair close to the bed. She sat there a long time, watching his chest rise and fall, rise and fall. Equipment surrounded the bed like anxious relatives. A clear plastic tube was taped to his hand; others disappeared into his nose and mouth. He'd been driving to a meeting when it happened, racing around the Beltway in morning traffic. She imagined him veering crazily into the breakdown lane, groping behind the seat for the mobile phone he kept in his briefcase.

She reached for his hand, the skin creased and spotted under the bright lights. It felt cool and light in hers, almost hollow. The cruel hospital light exposed the circles beneath his eyes, the lie that age is an attitude.

She touched his face, smoothed the sparse white hair at his temples. As a girl she'd known him dark-haired, in his vests and colorful shirts; she tried to remember him that way and found she could not. He had kept no photos of himself; there was nothing to remind her of what she'd long suspected and now knew: that she had only glimpsed the most alive part of him.

She laid his hand on the sheet. He would recover, the nurse had said so; but she would never forget this day: his chest rising and falling in the hospital bed, his secret false teeth in the plastic box, clearly labeled for her to see. He would wake up without them. She'd no longer be able to pretend not to know.

A luminous red line skated across the monitor, the mysterious workings of his invisible heart.

SHE DROVE home through rush-hour traffic, aware of the time. She was always there when Brendan came home from school; he would know immediately that something was wrong. On the seat beside her lay Ken's briefcase, across the backseat, the suit he'd been wearing when it happened.

She'd phoned home twice from the hospital. Both times the machine had picked up; Brendan hated answering the phone. Standing in the bright corridor, she'd wondered, briefly, if there was anyone else she should notify. Ken hadn't spoken of his other children in years. "They're grown now," he'd told Dinah once when she broached the subject. "They don't need me."

"They still need you," she protested. "Of course they do."

"Their whole lives they've been listening to lies about me. Lord knows what their mother's told them."

"They're old enough now," she persisted. "You can tell them the truth."

Finally he'd gotten angry, one of the few times he'd ever raised his voice to her. "It doesn't concern you, Dinah. Just leave it alone."

She had done as he'd asked. All these years she'd left it alone.

She parked in the driveway and took Ken's things into the house. Brendan's door was closed; she heard the shower running in his bathroom.

She hung Ken's suit in the bedroom closet, then opened his briefcase. Inside was his watch, a heavy gold Rolex she'd given him one Christmas. The watch had cost more than their monthly mortgage payment, but it was the only thing he'd wanted. It seemed ridiculous to pay for such a gift from their joint account; but she had no money of her own. She hadn't worked since before they were married.

She put the watch aside and opened his wallet—plain black calfskin, smooth as wax. Inside were receipts, credit cards, a crisp hundred-dollar bill. No photos of her or Brendan; she'd given him a framed one for his office but had never seen it on his desk. A scrap of paper fluttered to the floor. It had been torn from the corner of an envelope, a return address label in ornate script.

JODY KIMBLE, it read. 2323 BEECHWOOD TERRACE, ARLINGTON, VIRGINIA.

*D*on't do this," said Wayne. "You don't have to do this."

They sat in his truck in the country club parking lot, still dressed for tennis. Risky, but Dinah couldn't think of a better place. She didn't trust herself to go to his house.

"I can't live this way," she said. "I'm not this kind of person."

"You're just feeling guilty," he said.

"Of course I feel guilty. He almost died." Outside, the autumn leaves were at their peak. A plane buzzed overhead. Dinah imagined how it must look to the pilot, the hills spattered with red as if there'd been a terrible disaster.

"I have to get back," she said. Ken had an appointment with his cardiologist in an hour; she'd promised to drive him to the clinic.

"Wait." Wayne touched her shoulder. "I still want to see you. Can't we at least play tennis?"

"Maybe when things settle down." Her shoulder burned under his hand. "After the holidays."

"What are you going to do?" said Wayne. "You can't stay with him forever."

She thought of Ken the way she'd left him: lying on the living room couch, wrapped in his bathrobe like an old man. She had built her life around him; leaving him now would make her the sort of person she didn't wish to know.

"He's my husband," she said.

"Come on." Wayne's eyes sought hers. "You're miserable. You've wasted enough years on that selfish old bastard."

"Don't say that."

"Am I wrong?"

She looked away, at the cars racing along the highway.

"You can't divorce him; you've got a kid to think about. Fine. I accept that." Wayne reached for her hand. "I just want everything the way it was before."

"I do too," said Dinah. "But it isn't." She opened the passenger door.

"I've made mistakes," she said softly. "I married the wrong person. But you can't undo fifteen years."

"You don't love him," said Wayne.

"He's family," said Dinah.

ike every Saturday, Brendan slept in. When he came downstairs his mom was fixing his father's lunch on a tray.

"Why don't you go watch TV with your dad?" she said. "He could use some company."

"He's watching the news. I hate the news."

His mom sighed. "Go sit down and talk to him for five minutes. Ask him how he's feeling. Is that too much to ask?"

Brendan went into the living room. His father sat on the couch in a robe and pajamas, flipping through the channels.

"There's nothing on," he grumbled. He flipped past music videos, pro wrestling, a Mafia movie Brendan had seen twice but would gladly watch again. They had eighty-nine channels. There was plenty to watch.

"How are you feeling?" Brendan asked.

His father eyed him suspiciously. "How do you think I'm feeling? I can't just sit here staring at the television all day. I don't know how you do it." He tossed aside the remote. He had switched back to the all-news channel. "Tell your mother to come in here."

"Why don't you just whistle?" Brendan muttered.

"What did you say?"

"Nothing."

Brendan went into the kitchen. His mom was counting out pills from a bottle and placing them on the tray.

"He wants you to go in there."

His mom looked up. "Coming," she called out. And of course, she went.

She had changed. Since the heart attack, she waited on his father hand and foot; she came whenever he called her, like a trained poodle. His father didn't even appreciate it; he never said "please" or "thank you." If Brendan's manners were as bad as his father's, he'd never hear the end of it.

She seemed not to mind the old man's rudeness; she cut him too much slack, in Brendan's opinion. Though of course she cut Brendan slack too. She didn't care that he was fat. She called him queer things like strong and handsome, which was embarrassing but in a way nice because you could tell she meant it. It made him wonder about her, if she was blind or nuts or just needed to get out more; but hey, she was his mom. He supposed it was because she loved him.

She did cool things. She was an amazing skier, fast and ballsy, if you could call a girl that. She could play tennis; she had a huge garden. She insisted on making everything herself—bread, ice cream, yogurt, things other people just bought at the store. Sometimes she went overboard—she squeezed orange juice every morning and wouldn't let Brendan drink soda, which she said was full of chemicals—but she was a great cook. He would rather eat at his own house than at any restaurant in the world.

Compared to other mothers she was pretty. "Your mom is hot," his friend Guthrie said once when she took them to the pool and swam laps in her bathing suit. It was the last time they went to the pool with Brendan's mother.

He liked her best when she was going about her own business: rolling pie crust, canning tomatoes from the garden. The rest of the time she asked too many questions. Every night at dinner he was supposed to talk about his day at school. He said as little as possible, which made her mad. She didn't understand that talking about school was like adding minutes to his school day. Brendan couldn't think of anything worse.

He could sometimes avoid her questions by barging in while she was busy cooking. Then she'd put a knife in his hand and make him chop things. Later, when they sat down to dinner, she'd forget to ask about school; they'd talk about other things, as if she'd forgotten he was her son. Sometimes she talked about culinary school, dishes she'd made when she worked in a restaurant a long time ago.

When his father was home she didn't talk about anything; she just listened to the old man go on and on about his business deals. Luckily, his father worked late most nights; but once in a while his mom put her foot down. Then Brendan would hear them fighting through their bedroom door.

"Your son hasn't seen you in a week." Always in a whisper, as if Brendan couldn't hear them that way.

"What do you want me to do? Leave the office at five and sit in traffic all evening?" That was always his father's line, that by coming home at nine o'clock he was beating the traffic. This argument never got him anywhere.

"Yes," she would whisper. "That's exactly what I want you to do."

Then, for a week or two, his father would appear at dinner, usually just as she was taking something out of the oven. They'd make a big show of kissing—on the cheek, like married people on TV. Brendan would have to turn his head. He hated seeing his parents kiss.

At dinner his mother would be especially annoying, asking a million questions about his day. His father would sit there chewing his brussels sprouts, his mouth not quite closed. That was the other problem: his father was always on a diet. He loved terrible food: spinach, lima beans, always without cheese or butter. Worse, he watched everything Brendan ate, made him feel like a pig if he took seconds of anything. It drove him crazy to have a fat son. This made Brendan want to eat more and more.

T he house was silent Thanksgiving morning: no alarm clocks, no slapping sneakers on the treadmill. Ken slept deeply, hands folded across his chest, his heart pumping silently beneath them. Dinah crept out of bed and dressed in the dark. Dawn had broken; gray daylight peered from beneath the blind.

In the kitchen the massive turkey thawed in the sink. Dinah cut open the plastic and rubbed the skin with butter, the dimpled flesh cool beneath her hands. She hadn't cooked Thanksgiving dinner in ten years. Usually Ken booked them a table at a restaurant downtown. The traditional meal was too heavy for him; he hated the endless leftovers.

She chopped onion and celery and scraped them into a pan; in a moment the kitchen smelled of browned butter. Guilt nudged her; these were foods he wouldn't be able to eat. She thought of clots, lipids, the narrow passages to his heart.

You're just feeling guilty, Wayne had told her. As if guilt meant nothing, as if it weren't a feeling she'd earned and deserved. Three weeks had passed since she'd broken off their affair. She'd forbidden him to call; yet each time the phone rang her heart quickened, as though defibrillated. Meanwhile she brought Ken newspapers and drove him to the doctor's, filled his prescriptions and served his meals on a tray. Sometimes she caught a glimpse of herself—her reflection in the kitchen window as she counted out his pills—and wanted to laugh. A casual observer would call her a model wife; yet she'd betrayed him a hundred times over. She had watched the seasons change through Wayne's bedroom window. Five seasons: more than a year.

Ken's heart attack had changed everything. She was disgusted by how cynical her life had become. As if she were a spectator she saw herself waiting: for her time alone with Wayne, for the day Brendan went away to college and she could be truly free. Meanwhile, sleeping next to Ken each night, letting him touch her (not often, but still). The picture repulsed her.

She blamed herself for his hardening arteries, his heart starved of blood. Early in their marriage she'd cooked to his specifications—salads, steamed vegetables, dry chicken breasts. She'd tried to eat as he did but left the table hungry. Soon she was pregnant and ravenous; at night, after he went to bed, she devoured piles of pasta, mashed potatoes with gravy, grilled cheese sandwiches browned in butter. Her belly swelled; her breasts grew to the size of grapefruits. After Brendan was born, she cooked as she pleased. In recent years she and Ken seldom ate together. He worked late; most nights he assembled his own meal and heated it in the microwave. At restaurants he gave the waiters meticulous instructions: no oil, butter, egg yolks, or salt. His fastidiousness irritated her; it took all the pleasure out of eating. She dismissed as neurotic his fear of gaining weight. There had been nothing to suggest his concern was more than vanity, that he was worried about his heart.

"How did this happen?" she'd asked his doctor the one time they'd crossed paths at the hospital. "He takes such good care of himself. How could he have a heart attack?"

"Familial hypercholesterolemia," said the doctor. "I'm guessing, of course. In his parents' day nobody monitored cholesterol levels, so it's impossible to say for certain. But when a patient is this lean and this conscientious about his diet, and his numbers are still elevated, it usually indicates a genetic predisposition."

Later, when she confronted him, Ken seemed irritated by her concern. "Genetic tendency, my ass," he said. "My parents ate like field hands. There was nothing wrong with them that a little discipline couldn't have prevented."

His doctor recommended an angioplasty; the hospital sent him home the day after the procedure. For two weeks he'd moped around the house, complaining about the weather and the garbage on TV. He bought a blood pressure monitor and checked himself twice a day, announcing the results at lunch and dinner. The numbers never deviated from normal, but Ken kept checking; his health was his only hobby. Dinah suggested movies, drives in the country. Nothing interested him. All he wanted was to go back to work. Five years ago he'd sold his agency and started the Homes Project; he spent his days negotiating with loan officers and arguing with contractors, wheedling donations out of lumberyards and hardware stores. In between he fought downtown traffic, driving from one devastated neighborhood to the next. He'd been robbed twice, once at gunpoint. Still, he drove his Lincoln Town Car south of Pennsylvania Avenue, through the wasted streets of Anacostia. "I have to," he often said. "That's where the houses are."

She counted out six sweet potatoes, one per person: Jody and her boyfriend, Charlie and his girlfriend, herself and Brendan.

(Ken was careful with his starches.) He'd been stunned when she told him she'd invited his children to Thanksgiving dinner.

"You did *what?*"

"Charlie and Jody. I called and invited them."

His voice was oddly calm. "How did you find them?"

"I found Jody's address in your wallet." She chose her words carefully. "You never told me she wrote to you."

"Oh, that. A few years ago she sent me a birthday card at the office." Casually, as though it were a regular occurrence. "I thought I told you. I guess I forgot."

Dinah tore at a loaf of bread, a stale baguette she'd saved for the stuffing. She assumed he had regrets. They'd been babies when he left: Charlie six years old, Jody still in diapers. Dinah had known this from the beginning, but it hadn't seemed so bad then, before she had a child of her own. Before she knew what a six-year-old boy was: the sudden command of language, the stubborn independence that dissolved in a moment's fright. When Brendan was six he'd run off in a shopping mall. He was sobbing when she found him, clinging to the leg of a security guard. He'd shadowed her for days afterward, followed her from room to room. He wouldn't go to sleep unless she sat with him.

She broke an egg over the bread crumbs and added the onions and celery. She imagined Ken's remorse a tentacled thing, squeezing tight around his aging heart.

She heard footsteps on the stairs, the scuff of slippers.

"Ken?" she called out. "Is that you?"

He shuffled into the kitchen in his robe and pajamas. His fine hair stood out like a halo; his chin bristled with silver.

"How did you sleep?" she asked.

"Goddamn blood pressure pills. They give me nightmares." He

eyed the turkey. "Jesus Christ, that thing's enormous. Who's going to eat all that? As if I didn't know."

"Don't start," she said. "It's Thanksgiving. He can eat as much as he wants."

Ken grunted. "When is everybody coming?"

"I told Jody noon. Charlie and his girlfriend might be a little late." She rinsed the potatoes under the faucet. "Can I get you some breakfast?"

"Make me some coffee," he said, shuffling toward the living room. "I'm saving my appetite."

In the next room the television came on.

DINAH KNOCKED at Brendan's bedroom door.

"Can I come in?" she called out.

"I guess," he said.

The room was cool and dim, the navy blue curtains drawn across the windows, blocking the sunlight. Brendan lay on the comforter in jeans and a T-shirt, his back braced with pillows. The smell of roasting turkey seeped through the floorboards.

"Everybody will be here soon," said Dinah. "I wanted to make sure you were dressed."

"I'm dressed."

She glanced around. Piles of clothes everywhere, stacks of magazines near the computer. She sat on the bed.

"This has to be confusing for you," she said. "It is for me too."

"So why did you invite them?" He looked at her with her own eyes, clear gray flecked with green.

"For your father," she said. "Besides, they're your half brother and half sister. Don't you want to get to know them?"

"What for? They're his kids. Let *him* get to know them."

Amen to that, she thought. "That's the whole point," she said. She ran her hand across a section of bedspread, ironing the paisley pattern. There was a hole the size of a pencil eraser at the edge.

"Your dad has missed out on a lot," she said. "Charlie and Jody are adults now. He didn't get to see them grow up."

"Why not?" He stared at her. "Max's parents are divorced. He sees his dad all the time."

Dinah looked up at the ceiling. Years before, when he was little, she and Brendan had covered it with glow-in-the-dark stars.

"Times have changed," she said. "Back then fathers had very few legal rights in a divorce. Your dad and his first wife couldn't come to an agreement, so he lost out. It's sad, but that's what happened." It was the explanation she'd rehearsed, whether or not it was true.

His brow furrowed, a mannerism of his father's. "How come he never talks about them? I've never even seen a picture of them."

Dinah hesitated. For weeks she'd defended Ken to their son, tried to explain away things that didn't make sense to her either. She could tell from Brendan's face that he wasn't buying any of it. She rose to go.

"It's complicated," she said. "I don't understand it very well myself. But this is important for your dad."

Brendan frowned. She resisted the urge to touch his hair, smooth his forehead like she had when he was small.

"He's different since his heart attack," she said, in a tone she hoped was convincing. "Doesn't he seem different?"

Brendan leaned back into the nest of cushions. He placed a pillow over his face.

"No." His voice was muffled. "He's exactly the same."

C harlie hadn't seen Ken Kimble in twenty years, not since the night he and Jody had crept out of the house in Florida and ridden the Greyhound bus back to Virginia. The details of that trip—the stops in Atlanta and Charleston and Wilmington, North Carolina; the long walk from the bus depot to their mother's house—remained vivid in his memory, like a dream that lingers through the morning, shadowing everything.

He'd always known he'd see his father again. It was part of the structure of his life, the knowledge that Ken Kimble was somewhere in the world. Once, in college, he'd spent a spring break in Florida with some buddies. All that week he'd looked over his shoulder, waiting for the man to appear. Then, a few years ago, his sister Jody had seen Kimble's photo in the metro section of the *Post*. Apparently the man was living in Washington, a big-shot real estate developer. Charlie was a photographer for the *Baltimore Sun,* sent on assignments all over Maryland and northern Virginia. It seemed inevitable that their paths would cross. It was just a matter of time.

A thousand times he'd imagined their meeting. Always in a public place, always with an audience: he wanted the world to know what Kimble had done. He knew exactly what he'd say when the man introduced himself. *What a coincidence. My father was named Ken Kimble too. He abandoned my mother with two kids and never paid a dime of child support.* He imagined the man speechless, mute with shame.

He'd been working in his darkroom when the phone rang.

"This is Dinah Kimble," said a woman's voice. "Your father's wife."

Buzzing in his ears, an industrial sound. He saw that everything in his life had led to this moment.

"Are you still there?" she asked.

"I'm here," he said.

"Your sister gave me this number." She hesitated. "I'm sorry to bother you. I thought you'd want to know." There was a long pause. "He's had a heart attack."

He could have cut her off then. *I don't care,* he could have said. *I don't want to see him.* Something stopped him. Only later did he realize what it was.

Ken Kimble was getting old. If he didn't see the man now, he might not get another chance.

THEY DROVE to Great Falls on Thanksgiving morning, Charlie and his girlfriend Anne-Sophie. He fumbled in his pocket for a cigarette.

"Charlie!" she cried. "What's wrong with you?" He hadn't smoked in a year. He'd bought a pack just for the occasion.

She rolled down her window. "You were doing so well."

They rode in silence. Once, twice, he glanced across the seat at her. That summer they'd gone to visit her parents in France. She'd been a different person there, gesturing, laughing, her mouth moving in a strange way. It explained certain things about her face, the way her lips always appeared to be pursed, even when she was asleep. He'd fallen in love with the shape of her mouth. Now he knew that half the women in France had it too.

"You never kept in contact with him?" she asked.

"I haven't seen him since I was eleven years old."

She frowned. "How did he find you?"

"His wife tracked down Jody. I didn't get the details."

"He has married again?"

Charlie laughed. "He's always married. This is the third wife that I know of. There may have been others I didn't hear about."

The exits flew past.

"It's a special situation," said Anne-Sophie. She'd never quite grasped the English usage of the word.

"Very special," said Charlie.

"Does your mother know you are seeing him?"

"Good Christ, no. You can't mention his name in her presence." He inhaled deeply. There was a pleasant tingling around his mouth, a familiar jolt to the nerves along his spine.

"But they are divorced a long time," said Anne-Sophie.

"You don't know my mother." He signaled to change lanes. "She fell to pieces when he left. She never recovered from it."

"Is that why you hate him so much?"

"It's on the list." He tossed his cigarette out the window. "My mother had no business raising kids on her own. She's like a child herself. He was married to her for eight years; he must have known that. He left us with her anyway."

Anne-Sophie watched him. "Is this the reason you don't want to get married?"

"Do we have to discuss that now?"

She stared out the window.

"I'm sorry," he said. "It's not a good time."

"It's never a good time," she said.

GREAT FALLS was a money town. Charlie had gone there once to photograph a disgraced fed, a corrupt cabinet secretary indicted for taking bribes. He remembered the massive new houses crowded together, the wide dead-end streets, the green lawns reeking of herbicide.

This is a terrible mistake, he thought. Years before, he'd been flying home from an assignment in California when the plane made an emergency landing in a field of onions. Time slowed; he spoke softly to the hysterical grandmother sitting next to him and helped her assume the crash position. Before, he'd wondered how he'd behave in the face of death, whether he'd panic or pray. That day he discovered that his deepest instinct was to be pleasant.

He found the address easily, an imposing Tudor at the end of a cul-de-sac. He parked in the curving driveway and stared at the house.

"Is everything okay?" said Anne-Sophie.

"Fine," he said. The man was loaded, that much was clear. He thought of his mother, working for minimum wage at Shively's Cleaners in town. They'd kept her on for years despite her constant lateness, her frequent absences. On her slim paychecks she'd fed and clothed him and Jody, with no help from Kimble. She was too proud to sue for child support or alimony; she'd never asked their father for a dime. Charlie thought of the speech he'd prepared, how he'd shame the man, make him admit every despicable thing he'd done. *You kidnapped us. You lied to my mother. You said you were coming back.*

"Ten minutes," he told Anne-Sophie. "Ten minutes, and we're out of here."

They walked up the curved driveway, lined with bare trees. Anne-Sophie wore a thin sweater, leather pants that cupped her behind. Charlie chafed under his collar. She had talked him into a tie.

He lifted the brass knocker and held it for a second. He could still leave, turn around and drive away. They could call the house from a pay phone somewhere. *This is Charlie. I'm sorry. I couldn't make it.*

"What's the matter?" said Anne-Sophie.

"Nothing," he said.

He knocked firmly at the door. Music inside, soft footsteps; then a woman opened the door.

"Welcome," she said. "I'm Dinah." She looked about Charlie's age—tall and blond, the sort of woman he'd turn around to look at in the street. He felt suddenly sick.

"Charlie Kimble," he said, extending his hand.

"Welcome." A ray of sunlight cut sideways across her face, lighting the pale down of her cheek. A strange flush covered half her face. Her hand was warm and surprisingly strong.

"Come in." She was barefoot, her jeans streaked dark at the thighs, as if she'd wiped her hands on them. "The thermometer just popped. Charlie, can you carve a turkey?"

"Sure," he said.

They passed through a large dining room: high ceilings, golden wood floors. A long table was set with china and silver. His house, Charlie thought. I'm in his house.

"Ken and Jody are in the living room," said Dinah. "Brendan is upstairs."

Blood pounded in his ears; Jody had told him there was a son. He thought again of the plummeting airplane, hurling toward the earth.

They went into the living room. Ken Kimble sat in a leather armchair near the fire. He got briskly to his feet.

"Charlie." He offered his hand.

Charlie's heart raced. They stood eye to eye; their hands were the same size.

"Good of you to come." Kimble stood very straight, his chinos sharply creased. For an instant Charlie remembered him lean and suntanned, running along the beach.

Charlie nodded. He felt paralyzed, incapable of speech. Sweat trailed down his back.

Jody rose from the sofa. She wore a skirt and high heels, a phenomenon he hadn't witnessed in years. Even dressed up, she looked like what she was: an athletic, horse-loving tomboy with muscular legs and a round, open face.

"Charlie," she said, embracing him. "It's about time."

"Hey, Jo." He clasped her quickly, grateful to turn his back on the man. Then he turned to the wife.

"Didn't you need some help with the turkey?"

DINAH LED Charlie into the kitchen, an ache in her throat. How alike they looked: the same long face, the same nose and forehead and jaw. Jody favored her mother, red-haired and buxom. Charlie was the picture of Ken.

He stood at the window, examining the shiny leaves of a

bromeliad that bloomed in a corner. He seemed more interested in her plants than he'd been in his father.

"I'm so glad you're here," she said. "We both are."

"Thanks." He looked ready to run, like an animal caught in a trap.

"Let's have a look at that turkey," she said.

Together they lifted the bird out of the roaster. The skin was golden brown; dark juices pooled in the pan.

"It's huge," said Charlie.

"You sound like your father." He said nothing. A spot of red appeared in each cheek.

Dinah tilted the roaster and poured the drippings into a saucepan. "He's doing much better. He was pretty weak at first. Exhausted. But he seems to have his energy back."

Charlie stared at the floor. A flush crept up from his collar.

"That's good," he said finally.

"I'm sorry," said Dinah. "This is all so bizarre. It must be very confusing for you."

"I'm not sure why I'm here." At last his eyes met hers. "I haven't seen your husband in twenty years. He's a complete stranger to me."

Your husband. The coldness of the words shocked her.

"That's a long time," she said.

Charlie took the knife from her hands and inspected the turkey; he made a neat incision into the breast. A lock of hair spilled over his brow—thick and curly, a dark auburn. That, at least, was his mother's.

"Your hair got darker," she said without thinking.

He stared at her quizzically. His cheeks were now violently red, as though he'd been slapped. "How would you know?"

She took a deep breath. "I knew you when you were little. You and Jody. You probably don't remember."

He frowned.

"I was Dinah Whitacre then."

"Dinah," he repeated. Then his brow cleared. "The baby-sitter?"

"Yes," she said, relieved. "I was going to tell you on the phone, but I wasn't sure how you'd react."

"The baby-sitter." He began to laugh. "He married the baby-sitter."

Her cheeks burned. "That was years later, of course."

Charlie laughed harder, a deep sound that ended in a cough. He seemed to be choking. Finally he dabbed at his eyes.

"I don't know why I'm laughing," he said.

"It's quite a coincidence," she admitted, turning away.

"I'm sorry," he said. "That was rude. I didn't mean to offend you."

"It's okay." She busied herself at the stove, heating the pan drippings for gravy. When anyone asked how she and Ken had met, she jokingly described it as a hit-and-run. The details of that afternoon outside Emile's—the ice, her broken ankle, the drive to the hospital—came easily to her, the words familiar from years of repetition, like a hymn learned in childhood. Yet she never told the other part of the story; even their oldest friends weren't aware that Dinah and Ken had known each other before. *He married the baby-sitter.* She'd never thought of her marriage in quite those terms. It sounded to her like the stock plot of a porno film, incredible and slightly obscene.

"How is your mother?" she asked, changing the subject. "Ken told me once that she'd moved to the country. That was years ago."

"She's still there. Not much has changed with her." His eyes met hers. "She still drinks."

Dinah thought of her last evening baby-sitting at the Kimbles'. Ken had already left by then, run off God knew where with one of his students. Mrs. Kimble came home late that night, wet and bedraggled, her shoes in her hand. At the time Dinah had suspected, but wasn't sure, that the woman was drunk.

"She drinks?" she asked, stirring the gravy.

"Has for years. Since they got divorced." He seemed to speak more easily now that her back was turned.

"I'm sorry," she said softly. "I didn't know."

"It's not the kind of thing he would have told you." He handed her the platter of turkey.

"No," she agreed. "It isn't."

They brought the food to the table: turkey, potatoes, cranberries, stuffing. Odors rose from the table, familiar as rain; Charlie thought of his grandma Helen's table, laden with food. It astonished him, that Thanksgiving dinner could smell the same even here.

He heard footsteps on the stairs.

"Brendan," Dinah called. "Come and meet Charlie."

The kid appeared on the stairs, like a wild animal lured by food. He was nearly Charlie's height but much heavier, with pudgy forearms and big soft hands. He had an odd haircut, long on top, shaved around the sides. A crop of pimples bloomed near his mouth.

"Hi," said Charlie.

"Hey." The kid was badly, expensively dressed: baggy jeans, a sweater with an emblem over the chest. His high-top sneakers were perfectly clean, as if they'd lived their lives indoors.

"Do you care where I sit?" he asked his mother. His voice was deep and slurry, his mouth full of braces.

"Wherever you want," said Dinah.

The kid sat heavily in a chair. He kept his head down as the others trickled in: Jody, Kimble, Anne-Sophie. Only his eyes moved, following Anne-Sophie's ass in the leather pants. Charlie wanted to laugh. He remembered that age, the world full of female parts, how one of his mother's hairstyling magazines could keep him busy in the bathroom for a month. For you, pal, he thought. Happy Thanksgiving.

They arranged themselves around the table: Kimble at the head, Anne-Sophie next to him. Charlie sat at the opposite end next to Dinah, avoiding her eyes.

"Would anyone like to say a blessing?" she asked.

"Not me," said Kimble. "I got out of that racket years ago."

That racket, Charlie thought. How inspiring.

"Charlie?" said Dinah.

"No, thanks," he mumbled, coloring.

She shrugged. "Let's dig in, then."

The dishes circulated. Kimble decorated his plate with small dollops of vegetables and stuffing, a slice of corn bread. Then he mixed the foods together with a swirl of his fork. Charlie felt a flash of recognition, like a sudden headache: the tiny kitchen of their house in Richmond, his father mixing meat and potatoes in a single pile. He felt something break in him, a flat stone skipping across the surface, sinking to the bottom.

"I'm sorry your boyfriend couldn't make it," Dinah told Jody. "Russell, isn't it?"

"He's not feeling well," said Jody. "The flu, I think."

Flu, my ass, Charlie thought. Russell was a married doctor Jody had met at work; he was probably at home, celebrating the holiday with his wife and kids. Jody had been saying for years that the marriage was on the verge of collapse. He wondered if she still believed it.

Dinah filled the wineglasses; at the other end of the table, Kimble chatted with Anne-Sophie. He was done with commercial development, he told her; made his money and got out while the getting was good. He was working on a new project, subsidized housing for low-income families. "In my dotage," he said, as if he were so confident of his youthfulness that he could afford to make fun of his age.

"You're retired?" said Anne-Sophie. "I can't believe it."

Kimble beamed. "Semi-retired. I'm sixty-five, sixty-six in January. Dinah is my child bride."

Charlie stared at his plate.

"I read somewhere that the French have a formula," said Kimble. "Have you heard this? For marital happiness. The woman should be half the man's age, plus seven years."

Jody giggled. "That's silly."

"It's the ideal over there." Kimble winked at Anne-Sophie. "Am I right?"

"I've heard something like that," she said. "But it's a joke. It isn't serious."

"Of course not." Jody doused her potatoes with gravy. "It doesn't make sense. If both people are the right age now, what happens in ten years? The numbers don't work."

Kimble smiled. "In ten years Dinah will be too old for me."

Charlie glanced at Dinah.

"Have some more stuffing," she said, handing him the plate.

"I don't get it," said Jody. "Then how is anything supposed to last? More than a couple of years, I mean."

"It's not serious," Anne-Sophie repeated. "It's just an expression. Something old men like to say."

Ken Kimble laughed.

It seemed to Charlie that everything froze at that moment: the chewing and passing, the silverware noises.

"My dear," Kimble said to Anne-Sophie. His cheeks looked pink and healthy; his eyes twinkled. "How on earth can you blame us?"

Charlie felt a flash of heat. He pushed his chair away from the table.

"Is that what happened with you and my mother?" he asked.

"Excuse me?" said Kimble.

"Charlie, *don't,*" said Jody. She had the same transparent red-head's skin as their mother. Her cheeks looked full of blood.

"Don't what? I'd like to get in on this conversation." He turned to face Kimble; he felt strangely calm. "How old was my mother when you married her?"

"I don't recall," said Kimble.

"She was eighteen," said Charlie. "And you were how old?"

"Thirty-two," he said stiffly.

Charlie gave a low whistle. "A little young for you, no? Even by the French standard? But then, you like them young."

"Stop it!" Jody cried. A tear ran down her cheek.

"What do you want from me?" said Kimble.

Charlie's heart was loud. "I'd like you to explain yourself."

"What good would that do?"

Charlie laughed. "Absolutely none. But it might be entertaining."

Kimble spread his hands. "Son, I have nothing to say."

Charlie got to his feet.

"I'm going to get some air," he said. "And I'm not your son."

. . .

ALL ALONG the cul-de-sac the houses radiated light. Imported sedans lined the curving road. Charlie was startled to see his own car in the driveway. It seemed that days had passed since he'd driven down from Baltimore; weeks, months. The light was waning. In another hour it would be dark.

He sat on the front step. The wind had kicked up; he smelled pavement, exhaust, snow on the way. The fabric of his shirt breathed turkey and cooking herbs. A catering truck idled in the next driveway; young men in white shirts loaded it with boxes. That was more what he'd expected from a Great Falls Thanksgiving: hors d'oeuvres, catered food. Dinah had surprised him with her blue jeans, her plants hanging in the sunny windows, her copper pots steaming on the stove.

He inhaled deeply, picturing the way she'd once looked: the blond hair in braids, the purple stain covering her eye and cheek. She was a girl then, barely a teenager. He wondered, briefly, how it all happened, how she and the old man had gotten together. Then he realized he didn't want to know.

He walked around to the rear of the house. The lawn was impeccably tended, lined with shrubs. A dormant garden sat out back. In the distance he saw flashes of light, cars speeding along Leesburg Pike. The yard would be secluded in summer, protected by lush woods. Everything was dead now, the trees starved and bare.

He glanced back at the house, the kitchen windows ablaze with light. A figure crouched beneath the underpinnings of the deck. It was the kid, trying to light a cigarette.

"Hey," said Charlie.

The kid put the cigarette in his pocket. He looked stunned. He thinks I'm going to tell his mother, Charlie thought. He thinks I'm an adult.

He reached into his pocket and tossed the kid his lighter. "Try this."

The kid stared at him for a second, then took the cigarette from his pocket. He tossed the lighter back to Charlie, who took out his own pack.

"Thanks," said the kid.

They leaned against the house and smoked, hiding from the wind. Charlie was grateful for the cold, the bricks at his back, the quiet. The silence soaked in like an ointment.

"Hell of a dinner," he said finally. "Your mom can cook."

"Yeah," said the kid. "She's good."

Charlie tugged at his tie and stuffed it in his pocket. "I'm sorry about all that in there. You shouldn't have to hear that. For all I know he's a great father to you."

The wind whistled through the bare trees. The kid smoked his cigarette down to the filter. His big hands were as soft as a girl's, the nails bitten to the quick.

"He isn't," he said finally.

"Isn't what?"

"A great father."

Charlie watched him.

"He's never home." The kid shrugged. "Fine by me; I like it that way. But my mom is alone too much."

Charlie squashed his cigarette with the heel of his shoe. "Mine too," he said.

The kid flicked his cigarette butt into the yard. "Did she ever get married again?"

"Nah." Charlie shrugged. "I think he cured her on marriage forever."

The kid took another cigarette from his pocket. "Your girl-friend's pretty," he said. "Where's she from?"

Charlie tossed him the lighter. "France. She's French."

The kid lit his cigarette. "I was going to take French. I took Spanish instead."

"How do you like it?" said Charlie.

"I'm failing. It sucks."

"I failed French. It sucked too."

The kid laughed, a barking sound. He kicked at the ground with his sneakered toe. "Is it true you haven't seen him since you were six years old? That's what my mom said."

"Almost." He was surprised, somehow, that she'd told him. "We went to visit him once when he was living in Florida, me and my sister. I was ten. We stayed for a couple of days. Then we ran away."

"No shit?" The kid seemed impressed. "My mom didn't tell me that."

"She probably doesn't know. He was married to someone else then." He thought of Joan in her flowered caftans, Joan who'd bought them flip-flops and taken them to Disney World.

"The one that died?" said Brendan.

Charlie stared at him. "She died?"

"Yeah. She had cancer. That's what my mom says."

Charlie nodded. He felt dizzy and slightly sick, nerves and nicotine.

"What was she like?" the kid asked.

"Joan?" He remembered the sixty dollars he'd stolen from her purse. He'd felt bad about it for years afterward.

"She was nice," he said.

. . . .

DINAH CLEARED the dishes from the table. Brendan had left a slice of turkey on his plate; he'd excused himself after Charlie's outburst at the table. *How old was my mother when you married her? But then, you like them young.* The revelation had stunned her; she'd never imagined Ken's first wife was so young—eighteen when he'd married her, a teenager. What sort of man falls in love with a teenager? she wondered. And then, not for the first time: What kind of man is he?

She cleared the stuffing and sweet potatoes, brushed away the succotash and corn bread crumbs surrounding Ken's plate. Everyone had eaten well; they'd all had seconds except Charlie's girlfriend. Dinah thought of the girl as she'd been at dinner, absorbed in Ken's stories: deals he'd brokered, others he'd wisely passed up. He'd warmed under her attention, laughed as he hadn't in weeks. At one time Dinah would have been jealous. Now she was only grateful. It pleased her to see Ken interested in something besides his work, his failing health. He hadn't mentioned his blood pressure all day.

She went back to the dining room for the platter of turkey. The gravy boat had left an oily ring on the tablecloth. Charlie appeared in the doorway.

"Let me get that." He took the platter and followed her to the kitchen. He smelled of outdoors and cigarettes; he radiated cold.

"Where is everybody?" he said. "You shouldn't be stuck with the dishes after all that cooking."

"I don't mind. I enjoy it." She transferred the leftover turkey to a plastic container. "I rarely get to cook a real dinner. Your father—" She stopped herself, reddening. "Ken works late, and he hates a big meal before bed."

Charlie filled the sink with hot water. "I thought he was retired."

"He was, for about a week." She put the leftover turkey in the refrigerator. "After he sold the brokerage, he started a nonprofit company. He buys old houses and fixes them up, then sells them to poor families for cheap. He even helps them get mortgages. It's a terrific project."

"No kidding," said Charlie. "What's in it for him?"

Adulation, she thought. His picture in the paper. He gets to be a hero. Ken never spoke of the families he helped; he talked only about making deals, the way he always had. She remembered him in bed the night before his heart attack. *Miz Watkins and her struggling family.*

"Well," she said, "he doesn't make a dime off of it, if that's what you mean."

Charlie smirked. "So he does it for the satisfaction? Out of the goodness of his heart?"

"You could say that." Dinah scraped the plates at the sink. When she looked up, Charlie was staring at her.

"What?" she said.

"You look different."

Dinah smiled. "You mean my birthmark. I had laser surgery many years ago."

"Why?"

She cocked her head. "That's funny. I've never had to explain it to anyone before."

"Sorry. I shouldn't have asked."

"No. It's a great question." She stacked the plates in the dishwasher. "My whole life I thought something was terribly wrong with me. I figured everyone else thought so too."

"I didn't." He shrugged. "I was just a kid, but I never gave it any thought at all. To me it was just the way you looked." He placed a pot in the drainer.

"It was a fantastic dinner," he said. "Thank you."

"My pleasure. We have so little family, I rarely get a chance."

She sensed him stiffen next to her.

"I'm sorry," she said. "That was presumptuous."

He draped the dishcloth over the faucet. "He's not my father, you know. I don't think of him that way. I never will."

"But he *is*," she said. "Like it or not, he *is*."

"How do you figure that?" His eyes met hers. "Look, I know you mean well. But you don't know the first thing about me."

"So tell me," said Dinah.

"What do you want to know? The man walked out when I was six years old and never looked back. And I won't even get into what he's done to my mother." Charlie turned to face her. "The point is, he's never given a damn about me or Jody, from the time we were little."

Dinah's face burned. She'd hoped, naively, that the family could be reunited, that it wasn't too late. She was ashamed of her blindness.

"Jody called him once," said Charlie. "Did he ever tell you that?"

"No."

"About ten years ago. She was in college then. She had a few drinks to work up her nerve. She left a message on his machine at work."

Dinah frowned. Ten years ago she and Ken were already married, living in the house in Georgetown. He'd never mentioned a call from his daughter.

"What did she say?" she asked.

"She gave him hell. I guess she was pretty bombed. She probably didn't make any sense."

"Did Ken call her back?"

"No," said Charlie. "He didn't."

From the next room Dinah heard Ken's voice, female laughter; the false enthusiasm of a TV sportscaster. She was mortified: for defending Ken when she and Charlie both knew better; for her pathetic attempt at a family Thanksgiving. Ken's children had suffered enough.

"Oh, Charlie," she said. "I'm so sorry."

He shrugged. "The only thing I can't figure out is, why now? Why did he invite us here, after all these years?"

Because he cares about you, she started to say, knowing it was a lie. But she was sick of covering for Ken. Charlie was a grown man; he ought to know the truth.

"Because I insisted," she said, her heart hammering. "I thought it would be good for him."

"It figures," said Charlie.

"You're right," said Dinah. "He doesn't care one way or the other."

"I DON'T SEE why we had to leave so suddenly," said Anne-Sophie. It was raining again, the visibility poor as they merged onto the Beltway. "Before the dessert. It was very rude. You didn't even say good-bye."

"I said good-bye to Dinah." The name sounded strange in his mouth: the baby-sitter, his father's wife. *I'll be in touch,* she'd told him. Then she'd kissed him on the cheek.

"I thought he was charming," said Anne-Sophie. "He speaks French. Did you know that?"

"No," said Charlie. "I don't know anything about him."

They rode in silence.

"I talked to the son," said Charlie.

She smiled. "I didn't know he could talk."

"He's a smart kid. Smarter than I was at that age. He has no illusions about the old man, I can tell you that."

"Old?" said Anne-Sophie. "That's funny. To me he didn't seem old."

Charlie thought of the trail of corn and lima beans on the tablecloth, Dinah cleaning up after the man every day of her life, nursing him in his declining years. His whole life Ken Kimble had played musical wives; she was the lucky one sitting when the music stopped. Congratulations, he thought. You win. And he's quite a prize.

"I feel sorry for Dinah," he said. "In a couple of years she's going to be wiping drool from his chin."

Anne-Sophie shrugged. "It's an exchange. She has a beautiful house, a marriage, a family. For a woman that can be enough."

Charlie stared at her. "You're joking. Sharing a bed with that disgusting old man?"

"People get older. It's a part of life. Certainly Dinah understood this when she married him." She reached for his hand. "It seems to me she has a good life."

Charlie grunted. "Some life. You'd never settle for that kind of arrangement, would you?"

"If my choice is to spend the rest of my life alone?" Her eyes met his. "I don't know, Charlie. Perhaps I would."

. . .

DINAH WAS RINSING the wineglasses when Ken came into the kitchen.

"Good Lord," he said, eyeing the carcass on the counter. "That's a lot of leftovers. We'll be eating turkey till Christmas."

"It freezes well," she said.

He opened the cupboard above the sink and brought down a basket full of bottles; he counted out pills—a beta blocker, Lovastatin, a baby aspirin to thin his blood—then swallowed them in a single gulp.

"What happened to Charlie and Anne-Sophie?" he asked. "She got up and left suddenly. She never said good-bye."

Never mind Anne-Sophie, Dinah thought. What about your son?

"They had to leave." She took two pies from the refrigerator, pumpkin and cherry.

"None for me," he said. "I'm stuffed."

She cut into a pie. "Where's Brendan?"

"Haven't seen him. He's probably upstairs, sleeping off all those potatoes. Did you see the stuffing he put away?"

Don't, Dinah thought. Ken had grimaced when Brendan helped himself to seconds; she knew she'd hear about it later. "It's Thanksgiving."

"Every day's Thanksgiving for that kid." He replaced the basket of pills in the cupboard. "All those starches."

"He's still growing."

"He eats too damn much."

"*Stop it!* Do you hear me? Not another word."

Ken frowned. "What's the matter with you?"

"Me?" She put down the knife. "Charlie just walked out of here. You'll probably never see him again. And all you care about is what Brendan ate for dinner."

He shrugged. "I didn't tell him to leave. It isn't my fault."

"Nothing's your fault. You've led a blameless life."

"You're not making any sense," he said calmly.

She turned her back to him. "Get out of my kitchen."

T he locker room was nearly empty at that hour; the humid air smelled of shampoo, the showers of the early morning athletes. A few women lingered at the mirror, drawing lipstick mouths. Dinah unwrapped her ankle from its neoprene brace and stepped into the shower. She'd played tennis that morning, her first match since Ken's heart attack. After the Thanksgiving debacle she'd stopped playing nursemaid. He seemed to miss the attention; within a week he went back to work.

She stretched her arms overhead, grateful for blood and heat. Her opponent, a woman she knew from the club league, had a weak serve; Dinah had beaten her handily, barely breaking a sweat. Her muscles felt hungry inside her skin, starved for movement. She could have played for hours.

She stepped into the shower. Through the wall she heard deep voices, laughter from the men's locker room. She imagined Wayne on the other side of the wall, soaping his arms and chest. She remembered his body damp and slightly messy, a fragrant chaos of skin and hair. She'd noticed his truck in the parking lot and hoped they'd cross paths; she couldn't bring herself to call him. I'm a fool, she thought, remembering their conversation in his truck, the way she'd defended Ken. *He's my husband. He's family.*

She dried off and dressed. At the mirror she daubed color corrector over her left temple and cheekbone—green to neutralize the redness—then covered her whole face with foundation. Normally she ran out of the locker room barefaced, but she was meeting Ken at his office. They were going to Emile's to celebrate their anniversary. She'd planned the lunch weeks ago, before Thanksgiving. Now she dreaded it.

Outside, the morning was clear, the warmest December on record; for three days temperatures had climbed into the seventies. She rolled open the sunroof as she wove through the city. The Homes Project maintained offices just off Connecticut Avenue, in a renovated row house near the bus line. She found a parking space on the street and walked two blocks to the office. An evergreen wreath hung on the front door, losing its needles in the heat.

She went inside. Ken's old office—the top floor of a mirrored tower in Crystal City, Virginia—had intimidated her; she liked this place much better. The waiting room was small and cluttered, set with folding chairs. A little girl squatted at a toy workbench, banging with a plastic hammer. A red-haired black woman sat in the corner, an infant sleeping on her shoulder.

"How you doing, Miz Kimble?" said Val, the receptionist. She sat at a folding table overlooking the waiting room, arranging printed forms into neat stacks. A hand-lettered sign dangled from the table: "If You Need Help, Ask."

"I'm fine," said Dinah. "Is Ken ready for lunch?"

"He's in with the reverend right now. You want to set and wait?"

Dinah took a seat next to the plastic workbench. "Hi, honey," she said to the little girl, Val's granddaughter. "What are you making?"

"A car," said the child. She was absorbed and carelessly beautiful, her dark hair twisted into a hundred tiny braids. "I'm building Grandma a car."

Val laughed. "You hear that? I'm getting a car."

Across the room the red-haired woman eyed Dinah from head to foot. The baby breathed softly on her shoulder.

"He's a good sleeper," Dinah observed.

The woman shrugged. "He got to be. He been waiting all morning." There was something familiar in her wide cheekbones, the sharp cut of her jaw. Dinah remembered where she'd seen her: at the Man of the Year dinner the previous spring.

In the rear office a door creaked open: men's voices, heavy shoes on the bare floor.

"That's him," said Val. "Miz Kimble, you go on back."

Dinah got to her feet. The red-haired woman exhaled loudly, an angry rush of air.

"I'm sorry, Miz Watkins, but you got to wait," said Val.

"That's okay, Val," said Dinah. "She was here first. I'm not in a hurry."

"You go on back," Val repeated, in a voice that meant business.

Dinah went down a long corridor lined with stacks of cardboard boxes. Ken hunched over one of them, flipping through a manila folder.

"Hi there," said Dinah.

He looked up. "What are you doing here?" There was an unpleasant edge to his voice.

"Lunch," she said. "Our anniversary. Remember?"

"Now?" He looked flushed, irritated.

Dinah's jaw tightened. "It's lunchtime, isn't it?"

"I can't today. I've got someone here."

She peered over his shoulder. The office door was slightly ajar. A grizzled black man sat opposite the desk.

"Reverend Blanks?" she asked.

Ken glanced at his watch. "I'll call you later. It could be a late night."

"Fine." She turned to go. "There's a woman waiting for you out front. She's been waiting all morning."

"Let her wait." He went into his office and shut the door.

Out in the lobby the red-haired woman was gone.

MAS TREES, the sign read. FRESH CUT.

Dinah and Brendan parked in the lot. The air had turned cold; the car left a trail of vapor behind them.

Three years in a row they'd come to this busy intersection in Reston, where a family of tree farmers unloaded their pines and firs. The trees were overpriced and not very fresh, but deep in the suburbs there was nowhere else to go. When Dinah was a girl, she and her father had driven into the country for their trees, an all-day proposition involving lunch in a particular diner, roast beef sandwiches and gravy; then much deliberation before her father finally cut down the tree and loaded it into the truck. At home would be supper and Christmas carols, Perry Como and Bing Crosby on the hi-fi. Her father would sing along as he strung the tree with lights, his gruff baritone surprisingly tuneful. The trees were always too large, bushy and shapeless, but he delighted in their size. "Another winner," he'd pronounce once the lights were hung. "Another Whitacre special." She remembered her father young and strong, tossing the tree onto the truck as if it were a bag of old clothes; the early sunset as they drove back to Richmond, the pale winter sky. Her parents were far away now, living in a retirement community in Arizona; but she brought out the memory each year to admire, like a beloved Christmas ornament. It saddened her to think what Brendan would someday remember: a parking lot across from the Home Depot, traffic noise and diesel fumes.

But he didn't seem sad. He moved fast down the aisles of Scotch pines and Douglas firs, whistling. He was taller than most of the trees, nearly a man in his heavy jacket. They'd just come from the orthodontist; he'd suffered silently while the doctor tightened his braces. Now he seemed pleased to be outdoors, invigorated by the cold, his usual lethargy gone.

She'd hoped this year would be different, that Ken, somehow changed by his illness, would come with them to get the tree; but he was working late, as usual. They'd argued about it that morning while Brendan was still asleep, their harsh whispers more violent, somehow, than shouting.

"Just once," she rasped. "Just once you can come home at a reasonable hour."

"Christmas is a week away," said Ken. "I can't drop everything to get ready for some bullshit holiday."

Finally he'd promised to be home by nine, to hang the Christmas lights. It was better than nothing.

"Hey, Mom," Brendan called out. He struggled with a blue spruce, tall and shapely. "What do you think?"

"Nice," she said.

He took an awkward step back to examine the tree, still holding it upright with his outstretched arm.

"It's a girl tree," he said. "If you were a tree, this would be you."

Dinah laughed. There *was* something feminine about it, the graceful curves, the pear-shaped fullness at the bottom.

"Here's you," she said. She crossed the aisle and pointed to a towering Douglas fir. The tree was broad but shapely, the trunk straight and true. There were no bare spots. "The Brendan tree."

"You think so?" A rare smile pulled at his lips, red and slightly stretched from his braces.

"Absolutely. It could use a little trim up top"—a dig at his hair, which he'd decided to grow—"but all things considered, it's a pretty handsome tree."

Brendan stepped back and eyed the tree.

"You're right," he said finally. The smile cracked open, a glorious flash of silver and light. Dinah's throat tightened. "It's a pretty handsome tree."

They hauled the Brendan tree to the cashier. A man in a parka buzzed the stem with a power saw. "Fresh cut," he said. "Takes up more water."

Dinah reached for her wallet. A familiar voice called her name.

"Whoa," said Wayne Day. "That's a monster you've got there."

"Wayne. What are you doing here?" It was odd to see him off the court, his sinewy limbs hidden by street clothes. He wore the same corduroy jacket as Brendan, though Wayne's was old and worn and Brendan's was stiff and new.

"I've got my sister's kids," said Wayne. Over his shoulder Dinah saw the two little girls, laughing and racing through the rows of Christmas trees. He turned to Brendan. "Nice jacket," he said, offering his hand.

To her surprise Brendan smiled again, the same brilliant flash of silver. "Hey," he said, shaking hands. Years after he'd quit the club's juniors tennis team, Brendan admitted that for a coach, Wayne wasn't an asshole.

Wayne eyed the Brendan tree, lying like a fallen soldier. "You need some help with that thing? I've got rope in my truck."

"That's okay," Dinah started to stay, but Brendan interrupted.

"Cool," he said. "You can take Mom's end."

She watched them carry the tree to the car. Brendan covered the roof with an old sheet from the trunk; then, together, they hefted the tree. Wayne ran a rope through the open windows and wrapped it several times around the tree. He cut the rope with a pocketknife and wiped his hands on his jeans.

"Don't drive too fast," he told Dinah. "Up to fifty you'll be fine. Beyond that I can't guarantee."

"Thanks," said Dinah. He needed a shave; the skin of his throat looked rough and warm. A cloud of breath floated from his mouth.

"We should get home," she said. "Ken is waiting to put up the lights."

His eyes scanned her face. She'd put on makeup, knowing Ken would be waiting for them back at the house.

"I like you better the other way," he said. Without warning he bent and kissed her cheek. "Merry Christmas."

WHEN THEY pulled into the driveway, the house was dark.

"Your dad was supposed to be home," said Dinah. "To hang the lights." Her voice broke; she felt Brendan's stare. She never criticized Ken to him, never let Brendan say a word against his father. This time something caught in her. Tears burned behind her eyes.

Brendan reached for her hand. "It's all right, Mom. I can hang them." He stepped out of the car and began to untie the rope. "We'll manage without him."

They dragged the tree across the threshold and into the living room, leaving a trail of pine needles. In the hallway stood boxes of ornaments that Dinah had brought down from the attic.

"Where's the stand?" said Brendan. He rooted through a box and found it, the same painted metal one Dinah's father had used. Dinah held the tree upright while Brendan screwed the hooks into the base of the tree. It was a slow process, requiring many small adjustments, but he didn't seem to mind. He whistled softly under his breath.

"Done," he said finally. They stepped back to admire the tree.

"Carols," said Brendan. "We forgot the carols."

Dinah located the record in a box of tinsel. The year before she'd bought a copy on compact disc, but she missed the slow skip of the needle, the gentle static. "'O come all ye faithful,'" Perry Como crooned. "'Joyful and triumphant.'" Dinah hummed along with the record. Brendan rooted through another box for the Christmas lights. The telephone rang.

That bastard, she thought. He's not coming.

"Your dad," she said. "Probably stuck in traffic." She picked up the phone. "Hello?"

The line crackled. Loudspeaker voices droned in the background. She watched Brendan on the living room floor, patiently untangling a mess of wires.

"Ken?" she said. "Where are you?"

"At the airport." He sounded rushed, distracted. "I know this is short notice, but—"

"The airport?"

Brendan looked up sharply.

"I have to go to Florida," he said. Voices hummed around him; in the distance, a baby cried. "It's these deadbeat Cuban tenants.

My property manager has been trying to evict them, but they won't budge. We have to go to court."

"Florida," Dinah repeated.

"Just for a couple of days. Look, they're calling my flight; I have to go. I'll call you when I get there."

"Where are you staying?" she asked, but it was too late. He'd already hung up the phone.

he next day the phone rang three times. The first caller was Brendan's friend Sean Guthrie, inviting him to play a new computer game. The second, a woman named Charmaine Watkins, looking for Ken. The third, a receptionist in the dermatology department at Georgetown Medical Center, reminding Dinah of her upcoming appointment. Ken had scheduled it for her a few weeks ago, a consultation about the new procedure.

The following day it rang twice. A reporter from the *Washington Post,* hoping to interview Ken. Another call from Charmaine Watkins.

The third day it didn't ring at all.

eason's greetings, Dinah wrote. *Warmest wishes this New Year. Ken, Dinah, and Brendan Kimble.* Her hand shook as she wrote their names. Ken had been gone for four days.

At first she'd been furious, then concerned; she'd imagined him collapsed in an airport, his heart seizing in a crowded airplane. Finally she'd called the police.

"My husband has disappeared," she said. "He has a history of heart disease. I'm afraid something has happened to him."

The sergeant hammered her with questions. Were there marital problems? Had her husband done this sort of thing before?

"No," she'd answered calmly. "Of course not. Never before."

She sealed the envelope. Ken considered it ridiculous to write cards by hand—he said preprinted ones were easier and classier—but Dinah insisted; it was her favorite part of the holidays. One by one she crossed the names off her list: distant cousins, coworkers from her days at Emile's, a few of Ken's business associates. He had no living relatives, other than his children; his only friends were couples they both knew. In all their years of marriage, he'd never sent a Christmas card to Florida, let alone gone back for a visit. Dinah knew he owned property there—a time-share condo in Orlando, apartments near a golf course in Palm Beach—but never before had he mentioned any tenants.

She tucked the cards into her gym bag, to mail on her way to the club. She pulled a jacket over her tennis whites and was halfway out the door when the phone rang. It's about goddamn time, she thought. She grabbed the phone.

"Miz Kimble?" said a woman's voice. "This is Valerie Clark."

"Val." She took a deep breath. Surely Ken's secretary would know how to reach him. "What's up?"

Val hesitated. "Do you have a number where I can reach Mr. Kimble? We got a situation here . . ." Her voice trailed off. "I'm not sure how to handle it."

"I don't know where he is," said Dinah. "I was going to ask you the same question."

Val lowered her voice. "Miz Kimble, there's two gentlemen here. From the Department of Housing and Urban Development. They're asking a lot of questions. I think Mr. Kimble's in some kind of trouble."

"Trouble? What kind of trouble?"

"They want to see all the financial records. All the way back to eighty-nine. At first I said no, but I don't see as how I have any choice."

"Financial records," Dinah repeated. She stared out the window, at the white sky threatening snow.

"If Mr. Kimble calls, tell him I need to talk to him right away," said Val. "Tell him it's an emergency."

"Of course." Dinah's heart raced. "Val, that Charmaine Watkins keeps calling the house. Do you know what she wants?" She heard voices in the background. "Val, are you still there?"

"Miz Kimble, I got to go." Again Val lowered her voice. "About that Charmaine Watkins. She's been after Mr. Kimble for weeks now. He told me not to talk to her. He said she just want to make trouble for him."

She hung up the phone.

THAT AFTERNOON Dinah sat on the living room floor with a cup of coffee, wrapping Christmas presents and listening for Sean Guthrie's Jeep in the driveway. The snow had begun to fly. She wished she'd gone to pick up Brendan herself.

There was nothing to be done. She'd considered, briefly, going downtown to see the HUD people herself, but realized she had nothing to say. She knew little about the Homes Project beyond what she'd told Charlie at Thanksgiving. *It's a terrific project. He doesn't make a dime off of it.* For the first time she wondered if this were true.

Ken still had money. For a man who no longer took a salary or commissions, he had expensive tastes: exquisite clothes, a new Lincoln every year. He spent as freely as he ever had, and encouraged her to do the same. When she hesitated over a large purchase— Brendan's computer, furniture for the guest room—he seemed almost offended. "I'm your husband, Dinah," he'd say. "I've always provided for you." He had an inheritance from his second wife, some successful investments. He did their taxes himself, with the help of an accountant. Dinah's only contribution was signing the return.

They want to see all the financial records. I think Mr. Kimble's in some kind of trouble.

Dinah measured a length of wrapping paper and set to work on the presents. Clothes and books for Brendan, though he would have preferred computer games. Ken was difficult to buy for; he had no hobbies and liked choosing his own clothes. She thought of his elegant shirts, expensively custom-made by a downtown tailor. He'd left them all behind. He'd worn a pinstriped suit the day he left; it was the only thing missing from their bedroom closet.

He'd always been fastidious. She tried to imagine him in Florida wearing the same pants day after day, washing his underwear in a hotel sink. He'd have to send his shirt out every night to be cleaned. He was prone to food stains at the cuffs; in summer, armpit circles, dark stains beneath the collar. Florida would be warm in December. Ken had told her once that he and Joan had barbecued on Christmas.

She put down her coffee and went upstairs.

Ken kept two distinct wardrobes: dark wool suits for fall and winter, linen for summer and spring. The winter clothes he kept in their bedroom; the out-of-season ones, in the guest-room closet.

She went into the guest room, opened the walk-in closet and flipped on the light.

His summer suits and white bucks, his linen trousers and patterned sport shirts were gone.

*C*harlie hadn't always hated Christmas. As a boy, when his grandma Helen was still alive, he'd loved the weeks of preparation, the baking of gingerbread, the occasional, magical appearance of snow. After her death there was no more baking, no more carols; his mother didn't bother with a Christmas tree. She drank more around the holidays; if they were lucky she'd forget the day altogether. That way Charlie could eat dinner with Terence Mabry's family. If Birdie remembered it was Christmas, she'd make him stay at home.

The Mabrys had rabbit stew on Christmas Eve, venison if Terence's father had gotten a deer that year. They had buttered turnips, collards cooked with bacon, a sweet potato pie for dessert. Always under the tree would be a small gift for Charlie, mittens or a scarf. Maple, Terence's stepmother, was an industrious knitter; Terence had more sweaters than he knew what to do with. After dinner Charlie walked home with a good feeling. Then, at home, Jody would be waiting for him on the stoop; their mother would be passed out drunk in the bedroom. He'd hide his new mittens in his coat pocket, ashamed he'd gotten a gift.

As an adult he'd tried other ways of getting through Christmas—
twice he and Anne-Sophie had spent it in Bermuda—but guilt
pulled him back to the house in Montford, to his mother and sister.
There, the holiday unfolded the way it always had. His mother still
drank; he still tried to sneak away for a visit to the Mabrys. There
was only one difference.

Now, when Christmas was over, Charlie was allowed to leave.

ON THE EVENING of December twenty-third, he packed his
overnight bag: clean shirt, socks and underwear, a carton of cigarettes. Until now he'd bought only packs; the carton was an admis-
sion of defeat. He packed aspirin, toothpaste, soap. These were
things you couldn't count on Birdie to have.

His pulse quickened when the phone rang. Anne-Sophie, he
thought; perhaps she'd left something behind. He'd found one of
her cookbooks on his shelf, a hair clip between the cushions of the
sofa. They didn't seem like things she'd come back for.

He picked up the phone.

"Charlie," said a voice. "It's Dinah. I know it's the last minute,
but would you like to join us for Christmas dinner?"

Dinah: Ken Kimble's wife. After the Thanksgiving fiasco, he
figured he'd never hear from her again.

"That's nice of you," he said. "Does—" He broke off. "Does
your husband know you're inviting me?"

"He's out of town."

"For Christmas?" A bell rang downstairs: the frozen dinner he'd
heated in the microwave.

"It's a long story." She paused. "Will you come?"

"I can't." He zipped his overnight bag. "I have plans. I'm going to my mother's."

"How nice. Wish her a Merry Christmas from me."

Like hell I will, he thought. He had no intention of mentioning Ken Kimble to his mother, let alone the man's new wife.

"Brendan enjoyed meeting you," said Dinah.

"He did?" For some reason this pleased him. "I liked him too. He's a good kid."

"Thanks." She seemed reluctant to hang up the phone.

"Okay then," she said finally. "Give my best to Anne-Sophie."

"She's gone." He hadn't told any of his friends, only his sister. Why he felt the urge to tell Kimble's wife, he couldn't begin to explain.

"We broke up," he said. "She moved out last weekend."

"I'm sorry," said Dinah.

"Thanks."

A long pause, the wire humming between them.

"Well, Merry Christmas to you," said Charlie.

He hung up the phone. The house was deathly quiet. A bare branch rattled against the windowpane. Out of town, Charlie thought. What kind of man leaves his wife and kid alone on Christmas?

He went to the kitchen for his frozen dinner and ate in front of the television. When he'd first met Anne-Sophie, this habit had shocked her; after she moved in, they always ate together in the kitchen, a candle on the table between them. Now she'd taken the table with her, the queen-size bed they'd bought together. Charlie kept the stereo and television, the couch, the barbecue grill. They'd agreed easily about who would keep what. They had never wanted the same things.

. . .

HE DROVE to his mother's the day before Christmas. Other years he'd stopped to pick up Jody, but this time they took separate cars. Jody would stay in Montford until New Year's Day, or until Birdie drove her crazy and she left in a huff. When that happened—and it happened nearly every year—Charlie wanted to be as far away as possible.

It was late morning when he turned off the highway, the wan sky streaked with high clouds. He passed frozen fields, barns and houses, chimneys billowing smoke. In summer the fields would green, rise with corn, snow over with cotton. Now, in the low light, he saw only dirty golds, gradations of brown.

The house—his grandfather's house—was set back from the road, at the end of a dirt path that cut through a forest. Charlie nearly missed the turn. The path was overgrown, narrower than he remembered, shrunken by time. The house stood large and cock-eyed, needing paint; bare wood showed through in places, exposed to the damp. A shutter dangled from an upstairs window; it seemed to Charlie the old place was winking at him. When his grandfather was alive, he'd trimmed the shrubs to resemble sheep and rabbits. Since his death the hedge had grown in, forming a solid wall around the house.

He parked in the bare patch behind the house and walked around to the front, stopping to examine the trunk of a poplar. The tree was dead, struck by lightning the previous summer. He'd sent money to have it chopped down, but his mother refused to have strange workmen around, minding her business. He was staring at the tree when Birdie appeared on the porch.

"Charlie?" She patted her hair, slightly matted on one side. "Is it really you?" Her voice was clear and breathless, a love-struck ingenue from the matinees of her youth.

Of course it's me, he thought. Didn't I call and tell you I was coming?

She crossed the porch toward him, arms outstretched. She wore an old barn jacket over a faded housedress.

"Where are your shoes?" he asked.

"For goodness' sake! I must have left them inside." She stepped down from the porch and picked through the frozen grass in her bare feet. She tilted her head, like a girl offering her cheek for a kiss.

"Hi, Mama," said Charlie. Her face was downy and slightly sticky. She smelled of hairspray and something dark and musky, onions perhaps. Her face looked freshly painted: rouge, eye shadow, a round bright mouth like a child's drawing of a flower.

"Merry Christmas!" she chirped. "Merry, merry, merry! Come inside. I have a surprise for you." She took his hand, her nails digging into the flesh of his palm. The porch steps creaked under their weight.

"How you been, Mama?"

"Marvelous. I feel marvelous." She led him through the musty parlor, unchanged from his boyhood; probably uncleaned too. Heavy brocade curtains soaked up the light; thin rugs, worn bare in places, covered the floors. A long crack bisected the plaster wall, a jagged diagonal from floor to ceiling.

"I'm worried about that poplar," he said. "One good storm and it's going to come crashing down on your roof. When are you going to get someone out here to cut it down?"

"Soon," she said. "Just as soon as I get around to it."

The kitchen was bright and slightly malodorous, like food gone bad. The sink towered with dirty dishes; trash overflowed in a corner. On the small table were empty jelly jars, stacks of magazines, a portable television playing a morning talk show. There was a small clearing at one end, just large enough for a single plate.

"Surprise!" she cried.

Charlie looked around, confused.

"I've been baking for you all morning." She watched him expectantly. Her front teeth were smeared with lipstick; her eyes danced. She pointed to a metal tin on top of the stove. "Go on. Have a look."

Charlie opened the tin. Inside was a fruitcake, about eight inches across. It looked slightly burnt. He glanced around the room. It seemed impossible that one small, burnt cake had dirtied every pot and pan in the kitchen.

"Don't I at least get a kiss? After all that baking?"

Again he kissed her cheek.

JODY ARRIVED that afternoon, loaded down with bags from the Food Lion. Charlie helped her carry them from the car. She'd bought bread and milk and coffee, eggs and sausages, a premade frozen lasagna for Christmas dinner. That and all the Christmas trappings the store had to offer: two poinsettias, cookies shaped like Santas, paper plates and napkins printed with reindeer.

"Hi, Ma," said Jody. She looked around for a place to deposit the groceries. Finally she put the bags on the floor.

"Hello yourself." Birdie eyed the grocery bags. "What's all this?"

"I stopped for a few things. In case you didn't make it to the store."

Birdie laughed. "Who has time for the store? I've been baking all morning." She allowed Jody to hug her. "Girls your age don't understand. Baking from scratch takes time."

She stepped back and looked Jody up and down. "What's this you're wearing? A jogging suit?"

Jody smiled sheepishly. "It's comfortable."

"So is a bathrobe," said Birdie. "But this is Christmas Eve! If you're a young Grace Kelly, you can get away with traipsing around in a bathrobe, but the rest of us need to make an effort."

Charlie left them in the kitchen. He walked down the dirt road to the pond, frozen around the edges but still soft in the middle. One winter when it froze completely, he and Terence Mabry had walked clear out to the center and taken turns with an old pair of hockey skates.

The road stopped abruptly and Charlie hiked into the woods, grateful for his work boots, their deep treads gripping the frozen earth. He found the path easily, still worn and smooth after all these years. He and Terence had made it going back and forth to each other's houses. Now there were no children at either house, no one left to play in the woods. He wondered why it hadn't grown over like everything else.

He followed the path to the clearing, brushy now, that Pappy had used as a shooting range. "Not another house for ten miles," he used to brag. "Nothing out there but deer and squirrel and niggers, and if a stray bullet hits one of them, so much the better." The memory shamed him, a part of his grandfather he'd never understood. Pappy had loved Ella Mabry like family, and never came back from town without three chocolate bars, for Jody, Charlie, and Terence. It was only Terence's father he'd objected to. Pappy called him ignorant and lazy, though Curt worked harder than any man Charlie had ever known, year-round at the sawmill in Gretna and farming his own land besides.

Charlie peered through the trees. Lights glowed in the distance. The Mabrys' old bungalow had burned down years before; Curt had replaced it with a double-wide trailer. He'd added on a large front porch, planted the perimeter with rhododendrons and juniper bushes, so that from a distance it looked as permanent as a regular house. Since Maple's death he'd lived there alone, over the objections of Terence and his wife, who had a big new house near the army base in Richmond. In his quiet way, Charlie thought, Curt was as stubborn as Birdie: attached to the house decomposing around her, the floors buckling under the weight of her own dirt and clutter.

He crossed the clearing. Curt's dogs skulked out from behind the trailer, dragging their chains. "Hey, Rex," said Charlie. "Hey, Blondie." They were old yellow dogs, brother and sister, dead ringers for their mother, the original Blondie. Charlie climbed the steps to the porch and knocked at the door.

"Curt? You home? It's Charlie Bell." He'd always been Charlie Bell in Montford; his mother, too, was known by her maiden name. Nobody there had ever called them Kimble.

He heard movement inside the trailer. The door opened with a thin, metallic sound.

"Charlie Bell." Curt was just as Charlie remembered him, small and strong and wiry. They shook hands. Curt's palm was heavy and callused, thirty years of sawmill in that hand.

"I'm down visiting my mother. I was out for a walk and I thought I'd wish you a Merry Christmas."

"Been a long time." Curt glanced at the dogs. "I'm surprised they remember you."

"They got old."

Curt laughed, a deep bubbling sound. "Like all of us," he said. "Come on in. I just made coffee."

He limped slightly as he led Charlie through the neat living room. The trailer had a wonderful smell, fried potatoes and cherry pipe tobacco.

"What happened to your leg?" said Charlie.

"Arth-a-ritis in my knee," said Curt, giving it an extra syllable. "Guess I got old too."

He took the drip pot from the stove and poured two cups of coffee, dosed each one with sugar and cream.

"How come you're not up in Richmond for the holidays?" said Charlie.

Curt brought the cups to the table. "Terence and Yvonne took the baby to Chicago. Give the other grandparents a chance, I suppose." He sipped his coffee. "What about you, Charlie Bell? How old are you now?"

"Thirty-two," said Charlie. "Same as Terence."

"When are you going to settle down? What are you waiting on?"

Charlie smiled. "I'm not waiting. I like being single."

Curt dismissed this with a wave of his hand. "That's no life for a man. No kind of life at all."

"Some people shouldn't get married," said Charlie, thinking of his father. "I'm afraid I'm one of them."

"That's no way to talk," said Curt. "You'll be alone your whole life, you keep thinking like that. Pretty soon you'll be as old as me. Then what'll you have?"

"I try not to think about it." Charlie laughed. "What about you? Don't you get lonely out here all by yourself?"

Curt shrugged. "You get used to it. In the beginning I felt sorry for myself, losing Maple so young. But I had her twenty-three years. That's more than some folks get."

Charlie nodded. "I worry about my mama. She's getting older now. I wish she had someone to look after her."

Curt got up abruptly and refilled his cup. "Your mama is still a young woman. I'd say she can look after herself."

Outside, one of the dogs barked sharply.

"I don't know what's got into her," said Curt. "Excuse me for a moment." He disappeared into the living room. Charlie heard the screen door open, Curt talking to the dog in a low voice.

He took his cup to the sink. Curt's kitchen was immaculate. A clean frypan lay drying on a towel. Beside it were two glasses, two plates, two forks. A gold ring sat in a saucer next to the sink, as if someone had taken it off to wash dishes. Charlie picked up the ring and examined it. Two stones, garnet and topaz. He put the ring back in the saucer and went to the door.

"I should be going," he told Curt. "They'll have dinner waiting." He reached down and patted Blondie's head. "Good to see you, Mr. Curt."

"Give my regards to your mother," said Curt. "Tell her I said Merry Christmas."

Charlie crossed the clearing and followed the path to the dirt road. It was nearly dark, the blue dusk of early winter. The porch light was on. Jody sat on the steps in an old barn jacket.

"Where have you been?" she asked. "Shame on you, leaving me alone with her."

"Sorry." Charlie fumbled in his jacket pocket. "I went for a walk."

Jody eyed his pack of cigarettes. "I thought you quit."

"I did." He sat beside her on the step. "Where is she?"

"Taking a bath. I talked her into it. I don't think she's had one in a week."

An owl moaned in the distance.

"I worry about her," said Jody. "She doesn't take care of herself."

Charlie exhaled: two, three perfect rings of smoke. "Is she drinking?"

"I don't think so. But still. Half the time she doesn't answer the phone. I don't know where she could be." She took a cigarette from Charlie's pack. "How are you doing? Since Anne-Sophie left."

"The house feels pretty empty." He stared into the woods and thought of Curt on the other side of it, feeding his dogs.

"I don't get it," said Jody. "Why not do what she wants? Why not get married?"

"Why not? Go ask Mama. She'll tell you why not."

Jody chuckled. "No thanks. That's one conversation I can do without."

"I'm serious," he said. "Think of the misery she could have saved herself if she'd never married *him*."

"People get divorced," said Jody. "You can't blame him for everything."

"Sure I can blame him."

"Oh, please." Jody inhaled deeply. "Nobody could live with Mama. She's a disaster."

"How do you think she got that way?"

Jody shrugged. "What could he do? He fell in love with someone else." She stared into the distance. Charlie knew she was thinking of Russell.

"Well, isn't that the whole point of marriage?" he said. "You're not supposed to fall in love with someone else."

Jody exhaled loudly. "Do you think that's realistic?"

"No," said Charlie. "That's why I'll never get married."

Jody smiled. "I'd marry Russell in a minute, if he asked me."

No danger of that, Charlie thought. Russell would never leave his wife; Jody would grow old waiting.

The door opened behind them. Birdie stood wrapped in a flowered housecoat.

"Charlie Bell," she said. "Wherever have you been?"

THEY ATE breakfast for supper, sausage and eggs, the only meal Jody knew how to cook. Charlie cleared the table. He stowed the jars and magazines in the parlor, then placed the television on top of the refrigerator.

"Eat your eggs," Jody told Birdie. "You've barely touched them."

"I'm too excited to eat." She beamed at Charlie. "Having my children on Christmas Eve! It's just marvelous." She'd kept her red hair but needed a touch-up: under the bright kitchen lights, the roots were yellow-gray. Charlie looked at her hands, spotted like a ripe banana.

"Mama," he said. "Where's your ring?"

They'd bought it for her two Christmases ago. A mother's ring, Jody called it, set with their two birthstones, January and November.

Birdie looked down at her hand. "The jeweler's," she said. "One of the stones was loose. I took it to get fixed." She sprang up from her chair. "Time for dessert. Homemade fruitcake! Charlie's favorite."

Charlie and Jody exchanged looks. Fruitcake was not his favorite—nor, he believed, anyone else's. He dreaded the lacquered sweetness, the candied orange bits that stuck in his molars; but he accepted a slice. He stuck in a fork and encountered resistance, something stiff and unyielding at the bottom. He turned over his slice of cake. The bottom was lined with printed waxed paper.

THANK YOU, it read. FOOD LION IN-STORE BAKERY.

harlie left Montford the day after Christmas. He tossed his duffel bag into the trunk and went inside to say good-bye. Jody stood at the sink, washing dishes. Birdie sat at the cluttered table, watching television.

"I guess that's it," he said.

Birdie rose. "Charlie Bell." She took his face in her hands and kissed him tenderly on the cheek. He felt the imprint of her mouth, the waxy stain of lipstick. He studied her eyes, a murky green flecked with gold.

"I forgot to tell you," he said. "Curt said to wish you a Merry Christmas."

Her eyes widened momentarily, or maybe he imagined it.

"You ought to go visit him once in a while," said Charlie. "Him all alone in that house."

"I'm sure he's fine." Birdie turned away to adjust the antenna, sending a shower of static across the small screen. "It's not as if he's an old man. He's my age, for goodness' sake."

"Still." Charlie studied her back, the bow of her neck. From the rear she looked like a girl. Only the front of her had changed, sunk slightly, like a sackful of soft things. She was fifty-one that June.

"You drive carefully now," she said.

Jody turned off the faucet. "Let me walk you outside."

The afternoon was warm for December, smelling of moist earth, an early spring. Their boots dug into the muddy ground. Birdie's lawn was neatly trimmed. That fall someone had given it a good mowing.

"When are you leaving?" Charlie asked.

"I'm right behind you," said Jody. "I've got to get out of here. She's making me nuts."

His stomach lurched in the familiar way as he backed onto the dirt road. He punched the horn and waved to Jody and Birdie, who'd emerged from the house in her slippers. They stood on the porch an arm's length apart, their curly hair the same shade of red. It pained him to leave; at the same time he was grateful. The house felt crowded with the two women, the agitated air humming between them. It was something he'd never understood, why their mother pushed Jody away, why Jody kept trying. She called Birdie daily, averaged three visits to Charlie's one; yet the tension between them never abated. *Stop trying so hard,* he wanted to tell her. *She wants to be left alone.*

He turned onto the paved road, thinking of the mother's ring, left in a saucer next to Curt's sink. Birdie had grown up with Curt; he'd heard a hundred times how they'd built forts in the woods, colored Easter eggs, sat at the kitchen table making figures out of flour dough while Miss Ella fixed supper. Yet he couldn't recall seeing them speak to each other as adults. Occasionally, in town visiting over a holiday, he'd drive Birdie to the store; twice they'd bumped into Maple Mabry in the parking lot. Both times Maple had greeted him warmly. Birdie had responded with a stiff hello, averting her eyes.

He thought of the path through the forest, still worn bare after all these years. Well, why not? he thought. His mother must get lonely, and Curt was alone now too. No reason they shouldn't keep each other company. What he couldn't understand was why she'd keep the friendship a secret. When he'd mentioned Curt's name, she'd been visibly uncomfortable. Then again, his mother was a relic. She might not understand that times had changed, that a white woman could be friends with a black man. He felt better knowing that Curt was near, that his mother had someone to look after her. He thought of his own silent house, the empty spaces left by Anne-Sophie's things, not yet filled in by his own clutter. He imagined Birdie in her old barn jacket, plodding through the dark forest toward the lights of Curt's trailer.

Good for you, Mama, he thought. Good for you.

BIRDIE WATCHED her son drive away. That's it, she thought. The last I'll see of him for months. Her birthday was in June; if she wheedled enough, he might come and visit then. She heard clanging in the kitchen, Jody attacking the dishes. She was a clumsy girl; Birdie was just waiting for the family china to end up in pieces on the floor.

She went into the house. "Careful," she said. "Those are your grandmother's dishes."

"Don't worry." Jody rinsed a plate and set it in the drainer.

"They're irreplaceable."

Jody shut off the faucet. "Then maybe you should take over. I have to make a phone call." She wiped her hands on a tea towel and took the phone into the parlor, stretching the cord as far as it would go.

Birdie stared at the television. In ten minutes her soap opera would come on; she wished Jody would take a nap, a walk, anything so she could have a little peace. She thought of the bottle of wine she had stashed in the linen closet. She had not drunk in days.

She'd been good lately. It was, she thought, Curtis's influence: he never made her feel bad about drinking, would even have a glass with her before bed.

Jody reappeared and hung up the phone.

"Who did you call?" Birdie asked, adjusting the antenna.

"Russell."

Birdie had been hearing about this beau for years but had never seen any trace of him. She was starting to wonder if Jody had made him up.

"Are you sure you ought to call him?" she said. "Shouldn't he be the one calling you?"

"Says who?" Jody laughed. "Emily Post?"

"That was how we did it in my day."

"No advice, please. My relationship with Russell is going just fine."

"If you say so." Birdie adjusted the TV antenna; static sprayed across the screen. Of course the child was fooling herself. She'd dated this Russell for three years; if an engagement was forthcoming, Birdie hadn't heard anything about it. She was tempted to point this out, but her daughter took offense so easily. She'd learned to keep her mouth shut.

"Jesus," said Jody, scraping at a dirty plate. "How long have these been sitting here?"

Birdie flushed. She was sick to death of being lectured about her housekeeping; if Jody didn't like the accommodations, she could drive to Gretna and stay in the hotel. Then a thought came to her: If she's going to take over my house, I'm going to speak my mind.

"I guess I'm old-fashioned," said Birdie. "It would bother me terribly, dating a fellow for so long, and him never even meeting my family."

"It's a complicated situation," said Jody.

"Complicated how?"

Jody reddened. Usually Birdie was the one who blushed, but with her daughter she was cool as a cucumber.

"I'm just asking," she said sweetly.

Jody shut off the water. "If you must know, Russell is married. He and his wife have had problems for years. They're about to get a divorce."

"Married?" The floor seemed to move, as if the house had become unmoored. Birdie gripped at the wall, the table. She felt truly ill.

"He's miserable with his wife," said Jody. "He just stays with her because of the kids. He never loved her. He's in love with me."

Birdie remembered the girl who'd taken her husband away, the hateful Moira Snell. *I love him,* she'd said, so smug. *I'm in love with your husband.*

"In love?" said Birdie. "That's a reason to destroy a family? Because you're in love?"

"Mama—"

"How could you? After your father ran off with that young girl? After all he put us through?"

"Mama, sit down. I upset you." Jody touched her shoulder.

Birdie wrenched her arm away.

"Get out of my house," she said.

. . .

SHE LOCKED herself in the bathroom, splashed cold water on her face, and waited. She stared at herself in the mirror, the color high in her cheeks. Married, she thought. My daughter and a married man.

She listened to Jody's heavy footfalls in the bedroom next door, wire hangers jingling in the closet, a suitcase slamming shut. Soon she would be gone; then Birdie would find the bottle in the linen closet and set about the hard work of forgetting what she'd been told. She knew from long experience that it could be done. She'd already forgotten a lifetime's worth of painful things.

At the mirror she reapplied her lipstick, swatted her hair with a brush. Like every year at this time, she was ready for the holiday to be over. Her children's concern exhausted her; they treated her like an old woman who might fall down and break her hip. She peered out the tiny window overlooking the forest. The path was clearly visible through the bare trees. I'm not so old, she thought.

A knock at the door.

"Mama," said Jody. "Come out and say good-bye."

"Good-bye," said Birdie, not moving.

"Mama." Jody's voice sounded thick; she too had been crying. "I'm sorry. I shouldn't have told you that. I knew it would upset you."

Birdie waited.

"I'll call you tomorrow," said Jody.

Footsteps on the stairs; the front door closed with a thud. From the window Birdie watched Jody's car disappear down the dirt road. She came out of the bathroom and reached into the linen closet. The bottle was where she'd left it, behind a stack of towels.

In the kitchen she rooted through the crowded drawer for her corkscrew; she wasn't used to having so many clean utensils. The afternoon light was fading. At this hour her kitchen seemed lonely and sad.

She glanced out the window. An hour of daylight remained, perhaps less. She could wait an hour, but why? There was no reason to wait.

She left the bottle on the kitchen counter, pulled on her boots, and went out the back door. She made her way down the dirt road, pacing herself. Then, when she reached the forest, she ran.

She knew the path by heart now, every rock and gully and exposed root; she leapt over them easily in her boots. The air was cold on her bare arms; she had forgotten her coat. In a moment she wouldn't need it. His trailer was warm inside. She wouldn't need any clothes at all.

He was standing on his porch as if he'd been expecting her.

"Curtis," she said, catching her breath.

She had never come to him in daylight. But what difference did it make if nobody was there to see?

CHARLIE GOT HOME at dusk, heated himself a frozen dinner, and ate it in front of the evening news. He felt as though he'd been away a month; it surprised him to see how little had happened in the world. There'd been a house fire in southeast D.C.; a six-month-old baby had died on Christmas morning. A reporter stood before the burned-out house, the charred skeleton still smoking in the rain. The fire had started in the kitchen; the owner, a single mother named Charmaine Watkins, had been sleeping there with her three children, huddled around the gas stove for heat. The two older boys had escaped unharmed; their mother was in critical condition but was expected to survive.

"The cause of the fire is still under investigation," said the reporter. "According to reports, the Watkins family had lived without heat for several months even though the house was newly renovated."

Charlie dug into his Salisbury steak. The meat had begun to cool; the sauce had developed an oily skin.

"The house was purchased ten months ago from this man, District housing developer Ken Kimble—"

Charlie looked up from his food.

"—founder of the Homes Project, a nonprofit company that claims to provide affordable housing for poor families."

Charlie stared at the television. In the corner of the screen was a photo of his father, smiling broadly, dressed in a tuxedo.

"Kimble, who is already under investigation by the Department of Housing and Urban Development for alleged financial misdoings, could not be reached for comment."

The broadcast cut to a commercial; Charlie switched channels. The D.C. station offered expanded coverage of the fire. Charmaine Watkins had complained to Kimble's office for months about her furnace; it was defective when she'd bought the house. She couldn't afford to replace it herself.

The picture flashed to an impressive Tudor house. Another reporter, a handsome black woman, stood before it.

"WDC has tried repeatedly to contact Ken Kimble," she said, "who lives in this house in Great Falls, Virginia.

"Kimble left town the day before HUD announced its disciplinary action against him. His wife declined to be interviewed on camera."

His wife. Charlie wondered if Dinah was in the house, if she and the kid were trapped inside, hiding from reporters. He knew first-hand how brutal the press could be, drawn to scandal like hungry mosquitoes. He pushed aside his food and lit a cigarette, surprised to see that his hands were shaking. He'd wondered about Ken Kimble's business dealings, wanted to believe the man was crooked though there was no evidence to suggest it. *He doesn't make a dime off of it,* Dinah had told him at Thanksgiving. She had trusted the man. In that way she was just like Charlie's mother.

He thought of Birdie holed up in Montford. Her TV didn't pick up Washington stations, and Charlie had never known her to read a newspaper. His sister would find out soon enough, though, and when she did she wouldn't believe it. She was like every other woman Ken Kimble had hurt. Their mother. Dinah. Probably Joan down in Florida. The old crook had even charmed Anne-Sophie. Charlie thought of her at Thanksgiving, how she'd laughed at Kimble's jokes. *To me he didn't seem old. I thought he was charming.*

Is it just me? he wondered. Am I the only one who sees through him?

He took his plate to the kitchen, thinking of Dinah and Brendan alone on Christmas. He wondered how she'd explained it to the kid, where you'd even begin. How do you tell a kid his father is a criminal?

The kid. He, at least, would believe it; he wouldn't try to defend the man. My brother, Charlie thought.

Maybe that's what it took to see through a fraud like Ken Kimble. Maybe you had to be his son.

he newspaper sat on the lawn. Dinah peered out the window. The crowd of reporters had dispersed, though a strange green sedan still idled in the neighbor's driveway.

She decided to risk it.

She opened the door and hurried across the lawn. A short, stocky man got out of the car and ran toward her.

"Mrs. Kimble," he called. "I need to talk with you."

She grabbed the paper and ran back inside, slamming the door behind her. At the kitchen table she tore through the editorial pages. For two days straight there had been letters to the editor from Ken's former clients, low-income families who'd bought houses from the Homes Project. Charmaine Watkins's house wasn't the only one with problems. The others had faulty wiring, leaky roofs, appliances that didn't work.

She'd heard about the fire the day after Christmas. Early that morning a reporter had rung the doorbell. The cul-de-sac was crowded with cars; a van idled in the driveway.

"Mrs. Kimble?" the reporter had said. "Do you have any comment on the fire at the Watkinses' house?"

"Fire?" she said stupidly. "What fire?"

She saw it on the news later that morning: the blackened remains of the house, where a child had died because Ken wouldn't fix a furnace. She remembered Charmaine Watkins waiting in Ken's office, the infant asleep on her shoulder: his halo of dark hair, his perfect rosebud mouth. She thought, My husband killed that child.

The next day she'd called the investigators at HUD. "I want to meet with you," she said. "I want to get to the bottom of this." At their meeting the fire was barely mentioned; HUD was more interested in Ken's financial affairs. Apparently the Homes Project was nothing but a scam, a way to collect federal mortgage insurance. Ken had sold houses to people who couldn't afford them, had even loaned them money for their down payments. Most of his clients defaulted; when they did, he collected the mortgage insurance from HUD and resold the houses to someone else.

Dinah sat at the table, head in her hands, listening to the gentle noises of her house: the central air purifier, which made dusting unnecessary; the quiet hum of the dishwasher. She had no idea how Ken had paid for these luxuries. She'd never even wondered.

When the phone rang she let the machine pick up. Another reporter, she supposed, asking again when Ken would return. She was tired of saying she didn't know.

"You've reached the Kimbles," said her own voice, slightly distorted on the tape. "We're not here now, but please leave a message."

"Dinah?" A male voice, deep and resonant. "It's Wayne. Call when you get this. I saw the paper and I wanted to make sure you're okay."

She closed her eyes. Facing him was impossible, given what they both knew: that her husband was a fraud, that she was a fool. For years she'd lived alongside Ken, never suspecting. She had profited from his schemes; in a way she'd even collaborated. She thought of the Man of the Year dinner, the photograph that had appeared on the society page, her hanging on Ken's arm in the sleazy dress he'd bought her.

She glanced at the clock. Brendan had gone to his tutor's for a math lesson; soon she'd have to pick him up. She had already told him everything she knew: the fire, the baby's death, the HUD investigation into his father's affairs. *He doesn't need to know this,* a voice inside her said. *He shouldn't hear these things about his father.* For once she ignored the voice. The story was all over the television, the papers. She could not shield him from it.

Brendan had listened, stone-faced. "Was it his fault?" he asked finally.

"It looks that way," said Dinah. "We don't know for sure."

"He isn't coming back," said Brendan.

"He wouldn't just disappear."

He considered this for a moment. Then: "If they find him, will he go to jail?"

"He might."

Brendan turned away from her.

"They won't find him," he said.

SHE PUT ON her coat and hat, dark glasses to hide her eyes. In the garage she started her car, then opened the automatic door. The same green sedan was parked on the street, blocking her driveway. The stocky man got out of the car.

"Mrs. Kimble," he called. "I've been waiting all day to talk with you."

She rolled down her window. "Please move your car."

"First let me talk to you."

"Please." She glanced at the clock in the dashboard. "I need to pick up my son."

"I have to talk to you about your husband."

"MOVE YOUR CAR!" Tears rained down her face. "Right now, or I'll back into you. You think I'm kidding?" She threw the car into reverse and backed down the driveway. The brakes screeched, the bumper inches from the sedan's side panel. The cool air reeked of rubber.

The man got into his car and disappeared down the cul-de-sac.

*O*n New Year's Eve Charlie packed a box with things Anne-Sophie had forgotten: the cookbook, the hair clip, a silk kimono she'd left hanging from the bathroom door, still smelling of her perfume. He had no plans for the evening; there was nothing to celebrate. A coworker had invited him to a party, but showing up alone was impossible; he dreaded the sympathetic looks, the gentle inquiries about what had gone wrong. I'm what went wrong, he thought. He was defective in some basic way, broken in places that couldn't be fixed.

He found the address easily, an old brick apartment building off Dupont Circle. Anne-Sophie had lived in this same neighborhood when they first met. After moving in with Charlie, she'd commuted to Washington every day from Baltimore, forty minutes each way by train. She'd never complained. She was happy to merge her life with his.

He parked on the street and stood in front of the building, holding the box of her things. Her new apartment was on the second floor. The lights were on; shadows moved behind the bright curtains.

He buzzed her apartment from the lobby. "Come in," said her

voice over the intercom. She ought to know better, he thought. The city was full of freaks and predators. She ought to at least have asked who it was.

He climbed the stairs to the second floor. Anne-Sophie's door was open a crack; through it he heard soft jazz, voices, laughter. She was having a party. He left the box outside her door.

Afterward he sat in his car for a long time. The night was cold and clear; soon the fireworks display would begin on the Mall. He thought of Dinah and Brendan alone in the big house, another wife and kid his father had left behind. He considered calling them but decided against it; for a week he'd carried their phone number around in his wallet. He still hadn't used it. What in God's name would he say?

He took his mobile phone from the glove compartment and dialed Jody's number. She'd invited him to watch the fireworks with her and Russell. He couldn't think of a more depressing way to spend New Year's.

She answered on the first ring. "It's about time," she snapped. "Where the hell are you?"

"Relax, Jo. It's just me." For just an instant he felt sorry for Russell. That poor bastard's in for it, he thought.

"I'm at Anne-Sophie's," he said. "I came to drop off her stuff." A golden light appeared in the sky, followed by a tremendous boom. "Hear that? They just started the fireworks."

"Come on over," said Jody. "Russell should be here any minute."

"Nah, that's all right." Charlie reached into his wallet and fingered the slip of paper. *Dinah and Brendan.* "I'm wiped out. I think I'll just head home."

A shower of red exploded in the sky, leaving traces in the air.

. . .

ON NEW YEAR'S EVE Dinah packed Ken's clothes in a box: shoes, sweaters, winter coats. His suits she zippered into garment bags. On January 2 the whole mess would go to Goodwill. She knew he would never return.

The house was silent around her. For the first time in fifteen years, she was alone on New Year's Eve. Brendan was spending the night at Sean Guthrie's. Sean and another boy had come to pick him up; Dinah had watched the Jeep back out of the driveway and accelerate down the street. She'd been doing it too much lately, watching Brendan leave. One day she would see him for the last time; recent events had taught her that the day wouldn't announce itself. She had no memory of her last morning with Ken: whether they'd quarreled, whether she'd kissed him good-bye.

She sealed the box of clothes and glanced at the clock, thinking of Wayne. Parties would be starting; those with plans for the evening had already arrived at their destinations. She wondered if he had a date.

For the third time that evening, she dialed his number. This time she waited for the machine and left a message.

"It's me," she said, her voice quavering. "I called to wish you a happy new year."

She hung up the phone. I'll never be free, she thought. And then: How can I get a divorce if I can't even find him?

The doorbell startled her. Wayne: it had to be. She ran a hand through her hair and threw open the door. A short, stocky man stood on the step: the man from the green sedan.

"Mrs. Kimble," he said. "At last."

"It's New Year's Eve," she said, closing the door. "Don't you people have the night off?"

"Wait." The man grabbed the door handle. Dinah felt a flash of fear. He was powerfully built, with broad shoulders and large hands. She'd been an idiot to open the door.

"Who are you?" she said. The neighbors' windows were dark; if she screamed, nobody would hear.

"It's not what you think." He had dark curly hair; his brown eyes looked unnaturally large behind his glasses. She made a mental note in case she had to describe him to the police.

"I'm not a reporter," he said. "I'm a relative of your husband's."

"A relative?" She stared at him: the stout frame, the round face. He couldn't have looked less like Ken.

"Please," he said. "Let me come in. Here." He took off his glasses and handed them to her. "I can't see a damn thing. There's no way I can rape and murder you. I'm completely helpless."

She took the glasses, her heart racing. This is insane, she thought; but she couldn't help herself. The thought that Ken might have a relative fascinated her.

"Come in," she said.

In the living room they sat on the sofa. The man reached for his wallet. "Before we start, some visual aids." He handed her a worn photo.

"Who's this?" she asked.

"My sister," he said. "That's Joan."

She stared at him, confused.

"Your husband's former wife."

Dinah studied the photo—square, with a white border. The woman was dark, with the bouffant hairdo of twenty years ago.

She sat next to a swimming pool in a colorful caftan, her shapely legs crossed at the knees.

"My name is Ben Cohen," he said. "I live across the river, in Bethesda. I haven't seen your husband in years, but I've always wondered what happened to him. When I saw all this business in the newspaper, I had to get in touch with you."

Dinah handed him his glasses. "You knew Ken?"

"I wouldn't go that far. He's a hard guy to know."

You're telling me, she thought.

"He and Joan were only married for a few years. I met him two, three times." Cohen put on the glasses. "The first time was at my father's house in Florida. My father died that year, and my sister was staying in his house.

"I flew down from New York to see her at Christmas, and there she was, living in my father's house with this guy she'd just met. I was shocked. It was 1969. You didn't see many unmarried couples living together in those days, and Joan—she wasn't that kind of person. You're probably not old enough to remember how it was, but that's how it was."

Dinah nodded, calculating. In 1969 she was fourteen years old, living in Richmond, still baby-sitting for Ken's children. He had run away with Moira Snell that spring. Yet by Christmas he'd already moved in with Joan.

"It was bizarre." Cohen leaned forward in his chair. "I could see she was crazy about this guy, but he wasn't her usual type. She was very sophisticated; she had traveled all over the world—London, Paris, you name it. I was used to her dating lawyers, Wall Street guys. But this one had long hair and a beard. A hippie." He sat back in his chair. "That was the first time I met your husband."

Dinah blinked. For no reason she thought of Ken shaving, the meticulous way he went over his long face, how he never missed a hair. Ken with a beard seemed impossible.

"Mrs. Kimble?" said Cohen. "Are you with me?"

Dinah hugged her sweater around her; she was suddenly freezing. "Yes. Please go on."

"Well. I went back to New York, and a few months later I got a wedding invitation in the mail. In the mail! Her own brother, and she couldn't even call and tell me herself."

"How strange," said Dinah.

"It was," Cohen agreed. "But what could I do? She was my sister. So I got on a plane and flew down there for the wedding."

The wedding: Ken's second. It was a strange thought. Dinah had never told anyone she was Ken's third wife; even her own parents didn't know. There was no reason they should, she'd rationalized; but the truth was more complicated. She and Ken had promised each other their lives; that he'd already made this vow to two other women cast doubt on its seriousness. Her parents, had they known, would have questioned the worth of her marriage. On some level she'd felt the same way.

"Well." Cohen rubbed his hands together. "I show up at the wedding, I take one look at the groom and I can't believe it. He's a changed man. He's shaved off the beard, he's working for my uncle Floyd selling real estate, and guess what? He's a Jew!"

"What?" said Dinah.

"You heard me."

"That's impossible," she said. "He used to be a minister, for God's sake. A college chaplain. He worked with my father."

Cohen burst into laughter.

"A minister! I knew the guy was a fraud, but I had no idea." He shook his head. "That's some chutzpah."

"I don't get it," said Dinah. "Why would he pretend to be Jewish?"

Cohen chuckled. "You'd have to know my uncle Floyd. He was a tough customer. Never finished the eighth grade, and he died a millionaire. He had two rules in life: pinch a penny until it screams, and never do business outside the tribe." He adjusted his glasses. "Your husband's a smart guy. I'm sure he picked up on that right away. It worked, too. Uncle Floyd loved him like a son."

"That's incredible," said Dinah.

"No kidding! He looked about as Jewish as you do. I don't know how he pulled it off. Anyway," he continued. "The wedding. The guy fakes his way through the ceremony, and afterward I find out Uncle Floyd has handed him the keys to the kingdom. The guy's selling real estate, which makes sense—he's a born salesman. And he and Joan are living in my dad's house, this ridiculous *Gone With the Wind* mansion. Unbelievable." He broke off.

"At least that's how I felt at the time. I was living in New York then, working at a homeless shelter, what they used to call a soup kitchen; handing out overcoats to homeless people, which they used to call bums." He smiled. "I was disgusted by my father's money, like any good hippie would be."

He clapped his hands, as if a genie would appear.

"But not this one! Here's this old beatnik my sister dug up God knows where, wearing a suit, spending my father's money. My father who worked himself to death so he'd have something to leave his kids." He stopped for a breath. "As you can see, it bothered me. I didn't want the money myself. But I didn't want this guy to have it either."

Dinah nodded. Suddenly it was something she could picture, Ken in Florida selling real estate, wearing a suit, living with Joan in a *Gone With the Wind* house. A picture of her husband emerged like a fresh Polaroid, an image appearing from swirls of gray.

"Then what happened?" she asked.

Cohen shrugged. "Who knows? For three, four years I barely heard from her. Birthday cards, holidays. Finally she does call me and tells me she's dying."

He removed his glasses. Without them his dark eyes were delicate as a bird's.

"She had cancer," Dinah said softly.

"Breast cancer. For the second time." Cohen's eyes brushed hers. "She never told anybody about the first time. Apparently it was why she left New York in the first place. She had the mastectomy all by herself and just left. None of us had any idea. Except your husband, I suppose. He was the only one who knew."

He replaced his glasses.

"I can't blame him for what happened to Joan. My mother had breast cancer too; I guess it's in the genes. But the guy took advantage of her. They spent, what, four years together? Five? And he walked away with millions."

"That much?" said Dinah, reddening. "I knew she'd left him some money, but I had no idea."

"It wasn't just hers. Apparently he talked my uncle into making him a partner in the business. When Floyd died, your husband got everything." Cohen chuckled. "Floyd's kids weren't too happy about it, I can tell you that. My cousin Ruth even hired a lawyer. I guess nothing ever came of it, though. Your husband knew he was in hot water. After Joan died he skipped town pretty fast."

Dinah looked down at the engagement ring on her left hand, the four-carat diamond Ken had given her.

"He was an opportunist," said Cohen. "Joan never saw it. She was in love with him."

Dinah examined the photograph in her hand. "When was this taken?"

"Right after they were married. The spring of 1970. Joan was thirty-nine."

"My age," she said softly, studying the woman's broad face, her lively dark eyes. "Who took this?"

"I imagine it was your husband."

She handed back the photo. "Ken never talked about the past. I knew his wife had died, but that's all. I never even knew her last name."

Cohen nodded. "That's why I came. I thought all this might interest you. I don't think Joan knew much about him either. She said that he'd been married before. I believe there was a child."

"Two," said Dinah. "He had two."

Cohen sighed. "I think Joan wanted kids of her own. She just ran out of time." He replaced the photo in his wallet. "Do you have children?"

"We have a son." She thought of Brendan, glad he was away at Sean Guthrie's. Lately he'd refused to talk about his father; he got angry when she mentioned Ken's name.

"Pardon me for asking," said Cohen, "but what's going to happen to your husband?"

"That depends," said Dinah. "HUD is still investigating his business dealings. As for the fire at the Watkins house—" She paused. "They could charge him with negligence, involuntary manslaughter. He could go to jail. Of course, they'll have to find him first."

Cohen's eyebrows shot up. "The owner of that house must have an attorney by now. She could sue you for everything you've got."

"I don't blame her," said Dinah.

He looked around the room: the paintings on the walls, the grand piano Ken had bought but never played. "Quite a crib you've got here," he observed. "It's no Tara, but it's not bad."

Dinah laughed.

"They'll find him." Cohen rose to go. "With this kind of money at stake, someone will find him. He'll have nowhere left to hide."

*B*rendan sat in the Jeep's cramped backseat, though he was bigger than the other boys and barely had room for his legs. Sean Guthrie drove. Next to him sat a friend from his old school, a boy he'd introduced only as Fog. Brendan had heard all about this Fog, how he and Sean used to get high every morning before school, how they hid inside the school one night and discharged all the fire extinguishers into the faculty lounge. How, after they were expelled, they hid strips of raw bacon in the library's heating ducts, causing a mysterious stench to waft through the corridors as the bacon slowly rotted. Hearing these stories gave Brendan a strange feeling, as though Sean had become boring and he, Brendan, was to blame. He and Sean had never done anything more adventurous than smoke cigarettes in the woods or steal beers from the Guthries' refrigerator. For Brendan this was excitement enough. No way was he brave enough to do the things Sean and Fog had done. His mom would have a fit.

"Hey," said Fog as they backed out of Brendan's driveway. "Your mom is hot."

"Wicked hot," said Sean.

Brendan said nothing. He reminded himself that Fog would be gone in two days. Fog's parents had sent him to military school in South Carolina; he was home on Christmas break.

On the way to Sean's house, they stopped at a grocery store. "Be right back," said Fog. He returned with a case of beer and a carton of Marlboros.

"How'd you do that?" said Brendan. They were all underage.

Fog reached into his pocket and showed Brendan a Florida driver's license. Right away Brendan's stomach felt queasy, like every time he thought of his father.

"'Richard Berens,'" Brendan read. "Is that your real name? Richard?"

"No, idiot," said Fog. Sean stifled a laugh. "You don't put your real name on a fake ID."

"I know that," Brendan lied.

When they arrived at Sean's house, the windows were dark.

"Where are your parents?" said Brendan. His mom had asked if the Guthries would be home; he'd promised they would. He hadn't lied on purpose; then again, he hadn't made any effort to find out one way or the other.

"Some party downtown." Sean parked in the driveway. "They're staying in a hotel tonight. My dad can't afford another DUI." Mr. Guthrie was a big cheese at the State Department; his drunk-driving arrest had made the papers. At the time Brendan couldn't imagine how it would feel, knowing your father had spent a night in jail. Now nothing surprised him.

They went inside and put the beers in the refrigerator. "Here," said Sean, handing them each one. In Sean's room they fired up cigarettes. The Guthries didn't care if Sean smoked, as long as he didn't stink up the rest of the house.

"Check this out," said Fog, reaching into his pocket. He tossed a plastic bag onto the floor. "I brought it up special from redneck country."

Sean picked up the bag to examine it. "Holy shit. This is, like, half an ounce."

Brendan felt sick. Sean had told him there would be no weed. Fog was drug-tested at military school; if he failed again, they'd kick him out.

"What about your drug test?" said Brendan.

Fog smiled, showing all his teeth. "After Thanksgiving I came up clean as a whistle. They never test the same guy twice in a row."

Sean reached into a desk drawer for his rolling papers; Brendan cranked up Sean's new CD player—a Christmas gift from his parents, his reward for getting through another semester at Godfrey.

Fog took the joint from Sean's hand. "Me first. Finder's fee."

He lit the joint and took a long drag, closing his eyes. Brendan studied his face: round and pale, his flabby lips glistening with saliva. He decided Fog wasn't doing himself any favor with that crew cut. A face that ugly needed some hair.

"They make you cut your hair that way?" Brendan asked.

Fog exhaled. "What do you think? I do it because I like it?" He passed the joint to Sean.

"Chill out, man," said Sean. "Hang on to that spliff. Have another hit."

Brendan watched them pass the joint. By the time it got around to him, they'd have smoked it down to nothing, which was fine with him. He'd smoked marijuana twice before with Sean. Both times he'd gotten a wicked headache.

Sean went downstairs for more beers. Fog sucked deeply on the joint, then handed it to Brendan. He ran a hand across his head.

"Bullshit Nazi haircut," he said. "I fucking hate it."

"It's not that bad," Brendan lied. He took the joint. It was very moist, slobbery from Fog's lips. Disgusting, but he took a hit anyway.

"What's it like down there?" he asked. "Military school. They make you march and shit?"

"Hell yes they make you march." Fog accepted a beer from Sean, who'd returned with an armload. "They make you call them sir. They practically tell you when you can piss."

"Sounds like jail," said Sean.

Brendan nodded, thinking of his father.

"Hey," said Sean, reading his mind. "Tell Fog about your dad."

Brendan flushed.

"Come on," said Sean.

"What?" said Fog.

"It's no big deal." Brendan felt a strange gnawing in his stomach. The pot, he supposed.

"If you're not going to tell him, I will." Sean cracked open a beer. "Brendan's dad is a fugitive. He's wanted by the FBI."

"What did he do?" said Fog.

"Real estate scam," said Sean. "Screwed the government out of, like, millions."

"No shit." Fog stared at Brendan. "That's fucking cool."

Brendan stared into his beer, wishing he could be anywhere else.

BY TEN O'CLOCK the beers were dwindling. Brendan had stopped at two; the pot was doing strange things to his stomach. Sean and Fog had plowed through a whole case; they'd gotten progressively louder and stupider. Sober, Brendan could barely stand them.

"Hey," said Fog, reaching into his pocket. "I almost forgot." He took out a tiny package wrapped in tinfoil, no bigger than a quarter.

"No way," said Sean.

"Way." Fog got up and disappeared into Sean's bathroom. After much clunking and scraping, he came back with a round mirror, the kind for shaving in the shower.

"What are you doing?" said Brendan.

"Watch and learn." Fog unfolded the foil package and emptied it onto the mirror, a small pile of white powder.

"Cocaine?" said Brendan.

"Bogota's finest." Fog reached for his wallet and took out the Florida driver's license. He used the plastic card to cut the powder into three lines. Brendan remembered what his mother had told him about cocaine: you could have a heart attack and die. She'd known somebody who had, a guy she'd worked with at a restaurant a long time ago. He thought of his father lying in the hospital bed, the monitors attached to his heart. That's all I need, he thought. To end up like him.

He got to his feet.

"What's the matter?" said Sean.

"I have to go," said Brendan.

THE NIGHT SKY was clear; a few stray snowflakes glimmered under the street lamps. Brendan breathed deeply. He'd burned through an entire pack of cigarettes, more than he'd ever smoked in one night. His throat was raw, his nose felt stuffed with a wool sock; but the air was sharp and clean against his face. He felt better than he had in weeks.

"Where are you going?" Sean had demanded when he got up to leave.

"Home," said Brendan.

"What?" said Fog, rubbing his nose. His eyes were very bright; he seemed to have sobered up immediately. "You have a curfew?"

"Yeah," said Brendan, though it wasn't true; he had permission to stay at Sean's overnight.

"Your mom won't care." Fog leered. "I'll bet she's out ringing in the new year."

"Shut your mouth," said Brendan.

Now he shoved his hands into his pockets, glad, for once, that his mom had made him wear gloves. He'd chipped in for the beer and cigarettes; now he had just a dollar in his wallet—not enough for a taxi, even if he'd thought to call one. His house was miles away, but he didn't care. If he had to, he'd walk all night.

Headlights behind him, the hum of an engine. Brendan turned. It was Sean's Jeep.

"Hey," Sean yelled out the window. "You can't walk home. It's freezing out."

"I'm fine," said Brendan.

Sean opened the passenger door. "Get in. I'll take you."

"You're drunk," said Brendan. "You shouldn't be driving."

"Come back to the house then."

Brendan turned and kept walking. The Jeep followed slowly behind him. At the stop sign Sean slammed on the brakes; the Jeep slid on the ice. This is nuts, Brendan thought. He's plastered. He's going to run me over.

He stopped and turned. "All right," he called out. "But I'm driving."

Sean slid over into the passenger seat; Brendan took the wheel. Fear gripped his stomach. He'd only driven twice, both times during the day, with his mom, on quiet country roads. Driving Sean's Jeep was something else.

He looked over at Sean, slumped in the seat. "Where's Fog?"

"Back at the house," said Sean. "He's pissed."

The motor idled. Just sitting in the driver's seat made Brendan's heart race. Suddenly he was in no hurry.

"Why do you hang out with that guy?" he asked. "He's an asshole."

"He's my friend," said Sean. "He's fun."

Brendan fastened his seat belt. "You used to do all that? The cocaine and stuff?"

"I only did it once," said Sean.

Brendan glanced in the rearview mirror. The street was deserted; there was no point in waiting. "Here goes," he said.

He shifted smoothly into first gear. Nothing to it, he thought. He drove to the end of the block, signaled and turned. The motor raced; he shifted carefully into second. The engine stalled.

"Shit," he muttered. He turned the key and hit the gas, taking it easy on the clutch. The Jeep lurched forward, then stalled a second time.

"What are you doing?" said Sean.

"Shut up," said Brendan.

Again he started the engine. In the rearview mirror, headlights appeared, a car turning the corner. In a moment the red and blue lights came on.

"Oh God," said Brendan. "The cops."

"I think I'm going to puke," said Sean.

He scrabbled at the door and got it open just in time. The cop got out of his car and approached the Jeep.

"Everything all right here?" he said, shining a flashlight into Brendan's eyes.

"Yes, sir," said Brendan, like Fog in military school. Beside him Sean retched loudly onto the sidewalk.

"Have you boys been drinking?"

"I had a beer a few hours ago," said Brendan. There was no point in lying with Sean puking out the passenger door. He glanced at Sean. "He's pretty wasted, though."

"I can see that." The cop looked closely at Brendan. "You seem all right."

Yes, Brendan thought: he was going to let them go.

"Please step out of the car," said the cop. "But first, I need to see your license and registration."

THEY LEFT the Jeep by the side of the road. Brendan had passed the sobriety test, but there was still the underage drinking, the driving without a license. The cop wanted to speak with his parents.

They rode in the squad car to Brendan's house. Sean huddled in a corner of the backseat, pale under the street lamps. "I want to go home," he moaned until Brendan kicked him in the shins. Fog was still back at Sean's house, with a half ounce of pot and a mirror dusted with cocaine. As much as Brendan disliked the guy, he wasn't about to send a cop to the Guthries' doorstep.

Brendan's house was dark. The cop rang the doorbell. When no one came he let Brendan open the door with his key.

"Mom?" Brendan called, turning on the light.

"Are you sure she's home?" said the cop.

"She must be." Then Brendan opened the door that led to the garage and saw that her car was gone.

"What about your father?" said the cop.

"Gone," said Brendan.

In the kitchen the telephone rang.

"I'll have to take you down to the station," said the cop.

A quick beep; the answering machine picked up.

"Dinah?" said a male voice. Static in the background; a mobile phone. "It's Charlie. I just got off the highway near your house and—"

"Let me get that," said Brendan, running for the phone. "It's my brother."

S pring came late that year. March was as cold as winter; along the Potomac, disappointed tourists searched in vain for cherry blossoms. Then, in the first week of May, the world warmed overnight. By Memorial Day the heat had set in, the hazy skies of full summer.

Charlie stood on Dinah's back porch, looking out over the yards of Falls Road, the manicured lawns the color of limes. Dinah's grass was two inches higher than the neighbors'; yet her vegetable garden was carefully tended. More than a garden: she had planted a small farm. He recognized chard and butter lettuce, broccoli and cucumbers, row after row of peppers and tomatoes. Dinah and Jody sat at the picnic table chatting and laughing, stripping the husks from ears of corn.

He lifted the cover from the grill and poked at the coals. "What do you think? Are they hot enough?"

Dinah came over to the grill and looked.

"Perfect," she said. "I'll get the burgers. Wayne will be here any minute." She gathered the corn into a paper bag and carried it into the kitchen.

"Wayne's the boyfriend?" Jody asked. She'd become the summer

Jody, a transformation Charlie witnessed every year: red hair hidden beneath a hat, nose smeared with zinc oxide. He detected the sweet coconut aroma of sunscreen, a smell he'd always associated with his sister.

"Yep." He'd met Wayne a few times; the guy was usually at the house when Charlie came to pick up Brendan. That spring Wayne had thrown a party for Dinah's fortieth birthday; he'd bought her a used Rototiller for the garden. Charlie had never seen a woman so delighted by a gift.

"He's a good guy," said Charlie. He poked at the coals, feeling his sister's stare.

"Do you ever think about him?" she asked.

"Who?" said Charlie, though he knew. For most of his life he'd thought of Ken Kimble every day: every time he spoke to his mother on the phone, every time he saw a jogger in the park. Now, strangely, the man rarely crossed his mind.

"Not much," he admitted. "Do you?"

Jody shrugged. "At first I did. It was hard not to, with his picture in the papers. But lately I never think about it." She glanced at her watch. "Russell was supposed to be here an hour ago."

"I've heard that before."

"Don't remind me." She fumbled in her pocket for a cigarette and came up empty. "Got any smokes?"

"Nope," said Charlie. He hadn't smoked in months; he and Brendan had made a pact to quit. They'd made a number of bargains since the night Brendan was stopped by the police. Brendan had agreed to stop smoking, to stay out of trouble at school; in return, Charlie would teach Brendan to drive. They'd gone out twice already, practiced three-point turns in empty parking lots. All the while Charlie thought of Curt Mabry, who'd taught him the spring he turned sixteen; who wouldn't let him take the driver's test until he could back up for a mile straight, the whole length of the dirt road in Curt's pickup truck.

"Have you talked to Mama lately?" he asked.

"I tried calling last night, and again this morning," said Jody. "No answer. I don't know where she could have been."

"Maybe she has a boyfriend." Charlie laughed. "Maybe she's off on a romantic weekend."

Jody giggled. "Can you imagine?" She reached for her sunscreen on the table and applied another coat to her nose.

"What about you?" she said. "Have you heard from Anne-Sophie?"

"Nope." His chest still ached at the thought of her. It's getting better, he told himself. He hoped it was true.

"She's seeing someone else. Some French guy." He poked at the coals. "In a few years I'll be sending Christmas presents to her kids."

"Oh, Charlie." They both smiled. There was nothing else to say.

DINAH SOAKED the corn in milk and added a teaspoon of sugar, an old trick to make it sweet and tender. She glanced out the kitchen window. Wayne and Jody stood chatting at the grill; in the yard, Wayne's dog stole a Frisbee from Brendan's fingertips. Brendan had grown that spring; he was almost as tall as Charlie. He'd slimmed down, too: his pants were finally too baggy even for him, and he'd agreed to let Dinah buy him new ones. Once she'd actually persuaded him to play tennis with her; he'd moved a bit sluggishly, but his serve was strong.

At times he still confounded her, but she was learning how to handle him: when to insist, when to back off. The tennis, for example.

She'd hoped to make it a regular thing; but when she'd proposed a rematch, Brendan had balked. "Let it go," Wayne advised her. "He'll play when he's ready." A month later Brendan had approached Wayne for lessons. Now the two played once a week.

He was an independent boy; she understood that now. It was a quality she admired, one she hoped to acquire herself. She was forty years old, a woman making choices. That spring she'd launched a catering business; she was tired of spending Ken's money. In Great Falls alone the potential was enormous: most of her neighbors used caterers several times a year. Wayne had helped her apply for a business license, shown her how to track expenses and revenue on Brendan's computer. He'd offered to keep the books for her, but she was a grown woman. It was time she learned how the world worked.

She watched Brendan fling the Frisbee across the lawn, a powerful throw; lately he spent an hour a day throwing Frisbees to Wayne's dog. Wayne joined them for dinner every night; afterward he and Dinah washed dishes while Brendan played with Buster. All through his childhood he'd begged for a dog, but Ken had claimed to be allergic. Dinah suspected a different reason. He'd always been vain about the house. Often she imagined Ken's horror at hearing Buster's toenails on the hardwood floors. The thought pleased her.

The house was messier these days, but it was the sort of clutter she liked: a basket of clean laundry near the back door, fresh from the clothesline; herbs growing in clay pots on the windowsill. Framed photographs decorated the front hallway; Charlie had given Brendan one of his old cameras, and they spent nearly every Saturday at his house in Baltimore, developing film in his darkroom. For the first time in years, Dinah's house looked lived in, though she spent less time there than ever before. Most weekends she had catering jobs; it bothered her at first, taking the time away from Brendan, but he didn't seem to mind. He had plans of his own: he'd transferred to public school that spring and had a whole new group of friends. Dinah had resisted the idea of his changing schools, but both Wayne and Charlie thought it a good one. She'd been surprised to learn that Brendan had been miserable at Godfrey from the beginning. "He's a good kid," Charlie had told her. "All he needs is a fresh start."

Since New Year's Eve, Charlie had been Brendan's hero. He'd appeared at the house within minutes, spoken with the cop, and stayed with Brendan until Dinah came home. At first she felt guilty—she'd been gone when Brendan needed her, off at Wayne's house instead of at home waiting for her son—but Wayne had persuaded her that it was for the best. She'd have gone ballistic seeing a police car in the driveway, he'd pointed out, and that wouldn't have done Brendan any good. Charlie, apparently, hadn't gone ballistic; he'd convinced the officer to leave Brendan with him; then the two of them drove Sean Guthrie home. According to Brendan he never lost his cool, even when Sean threw up in his car. Brendan had gotten off with probation; Charlie had even gone to his trial. The perfect older brother, Dinah thought. His resemblance to Ken no longer spooked her; only occasionally, in profile, did she catch a glimpse of his father's face.

She watched them race across the lawn, Ken Kimble's two sons. They'd inherited his height, his thoughtful frown; they had the same laugh. Their father's laugh; it had to be. Yet Dinah couldn't say for sure. Married to Ken Kimble for fifteen years, she couldn't recall hearing him laugh.

He was a deliberate man. For weeks after he left, she'd wandered around the house in a daze; then, one dark afternoon, she'd ransacked his closets, his home office, looking for proof that he'd loved her. She found no letters, no photographs, no mementos saved in a sentimental moment; only canceled checks, bank statements, receipts for things he'd bought. These were the only traces he'd left behind, a history of luxuries purchased and consumed.

She searched her memory. Fifteen years of ordinary days, meals eaten, Sunday mornings with the newspaper, holidays come and gone. Surely there had been a day, a moment, when he'd revealed himself to her: his deepest self, his capacity for love. She recalled an evening many years ago, in Richmond, sitting in his car in her parents' driveway. *Where did it come from?* he'd asked, touching the birthmark on her cheek. *You can get it taken care of someday. You're a beautiful girl.* He'd had nothing to gain from her; his concern, as far as she could see, was pure. He'd loved her better, then, than he did later, when she was just another thing that belonged to him.

"Come and get 'em!" Wayne called from the porch. Next to him Jody piled the hamburgers on a plate.

Dinah drained the corn and carried the pot outside. Just then the telephone rang.

"Somebody get that," she called. "I've got my hands full."

Wayne ran into the kitchen, the screen door slamming behind him. In the yard Brendan and Charlie washed their hands at the garden hose. The dog nosed around the grill, panting loudly. Inside the house the ringing stopped.

Dinah piled the steaming corncobs on a plate. The table was loaded down with food; but for once she had not cooked too much. She had a large family, and everyone was hungry. The dishes circulated, Dinah to Jody to Charlie to Brendan. Then Wayne appeared in the doorway.

"Dinah," he said. "It's the Florida state police. They want to talk to you."